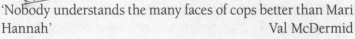

Praise for Mari Hannah

'Nobody understands the many faces of cops better than Mari Hannah'   Val McDermid

'Mari Hannah writes with a sharp eye and a dark heart'
                                                                                Peter James

'Truly absorbing'   Peter Robinson

'Thrilling, exciting and kept me on the edge of my seat. Expertly written and paced, pulling me from one chapter to the next, I couldn't put it down!'   Angela Marsons

'Mari Hannah is a consummate storyteller and her books genuine must reads for any serious crime fan'   Eva Dolan

'Emotionally captivating'   *The Times*

'If you read only one police procedural this year, make it *The Insider*. It deserves it'   *Daily Mail*

'Original and modern, rooted in the fast-changing relationships between men and women'   *Sunday Times*

'A pacy, gritty and authentic read'   *Heat*

Mari Hannah is a multi-award-winning author whose authentic voice is no happy accident. A former probation officer, she lives in rural Northumberland with her partner, an ex-murder detective. Mari turned to script-writing when her career was cut short following an assault on duty. Her debut, *The Murder Wall*, (adapted from a script she developed with the BBC) won her the Polari First Book Prize. Its follow-up, *Settled Blood*, picked up a Northern Writers' award. Her Kate Daniels series is in development with Stephen Fry's production company, Sprout Pictures. She is currently Reader in Residence and Chair for the Harrogate International Crime Writing Festival. Mari's body of work won her the CWA Dagger in the Library 2017, an incredible honour to receive so early on in her career.

Find out more by following Mari on Twitter @mariwriter or visiting her website www.marihannah.com

Also by Mari Hannah

STONE & OLIVER SERIES
The Lost
The Insider

KATE DANIELS SERIES
The Murder Wall
Settled Blood
Deadly Deceit
Monument to Murder (aka Fatal Games)
Killing for Keeps
Gallows Drop

RYAN & O'NEIL SERIES
The Silent Room
The Death Messenger

THE
SCANDAL

Mari Hannah

ORION

First published in Great Britain in 2019 by Orion Fiction,
an imprint of The Orion Publishing Group Ltd
Carmelite House, 50 Victoria Embankment,
London EC4Y 0DZ

An Hachette UK company

1 3 5 7 9 10 8 6 4 2

A CIP catalogue record for this book is
available from the British Library.

ISBN 978 1 4091 7409 7

Typeset by Input Data Services Ltd, Somerset

Printed and bound in Great Britain by Clays Ltd, Elcograf S.p.A.

www.orionbooks.co.uk

For Anne O'Brien

THE SCANDAL

Prologue

Some fear is real, some imagined. Nancy fled the building, flinching as the door swung shut behind her with a solid thump. The feeling that she was under surveillance – even as she drove through the staff car park – was like a knife plunged deep into her back. She'd left her resignation on her desk with little explanation. Circumstances beyond her control wouldn't cut it. Not a hope in hell. She'd been too vocal for her own good. Too vociferous in her defence of the defenceless. Hers was a just cause, one that had put her in danger more than once. This was not and never had been about her welfare.

In one way, the assault had clarified matters, a backhander so violent it had thrown her clear across the room, clattering across the floor, propelling her into a solid wooden chest. No witnesses; they were too clever for that. That slap, delivered with such venom, was counterproductive. A signal – if one were needed – that she couldn't change things from the inside. There was no other way . . .

She had to go.

It had taken months to make the decision. Using what she knew had ramifications. It would blow the lid off a situation that was out of control. To do it right meant meticulous planning, evidence collection and recording: photographic as well as the notes she'd scribbled frantically in her journal: names, dates and times. In the meantime, she'd sold up without telling a soul, moving to a place where no one knew her in order to distance herself from those seeking to silence her. Handing in her notice with immediate effect was only the beginning.

She'd have to be careful now.

As she drove teary-eyed from the estate, the faces of those

she cared for scrolled before her eyes like movie credits: Bill, Edna, Molly, George and countless others who'd gone before. Unloved in a lot of cases. The forgotten ones, she called them: isolated, indecisive, plain weak. When they found out that she'd gone without saying goodbye, they'd feel abandoned. Telling them was out of the question. Taking them into her confidence was never an option. A slip of the tongue would tip off the very people Nancy was anxious to expose, leaving those under her care and protection vulnerable – or worse, robbing her of the ability to blow the whistle.

She sighed.

Her colleagues didn't want to know. One by one, they had turned away, preserving their jobs, maintaining the status quo. Who could blame them? For years, they had been operating in a culture of fear. She wondered if they had been paid for their silence. Blood money.

How could they?

Nancy did blame them. Gutless, every one of them.

A single drop of warm liquid fell from her eye, dribbled down her cheek, hot and salty as it crept into her mouth. There would be no tears from the victims. Some had passed away already, unable to cry or complain. The rest would have forgotten her by morning. And yet she could hear them weeping, baffled by a sudden and inexplicable change in circumstances, waiting, wondering if she was ever coming back. That gut-wrenching thought was more than Nancy could bear.

If only it were possible to consign her own observations to oblivion. It wasn't. She felt guilty then. There was nothing worse than memory loss, but right now she'd give anything to be able to wipe her own hard drive. A despicable thought. Cowardly. It lingered in the back of her mind as she passed through the iron gates and out on to the open road, the decision to go gnawing at her conscience. She worried that her actions would leave those she might never see again caught

2

in a trap with no way out. At least not in the short-term . . .

Tears stung her eyes: the short-term was all they had left.

What Nancy did next would determine their fate and that of countless others; it was a responsibility that she alone seemed prepared to shoulder. Yet these were no isolated cases. There had been many prosecutions over the years, the accused lifted by police and put before a court of law, some sent to jail. And still it went on. Her actions weren't an exercise in conscience cleansing. At every turn, she'd spoken up. On each occasion, she'd been told to shut the fuck up or face the consequences . . . And the consequence had just rounded the bend in her rear-view mirror.

Oh God!

He'd found the letter sooner than she'd anticipated. She imagined him skulking around her office, opening drawers, his dirty fingers all over her stuff. Curious to know what was inside an envelope addressed to her boss, he'd have broken his neck to get over there, a sneer developing as he was sent after her . . . Nancy didn't want to think what his instructions had been.

'Deal with it!' most probably.

And deal with it he would.

Nancy's stomach took a dive, the stress of what he had in mind bringing on arrhythmia, a condition she'd endured since her early twenties, a skipped heartbeat that seemed to last forever, followed by a thunderous shake of the vital organ struggling to right itself beneath her ribs, like a car battery spurred into life by jump leads. She'd never outrun the Land Rover on this remote stretch of road, though she'd do her damnedest to escape the man in the car behind . . .

Or die trying.

Up ahead, a beam of light across the road. A lucky break . . . An articulated lorry on its way out of a stone quarry, slow-moving with a heavy load. Braking, she flashed him out. The vehicle moved forward, a lumbering beast, its cab moving one way, the trailer seeming to disconnect as the driver turned the wheel. Nancy waited . . . the Land Rover gaining ground.

She had one shot.

Just one.

Flooring the accelerator, she took her chance, pulling out, squeezing her Fiat Panda through the narrow gap between the lorry cab and trees lining the opposite carriageway. Blinded by headlights, Nancy pulled hard on the wheel, swerving to avoid oncoming traffic, missing the lead vehicle by a whisper, a long line of cars preventing the four-by-four from overtaking. An angry, elongated blast of a horn from behind.

Nancy stared wide-eyed into the rear-view mirror.

The lorry slowed in response to the maniac behind, frustrating the driver of the tailing vehicle. The Land Rover countered, poking its nose out to enable him to get a better view, disappearing as quickly, repeating the process over and over again in an attempt to get by. Nancy drew her eyes away, struggling to concentrate. More horns. Flashing headlights. Road rage might save her skin.

A clear image of the man chasing her arrived in her head: evil eyes like dark pools of hostility burned into her memory; callous hands gripping the wheel; foul mouth screaming abuse. He was not someone you messed with. Nancy glanced at the speedo; it was climbing – seventy, seventy-five, eighty – increasing the distance between them. She prayed that there would be no break in the oncoming traffic. If she could make it to Devil's Bend, she could take the back roads, switch off her headlights and call for help. It wouldn't be swift to arrive. This was rural Northumberland. No cops. Only robbers. She had more chance of dating Idris Elba than seeing a police car at this time of night.

The sadistic pig in hot pursuit would show no pity, Nancy knew that. Inflicting pain was his thing; thinking about it, doing it, was like an aphrodisiac to him. Carrying out someone's dirty work handed him the power and kept his employer's hands clean; the meaner he was, the better he liked it. Distracted by that scary reality, Nancy miscalculated the angle of the bend. She took the corner too fast, tipping her vehicle on to two wheels momentarily.

She opened her mouth to scream but no sound came out.

The Fiat hung in the air, seemingly in slow motion, before righting itself, crashing to earth with a thud on a dark dirt road, glancing off a tree, shaking the chassis like a toy. She almost lost control of the steering wheel as the car bumped over uneven ground, rattling the interior and her along with it.

Taking her foot off the brake, she killed the lights, her eyes stuck fast to the darkness where her wing mirror used to be, hoping that the lorry – and, crucially, the four-by-four – would coast by without seeing her. As it did, she blew out a breath, turned her lights back on and drove further into the wood.

Cutting the engine, she wept, white noise filling her head, fists clenched so tightly her nails dug into the palms of her hands. She was struggling to get breath into her lungs as she squinted into the forest, the trees like malevolent figures standing guard. An owl hooted, irritated by the disturbance. Shivering in the dark, Nancy fumbled her phone from her pocket, losing it in the footwell as it slipped from a shaky hand. A fingertip-search failed to locate it.

She tried again.

Nothing.

'Come on!'

Another car flew by on the road behind, a streak of light, like a comet in the Northumberland sky. Turning the light on to find the phone wasn't an option. It would act like a beacon in the pitch-dark forest, pinpointing her exact location in the event he doubled back. Stay calm. It has to be here somewhere. She tried again with her left hand, then her right, walking her fingers across rubber matting caked in dried mud. Her little finger nudged a solid object. The device had bounced, lodging itself on its edge under the door sill.

Finally! Using her thumb to activate the screen illuminated the car. A waste of time. What the fuck? No signal.

Nancy panicked.

If she had to wait till morning with the engine off, she'd freeze to death. Tonight, minus five was forecast. The road lit up behind her: headlights that sent a shiver down her spine. The beams didn't flicker or change as she stared at them. They were stationary . . .

Weren't they?

Nancy held her breath . . . one, two, three seconds . . . four. Switching off her phone, she scanned the surrounding vegetation, imagination in overdrive. Had he parked his vehicle? Was he heading out on foot, stalking her with intent to do her harm? No . . . The lights were on the move, inching closer and closer to the junction where she'd left the road. Out of the car now, she legged it. Fifty yards, no more. Ducking down, she waited, praying that the open door of the Fiat would give the impression that she was long gone.

From her position, she had a good view.

The approaching vehicle slowed, turning in, illuminating the dense and eerie forest, her car along with it. Momentarily, Nancy froze, her face pressed against the rough bark of the tree she was clinging to, senses on high alert. She shut her eyes, the better to concentrate. Geoff always did that when she read to him.

Blinded by headlights, she couldn't see the shape of the car clearly and prayed that this was not the one she was hiding from, that it was someone else, a couple of lovers perhaps, a clandestine rendezvous. In seconds, she realised she was wrong. There was no disputing the clunk of the door of a high-end motor.

The Land Rover.

Opening her eyes, Nancy shuffling sideways. A dark, menacing shadow passed across the headlights of the four-by-four. A twig snapped behind her. Dry-heaving, she swung round

6

to find the eyes of a stag staring back at her, ears pricked up, aware of the danger.

That made two of them.

As it bounded off into the forest, Nancy turned back. The figure was on the move, a torch in his hand, its beam sweeping left and right, left and right, like a searchlight looking for survivors in a deep and dangerous sea, except for Nancy there was no lifeboat crew to pull her to safety. The flashlight was now trained on her empty Fiat, then suddenly it changed direction.

Move, MOVE!

Nancy prayed that nature would provide enough cover. She crouched low, scrambling across rough terrain on her hands and knees, over the stumps of felled trees, snagging clothing, brambles lacerating her skin as she moved through the brush. In her rush to stand upright, her wedding ring caught on a branch as she propelled herself forward, dislocating her finger. The pain was excruciating, stopping her dead in her tracks.

The thought of Geoff – gone six years – gave her strength. In spite of the crushing grief of losing him, she'd kept her side of the bargain to carry on. He was a good man, a kind man. Irreplaceable. A voice, weak and croaky, arrived in her head. 'Without me around to hold you back, you can do anything you want.' He'd winked at her. 'You could go to law school, finish your degree, or take up the voluntary work you're always banging on about. Fight the good fight, Nancy. It's what you've always dreamed of. Whatever you choose, you'll be brilliant at it. Give it your all . . . Not for me or the kids . . . Do it for yourself.'

That conversation – the hospital ward in which it had taken place – was a memory so vivid, she could almost feel his bony hand attempting to squeeze hers. There was no strength in it. He was tired. Ready to say goodbye. She wasn't. Somehow, she'd managed a smile, a lump forming in her throat, their plans in ruins, the idea of losing him breaking her heart.

'Promise me you won't dwell on what you can't have,' he'd said.

'I promise.'

'We've had a ball, haven't we?'

'You bet.'

'No tears?'

God, how she'd wanted to bawl. A shake of the head was all she managed in reply.

Geoff winked at her. 'I'll be with you every step of the way, Nancy.'

'I know.'

Two days later, he was gone.

He'd known that, even as a kid, if she'd witnessed injustice, she felt compelled to confront it. Right now, she could be forgiven for thinking she'd picked a fight she couldn't win. A sob left her throat as she stared ahead through pools of water, propelling herself further into the forest, inch by painful inch, aware that with every step forward, the only exit was behind her. She'd have to find a place to hide, a crawl space in the undergrowth. Later, when the coast was clear, she'd double back to the main road, flag down a car and get a ride. The only alternative was to make for high ground where she might find a signal.

Might.

With superhuman effort and Geoff's encouragement urging her on, she hauled herself upright, prepared to do whatever was necessary to get out of there and finish what she'd started. Each time the flashlight reached her, she took cover, turning her body sideways to make herself invisible, setting off only when it moved away. She sprinted, arms like pistons, darting left and right. Better a moving target than a stationary one. The gunshot was a warning to stand still. In this part of 'the Shire' no one would hear, let alone question it: a poacher, gamekeeper, deerstalker – someone in for the kill on a lonely woodland track. Given her present predicament, the description was apt. The man with the firearm was a hunter, Nancy his prey.

1

One year later . . .

Slow-moving rush hour traffic. The biker cautiously weaved his way through a three-lane snarl-up on the city bypass, the north–west radial route. At this rate, it would be a while before Chris Adams reached his destination. He had stuff on his mind, not least of which was the possibility that frustrated drivers would forget to 'think bike' and change lanes unexpectedly in their rush to get home, wiping him out in the process. A momentary lapse in concentration had proved fatal to many who'd chosen two wheels over four. As a mode of transport, motorcycles were thrilling, but highly dangerous if caught in the blind spot of other road users.

Bringing his Suzuki to a stop, he dropped his right leg, resting his foot on the slippery tarmac. Rainbows of diesel glistened on the wet road, dark patches of death reminding him of the pal he'd lost a year ago, who'd hit an oil spill on a bend and spun out of control. Then there was the one that kept him awake nights, invading his dreams, an even closer friend, devoted wife and mother of two, a highly skilled rider who'd died when her bike hit a pothole, throwing her and her machine into the path of an oncoming car. Riding directly behind her, Chris had witnessed the fatality.

She was dead before she reached hospital.

After that, his mother had begged him to abandon his machine until the spring. Maybe she was right. Chris considered this as a gap in traffic opened up, allowing him to take a slip road off the central motorway and double back into town, but there was nothing like the thrill of two wheels, the exhilaration of an open road where he was free, not dogged by work-related preoccupation with criminal activity and the inevitable misery for victims that came with it. Much of his life had been pedestrian. Speed concentrated the mind – made him come alive – with only one consideration: survival.

He opened the throttle, a quick head check before moving off, keen to return to his office, wishing he had something that might put a smile on the miserable face of the man he worked for.

He didn't.

His day had been much like any other. A stuffy courtroom, a mixed list of prosecutions. Nothing sensational. No meaty cases that might catch the public imagination. Not even a serious faux pas by an ageing member of the judiciary like last Friday; an inappropriate remark to a female barrister from a High Court judge during a rape case that caused a sharp intake of breath from those assembled in the courtroom, followed by a demand from the victim to retry the defendant before a different judge and a swift complaint to the Lord Chief Justice by the Crown Prosecutor. The story had made the nationals and drawn outrage from feminists on social media who were demanding an immediate resignation.

They wouldn't get it.

Chris had spent the best part of two years on the press bench listening to people argue over criminal prosecutions: judges, lawyers, police, probation officers and other expert witnesses, an endless list of professionals with insight into the criminal mind and culture. Many in the dock were sad, disaffected and underprivileged, those who'd fought to survive a lifetime of abuse or neglect. Some had come full circle, making the leap from abused to abuser. And so it went on . . .

Depressing.

In the main, Chris was there to report on those at the other end of the spectrum, the public interest cases involving hardened criminals for whom violence had become a way of life, those who peddled drugs, raped or murdered, or had taken the view that the laws of the land didn't apply. If a repeat offender committed a heinous crime, all the better. There was nothing like blame to whip up a frenzy and sell newsprint, hard copy or digital. Those who failed to control the urge to inflict pain on release – physical, sexual and financial – were top of his target list.

Chris used to believe in justice and rehabilitation. That's what drew him to the job, but lately he'd become disillusioned. The criminal justice system was a game, the courtroom a theatre where the best legal minds in the country battled for supremacy to audiences who focused on the spectacle.

Where was the will to see due process prevail?

There were the usual voyeurs in court today, those who came, week in, week out to gawp at offenders in the dock or witness the grief etched on the faces of eyewitnesses during cross-examination, the gory details of murder and manslaughter providing free entertainment. There was no doubt in Chris's mind that some in the public gallery were switched wrong. The majority viewed criminal trials as real-life versions of the courtroom dramas they had seen on screen. They'd have bought popcorn if it was available.

As he passed by, he glanced at the iconic 24-carat gold Rolex clock outside the Northern Goldsmith's. He was late. Much later than he thought. Dropping a gear, he turned down a back alley, parking up to the rear of a large office block. Pulling his motorcycle on to its stand, Chris removed his helmet and ear-plugs, ran a hand through his hair in an effort to make himself halfway presentable. Securing his bike with an alarmed disc lock – a gift from his mother on his birthday – he stowed his skid lid and gloves in the pannier and rushed inside, legging it up the stairs two at a time, pushing open the door to an open-plan office.

Reporters caught up in the usual frenetic activity of the newsroom ignored him as he moved swiftly towards a door marked Mark Fox: Editor-in-Chief – the sign picked out in bold black letters, polished every day by the office cleaner. Chris could see the great man himself through the blind of the internal window that allowed him to keep a close eye on his staff. A stickler for punctuality, Fox had a face like a slapped arse. He was sitting at the head of a large table impatiently tapping his pen, while the four men and two women who made up the editorial team looked on.

They had started without him.

Taking a deep breath, the court reporter knocked on the door.

A bark came from within. 'Come!'

Turning the handle, Chris entered, sweat sticking to the shirt he was wearing beneath his Belstaff jacket. If an atmosphere in a room could be described as a colour, this one would be gun-metal grey. The editorial meeting obviously hadn't gone well. Heads were down. Fox's expression was stern, his default position.

No change there then.

What Chris had to say wouldn't make it any better. As he moved into the room, Fox relaxed into his chair and made a meal of showing his irritation.

'Nice of you to join us,' he said.

'Sorry to keep you waiting. Traffic was a bastard.'

'Take a seat.' It was an order, not a request.

Taking off his jacket, Chris pulled a pen and a crumpled notepad from the pocket of his jeans. Flipping it open was a mistake; the page was covered in doodles and very little else. Blushing, he glanced around the room, noticing that everyone assembled had homed in on his untidy scrawl. Trish, the female features editor who'd taken him under her wing when he joined the paper, sent him an unspoken message to get on with his input. This late on a Friday afternoon, she couldn't wait to get out of there. Chris felt sorry for her. She'd been there fifteen years. The provincial newspaper was now in trouble, according to those in the know. Heads would roll before long.

His probably.

He'd been looking over his shoulder for weeks, hanging on to his job by his fingernails, feeling undervalued and under pressure. Some journalists were seeking work elsewhere. Pay was frozen. Fox was in denial. If he was looking for a punch-bag to vent his anger on, Chris would do nicely.

'Do you have anything of interest to contribute this week,' Fox said, 'or have we been sitting here twiddling our thumbs for nothing?'

'Guilty verdict on the Canning Street burglaries,' Chris began. 'Foregone conclusion, given that the cops found the defendant asleep on the premises . . .' A chuckle made its way round the room. Fox was the only one with a straight face. The guy needed to lighten up. 'His defence was laughable,' Chris continued. 'Claimed he was so drunk, he'd wandered into the wrong house, hence the "Not Guilty" plea. The judge took one look at his form – a list of breaking and entering convictions as long as the Tyne – and sent him down for twelve.'

Fox glared at him. 'I wish you wouldn't talk in shorthand.'

'Twelve months,' Chris confirmed.

'And Armstrong?' The editor was referring to a man due to stand trial for Section 18 Wounding. His victim – a young woman he was having a relationship with – had suffered a serious skull fracture that very nearly ended her life. Too frightened to press charges following a lengthy spell in hospital, she'd become hostile in interview, refusing to point the finger at the man responsible. A concerned neighbour who'd witnessed the attack from her bedroom window made an official complaint and gave the police an in, a chance to put a violent man away without compromising the girlfriend.

'He walked,' Chris said. 'The prosecution accepted a plea to ABH.'

'What?' Fox was appalled.

'Actual bodily harm, boss.' As the piss-take landed in his boss's lap, Chris didn't make eye contact with anyone else in the room. If the editor-in-chief wanted longhand, then that's exactly what he'd get.

'I know what it is, you idiot—'

Chris cut off the stream of abuse he suspected was coming his way. 'The judge swallowed the sob story peddled by his barrister. The usual bollocks: unfortunate upbringing; in with the wrong crowd; spent time in care, unloved and un-supported by family.'

'Sounds familiar,' Fox said.

The subtext of his comment stung.

Biting his lip, Chris swallowed down his anger. 'Armstrong put his hands up to slapping the IP – I mean Injured Party. The case hinged on his intent to do her serious harm. She'd fallen backwards, hitting her head on a ceramic garden pot, an undeserved misfortune that made him sound like a halo short of a saint.' Adams struggled to keep the edge from his voice. 'Oh, and you should know he's turning his life around. The couple are expecting a baby. Medics found that out when she was laid up in hospital. Armstrong also has a job interview – the first for a decade. Pound to a penny it'll have vanished before he swaggered from the building with his entourage.'

'What did he get?' Fox queried.

'Conditional discharge.'

'You're kidding,' three colleagues said in unison.

'Nope. There were ructions in the courtroom.'

'Hardly surprising,' Trish said. 'Everyone knows the guy's a thug.'

Fox glanced at his watch, then at Chris. 'If there's nothing in it for us, couldn't you have phoned it in?' There was no pleasing him.

'Not if you wanted all the results, Mark. I was covering more than one court.'

The informality displeased the man at the head of the table. 'What about the murder trial in court four?'

'Jury failed to reach a verdict. They've been sent home for the weekend.'

'That sounds like an idea.' Fox looked around. 'Are we done?'

The editorial team were nodding, the first display of genuine enthusiasm since Chris walked in to the room.

2

The job asked too much sometimes. There were moments when Detective Sergeant Frankie Oliver felt she might go into meltdown, that one more call-out would tip her over the edge; times when the need to ignore her mobile phone competed with a compulsion to answer. Tonight, the sound of the device vibrating on the table evoked a sense of dread so immediate and profound that it caused the hairs on her bare arms to lift. She knew instantly that it was a duty call – even before she checked the home screen. Like every other force in the country, Northumbria Police expected, no, demanded, the attention of those who'd taken the oath to Queen and Country.

Who wanted a private life anyhow?

With half an eye on her host, Frankie picked up the phone, jabbing at the button that would connect her to her SIO, Detective Chief Inspector David Stone. He cut straight to the chase, no pleasantries or apology for the interruption to her evening.

'We're on,' he said.

The word 'dead' was a given or he wouldn't have troubled her. Swearing under her breath, Frankie threw an apologetic glance at her host. As Stone's second-in-command on the Murder Investigation Team, Frankie's presence was mandatory. Her private life took a back seat where the job was concerned. She listened carefully as he gave a brief summary – another crime scene, another pointless death – a stabbing this time. No weapon had been found. No ID on the body either. As was often the case, details were sketchy. In the early stage of an investigation, many victims were nameless, empty vessels. It was up to detectives in any Major Incident Team to fill in the blanks; to get to know the deceased post-mortem; to identify the IP and inhabit their lives in order to understand their deaths. Murder bound victim to investigator, a seal impossible to break.

David was still talking . . .

'The victim is of mixed race, early thirties or thereabouts. He was found in Northumberland Place, Newcastle. Breathing, only just . . . and not for long. Pronounced dead at the scene by an off-duty paramedic who happened to be passing and noticed him lying in the alleyway. He called it in at 22.05.'

Frankie glanced at her watch. It was only half past. David lived in a rural area forty-five minutes from the city centre, thirty if he was really pushing it. She said, 'What did you do, fly there?'

'I was already in town.'

'You have a life? That's news to me.'

He laughed.

He'd left his Northumberland home to join the Metropolitan Police fifteen years earlier, making a life in London, losing touch with old friends. Since he'd returned to his roots a few months ago, he'd been working round the clock, too busy to remake their acquaintance. There were few people he associated with outside of work and he hadn't mentioned any arrangements during the day. It had her wondering if he'd met someone and if that someone was a woman. He sidestepped the question she was dying to ask . . .

'The pathologist will meet us there.'

'Us?'

Frankie's eyes flew across the room to where her sister-in-law – Inspector Andrea McGovern, a Traffic cop she'd known since training school – was splayed out on the sofa, shoes off, a remote control in one hand, a glass of red in the other, waiting patiently for her to get off the phone.

'Guv, it's movie night. Andrea and I have popcorn and everything!'

'Nice try, Frank. Now get a wriggle on. I could do with some help. If you've had a drink, I'll send a car.'

'No need. I'm sober . . . Saving myself for Santa.'

David laughed, making light of her seeming reluctance to drop everything and come running. In spite of what she'd said, he knew she didn't mean it. She was already feeling the adrenalin rush, a physical reaction that came with every new investigation. For her, duty was everything, part of her DNA. She was already pulling on her coat, scooping up her car keys, miming apologies to her in-law, questioning initial intelligence as she readied herself to leave. As a third-generation cop, it had been drilled into her by her father and grandfather never to take anything at face value. An open mind was key to any murder case.

'Any witnesses?' she asked.

'Not to the incident, though the town is heaving. You know what it's like on a Friday night. The blues and twos drew quite a crowd. A rowdy bunch, as you'd expect, the majority of them still hanging around when first responders arrived on the scene – you'd think they had no homes to go to.'

'Anything else?'

'They don't know the victim—'

'They probably don't know how to tell the truth either.' It was out of Frankie's mouth before she could stop it. Some minds were more open than others. She leaned over, kissed Andrea's forehead by way of apology and made for the door. 'Hold on to your audience, guv. I'm on my way.'

By the time she arrived, the crime scene was flooded with police vehicles, the area already locked down. David watched her climb out of her car, pull her collar up and push through a growing crowd of onlookers. She was casually dressed, jeans and boots, a thick red scarf wrapped around her neck, police-issue gloves and laser eyes that could bring down a Boeing if she tried real hard. As she walked towards him, he

received her unspoken message: another Friday night ruined
. . . coppers were entitled to a social life. Had he not known
that she didn't believe that any more than he did, it might
have made him feel guilty. As it was, beneath the veneer of irritation, he detected a mixture of emotions: the thrill of being
part of an elite murder squad competing with the anguish
that another violent death had taken place on the streets of a
city they both loved.

Acknowledging him with a nod, she ducked beneath the
outer cordon and sauntered up the slight incline of the side
street, passing through a row of bollards preventing vehicular
access, ignoring a wolf whistle as it rang out behind her. In
any other situation, she'd have retraced her steps to challenge
the sexism of the brainless moron belittling her. Tonight, her
priorities were more important than personal feelings.

The SIO was standing east of a Moss Bros shop, close to a
couple of phone boxes. A crime scene screen had been erected
to keep prying eyes out; he stood aside to let Frankie enter.
She pulled up sharp as she neared the body, her focus at
ground level, blue strobe lighting flashing across her solemn
face. The victim was lying face up, close to the wall, about
a quarter of the way between Northumberland Street and
the city's Central Library, a wound to the chest, a smart grey
jacket stained the colour of beetroot.

David watched the grief appear on Frankie's face. Any life
taken by force was distressing. More so, it seemed, in the
festive season. There was no job worse than giving the death
message to loving parents in the presence of a twinkling
Christmas tree, in a home decked out to welcome family
and friends. It wasn't only that that had upset her. There was
something else, a definite shift in her mood that put him on
alert.

He studied her carefully.

While she was saddened by every unlawful fatality, this
one was different. Ordinarily, she'd have crouched down

to examine the body, offered an opinion, taken a good look around, sharing insight into what the scene was telling her, photographing everything in situ even though the crime scene photographer was on site doing it. This evening, in this back lane littered with fag ends and discarded rubbish, there was none of that. It worried the DCI. She was rattled, frozen to the spot and it had nothing to do with the plummeting temperature.

Something was up.

He moved closer, dropping his voice to a whisper. 'Frank? What is it?'

She didn't answer immediately.

Pulling the scarf away from her neck to get some air, she allowed it to hang loose to her knees, unbuttoned her coat, her gaze fixed on the deceased, a mop of dark hair, a strong jawline, brown lifeless eyes. Frankie seemed to age instantly. She looked like she might drop to her knees and start wailing. She hung on.

'His name is Chris Adams.' She didn't look at him.

Her tone of voice was professionally detached. David hated that phrase. It was meaningless. And untrue. No detective he knew was that hard-boiled. Underneath the inscrutable, cool-headed veneer, they were as emotional as everyone else. Detectives felt the pain, the tragic loss for those left behind, even if they locked it in during a shift. In the small hours, time and again it would come back to haunt them when they least expected it. David often woke sweating and gasping for breath having rerun an awful crime scene during sleep. It made a mockery of the advice not to take your work home with you.

Frankie was no different. David knew that. Except tonight her expression was tinged with nostalgia, as if a million memories were competing for space in her head. She turned to look at him, her jaw rigid, anger distorting her soft features, hands balled into fists of pent-up aggression.

'We were neighbours,' she said.

'Jesus! I'm so sorry—'

'Yeah, me too.'

'Were you close?'

'Very . . . once upon a time.' There was a hard edge to her voice. 'I . . . sorry, guv, I'm finding it hard to process this. His mother . . . oh, God! How the hell will I tell his mother?'

'You won't have to, Frankie. I'll take care of it.'

'No, you don't understand. How could you? It's complicated.' She stared at the victim, closed her eyes, then opened them again, a white cloud visible in the darkness as she blew out a breath, an attempt to gather her resolve. And still she wasn't in any fit condition to do her job. She sucked in a breath. 'Guv, I'm sorry. I'm OK, I just need a minute.'

David caught the eye of the uniformed officer guarding the tent. Flicking his head to the right, the SIO sent him packing. The PC scurried off without a word. David was about to reach out and rest a comforting hand on Frankie's shoulder, but then he thought of all the prying eyes and phone cameras trained on them and how such an action might be misconstrued.

Another whistle, a cackle of laughter from behind.

Frankie swung round. 'Does that arsehole think this is funny?'

'Let it go,' David said quietly. 'In fact, stand down. I'll call Abbott out—'

A filthy look. 'The hell you will.' She was appalled by the suggestion that she wasn't up to the job because she had prior knowledge of the victim. 'I'm here now and I'm going nowhere.' She glared into the crowd, her eyes homing in on the kid giving her grief. 'Keep that fucker away from me or I'll deck the bastard.'

'Go home, Frankie.'

'No. Andrea will be halfway through *Killing Ground* already.' Seeing his reaction, her eyebrows almost met in the middle.

David spread his hands. 'I'm saying nowt.'

'You didn't need to. Your eyes did it for you. So, you found me out. I'm a sad fuck who spends all day dealing with shite like this and then goes home to watch it on TV. It doesn't make you a bad person. It relaxes me. It's something Andrea and I have done since we were at training school together—'

'Frankie, stop!'

She already had, her attention straying to Northumberland Street where a helter-skelter rose up from the pavement to celebrate the joy of Christmas. She seemed lost in another time, another memory. She turned to face him, clearing her throat. 'Chris's mum brought us here when we were kids. She let me push his buggy. I was seven. He was three. I've never ever seen a bairn so excited.'

David needed no further explanation. For over a month, a crocodile of children and their parents had formed an orderly queue across the road to stand in wonderment at the famous Fenwick's Christmas windows, an annual trip for thousands of kids. Frankie's melancholy expression changed to one of disgust as she noticed a group standing in the foreground beyond the cordon, baggy trousers at half mast, baseball caps worn the wrong way around, skinny frames, screaming skulls; drinking, smoking and smirking, as if a young man's death was inconsequential, something to laugh about.

David sensed trouble as he followed her gaze.

Shivering in the cold, hands jammed into their pockets, a crowd of mostly young men had formed, an interruption to their crawl around the city's clubs and public houses. The youngest of the group, a kid with flame-red hair, gave them the one-finger salute, mouthing off to impress his mates, all of whom were high on alcohol and thought he was hilarious. Instinctively, the SIO knew that he'd be the one Frankie would single out to talk to. There was nothing surer. Unless she had eyes in the back of her head, she couldn't know that this was the same lad who'd whistled at her when she'd arrived a moment ago.

'Ignore them,' David said. 'Go and watch your movie, if you can still stomach it. I can manage here.'

'I said I'm fine. And, for the record' – she flicked her head towards the rubberneckers – 'unlike the scumbags beyond the tape, I have respect for the dead and can tell the difference between fact and fiction. If they saw anything, we need these people processed. Otherwise, we need them shifted.' Catching the eye of a uniform hiding over David's shoulder, Frankie raised her voice to attract his attention. 'Excuse me?'

The copper pointed at his chest.

A nod from her. 'What's your name?'

'PC Joe Taylor.' He walked towards her.

'OK, Joe. I'm DS Frankie Oliver. Keep hold of Mouth Almighty with the ginger hair. Take the details of the rest and move them on . . . all except her.' Beth Collingwood, Home Office pathologist, had emerged from through the crowd and was heading their way at a fast pace.

3

David had the floor. The incident room was half-empty, despite his call putting the Murder Investigation Team on alert that he wanted them in bright and early for a briefing. Detectives had fallen like ninepins in the past week with a winter bug that was proving hard to shake. To say they were thin on the ground was a gross understatement. The whole force was understaffed and under pressure, including other Murder Investigations Teams he might have called upon to help. Fortunately for the SIO, key personnel had survived the lurgy and made it in to work: DS Dick Abbott, a detective with twenty-five years' experience; DC Ray (Mitch) Mitchell, a rookie brimming with enthusiasm and eager to impress; PC Indira Sharma, their new aide, who had her eye on a transfer to the CID, and a few others. They could manage . . .

Just about.

David waited for the hum of conversations to die down, keen to crack on. 'As you all know, the body of a young male was found in Newcastle city centre last night. On a busy Friday, it goes without saying that canvassing the area for potential witnesses is going to be a 'mare for us. Frankie identified the victim at the scene as Chris Adams. The post-mortem was carried out in the early hours of this morning by Beth Collingwood. A full report will follow, but I can give you the gist of it. The IP sustained a fatal penetrating trauma to the left chest, puncturing the heart, causing massive blood loss.'

'Any news on the type of weapon used?' Abbott said.

'Not yet. Beth seems to think it's unusual.'

'In what way?'

'Apparently, it's not something your average punter who

carries an offensive weapon would have on their person, or in a kitchen drawer for that matter. She isn't even sure it's British. Fortunately for us, there's been some in-depth research into knives that might help us. Beth's looking into it. In the meantime, please familiarise yourself with this . . .'

He was pointing at the murder wall, a visual aid to their investigation where lines of enquiry, scenes of crime photographs, victim information, location maps and potential leads would be posted over the coming days and weeks. It had replaced the old-fashioned version, a glorified whiteboard, littered with cards and scrappy notes. The modern equivalent was digital, a giant smart TV screen attached to the wall of the incident room, linked to a computer where evidence strands could be pulled up, overlaid and linked by the touch of a button as the enquiry progressed.

Frankie had uploaded stills taken at the crime scene. She could hardly bear to look at them. Mitchell raised a hand, eyes glued to the image of the victim. Chris Adams' eyes were open, one of them bloodshot, a scuff above his right eye. Mitch glanced at the SIO.

'Are the injuries to the IP's face fresh, guv?'

'No,' David said. 'They're at least a week old, so we have work to do.'

'Maybe his parents will know how they got there.'

'Parent,' Frankie corrected him. 'His father is dead and we've yet to locate his mother.' She glanced at the SIO. David gave her the nod, her cue to take over. She stood up, the better to see and be seen. 'Susan Adams didn't answer the door last night, so we're not releasing the victim's name to the press until she's found, informed and formal identification is complete.'

'Any siblings?' Abbott asked.

'None,' Frankie said.

'You seem to be very well informed.'

'Sadly, I am. I knew the victim personally, *knew* being the operative word. Unless the guv'nor has anything more to add, I'll fill you in on what I know of his antecedent history.'

David signalled that she should proceed.

All eyes turned in Frankie's direction, registering that she had no notes, a heavy hint that she knew the victim well enough not to need them.

'Chris and I lived across the road from one another as kids. We practically grew up together, though he's four years younger than me. Our parents were the best of friends. His mother is a recovering alcoholic; his father, an African American war correspondent, now deceased. Stan Adams was killed on assignment in the Middle East. Susan Adams was pregnant at the time and never got over it . . .' Frankie paused, a sad look on her face. 'Long story short, she went into meltdown, began killing herself with alcohol soon after her son was born, a downward spiral that saw him in care on more than one occasion. She'd dry out, get him home, then repeat the process . . .' The DS made winders with her hands. 'This went on for years, a story we're all too familiar with.'

Frankie perched on the nearest desk, a relaxed pose, one leg dangling over the edge. Her body language didn't fool David. He sensed the tension, despite her valiant attempt at hiding it. Fleetingly, he wondered how close she'd been to the victim, if there was more to their relationship than she was prepared to share with the team. Even if Chris Adams was younger than her, the older they got, the less it would matter. If they had ever been an item, it must've been a long time ago. She'd never spoken of him in general conversation, but that meant very little in the scheme of things. When it came to his 2ic, in spite of her extrovert personality, getting personal information out of her was like mining coal.

A pick and a shovel were a must.

'That said,' she continued, 'Chris was lucky. Unlike a lot of kids, he survived periods in foster care unscathed. At home he had a rough time. Parent/child roles were reversed: he was the carer, his mother the one who needed looking after. Consequently, he lost a lot of time at school, through no fault of his own, and got into college by the skin of his teeth.'

'Locally?' Mitch was notetaking.

'Newcastle College.' Frankie glanced in his direction. 'He wouldn't leave his mum. That was the kind of lad he was.'

David thought he saw her falter then. She recovered quickly. If there had been any recent relationship between victim and investigator, it would rule her out of involvement in the case. He didn't want that, and Frankie had made it perfectly clear that there was no conflict of interest – he'd have a fight on his hands if he pushed her on the subject.

'There was no wallet found on his body?' Abbott asked.

Frankie shook her head. 'No cash, bus pass or railcard either. No mobile phone or car keys. The lack of ID and means of communication would lend itself to the theory that he'd been rolled for his possessions. We need to know how he arrived in the city and how he was intending getting home.'

'Unless he walked in,' Mitch offered.

'That's possible,' Frankie said. 'As far as I'm aware, he still lives with his mum in Woolsington, so it would have been a bloody long walk. Her address is on my desk. Get on to the DVLA and see what vehicles are registered to the property, then check the details against the ANPR. I know for a fact that Chris drives, so his car might be sitting in a parking bay somewhere. If he wasn't alone, there might be evidence to collect. I want it found.'

'Do we know what make of vehicle he drives?'

'No, sorry.'

'If he still lives with his mum, and she can't be found, can't you call your old man?' Mitch said. 'He'll have clocked the car, for sure. I mean, not much gets past him, does it?'

Normally, Frankie would have laughed. Although he was now retired, her father was a legend in Northumbria Police. She hesitated. David knew why and so did Dick Abbott. Mitch had no idea what he'd stepped in, only that he'd touched a raw nerve.

He backpedalled swiftly. 'As you were, Sarge. It's probably best to wait until we find and inform next of kin.'

David stood up to face the squad. 'Now it's your turn. First impressions . . . anyone?'

Abbott raised a finger. 'Based on the absence of personal possessions, it sounds like a botched robbery to me, rather than the result of a fight – that's if I can trust my gut.'

'Sometimes that's all we have,' David said.

'Works for me,' Frankie added. 'Anyway, Chris wasn't the type to involve himself in violence. He was always the peacemaker, never one to retaliate if someone took a pop at him – and they often did – in and out of school, for all sorts of reasons. His mother sent him in in dirty kit, no lunch money or note for being absent.'

'He was bullied?' Abbott asked.

'A long time ago. You know how cruel kids are.'

'Could that be relevant?'

'I doubt it.'

'That eye injury came from somewhere.'

Frankie met Abbott's gaze across the incident room. 'That's a valid point, but the Chris I knew was always one of the good guys. Unless he's undergone a personality transplant in recent years, I can't see him scrapping in the street; a) it's not his style and b) there are no defence injuries that would suggest an attempt to ward off an attack. I think it's more likely he was caught by surprise.'

'How long since you last saw him?' Another question from Mitch.

Frankie was proud of her protégé. She'd taught him to question everything, just as her father had taught her. Right now, the young detective was doing a great job. She turned to face him. 'I'd see him now and then after I left home to go to training school, but weeks turn to months, months to years and then . . .' She paused. 'Last I heard, he was working for the *Corchester Herald* as a court reporter. Still does, I checked that out on my way in. That's where the guv'nor and I are heading next.'

A voice from the back of the room. 'Any witnesses to the attack?'

'Yeah, they're queueing up,' David said drily.

'No one?'

The SIO shook his head.

'Someone must have seen something.' Abbott again.

'Whether they're aware of it is another matter,' Frankie said. 'The town was lively last night. According to Mason Carter, the off-duty paramedic who happened to be in the area and tried to help, Northumberland Street was busy. There was no one else in the alleyway when he saw Chris lying there. People began showing interest when panda cars raced to the scene and not before. A crowd was building by the time the boss arrived, so either the incident went unnoticed, or people weren't aware of how seriously injured the IP was and walked on, preferring not to get involved.'

'Very public spirited,' Rob Mather muttered under his breath. He was the office anchor. Every statement that came in would pass over his desk in the course of the enquiry. He was the wrong side of forty, a man set in his ways. In his eyes, things were black or white; there were no grey areas.

'Can you blame them?' Frankie said. 'Piling in to someone else's fight is a risky business. You know as well as I do that Good Samaritans get hurt or end up in court charged with affray. Even if a pedestrian did see something, who's to say they'd realise what they were witnessing, let alone how serious it was? Chris died from a single stab wound. In a dark alleyway, a blow to the chest could look like a push or a punch – it would be over in the blink of an eye.'

'Frankie's right . . .' David had left the scene before her and suddenly remembered something. He caught her eye. 'How did you get on with that ginger kid?'

'Ginger kid?' Abbott queried.

'Michael Brent,' David explained. 'Teenager shouting his mouth off at the scene. Frankie didn't like the look of him.'

'Convenient punchbag?'

David shot Abbott down. 'I think you know her better than that.'

'Relax, guv. He was joking,' Frankie said. 'Otherwise, as big as he is, he'd be flat on his back.'

Everyone laughed, including Abbott. He and Frankie were close. She wouldn't miss the opportunity to get stuck in if the situation demanded it – everyone knew that – but she'd never vent her anger on a member of the public, no matter the circumstances or what mood she was in.

That wasn't her style.

'My conversation with Brent didn't take me anywhere, Dick. He was legless but harmless, less vocal when I put him in the back of my car. I gave him a good talking to. He tripped over himself to apologise for his behaviour.'

'Is he known to us?'

'No. I checked with Control before I let him go. He's now in the system, should his description come up again. And it will if he was anywhere near that scene before Chris was set upon. With hair that colour, he'd be hard to miss.'

'I've put out an appeal to get the ball rolling,' David said. 'Let's hope the phones start ringing soon. Anything else?' He was looking at Frankie. 'I'm keen to trace Mrs Adams and inform her of her son's death before someone does it for us.'

'There is one thing,' she said. 'En route to the crime scene, I observed a number of rough sleepers, at least two in the vicinity of Northumberland Place. If I know one thing about Chris, it's that he'd give anyone his last penny, especially someone in need. Assuming for a moment that he got his wallet out, and I have no proof that he did, his kindness may have cost him his life. You know what it's like at this time of year. People are desperate. Some poor sods have nowt to eat, no roof over their heads or access to help. They sit on the street with their hands out for loose change because that's all they can do. Others though are more aggressive. They're out in force, on the lookout for an opportunity, stealing to live—'

'There's a damn sight more out there living to steal,' Rob Mather said. 'They'd roll their granny to line their pockets.'

'That attitude isn't helpful,' Frankie snapped.

'A social conscience is not in Rob's toolbox,' Abbott said. 'Maybe we should have a whip round and give him one for Christmas.' The team laughed, a chance to let off steam. Dick wasn't done. He kept his focus on Mather. 'Maybe you should look up the difference between homeless beggars and thieving arseholes. In our region alone, the number of rough sleepers has doubled in three years.' Now he turned to face Frankie. 'You're not seriously suggesting the victim was rolled for his cash by one of them?'

'No—'

'We have no proof that he wasn't,' Mather said.

Dick rounded on him. 'Did I ask you?'

'Pack it in, you two.' Frankie eyeballed the two men. 'In-fighting isn't going to get us anywhere . . .'

Stone let her deal with it, tuning her out as she told them to button it. After a shaky start, the team he'd inherited since moving north was beginning to gel. There were still a few rough edges that needed smoothing over but he could count on his 2ic to get the iron out.

Like every other member of the MIT, Mather had earned his spot. He might not be good at the face-to-face stuff, but everyone, including Abbott, knew that he was a first-rate statement reader. Analytically, no one could touch him. Dick, on the other hand, was a people person. His skill lay in the sharp end of policing, dealing with the public, hands-on. Like Frankie, he was a detective with the experience, knowledge and instinct to turn a case on its head, not one to sit poring over statements all day long.

'We have no proof of what took place in that alleyway,' Frankie said. 'Only that it ended tragically. Most rough sleepers beg – that's how they get by – but aggressive begging is counterproductive. They know that it'll get them moved on. The reason I mentioned them is to highlight the possibility that among them we might find a vital witness, not a perpetrator. They may not have seen what happened, but they might have seen the person who stabbed Chris Adams leaving the scene. As far as I'm concerned, they're our eyes and ears on the street.'

'I agree,' David said. 'I want the outside team down there tonight asking questions.'

'Won't they have scarpered by now?' Mitch asked. 'The rough sleepers, I mean.'

'Not necessarily,' Frankie said. 'Many have a favourite spot, a doorway that offers a bit of shelter from the elements with plenty of foot traffic, a place they return to night after night. To them it's home, if that doesn't sound ridiculous. I'd be surprised if a death in the area would put them off. Male or female, they live with danger every night they sleep on the street.'

'Frankie has a point,' David said. 'If they're still there, I want every one of them spoken to. If any are missing, I want them found. Chris Adams may have been the target of a robbery that went horribly wrong, or God forbid a hate crime. It's our job to see his murderer doesn't get away with it. For the time being, theoretically speaking, that's all we've got in terms of motivation.'

David pumped the theories: a young man of mixed race on his own in the city would be vulnerable among large groups of drunken youths; some had racist tendencies, others would seize any chance to take a pop at someone they didn't like the look of. If Chris was seen handing money to someone on the street, he may have unwittingly signed his own death warrant.

'Guv?' Frankie said. 'I think robbery is the more likely scenario.'

David turned to face her. 'Why?'

'He may have withdrawn cash last night.' Using a remote control, she uploaded a map of the area around the crime scene. 'There are three ATMs around the corner at the NatWest Bank on Northumberland Street, within a hundred yards of where he was stabbed. Thanks to the paramedic who found him, we know the exact timescale. He called time of death at 22.05. Collingwood said Chris wouldn't have survived more than a few minutes after he was stabbed. Given that he was still breathing when the paramedic arrived, that narrows it down considerably. The scene is still being processed. Initial reports suggest that he died where he fell, so we can be quite prescriptive when we check the cashpoints. I'd like to explore the possibility that he made a withdrawal and see where that takes us.'

'Good. Now we're getting somewhere.'

4

Frankie tried Susan Adams one final time, then rang her own mother and left a message on her answer machine before leaving Northern Command HQ – or Middle Earth as it had been nicknamed by those who worked there – David having made an appointment to see the victim's editor, Mark Fox, a man they knew of but hadn't met in person. Progress was slow on the way to his office. They got stuck at the bottom of the coast road in nightmarish roadworks that had gone on for months.

Frankie checked her watch: nine thirty. 'We're going to be late.'

'It's the arse-end of rush hour. What did you expect?'

'I'd have expected a detour . . .' She grinned at him. 'It's called anticipation, guv. You should try it.'

They were like an old married couple sometimes: tit for tat in conversation, mostly good-humoured, though not always. Since they'd started working together there had been a few all-out rows and no-holds-barred shouting matches, but as a professional unit they remained tight. Stone was a good investigator, a good bloke; in Frankie's opinion, a keeper.

The stream of brake lights ahead didn't bode well.

David swore under his breath, as frustrated as she was that he was unable to make headway. Deciding to take the next slip road, he indicated, crossing from the middle to the inside lane, taking her kidding that he should have chosen another route. As he attempted to manoeuvre into position, an angry horn blasted from the vehicle behind. The driver put his foot down, preventing David from claiming the space.

'Look at this idiot!' David said. 'I fucking hate road rage!'

Frankie stifled a grin. 'Was that supposed to be ironic, guv?'

Ignoring her, he edged out further . . . and further still, until he was a few millimetres from the offending car. Another blast from his rival angered his 2ic. She leaned forward, checking her wing mirror. The red-faced driver inched forward, hurling abuse through an open window, one hand spread out in a gesture of discontent – and that was putting it mildly.

'He's lost it totally. Hold your line, guv.' Frankie wound her window down and stuck her head out. 'You got a problem, mate?'

'Yeah. My side, your side,' he yelled. 'Tell your boyfriend to fuck the fuck off.'

'I'd really like to help you out. Unfortunately, that would be insubordinate. He's not my boyfriend, he's my boss.'

'I don't give a shit who he is, he's not getting in, so he may as well stop trying.'

'Even if I ask nicely?'

'Even then! If he scratches my fucking car, he'll wish he hadn't.'

'Is that right?' Frankie grimaced. 'I'd swear too, only that would be conduct unbecoming a police officer.' She held up her warrant card. 'Now back the hell off.'

The car came to a sudden stop, allowing David in.

Frankie relaxed into her seat and crossed her arms, a big smile on her face. That small leather wallet with the shiny Northumbrian Police badge inside was as effective as any blue light. They had just got moving when her phone beeped an incoming text.

She scooped the device off the dash.

The word MUM appeared on the home screen. Frankie had told her mother only that she needed to speak to Susan Adams urgently. As a retired detective's wife, Julie Oliver knew better than to enquire further. Her message was short and sweet:

Susan's back.

Frankie typed a one-word reply: **Sober?**

For ages – and in good spirits.

Thanks, I'll be right there.

Anything I can do?

Sit tight. She's going to need a friend.

Understood.

'Change of plan,' Frankie said to David. 'Susan Adams is home.'

'Right.' He took his phone from his pocket and handed it to her. 'Call Fox and put him off. I didn't tell him why I wanted to see him, only that it was important. If he asks, make something up. No, on second thoughts, tell him the truth. We've been delayed on a priority job and will be there as soon as we can.'

Frankie was already making the call.

Completing a swift U-turn at the roundabout, heading back towards the coast, David took the A19 north, the A1 south, before finally heading west on to the A696 towards Newcastle International Airport, leaving the cityscape behind. The village of Woolsington was nine miles away. Frankie remained silent the entire journey. She was steeling herself for what would follow, drowning in her own dark memories.

Twenty-five minutes later, they reached their destination. Frankie glanced at the front door of her parents' semi-detached as the car coasted by, reliving her childhood memories of the death message being delivered. Two tragic events – now three – on opposite sides of this quiet avenue went way beyond bad luck.

Death was the glue that had bound her mother to Susan Adams. In 1992, eight years after Susan's brave and doting husband had been struck down, Frankie's much-loved sister, Joanna, had died at the age of fifteen. Hers was no accidental death, nor the result of an incurable illness; she'd died at the hands of someone who'd never been caught, a killer who'd blighted the lives of her whole family, defining Frankie's life and choice of career. And now Susan's only child – the one remaining link to her late husband, her reason for living – was dead too. Another stabbing; another cruel twist of fate, impossible to bear.

Sensitive to the feelings that a visit so close to home might awaken in Frankie, David pulled gently to the kerb a few doors down, outside a smart semi-detached house. As the car came to a stop, he made no attempt to leave the vehicle.

He turned to face her. 'You OK?'

Frankie didn't feel OK – she had an acute pain in her chest – but she managed to nod a reply. She stared at his hands, still resting on the steering wheel, avoiding eye contact. He was giving her an out, should she need one, and she was sorely tempted to ask him to drive away – and keep on driving – but instead she unclipped her seat belt. 'We need to get in there,' she said.

'OK . . . When Susan comes to the door, take her inside. I'll tell her what happened. You support her afterwards.'

Frankie shook her head. 'I know her, David. It'll be better coming from me – if that doesn't sound absurd.'

'If you're sure.'

'I am.'

She didn't look it.

Didn't feel it.

She climbed out of the car, hesitating at the gate. It squeaked as she pushed it open. Her heart began to beat faster as she walked up the paved driveway, a well-tended garden on either side, therapy for Susan when she was well, a shared hobby when her husband was alive. Time stood still as Frankie approached the blue front door with a feeling that one or both of her parents might be watching from her father's den on the opposite side of the street.

Her palms were sticky with sweat.

She pushed the bell and heard it chime inside.

David glanced at her. 'You sure you want to do this?'

A split-second hesitation. 'I have to do this.'

Frankie's ambivalence towards the woman melted away as she heard the chain slide back. Susan had obviously seen her through the spyhole, a smile developing as she opened the door . . . before the lights went out. It wasn't the sight of Frankie – a frequent visitor in the past – but the handsome male with short-cropped hair and the penetrating eyes of a policeman that frightened her.

She knew.

Her legs gave way.

David caught her before she hit the deck.

Helping her into the living room, he sat her down on a sofa in front of a wood-burning stove. Frankie couldn't help noticing the transformation – in Susan, but more so in the house. It was a home now, where once it had been uninviting. Last time Frankie had been inside, it lacked warmth. Gone was the sofa Susan used to sleep on day and night, the empty bottles, a thick film of dust, the dishes piled in the sink until they turned green and mouldy. Chris had tried his best to keep on top of the mess, but Frankie had witnessed his struggle growing up and had to admit she'd resented his mother for it.

Her mum was right. Susan Adams was sober. Frankie was astonished at the transformation. It would appear, on the surface at least, that she'd got her shit together and completely turned her life around. She was well dressed and made up. Gone were the effects of alcohol abuse, the detrimental appearance of a heavy drinker, the bleary eyes, the sense of being out of it. Physically, she looked better than Frankie had ever seen her.

She'd look very different tonight.

The strangulated wail that left her mouth as Frankie confirmed that she'd never again see her son alive could've been heard across the street. Frankie pictured her parents' hands finding each other, their own misery flooding back, twenty-five years gone in a flash.

The widow wept, a choking sound that Frankie had heard from her own mother all those years ago. There was no point trying to talk to Susan until she'd released the anguish that such devastating news had brought to her door, until the enormity of the situation had a chance to sink in. In the days and weeks ahead, she'd be lost in a fog of desperation, confused, unable to function, her life – or what was left of it – on hold as she tried to readjust. No easy feat.

Frankie suspected that she was staring at a dead woman.

There were photographs of Chris and his father on the mantelpiece – almost a mirror image of one another, although Stan Adams had a much darker skin. Frankie glanced at David, pain etched on her face. He was visibly paler than when they entered the house. They hated their job sometimes. And Susan didn't yet know the half of it . . .

She wiped her nose with the back of her hand and sat in silence, unable to comprehend what had taken place – a feeling of disconnect that Frankie had experienced herself. Shock had rendered the woman incapable of speech, let alone conscious thought. A mixture of emotions flashed across her face – anger, sadness, disbelief – as she tried to assimilate information she didn't entirely understand. If Frankie had to describe her, only one term would suffice: shell-shocked. She imagined the questions she'd be asked.

David left them for a moment, reappearing with a glass of water.

Susan looked up as he passed it to her. She could barely

hang on to the glass. 'How?' She choked on the question, her voice barely audible. 'Was he in the car?' She was struggling to get her words out. 'I've told him so many times to take care. Don't tell me he'd been drinking.' She was wide-eyed, searching Frankie's face for answers. 'Is that why you're here?'

'No, Susan . . .' Frankie had never stalled when in this situation. For a moment, she thought she might. She drew on her reserves. Experience had taught her that there was no other way to convey the awful truth but to come right out with it. 'Chris's death wasn't accidental.' She gestured to her boss. 'This is my guv'nor, Detective Chief Inspector David Stone. We work in the Murder Investigation Team.'

'Murder?' Susan repeated the word no parent wanted to utter, as if she didn't believe she'd heard right the first time.

Frankie wanted to take it back, but she had a job to do, part of which was to transmit the awful truth of what had happened to Chris. Susan turned her head in slow motion, a pair of vivid blue eyes staring directly at the SIO, like he was an alien being, as if it was the first time she'd set eyes on him, an accusatory expression. Receiving news like this was more than any mother could bear.

Another wail . . .

This one would keep Frankie awake tonight.

She kneeled on the floor, taking hold of Susan's hand. It was cold to the touch. The detectives were 'sorry for her loss' but this was no time for platitudes. The woman was broken, eyes filled with big tears that spilled out and rolled down cheeks already streaked with mascara. What she said next knocked Frankie sideways, though she tried hard not to react.

'Chris always liked you, Frankie. More than liked, if I'm honest.'

The lump in Frankie's throat grew bigger, threatening to cut off her air supply. 'He was a great lad,' was all she managed by way of reply. 'I'm so very sorry.'

'He once told me that if he had a big sister, he'd want her

40

to be like you. I knew there was more to it than that.' Susan's expression morphed from regret that her son had never had the guts to voice his feelings to blind panic. 'Oh God . . . Forgive me, Frankie. I'd never upset you for the world.' She grabbed at Frankie's arm. 'I didn't mean . . . I'm sorry . . . You've been through so much.'

Frankie's mouth dried up.

Trying to push away the image of her dead sister, she reached out and gave Susan a comforting hug, meeting David's sympathetic eyes over her shoulder. His expression made her both sad and angry. The last thing she needed from him was pity, especially now when she had a job to do. A mirror image of her mother sitting on a sofa not a million miles away popped into her head.

Déjà vu.

Susan pulled away, eyes fixed on her ex-neighbour, a plea almost. 'You looked after Chris when I wasn't capable. Promise me you'll look after him now.'

It took all of Frankie's resolve not to weep.

5

Susan refused point-blank to go with Stone and Oliver to identify her son. She couldn't bring herself to do it. This was a mistake, in Frankie's opinion. In the aftermath of her husband's death in 1984 Susan had been denied the opportunity to say a proper goodbye. Logistically, it was impossible and, once his body had been repatriated, given the extent of his injuries, she'd been advised against viewing his remains. Heartbroken, she'd gone into decline and taken to the drink once she'd given birth.

To avoid history repeating itself, Frankie made a call, an attempt to persuade Susan's brother to accompany her to the morgue, explaining why it was so important to do so. Agreeing that in the long run she might benefit from making that traumatic journey, he came straight over, promising to act as escort, as concerned as Frankie was that Susan would live to regret her decision not to see Chris one final time.

Once the bereaved mother had entered the viewing room and seen her son, she didn't want to leave him. Frankie had watched her carefully, relieved that she'd taken the opportunity to view the body. If Susan had but one image in her head, it would be a positive one. Unlike last night, Chris's eyes were closed. He appeared to be at rest, though Frankie didn't believe in all that garbage. Dead was dead as far as she was concerned.

Where was Jesus when you needed him?

These days, Susan wasn't a religious woman either. Brought up a Catholic, her faith had been tested in the worst way possible, vanishing long ago. Once the formalities of identification had been taken care of, she had many questions she wanted answers to; top of that list, the one Frankie had been dreading, the first out of the mouths of most parents when they had lost a child, at whatever age and in a myriad of awful circumstance.

'When can he come home?' Susan asked.

Frankie hesitated, her mouth drying up, even though she'd anticipated the question. David was about to come to her rescue. Somehow she managed to answer as sensitively and factually as she was able. There was no room for error, no way she would attempt to gloss over what was, for some, the most traumatic part of the procedure, regardless of how distressing it was for those left behind.

'There's been a post-mortem,' Frankie explained. 'An inquest will be opened and adjourned.'

'Why?' Susan covered her mouth with her hand. She shut her eyes, then opened them again, a flash of anger as her gaze flitted back and forth between the detectives, finally coming to rest on Frankie. 'You said his death was no accident. He didn't die of natural causes, misadventure or suicide, did he? Surely there can only be one verdict—'

'There's a legal process to be gone through,' Frankie added. 'In cases of sudden or violent death, a coroner must gather the facts and determine cause. A verdict of unlawful killing must be decided beyond reasonable doubt. Though it pains me to say it, we're unable to give you a timescale for the release of Chris's body—'

'Then how do I arrange . . . ?' Susan let the sentence trail off, as if she'd suddenly come to her senses, realising that funeral arrangements would have to wait. 'I'm sorry,' she said. 'I knew that . . . what was I thinking? It's not the first time this has happened to me, is it?' She glanced at her son's corpse, then at Frankie. 'It's just, just . . .' The words stuck in her throat. 'He's my child and he's been through enough already. I can't bear the thought of him being kept here, or anyone touching him.'

Frankie understood. 'I want you to know that the pathologist is one of the very best in her field of expertise. She'd look after him, I promise you. But I must warn you that it might be a lengthy process. If— I mean *when* we apprehend the person responsible, his or her defence team may request a second, independent medical examination if they're unhappy with post-mortem results. I'm very sorry. They're entitled—'

'Entitled?' Susan spat out the word. 'Good God, they've taken my boy and they have rights?'

'As hard as it is to accept, I'm afraid so.'

Susan glared at Frankie as if she was personally responsible for the legal procedure. As if she was standing up for the bureaucrats who made the rules. It was a reaction both detectives had seen many times in situations like this. It was tough to witness, harder to take, almost impossible to gauge the potential long-term effect of such a delay on a recovering alcoholic.

This wouldn't end well.

A tear rolled from Susan's right eye, her focus returning to her son.

It broke Frankie's heart to witness him lying there. They used to be so close, sharing secrets, doing everything together. When things got tough, as they often did, her door would be the one he'd knock on. She'd grown up feeling responsible for him and had become the sibling he never had. And here he was, a shell of the young man she once knew.

Frankie felt sick.

White noise filled her head. Images scrolled before her eyes, memories of when they were children, like the time her mother had put on a birthday party for him because Susan was too pickled to remember what day it was; the look on his face as they walked into her house, unaware that her family were hiding in the living room, waiting to spring a surprise on him. He'd burst out crying and fled from the room. It was too much for a kid who could only imagine what it was like to

44

be surrounded by a 'real' family for whom celebrations were a big deal.

He was eight years old.

Frankie had found him in their secret den on the edge of the park, hidden deep in the bushes. A year earlier, in the aftermath of Joanna's cold-blooded murder, she'd run away to the exact same spot. Chris had come looking, crawling into the safe space they had built themselves . . .

'Frankie, are you OK?'

Nodding, she didn't look at him.

'Shall we go home now?'

'Soon.'

'Your mum and dad are looking for you.'

'I don't care!'

'Is Joanna ever coming back?'

Frankie shook her head.

'Why? Has she run . . . ?' Seeing her angry reaction, Chris stopped talking, the rest of the sentence lodged in his throat.

Frankie turned to face him. 'She's dead.'

He recoiled, his face crumpling. He liked Joanna. Everyone did. With a tear running down his cheek, he parted the bushes, eyeing the telephone box across the road from their bolthole, a direct line to her father, the one they turned to if they needed help. Chris opened a sweaty hand, revealing a few coins he'd stolen from his mother's purse.

'I'll call Uncle Frank—'

'He's not your uncle. He's not anyone and I don't want to see him . . .' She never told him why. 'Get lost. I didn't ask you here.'

'Can I stay?'

'No.'

'My mam's pissed. I wish she was dead!'

It was the first time he'd ever said it.

The words shocked Frankie. He hadn't meant it. He loved his mum but was scared that social services would take him away again. He was sick of finding her half-cut when he came in from school, dead to the world, completely still and pale from having ventured no further than the nearest off-licence to top up on booze and fags. Frankie remembered thinking that life was unfair: Susan wanted to die and was useless to anyone; Joanna had died when she wanted to live.

At the time, Frankie wanted to die too. Her parents had denied her the opportunity to see her sister's dead body, preferring that she remember Joanna as she was: vibrant, cheeky, smart. In protecting Frankie, they had inadvertently robbed one daughter of her chance to tell another how loved she was and say a final goodbye.

Susan's voice dragged Frankie from the past to the present.

'If they have to conduct a second post-mortem, will you be there?' Her hand covered her mouth as she struggled to finish what she'd started. 'Frankie, I need you to do this one last thing for him.' She was practically begging.

Frankie said, 'Yes, of course I will.'

Susan glanced at Stone and seemed to take comfort from his nod of confirmation. She stepped forward, laid a cold hand on Frankie's forearm. 'You're a good girl . . . You always were . . .' She said it the way she used to when Frankie was a kid, acting as Chris's childminder when she was incapable of doing it herself. 'No wonder your mum and dad are so proud of you.'

An invisible hand closed around Frankie's throat. Unable to breathe, she looked away, the years rolling back again. Fleetingly, she was a girl taking care of a drunken neighbour's kid, taking him to the park to play while her mum did her best to sober Susan up enough for her to function as a mother to the boy. Chris was in and out of Frankie's house. There was no reciprocal arrangement. Her mum and dad had banned her from his home, wanting to protect her from the worst of it. Consequently, she'd seen Susan comatose only the once – very soon after Joanna was murdered – having snuck away to find her friend, letting herself in through the rear door.

Chris was mortified, and so was she.

And suddenly, Frankie was back in the moment, in the viewing room, with a feeling of disconnect, like she wasn't really there but watching proceedings from a distance.

If only that were true.

They headed to Woolsington, David explaining the need to search Chris's room. Though the Murder Investigation Team were working on the assumption that the lad had been killed by an opportunist thief – wrong time, wrong place – as Senior Investigating Officer, it was his job to explore every avenue, every angle of the victim's life in case they were wrong. To do that effectively, it was vital to connect with him, to gather as much information about him as was available from his private living and work space, to get a handle on his friends, male and female, real and virtual; business and personal acquaintances, past and present. There might be something there that could aid their investigation.

Without hesitation, Susan gave permission.

Frankie made a call, arranging a methodical search of his room, calling in Crime Scene Investigators to turn the place over, though she didn't put it quite like that in front of Chris's mum. In a few hours, the place would be crawling with a white-suited forensics team.

As the car sped westward, Susan stared blankly through the rear passenger window without seeing, Frankie by her side. Her hand felt cold and clammy. There were no tears now, only sadness, a lifetime of loneliness stretching out ahead of her. She glanced across the back seat of the unmarked pool car, Frankie the focus of her attention, a question in her eyes, sympathy too.

Instinctively, Frankie knew what was coming.

'How can you put yourself through it, Frankie?'

It was a difficult thing to explain, a question the DS had

asked herself many times. The truth was, she did it because she knew she could do it better than anyone else. She did it for her mum and dad – for Joanna and Rae, for herself – most of all for the poor souls who had to face it. Grief was universal. It affected everyone. Many good cops couldn't handle this part of the job. David had been right to let her take the lead and, although it was the last thing she wanted to do, she'd do it to the very best of her ability. She cared deeply for the families of murder victims, this one in particular. At moments like this, she managed to dig deep and find the right words.

'Someone has to,' she said. 'How does anyone? How did you?'

Susan understood what she was saying. Before her husband died, she'd worked in a hospice, day after day, nursing the terminally ill. Her husband reported on the ravages of war – and lost his life doing it – her brother worked in a prison with inmates who'd never be released back into the community. None of these things were easy. It was a test of human endurance.

Susan cleared her throat. 'Does your mam know . . . about Chris?'

Frankie shook her head. 'Would you like her to come and sit with you?'

'No. Please don't trouble her. Tell her, by all means, but I couldn't ask her to do that, not after what she went through with your Joanna.'

'That's what friends are for. Will your brother stay with you?'

'No. His wife is terminally ill . . .' Susan let out a heavy sigh. 'Despite appearances, we're not that close.' Her grip tightened on Frankie's hand. 'Can you hang around for a bit?'

'Of course.'

'A Family Liaison Officer is available to you if you prefer someone other than Frankie or her mum,' David said. 'She'll keep you abreast of what's happening and answer any questions you may have.'

'I'd like that, thank you.'

What Susan didn't know – and didn't need to know – was that he'd already appointed Melanie Fitzgerald, an experienced FLO. She'd been instructed to keep a close eye on Susan and report back if she hit the drink. They were going to have to treat her with kid gloves. She was fragile, in a way not all parents were. Frankie couldn't let whoever killed Chris kill her too; she could only hope that her incentive to stay off the bottle hadn't died with her son.

Susan turned to face Frankie. 'And thank you for everything you did for Chris when he was alive.'

'We were mates. There's no need for thanks.'

For a while, Susan didn't speak.

When the impasse ended, she talked about Chris, telling Frankie how proud she was of him. For a lad who'd not had the best of starts, he'd made something of his life. Frankie was desperate to know if he was happy. She didn't have the heart to ask. There were more pressing questions she needed answers to. If only she knew where to start . . .

'Susan, do you have any idea of how Chris came by the injuries to his face? I was wondering if they occurred naturally, with no other person involved, a minor accident perhaps.'

Susan's eyes misted over, pride mixing with grief. 'He got them playing football last weekend, an elbow as he went up for a header. He scored from it, apparently. A good goal, he said. He's top scorer this season. When he was playing at home, I used to go along and watch sometimes.'

Her bravery amazed Frankie. It was good to talk, even better to get an explanation for the injuries to Chris Adams' face. 'And how did he seem to you when you last saw him? What frame of mind was he in? Was anything worrying him?'

'I don't think so. If anything, I'd say he was upbeat. Unusually so.'

'Do you know why?'

Susan frowned. 'Don't you?'

Frankie shook her head, confused by the question. 'Chris and I haven't seen each other in ages.'

'He never said.'

He must have.

Susan was staring at Frankie. 'Had you two fallen out?'

'No. Nothing like that . . . but we'd drifted lately.' For a moment, it felt like they were talking at cross purposes, as if the intervening years had disappeared and the two were still in regular touch. Shock affected people in mysterious ways. Maybe Susan wanted to hang on to the past, choosing to believe that they were as tight as they used to be. 'I wish it had been different.'

'Regret is a killer, such a wasted emotion. I learned that in therapy. It took years to understand it, let alone accept it. You don't have to explain yourself to me.'

Frankie did . . .

And therein lay the problem . . .

She couldn't put her finger on why she and Chris hadn't seen that much of one another, beyond the fact that each was busy getting on with life and career. Guilt wormed its way into her thoughts. She wondered if he'd still be alive if she'd called him. A ridiculous logic, one that occurred to her when she first saw his body in Northumberland Place. From that moment on, she hadn't been able to get that image out of her head.

'You did know he was on a mission?' Susan said.

Frankie glanced across the back seat, confused by the statement, catching David's eye in the rear-view mirror. The comment had blindsided them both. He wanted more and was urging her to keep going while Susan was in a mood to talk. Her attention had strayed out the window to a group of young people emerging from a pub, Christmas jumpers on, laughing and chatting. The world might have tilted in the past few hours, but it was going on as normal outside the car.

'Susan? What do you mean "he was on a mission"?'

The woman turned her head, a shrug almost. 'He didn't tell you?'

'No, he didn't.'

'He was trying to impress his editor. I don't know what it was about. He wouldn't tell me. A public interest case, he said. He seemed to think that it was the story that would make his name . . .' She was floundering. 'Though Stan died before he was born, Chris was very like his father in nature: curious, ambitious, interested in political change, in people generally. There was someone helping him. I know that much—'

'Did he tell you who?'

'No . . . I did ask. He said he wanted to finish what he started and then let me read it. He was secretive, like his dad. Stan never ever discussed his work with me until after the fact. I used to think it was because it would upset me, or that it was too stressful for him to talk about. I'll never know now, will I?'

David stopped the car at traffic lights, his focus very firmly in the car, rather than on the road. Intrigued by the conversation going on in the rear of the vehicle, he chanced another glance at Frankie, urging her to keep on it before Susan went off-piste into a world of melancholy.

'He never brought his contact home?' Frankie asked.

'No, but it was a she . . . I thought it might've been you.'

Frankie locked eyes with David, a slight shake of the head: It wasn't her.

'Is it possible he went out to meet her last night?' Frankie asked Susan. 'I assumed he was in town socialising. Didn't he always do that on a Friday night?'

'Most weeks. He had his work head on last night.'

'He told you that?'

'Not in so many words, but if he was off out with the lads,

he'd have put his car away and used the Metro. He didn't, so he definitely had other plans. He was like a dog with a bone lately.' Susan's expression changed suddenly, as if an idea had just occurred to her. 'You don't think he was killed because he was poking his nose in where it didn't belong?'

'We don't know, is the honest answer.' The car began to move. 'We will find out, and you'll be the first to know when we do. Can you remember what time he arrived home, what time he left the house?'

'He got in as I was leaving. Around six thirty. I'm in a book group in Bank Foot that starts at half past seven. My car is playing up. He offered me a lift. I said I'd rather walk. It's not far and he was in a tearing rush to jump in the shower and get out himself, so I left on foot.'

'And he wasn't in when you returned?'

'I didn't go home. After the book group, I had dinner with a friend who lives on Main Road. She'd asked me to stay the night. I often do if Chris can't pick me up and he'd said he might be late. He didn't like me walking back alone.'

'He knew you were planning to stay out?'

'Yes. He wasn't here when I got in this morning. I assumed he'd been and gone. His towel was on the floor in the shower. It never occurred to me to check his room to see if his bed had been slept in.'

Through the rear-view mirror, Frankie sent an unspoken message to her boss: *We should talk to his editor.* The rest of the journey was a blur.

6

Stone and Oliver had to wait for an editorial meeting to finish before they could see Mark Fox. As journalists filed out of his spacious office, the detectives were ushered in. The editor didn't hang about. He was a stony-faced man, around fifty years of age with a shifty appearance and thinning hair he was trying to hide with a comb-over. His office was hard on the eye, an untidy shambles of national newspaper cuttings, a semicircle of chairs around his desk, used coffee cups and an overflowing wastebasket of screwed-up, discarded copy, some of which had spilled over the edge and littered the floor.

'Excuse the mess,' he said, pushing a pile of papers out of his way.

'You're busy, we're busy.' Stone waved away the apology. 'I did tell the girl on the desk that it was urgent.' It was a heavy hint that he didn't like being kept waiting. He had a murder to solve.

Fox didn't apologise for the delay.

Picking up a remote, he muted the sound on two televisions mounted on the wall in front of him, one tuned to a BBC news channel, the other to CNN. A third screen was logged in to TweetDeck, a steady stream of posts on all manner of topics racing down the monitor in real time. Throughout the ensuing conversation – and despite the grave subject matter – Fox was inattentive, his eyes flitting over the heads of the detectives as breaking headlines marched across the bottom of the screens spouting news from across the globe.

For a provincial newspaper editor, it seemed like overkill to David, making him wonder if Fox had once been in charge of a more prestigious publication and was hanging on to old habits. His only reaction to the news that a staff member had been murdered was to close his laptop, scribble a note of it and presumably take him off the payroll. The incident would fill a column later. David had the distinct impression that it would only do so if Fox had nothing better to report.

That thought may have crossed Frankie's mind too. Her hackles were up – and it showed – a pair of unfriendly eyes locking on to the man they had come to see. And when David mentioned Susan Adams' claim that her son was working on something big, a story that might make his name, Fox sat back in his chair, eyeing them both with a mixture of suspicion and amusement.

'Don't take this the wrong way,' he said. 'I'd hate to speak ill of the dead—'

'Then please don't, sir.' Frankie said sharply. 'We're here to gather facts, not hearsay.'

Meeting her malevolent gaze across his desk, Fox climbed down. 'Look, Adams was a nice enough lad, conscientious and enthusiastic. As a court reporter, he was good at his job, but that was it. There was no scoop. If there had been, I'd have known about it.'

'How can you be so sure?' Frankie asked. 'If it was important, he may have been working under the radar.'

'My DS has a point,' Stone said. 'Perhaps he was still reviewing, not yet ready to disclose the nature of his investigation.'

'To me?' Fox laughed. 'I can assure you, there was no investigation. Nothing goes on around here without my say-so. If he was researching on the premises, there would be an audit trail and there isn't. I monitor my staff on a daily basis.'

From the look on her, Frankie had already made up her mind that she didn't like Fox. The editor-in-chief hadn't shown an ounce of regret over Chris Adams' death, let alone enquired after his next of kin. Before leaving the victim's home, the detectives had popped into his room for a quick look around ahead of the forensics team's arrival. She'd pointed out a framed photograph of his father on the wall, and another of his paternal grandparents sitting on the veranda of a duck-egg blue, clapperboard house fashionable in some parts of the States. They too would be devastated.

David kept his voice level. 'You have reason to believe that Chris was lying?'

'I wouldn't put it quite like that,' Fox said, 'though he's done it before—'

'What does that mean?' Frankie asked.

'It means he arrived here last Monday looking like he'd gone ten rounds with Mike Tyson—'

'Yes,' she said. 'An injury he sustained in a football match.'

'Did that information also come from his mother? Because if it did, you've been misled. I play squash with his coach every Sunday night. Adams never turned up for his match last weekend, so I knew he was deceiving me as soon as he opened his mouth. I don't blame the lad. We've all had a scrap and come off worse. He was probably trying to save face. He was an arrogant little shit at times. You do know his mother is a drunk?'

A flash of anger from Frankie.

Seeing her reaction, Fox hesitated, considering whether or not to continue trashing the reputation of their victim and his distraught mother. Focusing on the SIO – rather than his subordinate – was a decision he might live to regret.

He did it anyway. 'Detective Chief Inspector, without being too unkind, Adams was a dreamer, driven by a need to live up to his late father's reputation as a serious journalist. I wouldn't go as far as saying that he was delusional—'

'You didn't think he was going to make it?' David said.

'That about nails it.'

'Why not, if he was so diligent?' Frankie wanted a straight answer.

Fox wasn't playing ball.

David gave her the side-eye, a warning to back off and let

the editor say his piece without further interruption. If they riled him, they'd be shown the door.

Pretending not to notice, she delivered a shove: 'Mr Fox?'

'Because he didn't have what it takes.' Again, he favoured Stone. 'Did I miss something? I'm trying to answer your questions as sensitively and honestly as I can. For some reason, I seem to have got off on the wrong foot with your DS.'

David backed her up. He didn't want the editor knowing that Frankie had ever been acquainted with the victim. 'It's a reasonable question to ask, sir. You said yourself that Chris Adams was reliable. It's clear that there was no love lost between the two of you, so how come he was still on the payroll?'

'As I said, he was good at what he did.'

'With respect, you don't strike me as the type to keep someone on if you didn't like him.'

Once again, Fox's attention strayed to the television screens, currently displaying the wildfires sweeping through Southern California. Drawing his eyes from the shocking footage, he eyeballed the detectives. 'Commitment and dedication will only get you so far on the career ladder. There's good, there's exceptional, and then there are those who possess the killer instinct required to make it to the top. It's the same in any organisation, especially so in yours, I imagine. So, at the risk of being taken in for interrogation, I'll try again, shall I? The point I make is that a burning desire to investigate a public interest case is worthless if you haven't the ability to pull it off.'

'In your opinion,' Frankie said.

'Round here, mine is the only opinion that counts.'

Finally, she let it drop. 'Sir, tomorrow is Sunday. If you're not working, would you mind giving me a contact number in case anything of interest comes up.' When Fox handed over a card, she thanked him and stood up to leave. She couldn't get out of there fast enough.

*

'What an absolute dick!' she said as soon they got outside. 'And I'm obviously not the only one to think so. Did you see the woman heading into his office as we were heading out? I was certain she was going to speak to me. Then he came to the door and she thought better of it. The guy's management style needs an update. He spies on his staff and obviously disliked Chris intensely. So much so, he didn't give a shit that he'd been murdered. Callous bastard.'

'Big fish, little sea, Frank. Don't let him get to you.' David blipped open the doors of the vehicle.

Frankie climbed in, yanking her seat belt across her chest. 'Yeah, well he might be top dog at the *Corchester Herald*, but we're bigger and have alternative ways of finding what we're after.'

'Wells and Ben?'

'Absolutely.'

'Y'know, that's not a bad idea.'

'It's a great idea or I wouldn't have suggested it.'

Smiling, David started the engine. Ben, his nephew, was in training under the guidance of one of the countries most revered investigative journalists, Belinda Wells. For years, she'd worked for a major broadsheet in the capital. 'If Chris was as ambitious as Susan would have us believe, it stands to reason that he might have introduced himself to her at the first opportunity.'

'My thoughts exactly. It's worth an ask.'

'Don't hold your breath.'

Frankie swivelled in her seat to face him. 'Chris was smart, David. If he knew Wells was in town, he'd have cultivated some kind of friendship, for no other reason than to learn from the best. If there's one thing I know about journalists, it's that they stick together, feed off one another, drink in the same pubs. A long shot is better than no shot.'

David pulled away.

Frankie was pushing at an open door.

Unable to raise Wells immediately, David updated the MIT. CSIs had been swift, handing over the contents of the victim's bedroom, his vehicle registration certificate and a stack of notebooks, all written in shorthand no one in the office could understand, a series of strokes, like modern hieroglyphics. As expected, they hadn't found a phone; more than likely it had been in the IP's possession and taken by whoever had robbed and killed him. Notable by its absence, there was no computer in his room.

David retained the notebooks, inviting Frankie to his office to discuss them. Dumping the lot in the middle of his desk, he moved to the small fridge in the corner of the room, took out a large bottle of sparkling water, pouring them both a drink. Handing a tumbler to Frankie, he sat down, pointed to the notebooks, grubby with having been thumbed a million times.

'What?' she said.

'There may be other ways of recording nowadays, but not in a British court of law. As a reporter, I'm guessing that shorthand was a job requirement for Chris, a fast and accurate way of noting down proceedings and other interviews. You didn't warm to Fox and neither did I. I take it you're not happy to use him to decipher them for us, assuming they even use the same method of shorthand—'

'David, you really are the king of the understatement.'

He returned her smile. 'OK, so rather than bring in an expert we don't know, with no guarantee they'll be able to decode it, I'm thinking of asking Wells. Working in the same industry, there may be things she'll pick up that a so-called expert won't, journalistic terms that outsiders might not understand. She's come through for us before and will do so again if I ask her nicely. OK with that?'

Frankie met his eyes over the rim of her glass. 'You trust her, I trust her.'

'Good. I'll keep trying her. I'm more concerned about the conflicting accounts in respect of the injuries to Chris's face. I'll get Dick to chase it up with his football coach first thing in the morning. Any theories on why Chris would lie about what happened?'

Frankie said, 'I've never known him to lie.'

'We all lie, Frank – even you!'

Frankie leaned back in her chair, considering. 'Maybe Fox was right then. Chris was merely saving face. No pun intended. And then there's the other matter: Susan's assertion that he was writing a story that would make his name, Fox's denial. Maybe Chris got too close to whoever he was about to expose.' Frankie's eyes settled on the notebooks. 'In which case, these could hold the key to our case.'

David sent the team packing, restating his priorities for the morning, not much further forward at the end of the day than when they had arrived at Middle Earth. Frankie left the office with the others, but she wasn't going home. Not yet. She had no plans for the evening and was desperate to talk to the homeless community herself, rather than rely on others to do it for her. She hadn't told David where she was going. He'd be furious if he knew she was on the streets on a Saturday night singled-crewed, but she wanted answers and her gut was telling her to look for them in the city.

It might cost her a few quid. That was OK with her.

Frankie and David were similar in many ways. As with any professional partnership, they had differences of opinion. On the one hand, he was a daft Geordie with a heart the size of a house. On the other, there was a hard side to his nature, brought on by fifteen years of policing the capital. His view that giving money to rough sleepers was feeding drug and alcohol dependency, contributing to the mental and physical decline of addicts, was one that Frankie couldn't argue with. It was easy to say and difficult to adhere to when you were passing someone in need. Her boss had spent far too long on the streets of London.

She'd have to work on him . . .

The sun was long gone, the temperature falling below zero. Though she was wrapped up warm, layered against the cold, Frankie was freezing. She parked on Dean Street and walked up Grey Street, its stunning historical and classical architecture drawing tourists to the area from far and wide, a good pitching spot for those savvy enough to appreciate that.

Her feet were almost numb as she walked up the hill towards Grey's monument and onward to her destination, fighting a tide of revellers making their way downhill to the Quayside. A scrawny woman was sitting cross-legged in a doorway around halfway up, a bony hand out begging for cash in fingerless gloves, a filthy ragged pink blanket her only protection against the elements.

Handing her some change and a small chocolate bar, Frankie asked a few questions. She knew nowt. Unsurprising. Her chosen pitch was too far from the crime scene. The woman's thanks were hardly audible, lost on a stiff wind, spoken through lips that had a distinctly bluish tinge. Frankie wondered if she'd survive the night or if a pedestrian would find her frozen stiff by morning – fat chance of anyone in *her* organisation doing it.

A depressing thought.

The police were stretched to the limit dealing with the prevention and detection of crime and the prosecution of offenders against the peace. In her father's time, good coppers would always check on the weak and vulnerable or stop for a chat with those on the fringes of society. It was something she'd done too. These days you'd be hard pressed to find a foot patrol in the current climate of fire brigade policing.

Whatever happened to the protection of life?

Frankie walked on, angry that more wasn't being done to help those in need. Rough sleeping had risen year on year in every major city in the UK. Poverty was rife, the statistics for homelessness grossly misleading. Council street counts represented only those unable to find sanctuary in emergency housing or a temporary hostel with an available bed. The city centre was a magnet for the rest.

As she walked on, she considered this. These unfortunate souls slept on park benches, in shop doorways, in multi-storey car parks and graveyards, anywhere affording them shelter from the harsh northern climate. Outreach volunteers and street preachers did their best to direct them to organisations that might help, but some in this vulnerable group were migrants, ineligible for financial support. Many others were ordinary working folk, unable to survive, caught between the minimum wage and zero hours contracts, rising rents and cuts in benefits, a disgusting state of affairs for a country that only last year was one of the fastest growing economies in the world. The UK's lofty position had slipped since then. It made Frankie's blood boil to think that in 2017, in Britain, people were losing their homes, drifting on to the streets, forced to beg in order to feed themselves.

Another doorway . . .

Another skeletal form looking for a handout . . .

This time, Frankie passed by, unable to meet the haunted eyes of the beggar for more than a split second. He wished her a good day and it didn't even sound sarcastic. Willing to help or not, it was impossible to give to everyone. With guilt clawing at her conscience, she was about to retrace her steps when her phone rang . . .

Stone was working late.

'David, what's up?'

'Where are you? I tried your flat—'

'What are you, my mother? I'm out for a walk.' It wasn't a lie.

'Our radio appeal bore fruit. A witness came forward. Susan Adams was wrong about Chris. He wasn't working last night. He was in a gin bar with his mates at nine o'clock, one of whom has been in touch.'

'Doesn't mean he wasn't working. I've met my snouts in all sorts of places, some of which I wouldn't admit to under oath.' Frankie sidestepped a group of guys coming the other way, a stag do by the looks of it, a night out in the party city Newcastle had become, the choice of many before getting hitched. One of them was wearing a Rocky Horror costume, complete with corset, suspenders, wig and fishnet stockings. As her eyes travelled down his legs to high heels he could hardly stand up in, he looked mortified. One of his mates stopped to chat with the man on the ground, handing him an open bottle of beer and a fag. The image warmed her from the inside out as David's voice took her back to her call.

'Frankie? You still there.'

'Yes, I'm here. Which gin bar?'

'Pleased to Meet You on High Bridge. I gather most people refer to it as PTMY.'

'I know it well.' Frankie was almost at the junction of High Bridge as he said it. She was tempted to cross the road, turn up the side street, go inside and ask around, but she'd rather get the low-down from the witness before talking to bar staff. She checked her watch. It was close to the time of Chris's death and she wanted to see who, if anyone, might have seen what happened, when it happened. It would be a wasted journey otherwise.

'Do you have a name?' she asked.

'Liam Wiley. He's a mechanic. Works at a motorcycle dealership on the West Road somewhere. Dick will text you the details.'

'Have you spoken to him?'

'Dick?'

'No, you divvi. The witness.'

'Not personally.'

'What's the plan?'

'Wiley's working tomorrow. Dick told him you'll be along to see him first thing. Fingers crossed, we've caught an early break. Enjoy your walk, Frank. It might be the last one you get for a while.'

'Did you manage to get hold of Wells?'

'Yeah, I'm meeting her in Revolution in half an hour.'

'I thought you were going home—'

'I thought you were.'

Frankie looked around guiltily, her eyes scanning both ways, wondering if he was watching her.

'You're busted, Frank. Your car is parked on Dean Street.'

Frankie grinned. Nothing got past him.

'Night, David.'

Before he asked any awkward questions, she hung up.

7

Northumberland Street was bustling with people making their way from the Haymarket Metro to eat and drink in the city centre, others going in the opposite direction, some with bags of Christmas shopping, heading for home. It was the usual Saturday-night crowd, many wearing no outer clothing, the girls displaying bare legs and short skirts, teetering on stilettos that would be off before the night was out, landing a few of them in A&E.

It made Frankie shiver, watching them.

She turned away, shifting her attention to the ATMs at the NatWest Bank. Like Northumberland Place, the machines were now off limits, crime scene tape creating an access barrier, the area having undergone forensic examination during the day. The reminder of last night's discovery seemed all the more poignant set against the backdrop of Christmas decorations and the mini fairground in the centre of Northumberland Street.

During the afternoon, the bank had confirmed that Chris's card had been used at the right-hand cashpoint, dispensing £100 at 9.58 p.m. Minutes later he was dead. Keen to help, the bank manager had supplied details of his bank account and an image to establish whether it was Chris or someone else accessing his account.

It was him.

The lump in Frankie's throat grew bigger as she imagined him standing there, placing his card in the slot; a quick glance over his shoulder before punching in his pin number; hearing the shuffle of money as it was counted; taking his cash and receipt and walking away, unaware that he was about to take his last breath. The ATMs were metres from the lane where he was found bleeding from a single stab wound.

In her head, Frankie superimposed the image of a queue in front of him, two further queues to his left, one forming behind. In the run-up to Christmas, all cashpoints were on overtime. Each and every person in those queues was now vital to her investigation. The MIT had been given a list to trace and question them all.

Reaching into her bag, Frankie drew out an A4 sheet, her eyes travelling down the page, taking in every name, every transaction, whether it be cash withdrawal, statement request or balance check. Nineteen people had used the ATM in the minutes before Chris made his withdrawal, a further ten before police arrived and locked the area down.

On the face of it, the bank had done all the hard graft, supplying names and addresses of everyone who'd used the cashpoint before and after Chris. In Frankie's mind, the typed list of names represented only half the story. It was crucial to establish who else might have seen the victim with-drawing cash, whether he was alone or accompanied when he accessed his account, what he wanted the money for and the details of anyone who might have been loitering nearby, meeting up with friends for a drink or, crucially, planning a street robbery.

The male standing behind Chris in the queue – Mr Ashley Sutherland – didn't know it yet, but he was now her star witness. As a matter of urgency, Dick Abbott had planned to speak to him in the hope that the two men might have exchanged a few words while they waited in line – a joke about Chris's black eye perhaps – but Sutherland couldn't be located.

It troubled Frankie that the victim had lied about his facial injury to his mother, handing Fox the opportunity to draw attention to the deceit, although Frankie only had his word for it and David wasn't content to rely on the editor's version of events. With Dick poised to corroborate the account with

Chris's coach and team mates, the MIT would know soon enough. If it turned out Fox was correct, they had work to do.

'Spare some change?' The voice had come from behind.

Frankie spun round.

A male of indeterminate age with grey-flecked hair and stubble on his chin was sitting on the pavement, inside the doorway of Sports Direct. He hadn't been talking to her specifically. He was trying to attract the attention of anyone prepared to dig deep and offer him a few coins. Like hers, his breath was visible as a cloud every time he exhaled.

Frankie took a couple of steps closer.

'Is this your normal patch?'

'Yeah. My other home is in Monaco.'

Frankie grinned, looking up at the sign above the shop doorway. 'You're not into footy then?'

The man on the ground returned her smile. Sports Direct was founded in the early eighties by Mike Ashley, the billionaire owner of Newcastle United, the city's beloved football team, a man fans wanted out. Most would choose to piss in the doorway rather than sleep in it.

'Any port in a storm,' the sleeper said.

'Were you here last night?'

'Aye, I was. Why? You're not going to move me on, are you?'

Frankie glanced down at her plain clothes. 'That obvious, eh?'

'Coppers usually are, in or out of uniform.'

'You're breaking my heart, mate. I'd like to ask you a few questions but you're safe to stay put.'

In the circumstances, Frankie realised how ridiculous that statement was. In the small hours, the guy would sleep with one eye open, only resting when it was safe to bed down on whatever insulation he'd managed to lay his hands on: flattened cardboard boxes, plastic bags, a discarded duvet, probably thrown out with the rubbish, lifted from a household bin or donated by a charitable organisation. Curiously, his sleeping bag was a good one. Expensive. It would keep the man on the ground warm. Nevertheless, he was vulnerable to ill health at this time of the year.

Crouching down beside him, she showed ID and introduced herself in case he couldn't read. 'I'm Detective Sergeant Oliver. A young man was killed across the road last night around ten o'clock. Did you happen to see anything?'

'No. I caught the headlines this morning.'

Frankie tried not to show her surprise.

It didn't work.

'Newspapers are available in the library,' the rough sleeper explained. 'The only thing I read nowadays. They let you in if you get cleaned up, behave yourself and don't fall asleep. I'm teetotal so I do OK. It's warm in there. Libraries are for everyone, right?'

Frankie felt guilty for having doubted him. His semi-dishevelled appearance could be hiding a degree of some kind, a better life, a wife and kids. She asked: 'Did you hear anyone shouting last night?'

'Only at me.'

'I'm sorry to hear that.' It irked her that people might abuse, or even worse, ignore the plight of the homeless community.

'Occupational hazard,' he said.

'For both of us,' Frankie joked.

'Besides . . .' He pointed to his left. 'With that racket going on I could hardly hear myself think, let alone make out what was going down over there.'

Frankie followed his gaze. Around thirty metres away, a busker was playing a harmonica badly, a box laid out in front of him for passers-by to deposit change. Unlike the man on the ground, he wasn't homeless. He was a chancer, performing for pin money to spend over the upcoming holidays. Frankie hadn't noticed him before. Coppers had the ability to tune out most things while interviewing suspects or potential witnesses. Now her attention had been drawn to him, it wouldn't go away.

'He's not making much.' She screwed up her face. '*Britain's Got Talent* can rest easy.'

Her rough sleeper chuckled. 'I scarpered when the police arrived last night. I didn't see what happened. It was obvious that something heavy had gone down. When you're on the streets, it pays not to get involved. Besides, that thing was blocking my view.'

Frankie turned her head, sharing his perspective.

He had a point. His line of sight into the lane where Chris met his death was blocked by a merry-go-round, part of the mini-fairground attractions on the street. And the opposite was true. When the off-duty paramedic went to Chris's aid, there was no way he'd have spotted the man taking shelter in the doorway. He'd obviously cleared off by the time David arrived, before she turned up to view the body and assist him. Besides, what reason did her rough sleeper have to lie? Still, by his own admission he was in the vicinity at the time of the stabbing, someone dispossessed with no fixed abode, a man she couldn't afford to ignore or lose sight of.

Slipping her mobile from her pocket, Frankie held it aloft. 'Would you mind if I take your picture?'

He looked unsure.

It occurred to her that he'd not been asked that question for a very long time. It made her feel like a complete shit for asking, reminding him of his status as a man few cared for enough to want to capture his image on a mobile phone.

She owed him an explanation.

'It's for elimination purposes. In case you're mentioned by another witness. Nothing for you to worry about, I promise.'

He relaxed, grinning through a set of good teeth. 'So long as you get my best side. If you fancy making it a selfie, I could always put this on.' He held up a Christmas hat.

Frankie liked this one. Snapping a couple of shots, she slipped the device into her pocket. 'Were there any other rough sleepers you noticed last night?'

'Dozens . . . but not here, none that I saw anyway.'

'What's your name?'

'John Doe . . .' Another cheeky grin. 'Stuart . . . Ryman . . .
Sarge to my friends.'

'How are you spelling that?'

'S-A-R-G-E.'

'Funny guy.' She grinned.

'R-Y-M-A-N,' he added.

'Unusual name.'

'It means servant of the king.'

'Is that right?'

A big grin. 'You weren't expecting a royal connection?'

'No, but I'm impressed.' Ryman was an educated man. God
forbid he was also an ex-copper. The idea that he might be
was more than Frankie could handle. She wasn't going to ask
for fear that it might upset him, then decided it might upset
him more if she didn't. She opted for the obvious. 'You're a
veteran?'

'RAF flight sergeant aircrew, at your service, ma'am.'

She didn't pry further, though she couldn't help wondering
what might have befallen him since he'd left the services. 'Do
you have a phone, Sarge?'

He shook his head – silly question.

Frankie tripped over herself to apologise. 'Is there any
other way I can contact you?'

'How's your semaphore?'

She laughed. 'I'll ask around then.'

'That'll do it . . .' The busker had started up again. Her
ex-serviceman had to raise his voice to be heard. 'I have no
funds to skip town.'

'Is there anyone else you think I should talk to?'

'You could try the Doc—'

Frankie frowned. 'The Doc?'

'Redundant hospital porter. Keeps his ear to the ground.
Sleeps in the underpass, bottom of Pilgrim Street. I wouldn't

recommend you go alone. If you want, I'll come with you.'

It touched her to think that he was as concerned for her welfare as she was his. 'Thanks,' she said. 'I'm planning to meet up with my boss.'

'Giving me the brush off, Oli?'

'Do I look like the kind of girl who'd turn down the kind offer of an escort?'

Ryman gave a description of his friend. 'You can't miss him.'

The rundown was so distinctive, Frankie didn't need to write it down. 'In the meantime, if you hear anything, call me on this number if you can find a phone, Sarge.' Frankie slipped him a fiver, some loose change for the phone and her business card.

He read the name and commented on the fact that she was part of the MIT. 'Impressive. What's the F stand for?'

'DS Oliver.'

He saluted her. 'I like Oli better.'

'Keep your ears open for me, Sarge. The young man who died didn't deserve it. If I don't hear from you, I'll be back tomorrow night.'

'Is that a date?'

'You bet. Take care.' She walked away. The fact that they shared the same sense of humour – and had both worn the three stripes denoting a sergeant – left her with an overwhelming feeling of sadness.

8

David, his nephew, Ben, and Belinda Wells had their heads together when Frankie arrived at Revolution. The pub, an old bank conversion, was overcrowded. They were deep in conversation and didn't see her walk in and push her way towards the bar. While she was waiting to be served, she removed her hat and scarf, unbuttoned her coat and slipped it off, glancing in their direction. As usual, Wells was holding court. Frankie couldn't wait to get over there and find out if she knew Chris Adams or could tell them anything that might help piece together the last few hours of his life.

Vertically challenged, Frankie had to stand on her tiptoes and shout above a crowd three deep in order to be heard: 'Hey! Have you got to be twelve to get served in here?' When sarcasm didn't work, she waved a note in the air, trying to attract the attention of bar staff.

A waitress nodded, a gesture that Frankie would be next. The guys leaning against the bar parted to let her in. She felt underdressed compared to everyone else in there. The waitress shut the till, wiped the counter down, then made her way towards her.

'What can I get you?'

'Single malt.'

'You have a preference?'

Spotting a ten-year-old Laphroaig, Frankie opted for that, rubbing her hands together. 'I need to warm up.'

'No ice then?'

'Have you been outside?'

'No, I heard it's parky. You want water?'

'No, I'll have it neat, thanks.'

The waitress nodded: good plan.

71

Paying up, Frankie took the whisky tumbler and threaded her way through the crowds, almost losing her bag in the process, but hanging on tightly to her Scotch. Wells was the first to spot her. She shoved along, patting the seat beside her, making room for the detective sergeant.

Frankie sat down, meeting David's gaze.

He wasn't surprised to see her. 'Enjoy your walk?'

'I did.' She had. 'Any excuse to be outside.'

'Yeah, right.' He wasn't buying that. 'Anything I need to know?'

'What? I don't have a social life now?' She narrowed her eyes, teasing him.

Is it a date?

An image of Ryman flashed before her eyes. Her rough sleeper had hidden depths, a story to tell. Frankie didn't know why it mattered, but she wanted chapter and verse on his fall from grace. It must've been something catastrophic. As a non-commissioned officer in the RAF, he'd have been well paid, a salary somewhere in the region of forty thousand or thereabouts. She'd googled it on the way to meet the others. Unless he'd been dishonourably discharged, he'd have been in receipt of a decent pension, so why the hell was he on the streets?

David tried again: 'Cut the crap, Frank. What have you been up to?'

He knew her so well.

'If you must know, I decided to hang around at the crime scene to see who was there and to find out if they were there last night.'

'Did you turn up anything of interest?'

She shook her head, deciding to hold back on her new friend. 'Now I come to think of it, I didn't see any of the outside team asking questions either, which is odd, given your brief to engage with the homeless community. Maybe I missed them and they're chasing other leads.' She bloody hoped so or she'd dropped them right in it. 'How about you?'

'We lucked out.' He glanced at Wells.

'You're screwed,' she said. 'Neither Ben or I knew the victim.'

'Are you sure?' Frankie handed over a picture of Chris.

'We've seen him around, though we were never introduced.'

'Do you know his editor?'

'Everyone knows Fox.' Belinda gave Frankie the lowdown. 'He's a worm . . . No one likes him. Mind you, to be fair, he hasn't got much to smile about. Rumour has it the paper is about to fold. Print is in decline, editorial cutbacks inevitable. A lot of consumers are jumping ship, choosing to move online. Add in cover-price rises and it's a woeful picture. I can't imagine your friend, had he lived, would've had a job for long.'

Frankie glanced at David: 'You told them? Thanks very much.'

David opened his mouth to speak.

Wells got in first. 'We're running the story—'

Frankie cut her off. 'We only released his identity a couple of hours ago—'

'Enough time for Ben to do a background check and notice that his mother lives in the same street as your parents.' The journo placed a manicured hand on Ben's forearm, her eyes fixed on Frankie's. 'He's smart, this lad. I think you owe David an apology, don't you?'

Frankie delivered, apologising to David for jumping to conclusions. Mention of her parents made her feel guilty. Her father had called three times since the press release had gone out. He hadn't left a message. What was there to say? He'd be beside himself, worried about the effect of Chris's death on her, in two minds over the appropriateness of her involvement in the investigation, but confident that she was the right detective for the job.

Frankie kept her attention on Wells and Ben. 'Can you put some feelers out? One of your colleagues might know him.'

'I'll do it,' Ben chipped in.

Frankie threw him a smile, before settling on Wells. 'When are you going to offer this lad a proper job?'

'When you stop begging,' she said. 'He's still on probation—'

'After eighteen months?'

'In between university semesters.'

'Yeah, but—'

Wells cut her off. 'Look, I love having this gorgeous hunk following me around all day . . .' Ben was blushing. He'd do a lot of that, working with her. 'It's politically sensitive. As I said, times are tough in our industry. There are trained journalists keen to move up. A queue actually. For some obscure reason, they all want to work with me. They're only human, I suppose.' Wells pouted red lips at Frankie, making them laugh. The journalist liked men and they liked her. She didn't take herself too seriously. In fact, she was a riot when she got going. 'Our paper is one of the few that isn't losing money hand over fist. I can't swing a permanent placement just yet. Ben understands the need to earn it, like I did.'

'A meritocracy?' David pulled a face: are-you-taking-the-piss? 'How quaint.'

'Belinda's right,' Ben said. 'No one should get preferential treatment.'

'Bollocks.' Wells nearly spat out her drink, eyeing her mentee across the table. 'You need to harden up, mister. The job is yours as soon as I can put the bite on my editor. I'm working on it.' She winked at him, then turned her attention to Stone and Oliver, leaning in, lowering her voice, a hint of mischief in her eyes. 'I happen to know that he's playing away and doesn't want his wife finding out that he's shagging a girl half his age. His wife is loaded. An undercover photoshoot should swing it for Ben and me. I hate to blow my own trumpet but I'm a dab hand with a camera.' A wicked grin appeared. 'Very soon, we'll have a friend for life and excellent job security.'

'Don't push it,' David said.

Frankie was sweating now, another layer coming off. She

took a sip of her Laphroaig. It went down a treat, though already she was regretting not asking for ice. She liked Wells a lot. She was late fifties acting twenty years younger. In the past year, the two women had grown fond of one another. The older of the two had been an investigative journalist all her working life. She'd been a good friend to David when he was in the Met. Since their migration north, independent of one another – and purely coincidental – they had reached an understanding that if they could help each other out, they would. She'd passed him information that had helped solve cases. In return, he'd handed her exclusive material that had helped her to rebuild a career that was fast heading south.

Frankie loved Ben too. Discounting Chris Adams, he was the baby brother she never had. With both parents gone, David had stepped in as surrogate father to the lad, an arrangement that had benefitted man and boy in ways she never thought possible. In her book, family ties were everything. Wells had taken Ben under her wing on the understanding that he'd complete his English degree. He was planning to move out of David's cottage soon, or so he said, to a flat nearer the city, using some of his inheritance to put down a deposit.

The thought made Frankie sad.

She switched her focus to Wells. 'I know it's the weekend, but can you help us with Chris's notebooks?'

'Journalists never sleep,' Wells said.

She picked up her glass, toasting everyone with a bright blue cocktail Frankie recognised as Icelandic Iced Tea on account of the tiny flag poking out of the top. It was far from non-alcoholic.

'You've been in town ten minutes and already they have no daiquiri?'

David and Ben laughed.

Daiquiri was Wells' favourite tipple.

She raised her glass. 'I have it on good authority that this is the best thing to come out of Iceland since Björk,' she said.

9

There were better things that Frankie could think of to do on a Sunday morning than work: a wander through Amble's market; helping her grandfather on his allotment; a scramble up the dunes of Bamburgh beach with her mum and dad; taking a stroll along the Ouseburn Valley with Rae and Andrea; sinking a half of real ale. None of that was on her agenda today.

When she'd left Revolution at eleven last night, her car was white with frost. By the time she'd cleared the windscreen, her hands and feet were numb. All the way home, she thought of rough sleepers, her new bestie in particular. The image of the ex-serviceman remained with her as she climbed into a bed warmed by an electric blanket – her guilty pleasure – and still she reflected on what had happened to him.

No wonder she hadn't slept.

Before setting off to interview Liam Wiley, the guy who'd seen Chris Adams at the pub on the night he died, Frankie called Dick Abbott, asking him to do a PNC check on the witness. Wiley was from a rough area. He had no form. Not so much as a parking ticket to his name, which made her job easier.

Of the Murder Investigation Team, only Dick, Mitch and the SIO were in, apart from Indira Sharma who was putting in a lot of extra hours in the office. Information was coming in and leads were being followed up. So far there was nothing to get excited about. Frankie thanked Dick for the update and rang off.

Westgate Superbikes was smaller than Frankie had expected – no bigger than a triple garage. It was crammed with motorcycles in for repair and all manner of parts she didn't recognise. The man she'd come to see was a giant, six four at least, grey eyes and blond hair, cut short. He was covered in oil, a smear streaked across his forehead, ingrained in his fingernails. He was working alone on a green Kawasaki Ninja 650. When Frankie identified herself, he stopped what he was doing and looked up, grabbing a rag to wipe his hands. He slung a leg over the bike, leaving one filthy desert boot on the floor, the other on the footrest, freeing up the only seat in the place for her.

Frankie remained standing.

He dwarfed her – even sitting down.

'Sorry, I'm forgetting my manners,' he said. 'Can I get you anything? Tea, coffee? It'll have to be instant. That's all we have. I hope you take it black. We've run out of milk.'

Frankie had interviewed many a witness or family member who'd talk about anything – the weather, the state of the nation, how young she looked – rather than confront the issue she'd come to discuss, as if doing so would make the problem go away. It wouldn't. She glanced at the used mug on the bench behind the biker and decided not to risk it.

'I'm fine, thanks – and I'm very sorry about your friend, Mr Wiley.'

'Liam . . .'

He stuck out his right hand, then took it back, another wipe, this time on his shirt, before hooking his thumb inside the pocket of his jeans, a pose that Frankie found seductive. He'd look great in a set of leathers. The thought provoked a physical reaction deep inside her. She had to concentrate hard on what her witness had to say . . .

Liam sighed. 'I still can't get my head around it.'

Neither could she, but she kept that to herself. The concrete floor was as cold as a block of ice and her toes were numb. Trying not to shiver, she shifted her weight from one foot to the other. Wiley didn't seem to notice the cold.

'The detective you spoke to on the phone said that you saw Chris on Friday night in PTMY on High Bridge, that he was there until approximately nine o'clock. Is that correct?'

The biker nodded.

'I'm trying to piece together what happened to him between then and when he was found fatally wounded just before ten o'clock. Have you any idea what his plans were for the rest of the evening?'

A shake of the head was all the answer he gave.

'Did you not ask? It seems odd that he'd leave that early without saying goodbye or mentioning where he was off to.'

'I never had time to ask. It was my shout. I'd gone to get a round in and it took a while. The place was packed. When I got back, he was gone. Chris does his own thing. He told the others he had to go and said he'd see me at footy on Saturday – only he didn't turn up. Now I know why . . .'

Wiley dropped his gaze.

Frankie gave him a moment to compose himself. 'Any idea which direction he took when he left the pub?'

'No. As I said, he'd left by the time I returned from the bar.'

All day, and all day yesterday, uniform, Traffic and the ANPR team had been searching for Chris's car. Frankie suspected it would turn out to be parked up where he'd left it – assuming he hadn't taken the bus or Metro. His car keys were missing, along with the rest of the belongings he'd had on him. Whoever took them might be cruising around in the vehicle. 'Liam, do you happen to know where Chris usually left his car when he came to town?'

'The Gate, Times Square, sometimes in the multi-storey on the Quayside behind the Crown Court.'

'Can you excuse me a second?' Frankie pulled out her phone, calling David to update him. The conversation was brief. He said he'd send out the troops to investigate the locations Wiley had given and hung up, allowing Frankie to concentrate on her witness. 'Sorry about that. The sooner we find the vehicle, the better. Did you know Chris Adams well?'

'Aye, really well. We applied to the same university four years ago. I met him when we went to have a look around on open day. My mother got sick not long after, so I couldn't pursue my degree course. She has no one else. My old man left us when I was a young 'un,' he explained.

Every conversation had a subtext. Without actually saying so, was Wiley alluding to the fact that absent fathers and sick mothers was the glue that bound the two men to one another, the same way the loss of a loved one had cemented a relationship between Susan Adams and Frankie's mum?

'We had a lot in common,' Wiley added. 'Like me, he rides.'

Frankie was puzzled. She'd never seen Chris on two wheels, though that made sense. On the shelves in his room, above his small desk, were many books on biking, travel guides, motorcycle manuals, some classic, some new. On the wall was a signed poster of Superbike Champion Shane Byrne, though Susan hadn't referred to a motorcycle, only a car. 'No bike was found at his home.'

'It wouldn't be. He keeps it in a neighbour's garage.'

'His mum didn't mention it.'

'She wouldn't – she disapproves.'

'Any idea which neighbour?'

'No, sorry. I've never been to his home.'

That surprised her, given that Susan had turned her life around. If she didn't know where he kept it, Frankie knew someone who might. She sent a text to Abbott, asking him to look into it. He'd be on the blower already. He knew her father well. Slipping the phone into the back pocket of her jeans, she asked: 'Did Chris seem worried to you?'

'No . . .' Wiley cleared his throat. 'Quite the opposite. He was in fine fettle. It was a great night. Good music. A normal start to the weekend. I got to the pub at around seven thirty. Chris and some of our mates were already at the bar.'

'Male or female?'

'Both.'

'I'll need names, addresses. Would you mind?' Frankie handed him a notebook and pen. 'Phone numbers too, if you have them. As much information as you can give me. We need to talk to them urgently.'

With his mobile phone to aid his memory, Wiley wrote down the details, some of which were sketchy. Addresses were few and far between. What he passed to her were mobile numbers mostly, Twitter usernames, WhatsApp identities and a Facebook site that Liam told her had been created in part by the British Motorcyclists Federation, the modern means of communication for bikers, all of which she intended to follow up when she got to Middle Earth.

'How would you describe Chris? As a person, I mean.'

Wiley let out a big sigh. 'He was a laugh, always the centre of attention. Beats me why anyone would want to hurt him. It was an ordinary night. Six of us are . . . were, planning a European road trip next spring. We chatted about that mostly. He was really excited by it and so was I. We all were.'

'Was he drinking?' Frankie knew the answer. There was zero alcohol in his bloodstream.

Wiley was shaking his head.

'Did he ever?'

'Not much. He tends not to if he's working on a weekend.'

That didn't surprise her. Susan's alcoholism had ruined Chris's early life. He rarely indulged and, on the occasions he did, he'd stop at two. It made Frankie wonder why his mother had asked if he'd been drinking when she and David called at the house. Maybe Mitch was right: people change, except that flew in the face of everything she knew about her one-time friend.

Working?

'Did Chris have more than one job?'

'Not that I'm aware of.'

'Then where would he be working on a Saturday? Apart

from overnight arrests, the courts are shut on a weekend.'

'He used to go in sometimes to see what was going on. The job bored him senseless at times, but he reckoned the best stories came from nowhere, something he'd see or hear between cases. You think that's what got him killed?'

Frankie sidestepped that one. 'Sounds like he took his work seriously.'

'Aye, he took everything seriously. I have no proof that he was planning to go in on Saturday, but I can't think of any other reason he'd take off early when we were enjoying oursleves. I wish I'd gone with him now.'

'Did he ever talk about his work?'

'He talked about the writing more.' Wiley faltered, the expression in his eyes a mixture of misery and sadness, mourning lost opportunities and a life cut short perhaps. 'In fact, outside of our trip, that's all he talked about. To hear him tell it, he was penning a bestseller.'

The comment threw Frankie. 'He was writing a book?'

'Not any more.'

His brief answer was like a punch in the gut. Even though Frankie had seen their former friend's body lying dead on a city street, Wiley's stark reply underlined the senseless ending of his life, the wasted potential, the obliterated dreams. Chris would never marry or take that European road trip he'd been planning or emulate the achievements of a father who'd died before he was born. His mother had been robbed of the joy of grandchildren . . .

The list went on.

Frankie cleared her throat. 'Did he tell you what his book was about?'

'Beyond the fact that it was a thriller, no. He loved it though. It gave him a real buzz, putting words together. He was good at it too. He's had a few short stories published. Have you read any of his stuff?'

Frankie lied. 'We're looking into it.'

'He'd been really excited lately, like he'd found his niche and was finally making headway. I was green with envy. If things had been different, that could've been me.'

Frankie wondered if her witness – a man who, by his own admission, was with the victim an hour before his death – had realised that he'd handed her a motive? Envy was responsible for many a killing. She parked the thought, though this charismatic biker was suddenly less attractive to her than he'd been a moment ago. She made a mental note to check out his movements, especially the time he left the pub on Friday night.

'Fiction aside, do you happen to know what he was working on in his day job?'

'No, most of it was mundane. Taking down court results. It didn't fire his jets, I know that much. If it was a big case, he kept his cards close. He cared about victims and had more integrity than to make himself look big by exploiting their grief. He'd never sensationalise a story to sell newspapers and had the gloves off over it with his editor a time or two. I gather they didn't get on, though God knows why. Chris was a good bloke. Ambitious – but not at any cost, if you see what I mean.'

This was the Chris Adams Frankie knew too, a far cry from the lying, 'arrogant little shit' Fox had described. It occurred to her that the editor had some other reason for disliking him. He'd made no attempt to hide his opinions on the court reporter and was one of the last to see the lad alive. Whether he too was a potential suspect was open to question.

She refocused on Wiley. 'Do you recall anything unusual happen during the evening?'

'No . . . actually, yes. Not long before Chris left, he was nudged from behind and spilled his drink down his shirt. We all fell about laughing at first. He was a bit of a snazzy dresser.'

'A fight?'

'No, though for a moment we all thought there might be.'

'I thought you said he wasn't drinking.'

'It was tonic water,' Wiley explained. 'He brushed himself down and glanced over his shoulder to see who'd bumped into him. There was this guy. Well-built, tats, early thirties. He gave Chris a strange look. It was obvious to everyone that they knew each other. Chris never said anything to me, but I could tell he was uneasy.'

'Had you ever seen this man before?'

'No.

'And he nudged Chris on purpose?'

Wiley nodded. 'A deliberate attempt to provoke him. I remember thinking that he might've been responsible for Chris's mysterious eye injury.'

'Chris didn't mention how he came by that?'

'No. He was deep, a very private person. If he wanted to share, he would. If not, he kept schtum. If you're who I think you are, you'll know that already.'

Frankie frowned. 'Excuse me?'

Wiley gave her hard eyes, one sceptical eyebrow raised: *You know exactly what I'm on about.* 'There can't be many detectives called Frankie Oliver on the force. He talked about you non-stop. Not to everyone, only to me. There are some things too painful to share. You were the one. He never told you, did he?'

She shook her head, the sucker-punch almost knocking her over, confirmation that she was still important to Chris Adams – more so than he was to her. Frankie could have denied knowing him. What would be the point? It was out there now. Wiley couldn't retract it even if he wanted to.

'Chris and I hadn't seen each other for a very long time,' she said.

'Aye, he told me that too . . . He couldn't bear to see and not have you. I told him time and again to get in touch. He couldn't bring himself to do it. Ever ask yourself why you didn't bump into him when your parents live across the road? He used to hide if he knew you were visiting your folks.' Wiley put her out of her misery. 'Anyway, he didn't rise to the incident in the pub. The guy who'd spilled his drink fucked off. No apology or owt—'

'No words were exchanged?'

'None.'

'And Chris didn't tell you who he was?'

'No. He didn't stick around long after that. You think he might have been followed?'

That thought had occurred to Frankie too, but she was still reeling from the words spoken a moment ago by her witness. 'We'll look into it. Thanks, Liam. You've been very helpful. If you think of anything else, call me.' Handing him her card, she left as fast as her wobbly legs would carry her.

10

David emerged from his office feeling pretty positive after a call from a uniform cop who'd found Chris Adams' car. The search for his motorcycle was ongoing. The SIO's day was shaping up nicely. As he entered the incident room, Frankie was standing with her back to him, talking to DC Mitchell. Something about her body language wasn't quite right. Mitch acknowledged David's presence over her shoulder, pulled his coat off his chair and left the office in a hurry. As Frankie turned to find out who was standing behind her, she looked rattled, and that wasn't like her. David wandered over to find out what was troubling her.

'Guv.' Her tone was flat.

'What's going on?'

'I sent Mitch out to follow up on a lead.'

David glanced at the door Mitchell had walked through. 'What lead?'

'We need the CCTV from PTMY. I told him that's his only reason for breathing today. There was an incident there on Friday night, enough to warrant further investigation—'

'Then you'd better call him back. Dick's already on it.'

Frankie frowned.

'He took a call from a young woman in Chris's company on Friday night,' David explained. 'She told us all about it.'

Frankie took a couple of paces to the exit, glancing along the corridor. No sign of Mitch. Pulling out her phone, she made a call, telling the young DC to stand down, apologising for wasting his time, then hung up, eyes on David. 'Sorry, I should have run it by you first.'

'Yes, you should. Half our crew are missing, Frank. It's like the *Marie Celeste* in here. Two more called in sick. We can't afford to send anyone out on a wild goose chase. Besides, I ordered that footage as soon as I found out Chris had been in there. I also put out an action to see what route he took to Northumberland Street to see if he was alone or if he had company. That's basic procedure . . .' He dropped his head on one side. 'Are you feeling OK? You seem distracted.'

She didn't answer.

'Frankie, you need to concentrate.'

His gentle ticking off didn't touch her.

She had other things on her mind.

'Anything else?' she asked.

'As it happens, Chris Adams' car has been located in the Quayside Car Park. Thanks for the tip-off.'

'Thank Wiley, not me.'

'I will, if I ever get to meet him.'

Frankie looked into the middle distance at nothing in particular, Wiley's words ringing in her ears. David didn't question it. She turned to face him. 'What time did he park up?'

'Eleven minutes past seven on Friday night, which meant his ticket was valid until eight o'clock Saturday morning. The vehicle was locked and secure. Apart from a ticket attached to the windscreen for overstaying his welcome, it appears not to have been tampered with in any way. The vehicle has been uploaded for examination.'

'That's great news.'

'So why have you got a face like a smacked arse?'

'I wasn't aware that I had.'

'Try looking in the mirror . . .' She was out of sorts and not thinking straight. 'What's wrong?'

'Nothing.' She looked away.

'Doesn't look like nothing. Did you check the murder wall on the way in?'

'No. I—'

'Why not?'

'I had other things on my mind.'

'Like what?'

'Like my meeting with Liam Wiley.' Stone listened carefully as she recounted the interview with the witness and his statement that there was a minor altercation in the pub everyone called PTMY. 'Does that tally with what the other witness said? He seemed very plausible.'

'It does, which is why Dick is down there now. I want to know who spilt that drink, whether it was deliberate and, more importantly, if anything untoward happened afterwards. Did Wiley say anything else?'

'No.'

'Don't you mean yes?'

'Yes then.' Frankie averted her eyes, a quick scan of the incident room. Indira was loitering. It wasn't her Frankie didn't trust. Stone had pulled in a couple of extra call-takers, people she didn't know that well. Both were within earshot. She turned to face him, lowering her voice. 'Guv, I'd rather not discuss it here.'

'Guv?' David was caught off guard. She wasn't in the habit of addressing him so in private conversations and her secrecy worried him. Intrigued, he led the way to his office, stood aside to let her in, then closed the door behind her. Parking his butt on the edge of his desk, he crossed his arms and waited. A dialogue she was reluctant to have in the open must be pretty damn serious. 'The floor is yours,' he said. 'C'mon, spit it out. It can't be that bad.'

She stalled. 'David, he talked about me.'

'Who did?'

'The IP.'

The sudden formality hit David like a brick. Since he'd launched the investigation into Chris Adams' death, Frankie had only ever referred to their victim by his first name and now suddenly he was the 'injured party', an attempt to distance herself perhaps. He allowed the silence to grow, waiting for a fuller explanation. It was a long time coming, so he gave her a shove.

'Chris talked about you to the witness?'

'Yes, and I swear I've not seen him for years.'

'Is that so unusual? They were mates after all . . . and so were the two of you.' David dropped his head to one side, another nudge for her to elucidate.

'I'm concerned about Chris's state of mind,' she said.

'I'm concerned about yours, but don't let that stop you.'

She didn't laugh.

'You've changed your tune,' David said. 'One minute, he's the salt of the earth, the good guy, and now you're not so sure.'

'With good reason.'

'I'm listening . . .'

Frankie appeared conflicted, on the verge of a disclosure but unsure whether she was ready and willing to repeat the conversation she'd had with Wiley. She did, word for word, including the personal bits. 'Chris was very deep, and yet he'd given Wiley and his mum the impression that we were still in touch when we weren't. Wiley said he talked about me non-stop.'

'Is that why the two of you drifted apart, because he wanted your friendship to develop and you didn't?' David locked eyes with her. Was she unaware of the effect she had on men? It wasn't the first time he'd posed this question in the privacy of his own head. He didn't know it, but she was about to give him an answer.

'No, nothing like that. That's what's so bizarre. He seems to have invented this fantasy figure and pinned my name to it, and yet I'm the only one he didn't confide in. There were no signs of it when we last saw each other, I swear, let alone hints that I might've picked up on . . . or maybe I'm too dim to have noticed.'

'Maybe you only saw what you wanted to see.'

'There is that . . . I mean, what idiot in their right mind would get involved with me, right?' She didn't stop for breath. 'Don't you dare answer that. The question is, should I withdraw from the investigation?'

'I don't see why. It's hardly your fault if Adams fantasised about a relationship he didn't have the balls to pursue. I've been there too, remember? We all have our hang-ups, Frank. Don't worry about it.' She was. He could see that. 'Hey! Don't think too badly of him. He's human, like the rest of us. We can't castigate him for having great taste, can we?'

'Sod off! My love life, or lack thereof, isn't a joke. Our line of work doesn't leave much time for romance or even a one-night stand. That's my excuse. What's yours?'

'Maybe I'm waiting for the right girl—'

Frankie made a crazy face. 'Did you just step out of the 1950s?'

He laughed.

The banter between them had raised their spirits, but their laughter soon vanished. Beneath her comedy routine, Frankie was mortified by Wiley's revelation and the perceived mess it had landed her in. David forced himself to concentrate. Despite her tendency to fly solo on occasions, she'd never jeopardise a case. She'd made full disclosure at the first opportunity and that was good enough for him.

'Forget Wiley,' he said.

'How can I? What's said can't be unsaid.'

'Frankie, let it go. In the time we've worked together, you've played with a straight bat. I know that.' He did. She'd never let her personal feelings cloud her judgement or risk the collapse of legal proceedings should they apprehend the perpetrator who'd cut short a life – and still she was fretting. 'Would it make you feel better if I ran it past Bright?' He was referring to Detective Chief Superintendent Bright – the head of CID. 'That way your back is covered.'

'Would you?'

'Consider it done.'

She relaxed. 'If he laughs, I want to know about it. And if my dad finds out, tell Bright I'll sue him for sharing confidential information.' Her father and Bright were the best of friends.

David pressed his lips together, fighting the urge to laugh. 'Anything else?'

'Isn't that enough?' she snapped.

'I can tell there's more and you know I'm no good at guessing games.'

'Susan Adams may have misled us . . . unintentionally.'

'In what way?'

'Wiley told me that Chris was penning a thriller. It had me wondering if that was the story that would make his name. Given our conversation thus far, it's entirely possible that the public interest case he talked about was imagined too, the synopsis for a novel he hadn't yet finished rather than a factual exposé. Writers are an odd species, don't you think?'

'That's a generalisation if ever I heard one.'

'Name me one that isn't.'

David put a finger to his lips. He was struggling.

'I'm suggesting that Susan either misheard or took it the wrong way,' Frankie added. 'You heard what Wells said: the paper was in trouble. Maybe he was trying to impress his editor by finding an alternative career, a chance to jump ship before he was pushed. Or maybe he was doing both, investigating an issue that needed telling and writing a novel. By the way, if I'm mentioned in his bloody shorthand notebooks, dead or alive, I'll never forgive him.'

She looked away, her expression hard to read.

David wasn't fooled by her indignation. It was an attempt to mask her grief and hold back the anger that bubbled to the surface every now and then. Frankie was in limbo, unable to move through the stages of bereavement until their investigation into Adams' death was resolved. He recognised the signs. He'd have to keep a close eye on her.

11

At Stone's instruction, Dick Abbott had pored over CCTV footage from PTMY and had found nothing of the minor incident two witnesses had referred to independently. It had not been caught on camera and can't have been serious if bar staff hadn't felt the need to intervene. At the risk of embarrassing Frankie, Stone had no choice but to ask Wiley to call in at Middle Earth and take a look at the recordings on the off-chance that he'd spot the man who'd bumped into Chris Adams an hour before he met his death.

A couple of hours later, with his help, the SIO had a name: Gary Armstrong.

Known to the rank and file, Armstrong had spent periods in care and detention, graduating to adult prison as he reached adulthood. With a string of previous convictions to his name – GBH; Going Equipped; Affray; Possession of Class A Drugs, and more convictions dating back over fifteen years since he was a juvenile, including one of attempted rape – he was no stranger to the police. Further back still, at the tender age of eleven, only just within the age of criminal responsibility, he'd been in court on three separate occasions for Causing Unnecessary Suffering to an Animal.

'Well, that comes as no surprise.' Frankie pointed the offences out to David on the computerised criminal record. Childhood animal abuse was often an indicator of worse to come. Clinical evidence had established a close link between that and other forms of cruelty, women and children bearing the brunt of it from violent men. She looked up from her computer, meeting his gaze. 'And I don't believe in coincidence, do you?'

'Meaning what?'

She nodded at the screen. 'Take a look at his most recent court appearance. Looks like the CPS lost their bottle again, accepting a plea to the lesser offence, reducing a Section 18 Wounding to ABH. It's the date that interests me.' She swivelled her chair round to face David and crossed her legs. 'Armstrong was in court on Friday, the same day we launched our murder investigation. Chris was also in court. It's conceivable that they were in the same courtroom, Armstrong in the dock, Chris on the press bench. Maybe his death wasn't a botched robbery, but something more sinister. Wiley told me there was history between the two. The wrong kind.' She threw it out there, hoping he'd take the bait. 'It begs the question as to whether Armstrong is mixed up in the story Chris was investigating—'

'If there is a story,' David reminded her. 'Fox denies there was a scoop. He said—'

'I know what he said,' Frankie interrupted. 'And what Wiley said about Chris turning his hand to fiction, but he didn't tell his mum a pack of lies to make her day. That's not his style, David. He's wasn't delusional . . .' She blushed. 'Well, maybe he was on some level, but he was as honest as the day is long in every other respect. Whether or not Susan misunderstood what he was doing in his spare time, there's more to this case than we first thought.' Frankie paused, a sad look in her eye. 'The day before yesterday, Chris was alive, enjoying the company of friends, planning a road trip . . . writing—'

'It would help if we knew what.'

'Whatever it was, this case hinges on finding out what he was hoping would make his mother proud. If Armstrong had anything to do with his death, we need to pursue him with every weapon in our armoury. He's a bully who thinks he's bulletproof. He should've been locked up on Friday. Instead, he walked free. If he hadn't, Chris might still be alive.'

'That's quite a leap.'

'Do you have any better ideas?'

'At it happens, no. Dig up what you can on him and check in with Chris's editor. Find out what courts he was covering. If we can put the two men in the same courtroom, with Wiley's statement that they' – he used his fingers as inverted commas – '"bumped into each other" in the pub that evening, that gives us cause to question him.'

'We already have cause.'

'Humour me.'

Frankie picked up the phone to access the number.

'Frankie?'

She looked up. 'What?'

'Be nice to Fox.'

She feigned innocence. 'Don't you trust me?'

'Not even as far as I can throw you.'

Smiling, she made the call, putting the phone on speaker so he could listen in.

From the minute Fox came on the line, he made it perfectly clear that he was busy and she'd have to make it quick. It took him no time to confirm that Chris was indeed present when Armstrong was sentenced and that he strongly disapproved of the court's decision.

'Were you aware of any animosity between the two?' Frankie asked.

'Chris thought he was a waste of space,' Fox said. 'We all do. That's not surprising, is it? The toerag seems to wriggle out of a hefty sentence every time he gets caught. It must be galling for your lot, hardly worth your while putting in the paperwork.'

'Tell me about it.' Frankie paused. 'How was Chris when he returned to the office?'

'Late,' Fox said bluntly.

'That's not what I meant . . .'

'Though it could be relevant,' Stone whispered, 'if words were exchanged afterwards.'

'He was full of himself,' Fox said. 'Same old, same old.'

Frankie wandered why he made it his business to disrespect, at every opportunity, a young man everyone else had warmed to. 'Mr Fox, could you put your personal feelings aside and stick to the facts? You're not the only one in a rush.'

Frankie rolled her eyes at David.

The editor continued. 'Chris was not in the best of moods. The case had been listed several times and adjourned for reports. When the judge summed up, I gather the victim's family were bitterly disappointed, not to mention being laughed at by Armstrong's entourage. His cronies are shite, the lot of them. The family were hoping that he'd be sent down, her chance to escape an abusive relationship. Chris said there were a few raised eyebrows in the courtroom, a few tears too, no doubt. The victim will be scarred for life and yet she stuck by him, refusing to give evidence. Stupid bitch.'

'It's not as simple as that,' Frankie snapped. 'She's obviously terrified of him.'

'Then she should do something about it,' Fox countered. 'Anyway, if her family were expecting justice for their daughter, they didn't get it.'

David shook his head at Frankie, a warning not to let the editor wind her up.

She held her tongue, though her instinct was to let fly. 'Out of interest, did Chris mention any reaction afterwards? Any harsh words from the defendant towards his girlfriend's family – or to him personally. It's not unusual for there to be a bit of humpy after a court appearance. In my experience, offenders like the press even less than they like our lot.'

'Are you suggesting Armstrong had a go at Chris?'

'We're covering the bases, sir.'

'Then no, he didn't mention any afters.'

'OK . . . it was just a thought. I'd appreciate it if you'd keep our conversation to yourself. We haven't an ounce of proof one way or the other. I hope I can rely on your discretion.'

'Of course.'

'Good, because anything that compromises our investigation will have serious consequences.'

'Understood,' Fox said. 'An interesting theory though. If it proves to be correct, I wish you luck in apprehending the bastard. It's high time Armstrong was put away for good. Now, I really must get on. Are you finished with your questions?'

'I am. Thanks for your help.' She ended the call, hard eyes on David. 'What an absolute moron that man is. And, in case you're in any doubt, I'm not talking about Armstrong.'

12

The area was grim, known to police as the Wild West: a lawless ghetto of criminal activity, violence, drug peddling and prostitution where the strong were in charge and the weak did their bidding. The street was littered with rubbish: newspapers sticking to the wet pavement, fag packets, used hypodermics and a whole lot more, some of it unmentionable in polite conversation. Old sofas dragged outside in the summer were still there in December, and would remain there, soggy and stinking until they dried out, then they would be sat upon as their owners slapped on UV protection, reached for stolen Wayfarers, a chance to fry in the sun and brainstorm their next game plan in getting something for nothing.

Frankie sighed as David parked the car. 'This used to be part of my patch when I was in uniform.'

'Nice.' He was being ironic. The conditions in the street were appalling.

Frankie glanced through the car window, then at him. 'It was more respectable then. People took pride in their homes and spoke to law enforcement without having to apologise for it. Good people. Some of them still live here. They have no choice, David. Moving on costs money they don't have. And those that did escape unwittingly made room for the scum to move in.'

'Familiar story.'

'Yup. One that's gone on for years. The area quickly fell into disrepute and now look at it.' Frankie pointed across the road. 'And that blue door, lucky seven, is our next port of call.'

David followed her gaze.

The Victorian terraced property was more dilapidated than most, a shabby front door, burnt black in places as if a blowtorch had been used on it – and not to strip the peeling paint. Most likely a muscle-flexing exercise, a message from a rival to establish a pecking order perhaps: watch out, there's a new kid on the block. For every thug like Armstrong, there was another limbering up to take his place. Stone and Oliver didn't need to see inside to know that the door was locked and double-bolted.

'Looks like Armstrong upset someone,' David said.

'Just a bit.'

Neither made a move to get out of the car.

'Apart from his CRO sheet, what do we know about him?' David asked.

'Our lot have been in and out of there for years, using a battering ram and the dog section to get in mostly. I checked the PNC before we left. There's a warning marker on the property flagging up a dangerous dog in 2012. The abused animal has since been destroyed, a five-year banning order still in force.'

'Weapons?'

'Probably.'

'Ready?' David said.

'As I'll ever be.' Frankie reached for the door.

Once out of the car, she made a beeline for Armstrong's place. There was no doorbell. She knocked and got no answer. Shading her eyes, she moved to the window and peered in. Nothing. No lights, TV or radio on inside. She could see the remnants of a got-out-of-jail celebration: squashed beer cans on the floor, empty bottles on the table, ashtrays overflowing on the arms of threadbare furniture, top-shelf magazines, a bong and associated drug-taking paraphernalia. In the current climate, with no boots on the ground, who'd ever see it? A sudden movement made her recoil swiftly.

'Jesus Christ!'

'What?'

'That!'

A Japanese Tosa, bred to show aggression, launched itself at the window, rattling the single-glazed panes, baring teeth that looked like they could rip arms off without trying.

'So much for the banning order,' David quipped.

Frankie glanced in his direction, an expression that said: do we really have to go inside? Blowing out a breath, she looked up. Weeds grew out of the gutter and mould stuck to the inside of the windowpanes on the floor above. Greying curtains yanked untidily across a filthy sash window had insufficient material to cover the glass, leaving a gaping V-shaped hole at the top.

Making a fist of her hand, Frankie struck the door side-on, three short bursts, then three more. Teasing the letterbox open, she shouted through it.

'Police! Open up.'

The dog was frothing at the mouth by the time it arrived in the hallway, snarling and barking, making the hair on her neck stand to attention. Another glance at Stone. 'We're wasting our breath. Even if he's in there, he ain't coming out. And, personally, I'd rather have that door between me and his new best friend.'

They were about to walk away when Frankie noticed someone she knew shuffling along the pavement, head down, hands in pockets. He was around fifty metres away, a scrawny kid she'd had dealings with in the past. A lad who'd been willing to trade information in exchange for her blindness when in possession of illegal substances any sensible copper might consider small enough for his own use. With any luck, he might do so now. And if not, she'd be unreasonable and haul him in until he saw sense.

'Oi!' When in Rome, Frankie thought. 'Come 'ere!'

The lad slowed his pace, a shifty expression. He pulled up sharp, a few metres away, mouthing the F-word under his breath, scratching his neck until it was red raw. Frankie watched him carefully. He was nineteen or thereabouts, though he looked much younger. His face was gaunt, eyes vacant, pupils dilated.

'Drugged up or tooled up,' she said to David. 'Take your pick.'

'Either one will do nicely,' he said. 'Who is he?'

'Thomas Baxter – Tomma to his friends.'

Thinking he was going to leg it, Frankie approached him at a fast pace.

'Relax, Baxter, we're not here for you. We're looking for Garry Armstrong, big guy, tats, Mr Angry, like his dog.' The animal was still going crackers in the house. If Armstrong was in there, sleeping off his party, he was wide awake now. Eyes on the user she hoped might give her what she wanted, Frankie thumbed in the direction of the front door she'd been knocking on a moment ago. 'He lives here. Do you know him?'

The subject of her interest took a step away, a quick glance over his shoulder. The street was empty. In the next few minutes, that would change. Time was limited. They both knew it.

'Hey! I'm talking to you. You know who I mean, right?'

'Are you fucking crazy?' His voice was barely a whisper as he spat the words out. 'At least make it look like I'm being searched or sommat . . . I want to live, know what I'm saying?' He turned his pockets inside out, holding on to the lining with the tips of his fingers, the nails bitten to the quick. 'I've got nowt, man!'

He'd never make it as an actor.

'Stand still!' Frankie played along, her turn to whisper. 'Let me make this perfectly clear, Tomma. I'd hate there to be any misunderstanding. Armstrong and I have something in common. You don't want to get on the wrong side of either of us, right? So, when you're ready to do what you do best, you're going to tell me where I might find him. Am I making myself clear.'

'Crystal.' He tried to shrug her off. 'Get off me! I done nowt . . . I just showed you, I've got nowt. Search me again if you don't believe me.'

Out of the corner of her eye, Frankie spotted a dozen or so kids emerging from the back lane to jeer at the detectives, like flies to a rotting carcass. There were more of them than she was comfortable with, but David had her back. Hearing their taunts, Baxter raised his voice, projecting a string of verbals like vomit from his foul mouth.

Eyeballing her, he dropped his voice to a whisper. 'Please, DS Oliver.'

'Then cough.'

'You cow!'

Frankie stood her ground.

Baxter didn't. 'He hangs out at the boxing club. That's all I got.'

The group were almost upon them. 'Which one?'

'Benwell . . . Now fuck off before this lot do something you'll regret.' Shrugging himself free, Baxter sprinted off down the street, lifting the middle finger of his right hand, giving the impression that he'd rather die than talk to her. The feeling was mutual.

13

The boxing club was located in a former garage that had closed down years ago and moved to new premises on Scotswood Road, the main area for car dealerships on the western edge of the city centre. The club itself was a cavernous industrial building with a grey corrugated iron roof. Coloured punch-bags hung on spring-loaded swivels from RSJ crossbeams, enabling many members to train at once. Separated off was an area housing various items of gym equipment: weightlifting benches, exercise mats and three treadmills that were being used to full advantage by kids, black and white, young and old, all working at maximum capacity.

The smell of sweat was overpowering.

David's eyes were drawn to the dull thud of leather connecting with leather. The boxing ring was at the far end of the gym, away from the door, where a couple of youngsters were sparring, the smaller of the two holding his own, with fast hands and lightning quick feet. Others waiting their turn were shadow boxing or skipping, enthusiastic, committed, enjoying the camaraderie of being part of something special.

'Nice to see so many here, girls too . . .' David glanced at Frankie, a question in his eyes. 'Ever fancy it?'

'Me?' she snorted. 'I'm seven stone wet through. Don't think I'd have got very far, do you?'

'You're a copper. You've done OK—'

'By using my brain, not my paws.' She held them up in front of her eyes, a classic boxing pose, moving her head from side to side as if she were attempting to dodge an invisible right hook.

David laughed. 'Behave. You may not be in uniform but

everyone in here knows what you do for a living . . . anyway, that's not how it works. These places are as much about developing willpower and nurturing self-control in the right environment as how to land a punch. A good coach can teach these kids so much more than how to stay on their feet—'

'I said I'd have made a shite boxer, not that I needed a lesson in the history of the sport. I'm well aware of the ethos behind these clubs. My granddad used to run one just like it.'

'I didn't know that.'

'Why would you? Believe it or not, it was in a rougher part of the city than this. He was passionate about combatting youth violence. He told me once that if he dissuaded one kid from turning to crime it was well worth the effort and I agree with him. The kids he worked with were the lucky ones. They learned stuff from him they didn't get at home, starting with good manners.'

'I bet they did.'

Frankie grinned. 'He put me, Rae and Joanna on the naughty step a time or two, I can tell you. And woe betide us if we moved before he said we could. He's no slouch when it comes to discipline.'

'He slipped up with you.'

'And he knows it.'

David smiled, taking in the activity all around them. 'Serioiusly, we need more places like these. Ironic, don't you think, that we're in here looking for a thug?' He'd noticed that she'd already locked on to her target.

On the other side of the room, Armstrong was loitering near the fire exit, bulging muscles on display, body free of hair, a genuine tan glistening under the harsh tube lighting. He was the exception to the unwritten rule that those who took up the sport should never lift their fists outside of a boxing ring – and never in anger.

'It's rude to stare,' David said.

Frankie gave him a sideways glance. 'It's hard not to. He's built like a tank.'

'That's steroids for you.'

'Yeah, well I hate to use a cliché, but someone should tell him that beauty really is skin deep.'

Frankie was right. It was what lay beneath the surface Armstrong had to fear: DVT, heart attack, stroke, liver problems and other side-effects, any one of which could kill him.

'You only need to examine his criminal record to see the psychological effects of the drugs he's taking.' Frankie dropped her voice a touch. 'He's switched wrong, unable to control his temper, even if he wanted to – which, more often than not, he doesn't. He's dangerous and unpredictable, so watch yourself.'

'You too.'

'I mean it, David. Inflicting pain is part of who he is and why he'll end up doing a stretch in prison one day.'

'For having a go at us, or for Chris's murder?'

'If not his, then someone else's. If he'd been put away earlier, there'd be a few more kids round here with their own teeth. He's a lifer in waiting, for sure.' Frankie turned to face him. 'Listen, he won't square up to me, not in front of witnesses, that would be far too spineless, the type of behaviour he reserves for the women he screws and always behind closed doors. He might kick off with you though. You want me to take the lead?'

'Given that we've not yet had the pleasure, I'd like to tackle him myself.'

'Oh, go on . . . I've not "had the pleasure" either.'

'Even so.'

She accepted his decision as final. David felt guilty for the lie. He had concerns that Armstrong might not be the only one unable to control his temper if riled. His 2ic was an excellent detective. She was also a live wire who'd mix it with the best of them if she had something to say. Even though she hadn't seen Chris Adams for quite some time, this case was personal for her in a way that others were not.

'As a courtesy, a word with the coach might be advisable,' she said. 'He might want us to take it outside.'

Nodding in agreement, David walked away.

14

'We're on . . .' David flicked his head towards Armstrong. 'I told the coach we'll have a quiet word and remove him if we get any humpy. He's happy with that. He reckons it'll act as a lesson to others not to get on the wrong side of the law. Apparently, some of the younger kids look up to Armstrong, undoing all the good work he does with them. He may well have a point. C'mon, let's get it over with.'

He moved towards the man they had come to question, Frankie following him across the gym wondering what reaction they might get. Armstrong was powerfully built. She had no doubt that David could handle him if need be, in spite of what she'd said a moment ago.

'Garry Armstrong?'

The Tank looked up. 'Who's asking?'

Like he didn't know. He'd clocked them the minute they stepped over the threshold, as they had picked him out from across the room. Like police officers, offenders were always on the lookout. Armstrong seemed unconcerned by their presence.

He knew the drill.

David caught the eye of the kid wrapping tape around his hands. 'Son, can you give us a minute?'

The lad looked at Armstrong.

Receiving a nod, he moved away.

David showed his warrant card. 'I'm DCI Stone, this is DS Oliver.'

'Fucksake, what now?' Armstrong glanced at the ID, acting as if the interruption to his leisure time was a minor inconvenience.

There was no immediate animosity. Maybe that was

because of the venue, the fact that younger kids were looking on – as was the coach. Frankie knew Armstrong didn't give a shit about that. He'd just walked away from a prison sentence. This was him playing the big man. He thought he was untouchable.

He wasn't.

'We'd like to ask you a few questions,' David said.

'Make an appointment. I'm busy.'

'So are we. We have reason to believe that you might be able to help us with our enquiries. We don't have time to hang around.'

'Is this a joke? I'm sick of you bastards hassling me.'

'Can you see me laughing?'

There was a hush in the club. The smaller kids had stopped sparring and skipping. Anxious eyes turned in their direction. Aware of his young audience, and with a reputation to uphold, the Tank raised his voice a touch. 'You should've done your homework, pal. I don't talk to the pigs.'

David stood his ground. 'Well, you can hear me out here or come with us and we can do it in the comfort of the nearest nick. What's it to be?'

'And if I refuse?'

'Do yourself a favour, Mr Armstrong. Don't make this more difficult than it has to be. If you've done nothing wrong, and we're satisfied with your account, we'll walk away.'

'Ask your fucking questions then.'

'You were in PTMY on Friday night around eight thirty, nine o'clock—'

'So?'

'We understand that you were giving someone grief.'

'Not true, I'd have remembered.' He didn't flinch. 'Next question.'

David made him sweat a while. 'What if I told you we have a witness to the incident.'

'What incident?'

'You bumped into someone in the pub, spilling his drink—'

'The half chat with the dodgy eye?'

'Is that what it was all about?' Frankie said. 'You didn't like the colour of his skin? Hate crimes are taken very seriously these days—'

'Not my style, pet. Ask the lads.'

The arrogant shit pointed at a couple of black lads working out nearby. He knew they'd cover his arse rather than risk the consequences of going against him. Adjusting the strapping to his left hand, Armstrong looked Frankie up and down, stripping her with his eyes, reducing her to a piece of flesh ripe for the taking, in the way that guys like him treat all women. He wasn't the type to show respect for her as a person or as an officer of the law.

He cracked his knuckles, a show of bravado.

It didn't faze her.

David seized the initiative. 'Don't suppose you know how the guy came by his eye injury?'

'Fuck, no. Makes you think that I would?'

'Just asking.'

'Well, you have your answer. Now piss off and leave me be.'

'That I can't do. Tell us what happened in the pub.'

'There's nowt to tell,' Armstrong acted the innocent. 'The place was heaving. Accidents happen. I was walking through the pub, minding my own, when the wanker backed into me. Nowt I could do to avoid him. I did try.' He grinned for the benefit of a couple of kids loitering nearby, close enough to earwig the conversation. Frankie moved them on as David cut off his showboating.

'The man you claim backed into you has a name you're familiar with—'

'No way! Now there's a coincidence. You're going to have to do better than that, Detective. As I recall, the idiot you're referring to walked in with that injury. Ask around. If I clocked him, others probably did too. As I said, what happened in there was unintentional. There was no blood spilt that night, only water as I recall. Try pinning that on me and you'll be laughed out of fucking court. I was there, I admit it. That's all I'm prepared to say without my brief present.'

David ignored the comment. 'It wasn't you who caused his eye injury?'

'No, I told you.'

'You're pretty handy with those.' Frankie pointed at his bandaged fists. 'Feet too, I heard. According to your criminal record, you've given women a good kicking more than once. In my book, only a coward would do that.'

'Do me a favour. From what I saw of the wimp in the pub, if I blew on him he'd fall over. If I'd wanted to hurt him, he'd have stayed hurt. It's the first time I've set eyes on the guy—'

'You mean outside of a courtroom, don't you?' David pushed.

'Who takes notice of anyone in court? Present company aside – I make it my businesses to look my accusers in the eye and commit their faces to memory . . .' He was clever enough to gloss over the not so subtle threat and cover himself. 'That way I can make a complaint if I'm pulled in too often. Persecution is tough to deal with when you're trying to go straight.'

David never wavered as he continued his questioning, though he was fighting a losing battle. Frankie knew it. No one would dare to speak out against this thug. Trying to find a witness who would stick their head above the parapet was a pipedream.

'The young man you described as a half chat is now dead,' she said.

'Not my doing.' The Tank looked away, feigning indifference.

He might have the luck of the Irish when it came to court appearances, but he was facing a life sentence if he'd killed Chris Adams. Even the most arrogant villain would be nervous about spending the rest of his days behind bars.

Frankie wasn't fooled by his bravado. If justice had prevailed and she was to add up the sentences he might have served, she'd calculated that he'd have spent a good few years inside already, the majority of his life. It made her wonder if crown prosecutors were so intimidated by his reputation that they went soft on him. It was gratifying to know that Stone was up to the challenge.

'Don't you even want to know his name?' he asked.

'Not especially.'

'Then let me jog your memory. It's Chris Adams, the same Chris Adams who worked for the *Corchester Herald*. You know, the newspaper reporter who's been on your case, poking his journalistic nose into your criminal activity. My DS googled their website. You're averaging a mention every couple of months. Any more and we'd be thinking you were a minor celebrity, not a small-time crook who keeps getting caught. *Now* try telling me you bumped into him by accident.'

Armstrong was rattled.

David kept up the pressure. 'Did you see or speak to Chris Adams in court on Friday?'

'See, possibly . . . Speak to, no. Why would I? I was too busy high-fiving my preening dickhead of a barrister who, by the way, is as black as coal.' He smirked at Frankie. 'See, I'm no racist. Some of my best friends are more coffee than cream. Ask around if you don't believe me. I guarantee you'll not find anyone to level that allegation at me.'

'I believe you,' Frankie said.

Armstrong knew she was being sarcastic. 'What time was it you said your victim died?'

'We didn't, but we'd like you to account for your movements between eight thirty and say midnight.'

'Now?'

'That's the plan.'

'I don't think so. Talk to my brief.'

Although the MIT had a definitive time of death – unusual

in a murder investigation – establishing a sequence of events before and after the fact was vital. During Frankie's police career, many potential suspects had fallen foul of this rule, concocting alibis for the periods beforehand, spouting off at length about their movements afterwards, when in reality that was of equal importance to police. A time when weapons or clothing might've been disposed of or discarded, a victim's personal possessions stashed, offloaded in a lock-up or deposited at the home of an associate. Embellishments and half-truths by those under suspicion were gold to any investigator. The more embroidery, the greater the chance of catching them out in a provable lie.

Armstrong was no different.

'I'm afraid you picked the wrong horse this time,' he said. 'After I left PTMY I went straight to Escape, the nightclub on Collingwood Street. I was standing in a queue for a good while too. If you look hard enough there should be witnesses. It's a regular haunt. I'm well known there.'

'And no doubt your best mate was on the door to corroborate what you say?' Frankie couldn't help herself. 'Mr Armstrong, if you're in any way responsible for Chris Adams' death, there'll be no "escape" for you. That's a promise.'

15

'He's lying, and not very well either,' Frankie grumbled as she strode off at a fast pace, keen to check in with the incident room for an update, hoping their car was parked where they'd left it and still had four wheels. Stone's voice came from over her shoulder, a plea for her to slow down. She came to a stop and turned to face him. 'Wouldn't you love to wipe that smug grin off his face?'

'There's nothing to tie him to the crime scene.'

'Yet.' Frankie strode off, lengthening her stride.

David followed suit.

'He's the only lead we have,' she said

'Agreed. Take is slow, Frank. If we can place him in the vicinity of Northumberland Street, at the relevant time, we'll have another pop at him. Then we'll see what the slippery sod has to say for himself. He has a point, though, he didn't deny the drink-spilling incident—'

'Because there were witnesses.'

'CCTV didn't capture him—'

'Yeah, but maybe someone with a mobile phone did. C'mon, Chris was dead within the hour—'

'That doesn't mean the two events are connected. Maybe he's telling the truth—'

'Yeah, and maybe NUFC are going to win the Premiership.'

Stone gave a wry smile. It was a tantalising thought. An impossibility this year. Their favourite footy team was languishing in the league below.

'He obviously knows more about Chris than he's letting on,' Frankie added. 'The profile fits: villain with a history of violence and intimidation—'

'He still may not be the one we're looking for.'

'Doesn't mean he didn't put someone else up to it.'

'Also true.'

Itching to prove him wrong, Frankie paused a moment, considering his words. On account of his name – and the fact that he'd returned to his Northumberland roots – Stone had been dubbed the Northern Rock. He could so easily have been nicknamed the King of Caution, but he was probably right to rein her in.

She backpedalled: 'OK, you win. I'm prepared to give him the benefit of the doubt for now.'

'You said that out loud.' He narrowed his eyes. 'Just now you were halfway to placing that black cap on your head.'

She laughed. 'Whatever gave you that impression?'

'Bring me the proof and he's all yours, Frank. If Armstrong knew Chris as well as we suspect he might, he'd have made his mouth go about how he was being portrayed in the news-paper, warning him off.'

'It didn't work.'

'No, it didn't.'

As they walked on, David's comment stuck with Frankie. Before they left the office, she'd made it her business to check out the articles Chris had written for the *Corchester Herald*, a documentary-style series of life in a Newcastle ghetto, one of which came very close to libelling Armstrong, though her former friend was sensible enough not to refer to him by name. Her attention shifted to an old man approaching along the pavement, a flash of recognition passing between them. He came to a stop, tipped his trilby hat, resting a shaky hand on a walking stick as he took a breather.

She studied him. 'Mr Wilks?'

'Close, but no cigar,' he said. 'Stanley Wilkins at your ser-vice. You've not changed a bit, pet. How long is it? Nine years, ten?'

'Much more than that.' A wide smile appeared on her face as she was transported to another time. Pounding the beat in this area as it slipped into decline was the short straw no copper wanted, but one she'd grasped with both hands. It was a scary experience on occasions but exciting and also a lot of fun. 'How the hell are you?'

'Can't complain.'

He never did, even when his community began to fall apart. Remembering that he lived around the corner, she glanced at David. 'Stan's tea is legendary in these parts, his wife's homemade cake the highlight of my day when I was a rookie on foot patrol.'

'Aye, we used to sneak her in through the back door,' the old man said, giving David a firm handshake. 'She's one of the good 'uns.'

'The best,' David said.

A nod. 'And so was her old man.'

Frankie beamed proudly. 'How's Sadie?'

The light instantly left the old man's watery eyes.

Wishing she could take it back, she placed a hand on his arm as he told her that the love of his life had passed away five years since, after fifty-one years of marriage, every one of them a treasure.

As his emotions got the better of him, he quickly changed the subject. 'If you're driving a blue Ford Focus, you'd better get a wriggle on.'

It was enough of a hint to make the detectives take their leave of him. Not before Frankie had checked that he was still living in the same house and arranged to call on him when she had the time.

He said he'd like that and hobbled away.

As she rounded the corner, she let out a yell. 'Hey! Get off the car!'

A huddle of kids surrounding their vehicle scarpered like rats disturbed in a sewer, jeering, gesticulating and laughing as Stone and Oliver reached the car. One of the buggers had drawn an indecent image across the bonnet and scratched

Fuck the Police in large letters underneath. A new paint job coming right up. Little bastards. Before Frankie could react, her phone rang, Abbott's name appearing on the home screen.

She took the call. 'Dick? What's up?'

'I've located Ashley Sutherland, the guy who stood behind our IP in the queue for the cashpoint.' He reeled off the details of a house in Tynedale, south-west Northumberland. 'You want me to head over there?'

'No, the guv'nor and I are mobile. We can be there in no time. Is he at home?'

'Yeah, he's an off-duty fireman. He said he'd wait in.'

'How did you get on with Chris Adams' coach?'

'Fox was right. Adams didn't get his eye injury playing footy a week ago. He was a no-show.'

'Did he call with an explanation?'

'No, which apparently is unlike him. I've got details of his teammates, so I'll keep on it in case one of them knows what kept him away.'

'OK, I'll tell the boss.' Frankie's eyes drifted to the bonnet of her pool car, in two minds whether she and David should return to base and switch vehicles. Deciding that a fireman would've seen a lot worse in the course of his duties, she checked her watch: 12.30. 'Tell Sutherland we'll be right there.'

16

Hexham was on the south side of the River Tyne, around twenty miles away, population somewhere in the region of twelve thousand, a market town famous for its magnificent abbey that began life as long ago as AD 674. As the landscape changed, becoming more and more rural with every mile travelled, Frankie relaxed into her seat, eyes on the dual carriageway ahead, David's attention occasionally straying out the passenger window at the surrounding countryside, eyes scanning a big sky and farmland, both arable and dairy.

He asked Frankie a question and got a one-word response. He suspected that she was still chewing over the personal stuff they had discussed in his office, or maybe the man she'd nicknamed the Tank. It was a sad fact that they had little else to go on. Until they found out exactly what Chris Adams was working on, assuming his mother was right and he was on to something big, they were pissing in the wind.

'Armstrong is a dead end until someone tells us otherwise,' he said.

'Yup, I'll put Mitch or Indira on it when we get back to base.'

'I like Indi,' David said. 'She has potential.'

'Yeah, she does. So, what's the plan?'

'We concentrate on the ATM customers and see if we come up with any other leads.'

Frankie turned to look at him, a raised eyebrow. 'That's a big ask, David. Who takes notice of anyone in a queue?'

He was more hopeful. 'With Sutherland, we might stand a half-chance. As part of the emergency services, he might prove to be a better witness than you think.'

'Let's hope so.'

She fell silent.

Turning left, they crossed the River Tyne, skirting the town centre, following the satnav David had programmed with the postcode before setting off. Reaching their destination a few minutes later, they pulled up outside a very different house to the one they had visited earlier, well kept with a long garden front and rear. A shiny grey VW Tiguan was parked on the wet driveway, recently washed and polished. It began to snow.

'Mind the rug-rats,' Sutherland said as he let them in. The sound of Leona Lewis's 'Bleeding Love' reached them as they stepped into the hallway and on into the house. It was warm and cosy inside, the smell of a Sunday roast filling a living room that resembled a children's nursery. With so many toys on the carpet it was hard to know where to tread. In among the coloured plastic shapes sat three almost identical toddlers with dark curly hair and big brown eyes like their father's.

'IVF,' the fireman said by way of explanation. 'Be careful what you wish for, eh?'

Frankie held out a hand. 'Looks like you have your work cut out. DS Frankie Oliver. This is my guv'nor, DCI David Stone.'

'Good to meet you both . . . I hope.'

He was early forties, a handsome man, around six three. He wore slip-on Vans on his feet, jeans and a navy sweatshirt with the Northumberland Fire & Rescue Service logo on the front, a dribble of baby sick on his right shoulder. Minus the vomit and with her own force badge, she had one like it at home.

'DS Abbott said you were MIT.'

'That's right, Mr Sutherland—'

'My mates call me Ash.'

Frankie glanced across the room, a huge Christmas tree lovingly decorated in one corner. The dining table was set with cutlery and wine glasses. She was starving, thoughts of food and the smell of it making her salivate. She'd skipped breakfast and so, she suspected, had David. A pub was where they'd be heading next, if she had her way.

'Is this a bad time?' she asked. 'We don't want to interrupt your lunch if you're about to tuck in.'

'No, you're fine. The kids need a nap. If they don't sleep, we don't eat.' Lifting his left arm, Sutherland checked his watch. 'We're good for another half hour or so.' He peered over his shoulder into the kitchen. 'Dee! We have visitors.'

A brunette with smouldering brown eyes appeared, wiping wet hands on a checked tea towel, her face flushed from a hot kitchen. She shook hands with both detectives and introduced herself as Sutherland's better half, a wink to her husband as she said it, extending a wide smile to her guests. She was dressed in jeans, Uggs and a green T-shirt matching the colour of her eyes. She was classy, a dead ringer for singer-songwriter Andrea Corr with the accent to match.

Frankie took to her straight away . . .

David was instantly in love.

His reaction to another man's wife should've worried his 2ic. It didn't. On the contrary, it gave her a warm feeling deep in the pit of her stomach. Having lost someone very special, in the worst of possible circumstances, he'd been dancing in the dark for a very long time. When they first met, he was in despair, though he'd chosen not to share that with her. The fact that he was approaching normality lifted Frankie's spirits.

As Sutherland and his missus bent to pick up the kids, Frankie gave David the side-eye, trying not to laugh out loud.

'Honestly, we can come back if this is not a good time,' she said.

'It's as good a time as any.' The fireman was now upright, a wriggly child in each arm. 'They should've been in bed by now.'

'And whose fault is it if they're not?' Dee narrowed her eyes at her husband, the third child fixed to her hip, a glance at the detectives. 'Big Lego is Ash's favourite pastime. If it was up to him, the kids would never get an afternoon nap. Give us a minute or two and he'll be right down.'

As the couple took the children upstairs, Frankie fixed her gaze on David. She'd never seen him so taken with any woman. 'You look hot, guv . . . but she's hotter – and married. Just saying—'

'Just looking.' He blushed.

'That's fine, so long as Fireman Sam doesn't catch you. Did you see the size of his pecs?' Frankie lifted an arm, clenching her fist, trying to accentuate hers. She punched Stones' arm playfully. 'Might be best if you ask all your questions today so we don't have to come back, eh?'

They stopped talking as the crew manager arrived in the room, moving piles of ironing off the sofa, creating space for them to sit down, kicking Lego bricks out of the way.

'Right, sorry. Can't say that I'm not intrigued. How can I help you?'

'We're investigating the murder of a young man,' Frankie said. 'On Friday night, minutes before he was set upon by persons unknown, he used the NatWest ATM on Northumberland Street. Our enquiries with the bank led us to believe that you stood directly behind him in the queue.'

'Blimey! Poor guy.'

'Do you remember him?'

'Not especially.' Sutherland's expression was blank. 'To be honest, I didn't really take much notice of anyone. I was aware of the guy in front of me, but all I saw of him was the back of his head, a light-coloured jacket, I think, a multi-coloured stripy scarf.'

'No overcoat?' David asked.

Sutherland shook his head. 'I don't know why. It was bloody freezing.'

'And what was his demeanour?'

'As I said, I didn't see his face. He was probably bored waiting like the rest of us. The machines were busy . . . I did notice one guy jump the queue at the front. I was going to have a word, then thought better of it. He was off his face. I don't think your guy even noticed. He wasn't jumpy, looking around or anything. He was too busy on the phone.'

David and Frankie exchanged a look.

'Did you hear any of his conversation?'

'As it happens, I did. He clearly didn't want to meet up with someone. I got the impression that whoever he was talking to was giving him grief – a girlfriend perhaps. I could relate . . .' Realising that his comment demanded an explanation, Sutherland glanced into the hallway to check the coast was clear, lowering his voice. 'Dee had been bending my ear before I went out. Our brood are a handful at the best of times. I'd come off nights and she'd averaged around three hours sleep the whole week. That's why I was heading home early.'

'The victim was arguing?'

'Not as such . . .' Sutherland frowned, trying to remember the content of the conversation. 'I can't recall it word for word. He was calm, not angry. If I had to describe his tone, I'd have said he was in the driving seat. He said something like, "I know what you've been up to." Like I say, I felt sorry for the guy.'

'Anything else?'

'Yeah, he said: "Maybe you should have thought of that before" or words to that effect.' Guilt flashed across the fireman's face. 'My missus had used a similar phrase as I left the house. Dee is the best there is. I'm lucky to have her, but if she has something to say she says it. Anyway, it made me feel like a shit, swanning off into town with the lads from my shift. It was me who wanted a kid in the first place. Neither of us was expecting a triple whammy.'

Frankie couldn't imagine anything worse. 'Did you happen

to notice where our victim got his bank card: jeans or jacket pocket?'

'Neither. He had a bag slung over his shoulder. I'm pretty sure he opened it when the phone rang and took his wallet out at the same time.'

'Definitely an incoming call?'

'Yeah, when I heard it ring, I went for my pocket thinking it was Dee. It wasn't.'

For someone who didn't take much notice, Sutherland was doing really well. It was amazing how much eyewitnesses remembered when walked through a series of questions. Thank God for cognitive interviewing, a technique Frankie had learned from her old man and David had picked up when he was a detective in the Met.

'I take it you didn't find it?' Sutherland said. 'The bag, I mean?'

Frankie shook her head. 'Mobile either.'

'You think he was robbed?'

'It's a line of enquiry we're exploring. Where did he put his cash and card after using the ATM?'

'I'm pretty sure he was still counting his money as he walked away.'

'In which direction did he walk?'

'South towards Pilgrim Street.' Sutherland was smart . . . and suddenly uncomfortable. 'The more I tell you, the more it drops me in the shit. Makes me your number one suspect, right?'

'Not unless you killed a man,' David said.

'I didn't.'

'Then you have nothing to be concerned about, except answering our questions. Was anyone waiting for him?'

Sutherland shook his head. 'Not that I saw.'

'You didn't see anyone hanging around in the vicinity?'

'Yeah, loads.'

'Anyone who stood out as up to no good? The IP was left for

dead yards from where he completed his cash transaction, so whoever killed him wouldn't have been that far away.'

'You reckon someone was staking out the ATM?'

'It's a possibility.'

'Look, I didn't see anyone or anything unusual. Everyone seemed full of Christmas spirit. I don't think your guy even looked over his shoulder. He stepped up, did the business and left. I'm sorry, I can't be more specific. I realise that's not a lot of help.'

'On the contrary, you did good.' Frankie handed him a card. 'Thanks, Ash. If you remember anything else, give us a call.'

17

The Rat was an eighteenth-century inn, a favourite haunt of David's and many other coppers, set high on a hill above Hexham in the small hamlet of Anick. The snow had already settled there and was getting heavier by the minute. Great flakes of the white stuff fell silently around him as he jumped out of the car, pulling on a brown wax jacket with a thick lining. Frankie climbed out too, turning up the collar of her grey overcoat, wrapping a scarf three times around her neck as they took in the amazing vista along the Tyne Valley, the snow falling all around them like confetti.

David's attention drifted to the steep bank he'd just managed to negotiate. He glanced at her, a childish twinkle in his eye. 'Where's a plastic bag when you need one?'

'You mean you have no sledge? I'm gutted. My old man never travels without one. Snow shovel, a bar of chocolate, a slab of Kendal Mint Cake if he can get his hands on one.' Frankie gave a three-finger salute. 'He thinks he's bloody Baden-Powell.'

He laughed. 'I have a lot to live up to.'

'You do.' She pulled on a red beret and gloves to match, brushing snowflakes from her eyelashes, rubbing her hands together to warm them up.

'The hat really suits you,' David said.

'Thanks.'

He glanced over his shoulder towards the pub. 'Do they have rooms to rent here?'

'So much for waiting for the right girl,' Frankie said.

He swung round, wide-eyed. 'It wasn't a proposition—'

'Chill out, man. I'm pulling your leg.'

'Still . . .' He pointed at the leaden sky. 'By the look of that lot, I reckon we might need a room . . .' He relaxed. '*Each,* in case you're in any doubt.'

She grinned. 'Careful, that was nearly a joke.'

He liked it best when they were larking around. Personal relationships aside, he found the idea of being snowed in with her appealing. A chance to kick back and forget about work for a day or two without the cloak of death surrounding them. As friends and colleagues, they had been good for one another, a diversion from a dark past.

He knew she felt it too.

As the snow continued to fall, they stood a moment, taking in the peace and quiet of the Northumbrian landscape, the river snaking its way eastward around the Roman village of Corbridge, disappearing around the bend on its way to the North Sea.

'I've known this pub since I was a kid,' Frankie said. 'Mum and Dad brought us one Christmas, a special treat. It was snowing then too. Me, Rae and Joanna had a magical time. It was our last Christmas together. God, I miss her, David.'

'I know.'

It was good to hear her talk about the past in positive terms. She'd never done that before, even though Joanna had been dead a long time. But since Frankie had shared the awful truth of what happened to her, it had taken the pressure off her shoulders. Her sister was no longer a hideous secret.

'I'm busting for the loo,' Frankie said. 'Shall we go in?'

'You go ahead, I need to make a call.'

'To whom?'

He sidestepped the question. 'You know what it's like in there on a Sunday lunchtime, Frank. It'll be packed to the rafters.' He slipped his phone from his pocket. 'What I have to say is confidential.'

'Mrs Fireman Sam didn't slip you her number, did she?'

He touched the side of his nose, a hint that she should stop digging. 'I need to update the team.' And talk to someone else whose name he wasn't about to mention. 'Why don't you grab a table. Mine's a sparkling water, if you're buying.'

'You're so hardcore.'

She turned, crossing the lane to the pub. Opening the garden gate, she glanced over her shoulder, a cheeky grin. What David had said was true. Rain or shine, inside the old drover's inn, it was impossible to move far from other customers, difficult to have a conversation without being overheard. In normal circumstances that wouldn't bother him. It did today. Batting her away like an irritating fly, he punched in Detective Chief Superintendent Bright's number, lifting his mobile to a frozen ear.

The call went straight to voicemail.

He left a message for Bright to call him as soon as he was able, then called Abbott, updating him on their interview with Sutherland in case Frankie should ask, suggesting that he might chase the victim's service provider. Whoever had called Chris Adams prior to his death was highly significant, possibly the last person to speak with him. David wanted them found and spoken to.

18

When David entered the pub, Frankie was standing in front of a roaring fire and she wasn't alone. Bright – the man he was so desperate to speak to – and a woman he didn't know, were leaning against the bar right beside her. Stone made his way towards them, registering a shot of whisky in Frankie's right hand, a slight awkwardness in her demeanour. He wondered why, given the fact that she was so well acquainted with the head of CID and the woman David assumed was his missus. Frankie's unease had nothing to do with the fact that they were in a pub while on duty – when were they anything else? – no, there was something else bothering her and it didn't take him long to figure out what it was.

It worried him too.

'Guv.' He stuck out a hand.

Bright grasped it firmly. 'David, how's life treating you?'

'Can't complain, sir.'

'This is my wife, Ellen.' Bright glanced at the woman standing by his side. 'DCI David Stone is my newest SIO, spent fifteen years in the Met before he came to his senses and returned north. For the life of me, I can't figure out what took him so long.' Bright was a northerner through and through. He'd spent his whole career in his home force and wouldn't want it any other way.

'Take no notice of him,' Ellen said. 'I've heard a lot about you, David – all of it good.' She glanced at her husband. 'Go on then, get the man a drink.'

Bright nodded to the barman, his cue to put the drink on his tab.

He took the order and turned away.

David smiled at Ellen, a woman of indeterminate age,

probably the wrong side of fifty. She had good skin, flame-red hair worn in a single plait that hung like a rope over her right shoulder. The colour of her hair matched her sweater perfectly. Frankie had mentioned her in general conversation. She was Bright's former PA, the relationship between the two developing after his first wife died, the only woman Frankie had ever come across who could put him in his place, bar one. Given their marriage, Ellen no longer worked for him or anyone else in Northumbria Police.

She swept a hand towards the only table that was free. 'Please, won't you join us?'

Frankie's eyes sent a message to David: don't you dare.

He glanced at the table, relieved to see that it was set for four and was already reserved. 'That's kind of you, Ellen, but you're obviously expecting company. We don't want to intrude. Frankie and I intend to eat and run, if it's all the same to you. We have a lot on.'

'Nonsense, I insist!' She looked at her husband. 'Don't we, darling?'

'We do now.' Bright was more amused than embarrassed by her informality. 'Besides, our friends bailed,' he explained. 'They were driving through from Durham and got stuck on the 68 in a foot of snow. They're unable to make it.' He glanced at Frankie. 'I called your father on the off-chance that he and your mum might come out and play instead. Unfortunately, they had other arrangements.'

The relief on Frankie's face was self-evident.

David wondered if her parents' 'other arrangements' involved babysitting Susan Adams. If he knew anything about the Oliver clan it was the generosity of spirit that set them apart from other families. From the look of her, Frankie was thinking the very same thing.

'Besides, it's us or the door,' Bright glanced over his shoulder. 'You're fully booked, aren't you, Dan?'

The barman, Dan Gennery, looked up. 'The way we like

it . . .' He focused on Stone. 'You may as well accept. There won't be any tables free for a while, I'm afraid.' The barman smiled at Frankie across the counter.

She didn't smile back.

Ellen giggled. 'I think Dan has an ulterior motive to keep you here, love. If you're interested, he's also unattached and looking to join the army.'

'Ellen!' Bright gave her a dirty look. 'Stop matchmaking.'

Winking at Dan, ignoring her husband, she said: 'That's settled then. Detectives have to eat, especially this one.' She was talking about Frankie. 'Look at you! You're wasting away. C'mon, let's eat.'

They all sat down, scanning the blackboard as well as the menus on the table, Bright and Ellen a lot more enthusiastically than the other two. Stone and Oliver's appetites had deserted them for different reasons. David didn't want company any more than she did. Questioning the head of CID on Frankie's fitness to continue with the case was not a conversation he could have with either woman present. It was nevertheless an exchange he needed to have, despite what he'd said to her in the privacy of his office. She had the know-how but was she too close to the victim? Bright was the man who'd handed her the opportunity to prove herself as a murder detective and David didn't want to be the one to take it away.

'How's the enquiry going?' Bright asked.

Frankie's face betrayed her.

Ellen noticed her hesitation and made the wrong jump. 'Oh God, here we go. Sorry, Frankie, I know you lot never switch off, but he really can't help himself. Let them eat, darling. Can't you see they're exhausted?'

Frankie smiled defensively, eyes on Bright.

Despite Ellen's dig, he was still waiting for an update.

'It's going nowhere, to be perfectly frank, guv.'

'Why's that then?'

A waitress arrived to take their order, the men opting for

roast pork and all the trimmings, the women choosing something lighter, Ellen adding that she wanted to leave room for sticky toffee pudding. As they waited for their food, they made small talk, though it was clear to everyone that Bright was itching to steer them in another direction.

Frankie looked out the window at the frozen landscape. 'Jesus! It's practically a white-out.' She turned, faking disappointment. 'We should get moving as soon as we're done, guv. We'll never make it to the main road if we hang around, let alone to Middle Earth.'

David backed her up – she couldn't get out of there fast enough.

The chit-chat continued over lunch. When they were done, David wiped his mouth and pushed his plate away, nudging Frankie's foot under the table, a hint that he was ready to leave and keen to put her out of her misery. He drained his glass, returned it to the table. He was about to stand up when Bright took his mobile from his pocket, checking the screen.

The F-word arrived in David's head.

Bright looked up.

Before he could ask, David offered an explanation. 'I left you a voicemail, guv. Would you have a moment tomorrow morning? There's a couple of things about the case I'd like to run through with you.'

'I wondered how long it would take you to come clean,' he said. 'Relax, will you? I know all about Frankie's friendship with Chris Adams.'

He'd been talking to her old man.

Bright's eyes found hers. 'Lucky for you, I also know that it lapsed a long time ago—'

'There's stuff you don't know,' she said.

'I know enough, so stop fretting. What I need right now is your mind on the job.' Bright met David's gaze. 'And yours too.'

'Yes, guv,' Stone and Oliver said in unison.

19

Indira called as Stone and Oliver left the pub. Wells had been working on the victim's notebooks and needed to speak to them urgently. They agreed to rendezvous at her place – and drove through a blizzard to get there – an apartment in a beautiful art deco building on the edge of the Town Moor, a parcel of common land larger than Hyde Park where David used to run when he was living in London. Belinda's home was well furnished, but unloved, a place to exist and lay her head rather than live comfortably. Having resided in the capital herself for many years, she'd got used to a different lifestyle, working from bars, cafes and libraries in the city, eating on the go wherever she happened to land.

Sunday newspapers littered the table where she invited them to sit. She looked as tired as the detectives felt, on account of working late into the night to give them what they were after, something she hoped would aid their investigation into a young man's untimely death.

David hoped so too.

In the car on the way over there, Frankie had expressed her relief at Bright's response to her former friendship with Chris Adams, though David still had reservations and intended to continue the conversation with the head of CID as soon as he was able. He eyed the untidy pile of notebooks scattered across the tabletop, keen to know what had prompted the journalist's call.

Before she began, Wells sipped at a glass of white wine, leaving a faint red imprint of her lips on the glass. She pointed at the notebooks. 'I could spend time transcribing these for you, but it'll cost you and I know your budget is stretched, so I thought I'd précis them to save time and money.' She tapped the summary of observations she'd made. 'Most of the content is as you'd expect, court-related: names of defendants and legal counsel; adjournments and results; idle doodles and not a lot else. I've written down all of the names your guy mentioned in case they're of interest. There are a couple of references dotted here and there that I didn't entirely understand. They're not all recent.'

'How long ago?' Frankie asked.

'Over a year.' Responding to the intrigued looks on the faces of her guests, Wells added. 'Don't get too excited. They're cryptic notes, nothing more.'

'About what?' Frankie wanted to know.

'There's mention of exploitation – more than once – which could be related to a case he was covering, perhaps a lengthy trial. That should be easy for you guys to check out. It's underlined where none of the other stuff is – possibly his method of highlighting it for future reference. I could be a mile wrong. It just sprung out at me when I read it.'

Wells pushed an A4 printout across the desk, consisting of a list of names. Frankie picked it up, her eyes travelling down the page. There were upwards of two hundred names there that needed checking out. At the bottom of the page Wells had compiled the notes she'd drawn to their attention a moment ago, all but one with corresponding dates attached:

Fraudsters targeting the vulnerable on an industrial scale.
Gross breach of trust – 11/16 – Wow!
Need specifics. 12/16
No further contact with N over Christmas – worried. 01/17
Unable to proceed. 100s/1000s? 06/17
Where is N? – 08/2017
No further forward. Where to begin? 10/17

'There are more recent entries here.' Wells slid one of the notebooks across the table.

130

Frankie recognised the handwriting from the time when she used to help Chris with his college assignments; from birthday cards she'd received from him over the years; from postcards he'd sent her when he was abroad on holiday. His homemade, illustrated cards were a thing to behold, each one scripted with love and care, a flowing style. Frankie loved the way he crossed his Ts deliberately. The written word had always been important to him.

Scanning the entries, her eyes were drawn down the page where entries stood out in bold lettering, presumably why Wells had highlighted rather than transcribed them like the others. Seeing was believing. They were written in such a way that it made the hair stand up on Frankie's neck. It was as if her former friend had been angry when he made the notes. Consciously or subconsciously he'd pressed down hard on the page, gone over and over the letters with more than one stroke, underlining them all twice as if he was angry. *JC: Illegal immigrant?* Next to this he'd written the word: *Trace*.

The last entry knocked her for six . . .

Police – speak to FO?

Shit!

Frankie's stomach rolled over – and not because this might be the break they'd been looking for. She kept hold of the notebook, unwilling to part with it.

'I need a drink,' Wells said.

So did Frankie: a strong one.

David looked at her. 'Let's take five then.'

Wells got up and left them alone, a brief but pointed look passing between the two women before she disappeared into the kitchen. A few minutes later, she returned with a pot of coffee and biscuits on a tray. David dived in. Having picked at his dinner, leaving half of it on the plate, he'd regained his appetite.

Frankie definitely hadn't.

Sensing an odd atmosphere, David's eyes flitted from Wells to Frankie.

He spoke with a mouthful of the biscuits his nan called Melting Moments, pointing at the typed list on the table. 'We need to run these names through the database PDQ,' he said, wiping crumbs from his mouth with the back of his hand. He leaned forward, gesturing for Frankie to hand over the notebook. Her heart was in her mouth as she passed it to him. She didn't want to be there when he read it. Another disparaging look from Wells. A hint of support too. Anticipating the drama that her find might cause, she gave Frankie an out.

'If you want to call Dick, there's a file open on my computer containing the exact same information. You can email him from my study, Frank. First door on your left as you came in.'

Thanking her, Frankie jumped up to remove herself from the room. Thinking time. Moving out into the hallway, leaving the other two alone, she shut herself in Wells' office, pulling out her mobile to make the call, beads of sweat appearing on her upper lip.

Abbott picked up immediately.

'Dick, I'm in trouble,' she said.

'What kind of trouble?'

Frankie explained. She liked Dick. He was a true friend with a clever mind and vast experience. They had been colleagues for years. Apart from David, there was no one on the force she trusted more. She could rely on his discretion and was desperate for his take on Wells' discovery before fronting up to her boss.

20

When Frankie finally arrived in the living room with Abbott's sound advice echoing in her head, Stone and Wells had their heads together, deep in conversation, whispering conspiratorially.

Standing on the threshold, Frankie held her breath.

Sensing her presence, David looked over his shoulder, giving her the thousand-yard stare. He was disappointed, itching to ask her what she thought she was playing at. Hauling herself off her chair, Wells left the room with the remains of their snack, rolling her eyes at Frankie as they passed each other going in opposite directions.

Her expression said: You're in deep shit, lady.

Yeah, like Frankie didn't know it.

She slid on to the chair the journalist had vacated, directly opposite Stone, the table acting as a physical barrier between them. Frankie needed one. Whatever the outcome, she wanted the conversation over and done with. Then she wanted the hell out of Wells' apartment.

A beat as David met her gaze.

Frankie shifted uncomfortably in her seat. Her SIO was on the edge of saying something she wasn't going to like. There was no doubt in her mind that she was facing a very different David than the one she'd arrived with, the one she'd been working with lately, the one she'd stood with in the snow outside The Rat. They had grown close. Very close. And now she had some explaining to do. There was no disputing the initials *FO* scribbled in a murder victim's hand. David had found her out and she'd blown the trust he'd placed in her.

She felt compelled to fill the silence but couldn't find the words.

David did it for her. 'Are you going to tell me what the hell is going on? Chris contacted you, didn't he?' When she didn't respond, he glanced at his mobile. 'Do I have to call Dick and ask him to pull up the IP's phone records in order to get an answer?' He raised his voice. 'DO I?'

Frankie flinched.

And he wasn't finished yet.

'Start talking, Frank.' There was a sharp edge to his voice. 'Am I the only one not in the loop here or did you redact your number before anyone else noticed it?'

Frankie wasn't sure what to say. She opted for the truth. 'Of course not. David, whatever you think of me, I didn't come clean for all the right reasons, I promise you. You have every right to be angry. I would be too in your position, so go ahead and put me on paper. I deserve whatever you have in mind to throw at me.'

'The right *reasons*?' He never took his eyes off her. 'Are you serious? What fucked-up reason could you possibly have to mislead me—'

'I didn't—'

'Yes, you did. Me and the rest of the team. There's no room for divided loyalties in any unit. You don't get to choose what you share, what secrets you keep.'

'There is no secret!'

'Really? *I* decide what's relevant to the case. And there's a reason for that: *I'm* the one who'll get it in the neck if the wheel comes off, not you.'

'OK!' Frankie huffed. 'You made your point. I do the grunt work, you're the boss—'

'And it's high time you remembered that—'

'Right!' Frank bit back. 'Like you're ever going to let me forget it.'

David gave her hard eyes. 'You're a piece of work sometimes.'

'That's why you picked me, as I recall—'

'Yeah, well everyone can make a mistake.' The impasse was

heavy with resentment. Hard to handle for both detectives and David was far from finished ticking her off. 'What the fuck is wrong with you? If you'd been honest at the beginning of this enquiry, instead of pissing in the wind, we might actually be making headway—'

'That's not fair—'

'No, I'll tell you what's not fair. Withholding crucial information from an SIO in a murder investigation isn't fair. That's conduct I might expect from others. Never from you. I need to be able to trust my 2ic. Clearly that's not the case. This is about as serious as it gets in my book.'

He was really bugging her now, his voice getting louder and louder. Christ knows where Wells was hiding. The walls of her apartment were paper thin. Frankie took a deep breath and dropped the attitude. David was right. She'd failed to live up to her own high standards. At the very least, he deserved an explanation. Then she went the wrong way about it . . .

'Have you any idea what it's like to have someone you care for die on you—'

'You said that out loud, Frank.' He wasn't joking.

His face was set in a scowl, his jaw rigid. She may as well have slapped him. Frankie should've engaged her brain before opening her big mouth . . . As soon as the words were out there, she'd realised that they had been misconstrued and wanted to take them back. A close colleague he'd worked with in the Met – a detective he was clearly in love with – had died in his arms having been shot at point-blank range by a jealous and violent former partner. That incident had changed the direction of his life dramatically, the reason he'd fled the south and come home to Northumberland.

'I didn't mean that. You know I didn't. Hear me out—'

'Why? So you can throw me another low-baller?'

Frankie felt bad for having raked up his grief in order to

defend herself against a flagrant breach of the rules. 'David, I didn't mean to hurt you . . . that was never my intention. You know me better than that.'

He was staring right through her. 'Y'know what? I'm beginning to think I don't know you at all.'

Frankie looked away, tears pricking her eyes. This from a man who knew more about her than anyone outside of her immediate family – more so than some – a friend and colleague with whom she'd shared her innermost secrets. She wanted to tell him what his friendship meant to her. He was the only one in whom she could confide.

He asked, 'Are we done?'

She looked at him. 'I really hope not.'

He caught the double entendre and didn't respond.

'David, I'm sorry. What I was going to say before you cut me off was, do you have any idea what it's like to have someone you love die . . . and not be able to find the person responsible? I've lived with that all my life. You know I have.'

'You were in love with Adams?'

'No! Yes . . . not in the way you mean. Had that been the case, I'd have fessed up right away. I wanted to help . . . to do something positive for Susan. I thought if I told you, you'd rule me out of the enquiry.'

'Damn right I would.'

'Yeah, well I'm not the only one who's withheld information, am I?'

'Meaning what?'

'I may not have your credentials but try to remember who helped put you on that pedestal, guv. I had your back. The question is, do you have mine?'

It was harsh. Still, Frankie was fighting for her life here. Being his 2ic meant more to her than he would ever know. He said nothing for a while. He knew exactly what she was getting at. They'd worked a case where he'd been practically unable to function due to personal issues surrounding the death of his ex-colleague and she'd been forced to cover for him. Now was payback time . . .

She hoped.

Lowering her voice, she used a gentler tone. 'All I'm saying is we don't always lead with our heads, David. Hearts come into it too, don't they?' She spread her hands, a shrug of the shoulders, a gesture that was self-explanatory. She'd played her last card and didn't know what else to say.

'You're well out of order—'

'I never spoke to Chris, I swear to you. He tried contacting me, out of the blue, a few weeks ago, but left no message. His phone records will confirm that I didn't return his call. So, before you hang me out to dry, please take that into account. We never spoke, in person, on the phone or online. I was busy with a case—'

'And now he is the case . . . A murder statistic.'

His words stung.

'Do you think I don't know that? If I'd taken action, he might still be alive.'

Frankie's heart was banging against her ribs. Her attempt to take the temperature down hadn't worked. She dropped her gaze. Having failed Chris in life, she'd felt a heavy burden to honour his memory. Her loyalty to the job she loved should've taken priority. Guilt was eating her up. She glanced out the window, avoiding eye contact, wondering why she hadn't told David before. He'd have understood. She knew he would. Spontaneously, his voice arrived in her head . . .

We all lie, Frank – even you!

She hadn't – and she wanted him to know it.

The silence was unbearable.

'My hands are up,' Frankie said. 'I didn't tell you about the missed call, I admit that. Everything else I said was true . . .'

David let her stew a while and then said, 'Give me one good reason why should I believe you?'

137

'Because it's the God's honest truth. I've had no contact with him for several years.'

'The call slipped your mind?'

Frankie dropped her head on one side. 'You know what, David? Sarcasm doesn't suit—'

'So why did he call?'

'I *don't* know . . .' She let out a frustrated sigh. 'Look, I was once his first point of contact if he was in trouble and, to some extent, he was mine. I suppose I thought that if he needed help, he'd call again.'

'So why didn't he?'

'Your guess is as good as mine,' she said. 'Ever since I saw his body at the crime scene, I've been asking myself the same question.'

'I suspect you already know the answer,' David said. 'You'd moved on and didn't have the time or wherewithal to hold his hand, is that it? Doesn't sound like the Frankie I know.'

She didn't respond.

He gave her a nudge. 'Tell me . . . c'mon on, don't keep me in the dark. To make sense of your indiscretion, I need to know. No matter what it is, I want the lot. I mean it, Frankie. You have one chance to redeem yourself.'

And still she hesitated.

'He was around when Joanna died, I presume.'

She nodded. He'd hit the bullseye.

'And? You were kids then.'

She ran a hand through her hair. This was killing her. She had to give him more. 'He saw me at my worst and never let me forget it, even as we grew up. He was a great lad, but he couldn't comprehend that if I kept picking at that particular scab, it would never heal. He wouldn't let me leave the past behind, didn't understand why I wanted, needed, to wipe the slate clean and get on with life. I suppose because his mother hadn't been able to get over the grief of losing his dad. Believe me, if I'd been old enough to drown myself in alcohol when Joanna died, I would have.'

'He wanted your help—'

'And I let him down—'

'And now you want to make it up to him.'

She nodded. 'I assume he wanted advice on the issue he was desperate to shine a light on. Well, he got what he wanted, didn't he? His name is in every newspaper on every breakfast table in the county. He didn't get to tell his story. He is the story.' Frankie wiped her face with her hand, her focus returned to the notebooks Wells had left on the table. 'Or maybe his notes were just another figment of a fertile imagination. Who the hell knows what was going through his mind? Maybe he wanted my advice with the thriller he was writing, ideas that occurred to him as he sat on the press bench waiting for court judgements perhaps. We've all been there, haven't we? It's dead time. There's nowt to do except scribble in a damn notebook.'

David said nothing.

Frankie had never seen him this pissed off. He was studying her, clearly in two minds whether she was telling the truth. He sat back considering his options and made her wait. Another glance at his phone. Frankie wondered if he might call Bright for advice. Who would she call: her father, her granddad, Andrea, or maybe Dick Abbott who'd be on standby, keen to know the upshot of her spectacular fall from grace? If David transferred her, or even worse, if Bright demoted her, what could she possibly say to any of them? And what would they say to her in return?

Frankie rubbed at her temples. The fall, if it came, would be devastating and public. Her father, grandfather and sister-in-law – all ex-police or serving – would never live it down . . . and neither would she. The word sorry was inadequate in situations like these. It didn't convey what she really wanted to say.

Reacting as if he'd read her mind, David's eyes softened.

He offered a two-word response: 'Apology accepted.'

'But I'm out, right?'

'Wrong,' he said. 'You have clearance from Bright. If you didn't call Chris, then as far as I'm concerned, nothing has changed. You're covered. I'm prepared to draw a line under it. Let's get one thing straight: no more secrets, you hear me? We work as a team or not at all . . . Now do your job.'

'Yes, guv.' Touched by the gesture, Frankie thanked him with her eyes, then stood up before she made a fool of herself. 'I'll see you at the car.'

Pulling on her coat, she left the room quickly, keen to avoid Wells on the way out. Closing the door quietly behind her, she blew out a breath as she walked out into a storm of a different kind – a snowy winter wonderland, equally icy – her mind instantly on the investigation she was desperate to resolve.

Who the hell were N and JC?

21

They didn't speak as they crawled back to base on ungritted roads, Frankie counting herself lucky that David had put his trust in her, allowing her the opportunity to continue investigating the death of Chris Adams. Her actions had been reprehensible. She didn't deserve a second chance. At Middle Earth, he left her to her own devices, peeling off towards his office, shutting his door, pulling down the blind on the internal window.

He may as well have hung a sign on it: keep out.

She did.

In the incident room, the murder wall was filling up with new intelligence. Frankie stood in front of it, hands on hips, taking in every detail uploaded there, following the information trail that would inform the future direction of the enquiry, fragmented sentences that represented Chris Adams' life, laid out in order of importance: Scene; Victim; Forensics; House-House; Family and Associates; Suspects and Miscellaneous. The blown-up images of the crime scene and the wounds inflicted on the victim distressed her more now than they had in reality. Maybe she had been too shocked to take them in.

Her eyes settled on two words: Injured Party. Male. Chris Adams (31); Cause of death, single stab wound to the chest. A dotted white line led to the words: Unexplained Eye Injury. She considered this a moment: footy, his mother said; not true according to his editor, corroborated by his football coach.

That bothered her.

Her mind was in turmoil as she tried to make connections between what she knew and what the MIT had found out since the investigation began. Nothing stood out or offered further insight into this pointless and violent death. There had to be something she was missing. It was probably up there, staring her in the face, hiding in plain sight. If only she could see it.

Another dotted line led to Forensics: DNA had been found on Chris's body. None that matched the database. A single strand of blond hair belonged to one of his pals, a female who'd been with him at PTMY. She had no form and was probably irrelevant. Perhaps they had kissed as she entered the pub. Perhaps not. Chris's car had been found locked and secure, the results of fibre lifts still pending. Ditto reports on the computer found in the boot of his vehicle. Hopefully, there were further clues there. No witnesses had yet been found to the attack. That didn't mean there were none. Only that they hadn't yet come forward.

Her eyes followed another dotted line to the IP's parents: mother, Susan; father, Stanley – deceased. There was little about the family she didn't know already. Frankie moved quickly on to Motive: Robbery? Hate crime? Other? There were answers here if only she could make sense of them.

She would . . .

In time.

Her gaze shifted to a column with the heading Significant Witnesses: Liam Wiley (friend/PTMY); Ashley Sutherland (ATM customer); Mason Carter (paramedic). Carter was the last to see the IP alive. There had been no verbal exchange between the two. Finally, Frankie reached the Suspects column; there was only one: Garry Armstrong, the thug who'd rob his granny for her pension money without a second thought. He had reason to hate a journalist who gave him bad press. He'd been in contact with Chris within an hour of his death and had racist tendencies. He was, in short, a violent recidivist offender, with low morals and a quick temper, a guy whose strong-arm tactics were legendary in the north-east.

She considered this.

Armstrong had been convicted of fraud. Could he also be involved in exploitation on a grand scale, as outlined in Chris's notebooks? If so, of which societal group? Was this why Chris wanted to consult with her? Had he perhaps been warned off?

Frankie glanced at the list of the most significant outstanding actions, the first of which was a TIE action.

Trace, Interview and Eliminate witnesses, male and female with IP at PTMY.

Everyone detectives had spoken to so far had corroborated Wiley's account of what happened in the pub. No fight, no words exchanged between the IP and Armstrong, a case of hard eyes, two men who didn't like each other.

What was Adams working on: novel or exposé?

Unregistered mobile: call to victim on the night he died. Who from?

Trace: Illegal immigrant, JC.

Trace: N.

The list went on . . .

The scoop, Frankie thought . . .

This had to be about the scoop.

Had Chris been punching above his weight? Were his old injuries a warning? Given the contents of his notebooks, Frankie would put money on it. As her mind wandered through the evidence, she found herself thinking of Joanna, her father's obsession with her death. She ached to bring both killers to justice, and she would if she didn't let her fear of failure get in the way. The forensics team had found an early photograph of Frankie among possessions they had lifted from Chris's bedroom. They had recognised her instantly. Why wouldn't they? She hadn't changed a jot as she'd grown up. The thought of the discovery depressed her. It had nothing to do with her personal connection to Chris, more the fact that she'd not kept a single image of him.

Abbott arrived at her shoulder. 'How did the guv'nor take it?'

She turned to look at him. 'I'm here, aren't I? And I still have my warrant card.'

He gave a wry smile. 'That's a plus.'

'Yeah, but I've let him down. I've let you all down. I can't pretend that this is one of my better days.'

'Forget it,' he said. 'No one here blames you. You screwed up. We've all done it. Makes you human like the rest of us.' He grinned. 'Who knew?'

Frankie forced a smile she didn't feel deep down. She was wired, feeling like she'd aged ten years in the last couple of hours.

Abbott added. 'He'll come around—'

'You reckon? I'm not so sure, Dick.'

'Keep your head down.' Abbott glanced at the murder wall. 'We're finally making progress.'

'Yeah, but what does it all mean?' Frankie followed his gaze. Wells' notes had been added to the puzzle. Frankie's eyes homed in on one in particular: *Unable to proceed. 100s/1000s? 06/17*. 'Hundreds and thousands of what? Are we talking migrant workers?' The slave trade in the UK was a growing problem.

'Could be prostitution? I wouldn't put it past Armstrong. He has his fingers in most pies.'

Dick stopped talking as David emerged from his office. 'I've had enough. I'm going home. You two get yourselves away too. We have a big day ahead of us tomorrow.'

Frankie's head went down.

He hadn't yet forgiven her.

22

Northumberland Street was almost empty, unusually quiet for the city centre. The appalling weather had kept most right-minded people indoors. Through a curtain of snow, Frankie watched two blurry figures trudging down the street, arm in arm, their laughter reaching her from across the road. They probably had a party to attend, beers to down, mates to meet up with.

Lucky them.

This wintry evening was no different to any other city the world over, filled with cheer for those with the financial resources to enjoy the season of goodwill, desperately depressing for the underprivileged. The thought lingered in her head as she walked on past the silent merry-go-round.

She pulled up sharply.

The doorway of Sports Direct offered little shelter tonight. At first, all she saw was a hump of uneven snow where the swirling wind had blown it into the gap between the entrance and the pavement, a drift in one corner around two inches thick. Frankie couldn't tell if the figure lying beneath it was ex-serviceman Stuart Ryman or someone else. She felt compelled to investigate, hoping, praying that whoever was lying there was still breathing.

Crouching down, she extended a gloved hand, pushing her fingers through the white stuff to find a thick layer of corrugated cardboard on which the snow continued to pile up. She pulled it aside to reveal Ryman's navy blue sleeping bag. She gave it a gentle prod. Nothing. A body without doubt, but unresponsive, like a corpse. She couldn't imagine a worse place to die.

'Sarge, is that you?'

No movement.

In her peripheral vision, a pair of heavy boots appeared on the pavement beside her. Frankie caught the strong whiff of alcohol. Expecting trouble, she looked up. Stood up. The owner of the boots was well built, around her age but taller. He leered at her through unfriendly eyes. Whatever he had a mind to do, Frankie knew she could take him. He was unsteady on his feet, a glazed look in his eyes, a pushover if he gave her any trouble.

'Can I help you?' she said.

'Depends . . . You one of them God types come to offer him salvation?' His speech was slurred. He gestured towards the indistinct lump in the doorway, inverting his hand, allowing the snow to settle on it, a quick glance at the sky above. 'If this keeps up, he'll be a goner by the New Year.' He pointed at the sleeping bag. 'He won't be enjoying the prospect of a white Christmas, will he? You, on the other hand, are in luck. I'm available if you're after a bit of rough—'

'I'm not.'

'C'mon. We could have some fun.'

'I doubt that.' As he took in every inch of her, Frankie realised that there was no one around for as far as the eye could see. Her hand tightened around the pepper spray in her pocket. She was never without it, not since Joanna.

'Move on,' she said.

'Hey! Don't be like that. I'm one of the good guys.'

'So am I.' She held up her warrant card. Her action backfired.

'Fucking bitch.' He took a step forward. 'Leave him be, why don't you? I thought you people were stretched. Go pick on someone who deserves it.'

'Move it,' she said.

'Or what?'

'Do you really want to know?'

The drunk swayed, then walked off, muttering under his

breath, plaiting his legs as he shuffled across the road, leaving a trail of footprints behind him, slipping and sliding on fresh snow that was falling even heavier now, disappearing up the alley where Chris had been found. Nice to know she wasn't the only one today who'd misread a situation and come off worse.

Once again, she crouched down.

A second prod.

'Sarge, wake up.'

The body in the doorway stirred, an ungloved hand emerging from the sleeping bag, then a head. Never before had she been so pleased to see a Christmas hat. Shading his eyes from the glare of street lights, Ryman took a moment or two to focus, a few seconds longer to realise who was standing there.

'Oli?' He rubbed his eyes. 'Sorry I didn't wait up. I thought you weren't coming.'

'You thought wrong.'

'I'm glad.' He sat up, pleased for the company.

Relaxing her grip on the pepper spray, Frankie slipped her hand from her pocket to wipe the icy flakes from her frozen cheeks. She wanted to weep. Ryman had nothing to show for a career in the RAF, and yet he was still smiling. After the day she'd put in, she'd retreated to the incident room to lick her wounds, ignoring the majority of the MIT, David's office out of bounds to everyone until their shift came to an end. In the scheme of things, her row with him was trivial. No one would die over it. A slapped wrist was more desirable than the alternative.

She thumbed over her shoulder. 'Fancy a pint, Sarge?'

'I don't drink.'

'Neither do I . . . unless I need to.'

He dropped his head on one side. 'Tough day?'

'You could say that.'

'Wanna talk about it?'

'No, though I could do with the company.'

147

'Blimey! You must be desperate.'

'Then don't knock me back. My ego couldn't take it.' She extended a hand to help him up.

Ryman extended his, then withdrew it. He scrambled from his sleeping bag, stretching his aching limbs in the same way a moth expands its wings ready to take flight as it emerges from a cocoon. It was the first time she'd seen him upright. He towered over her by a foot or more. Close up, she noticed he was clean-shaven. His bulk suggested he was wearing everything he possessed.

They took off in the direction of a café bar, part of an old cinema on the corner of Pilgrim Street and High Friar Lane, the only place Frankie could think of that stayed open late that wasn't a pub with a no-neck bouncer on the door preventing Ryman from entering. The Tyneside was one of her favourite haunts. She was fascinated with the old movie equipment on display there. The staff were always friendly, the food was right up her street, not that she was hungry after her spat with David.

'Damn it!' The place was closed.

'Maybe they knew I was coming,' Ryman joked.

Frankie apologised. 'I'd forgotten it was Sunday. It gets like this when we're working round the clock – hard to know which way is up. They close at six. C'mon, do you like Indian street food?'

'I like any street food.'

'I didn't mean—'

He drew out the word 'Reelax,' a wry expression on his face. 'I'm winding you up.'

Dabbawal was on High Bridge in the historic heart of the city, not far from PTMY where Chris Adams had taken his last drink. The popular street kitchen was open until ten thirty and was only a short slide away. The smell of spice hit them as they walked in.

Ryman headed straight for the gents.

Taking off her coat, Frankie shook it out. After hanging it over a chair, she sat down, perusing a menu she'd found on the table. Ryman was away a while. Fleetingly, she wondered if he'd bottled it and left via the rear door when she wasn't looking. Then he suddenly reappeared, minus his coat and several layers of clothing. His face had been washed, hair smoothed. He'd made an effort to look presentable and certainly didn't smell like he'd slept in his clothes. In fact, he scrubbed up well. For the first time, she noticed how blue and alert his eyes were.

Sitting down opposite, he hid his surplus clothing on the floor under the table.

She handed him the menu. 'Take your pick. There's plenty of choice.'

It didn't take him long to make up his mind.

Frankie gestured to a waiter she knew. She'd eaten there with David once or twice, with Rae and her partner Andrea, her dad and other coppers from the Murder Investigation Team. The waiter recognised her instantly, arriving at her side with a wide smile on his face.

'Nice to see you again, ma'am.'

'You too.'

'Are you ready to order?'

'Yes, can we get a large pot of English tea please?'

'Nothing stronger?'

'Not tonight. I'm on duty.'

'Of course.' He glanced at Ryman, a puzzled look on his face, his eyes homing in on the ragged holes in his khaki T-shirt, the ones Frankie had been trying not to notice since he'd sat down.

Frankie met Ryman's eyes across the table. 'Sarge, what d'you fancy?'

The waiter relaxed, probably thought Ryman was working undercover. The RAF veteran had come to the same conclusion. Stifling a grin, he ordered his chosen meal without batting an eyelid, as if his unkempt appearance was part and parcel of a covert operation.

'And for you, ma'am,' the waiter asked.

'No food for me, thanks.'

'You're not eating?' Ryman looked disappointed.

'I already did.' She didn't tell him that it was hours ago, or that she'd lost her appetite having gone ten rounds with her boss. *We all lie, Frank – even you!* The guilt returned. Having been frozen to the core when she came in from the cold, she was now overheating, though her burning cheeks had nothing to do with the temperature inside the restaurant.

The waiter moved away.

Shifting uncomfortably in his seat, Ryman's eyes continually checked the door. If Frankie hadn't known any better, she'd have guessed he was on the run. That wasn't the case. There were no outstanding warrants for his arrest. Only once had he come to the attention of police in Bury St Edmunds, presumably where he'd been stationed, an area covered by Suffolk Constabulary. The duty inspector had referenced him off as NFA: No Further Action. The acronym meant something entirely different now that Ryman was of No Fixed Abode.

'Did you check me out then?' he asked.

'On the PNC?' Frankie met his gaze across the table. 'What do you think the chances of me being here were if I hadn't?'

He smiled at her. 'Something you always do before a first date?'

'That would be against regulations.' She paused. 'Sarge, don't get the wrong idea. This is strictly business for me.'

'Understood. Anyway, you're not my type.'

What was his type? Had there been a woman in his past? Someone he thought about often? Maybe he was a father too. She thought he'd make a good one. When his food arrived, she expected him to scoff it down. He took his time, then thanked her.

'No need,' Frankie said. 'How long is it since you ate anything vaguely resembling nutritious?'

'I do OK. You wouldn't believe what people throw away.'

While she poured him a second cup of tea, he shared details of his brush with the law, an altercation with a group of locals who were giving a smaller kid a hard time. He'd intervened and was arrested for his trouble, taken to the nearest nick for questioning . . .

'It wasn't serious, a bit of pushing and shoving on both sides. Still, three on one didn't seem fair. Lucky for me, the kid ran home and told his old man. They came to the station to make a statement and the copper let me go, though a report went in to my CO. The others received a caution. You probably know that already.'

Frankie didn't admit or deny it.

The incident had taken place two years ago, so he'd been homeless less than that. He didn't offer an explanation as to how he left the services and she didn't ask. It wasn't her business. She figured he'd have told her if he'd wanted her to know.

She asked, 'Did you get grief over it?'

'Nah, my guv'nor was a good bloke.'

Frankie examined his empty plate. She was beginning to regret not having eaten with him. Other customers were enjoying their nosh and her stomach was crying out for food. Though she hadn't felt like meeting up with Ryman when she left the office, she'd promised she would. As wired as she was, she couldn't renege on the deal. Besides, she was after information.

He spoke up before she could ask him for it.

'What's your SIO like?'

'A good bloke,' she mimicked him.

'You like him?'

'I do today.' She didn't elaborate.

Ryman didn't quite know how to respond. He was clever

enough to know that there was subtext to her answer. He lifted his cup. 'Then here's to good blokes everywhere.'

Frankie said, 'So, now your belly's full and you've warmed up, what's the word on the street?' She half-expecting him to shake his head and tell her he'd lucked out, except the glint in his eye gave her hope.

He knew something.

'A mate of mine camps out round the back of the Plummer Tower on Croft Street most nights,' he said. 'Her name is Eva. She got an eyeful of a runner just after ten on Friday night. He frightened her as he ran around the corner. Shifty guy, she said, wearing jeans and a fleece jacket with the letters HH on the front. Could be Helly Hansen.'

'Why don't I hand over my warrant card and go home to my bed?'

'Who'll pay the bill?' Ryman grinned.

Frankie knew the place he'd referred to. The old drum tower was medieval, part of the old town wall, a defence against the threat of invasion by the Scots. On the western edge of the city some of the wall had been preserved. 'That's an odd place to pitch, isn't it? There's not much foot traffic down that way in winter.'

'Eva doesn't beg from there. It's safer for her at night for exactly that reason, if there is such a thing for people like us. She's built herself a small shelter, tucked away under the trees that only I know about. No one goes there.'

'Except those trying to hide, it seems.' Frankie was both intrigued and concerned. 'You said she saw him. The question is, did he see her?'

'Not at first.'

'Shit!'

'He was too busy craning his neck to see if anyone was following. When he turned around, he saw her standing behind him and approached. I gather she was too scared to run.'

'Did he speak to her?'

'No verbals. She got the message when he drew an imaginary knife across his neck and took off like a bullet. That's when she noticed the motif on his jacket. She's petrified that he might come looking for her.'

'She should be, if he's the arsehole I'm looking for.' Frankie gathered her thoughts. 'When you say he took off, was he on foot?'

Ryman nodded.

'Can you take me to her?'

'It'll cost you.'

'Didn't I buy you dinner?'

'You did, thanks – and it'll keep me going for a week . . .' He paused, his gratitude replaced by a much darker emotion. 'Eva's eighteen and tiny,' he explained. 'Even smaller than you. She couldn't fight her way out of a paper bag – not that I'm suggesting you can't. She has no rations, Oli. Even less money. She's really struggling. I was hoping you could help her out.' He pressed home his point. 'You have something she needs and vice versa . . . only, if her needs are not met, it could prove fatal.'

Frankie was moved by his concern. 'She didn't ask for payment, did she?'

'I did it for her.' Ryman was pushing his luck. 'Eva doesn't need your money, Oli. She needs warmth. I'd be really grateful if one of your mob would sling her in a cell overnight in exchange for intelligence. A bit of give and take is all I'm after.' He thumbed out the window. 'Even if your man fails to make an appearance, she'll never survive this.'

The RAF veteran had presented Frankie with a dilemma. In the past few years, many police stations had closed, which meant there were fewer cells available, especially in the city. Even if she was able to find a custody sergeant willing to take Eva in, what Ryman was asking for was out of order unless she'd committed an arrestable offence or was in imminent danger. It sounded like she might be but Frankie only had Ryman's word for it.

'The cells aren't a downmarket Airbnb,' she said. 'What she needs is a hostel.'

'What she *needs* is protection,' Ryman said. 'Besides, the hostels are full. Even if they weren't, they won't take her.'

'Why not?'

He sidestepped the question. 'Can't you offer her a place of safety?'

Frankie placed her elbows on the table and leaned in, making sure she couldn't be overheard. 'This is not you wasting police time trying to find her a crib for the night, is it, Sarge?'

'You think I'm dicking you around?'

The thought had crossed her mind. 'I didn't find you standing guard at Plummer Tower tonight, did I?'

Understanding her scepticism, he offered an explanation. 'I went there after dark. She wasn't there. Where I bed down is a lot more public. I figured if she needed help, she knew where to find me.'

'And yet here we sit having a cosy meal.'

'Because we needed to talk. I'm not lying to you, I swear.'

'Don't get arsy, Sarge. I'm fact-checking.'

'I know . . .' Resting his forearms on the table, Ryman moved closer. He had more to say about his friend. 'Eva's a troubled kid. She's not from round here and she's vulnerable to anyone who wants to take advantage.'

Remembering her encounter with the arsehole on Northumberland Street, Frankie could relate. And when Joanna's teenage face appeared in her head it was a done deal . . . almost. Unaware of the images she was seeing, Ryman was still trying to convince her . . .

'Her problems doubled the moment she set eyes on your suspect, Oli. If it is the man you're looking for, he won't want any witnesses.'

'And of course, she won't come to the station without her minder—'

'It's not that so much. She'll happily pass on what she knows, but her English isn't good. As it happens, I speak her language, a plus point of being in the RAF.'

Frankie dropped her head on one side. 'I thought you were flight crew?'

'Before that I was an intelligence analyst, translating radio comms, disseminating intel to commanders on the ground. It was OK, but no more than a glorified desk job. The role didn't fire my jets – in any sense. I wanted to be hands on, like you.'

'What the hell happened to you, Sarge?' She had to ask.

'That's not important. Maybe I'll find a winning lottery ticket, get myself straight and tell you about it over a drink sometime.'

'I thought you didn't drink.'

'I don't . . .' He quoted her. '"Unless I need to."'

She thought about what the drunk had said about Ryman being a goner by the turn of the year. 'You need a bed too though, don't you?'

'I'll survive. Eva won't.'

Ryman was talking sense. Statistically, homeless deaths on British streets were rising and no one was doing anything about it. The government needed to act. Frankie did too by the sounds of it . . . and fast.

Ryman was practically begging. 'If Eva had eyes on your man, you have cause to take her in for questioning, don't you? With your help, that can be a lengthy process. It might mean she needs a rest halfway through the interrogation . . .'

'We interview. We don't interrogate—'

'She's Russian. That's not how she'll see it.'

'Point taken.' Three scary letters popped into Frankie's head. The KGB might have changed their name to FSB, but they were as intimidating as they ever were to those who came to their attention, a frightening prospect for anyone, especially for someone so young.

Ryman looked at the clock on the wall. 'By my reckoning, that should take you – or whoever carries out the interview – most of the night, assuming you have someone available to question her. It would be a damned shame if your best lead croaked by morning.'

Frankie couldn't argue with his logic. Without actually saying it, he was telling her that his friend Eva was in the country illegally. People were on the move, crossing national borders at a rate of knots, a problem for immigration officers countrywide. Ryman was smart enough to know that if he mentioned her status specifically, Frankie would be duty bound to take appropriate action. Eva now faced an added danger. The man Frankie was looking for had taken one life. He had nothing to lose by killing again.

23

There was a lull in the weather as Frankie and Ryman left the street kitchen and walked down Market Street, an area undergoing regeneration. Many buildings of historical significance had been retained. The intention was to breathe new life into a part of the city that badly needed it.

There was no one about.

On the way down the road, Frankie eyed what used to be a CIU club her father and grandfather referred to as 'the bottom office' where they'd have a pint with their colleagues after work. Ryman's voice brought her into the present . . .

'Did you manage to speak to the Doc?'

Frankie shook her head. 'I drew a blank there, I'm afraid. It seems he's moved on.'

'That's news to me.' Ryman stopped walking. 'He wouldn't just take off. Something must have happened to him. Is there any way you could check the hospitals and let me know? They'll tell me nowt. I'd be wasting my breath asking.'

'That I can do.'

And she would.

They walked on, turning into Croft Street and on towards Plummer Tower. To the left, around the back, was a small area of greenery, overgrown with weeds affording some shelter. Frankie used her flashlight to illuminate their way. Eva was asleep under a makeshift tent that sagged in the middle from the weight of the snow. She woke with a start as Ryman bent down and gave her a shake, speaking in Russian, a language Frankie would never get her tongue around.

The waiflike figure sat up. She made no move to leave her sleeping bag. She had delicate features, an angular face and haunted eyes that darted past Ryman and Frankie, checking the area beyond. She spoke quickly in her mother tongue, an urgent tone.

Ryman answered, gesturing towards Frankie.

Stepping forward, the DS handed Eva a sandwich the waiter in Dabbawal had kindly made up for her, a takeaway coffee in a paper cup and a squashed pack of Marlboro she'd bought on her way to meet Ryman. Receiving the unopen pack, Eva formed her hand into a fist, using her thumb to ask for a lighter. Feeling foolish, Frankie spread her hands to indicate that she didn't have one.

She glanced at Ryman.

He shook his head. He didn't smoke.

Eva rifled through the tatty shoulder bag attached to her person with a diagonal strap, searching what appeared to be a bottomless pit of bits and bobs, eventually pulling one out. She sparked up with shaky hands, leaving the cigarette in her mouth as she spoke to Ryman. A cloud of smoke drifted into her eyes and through long brown hair she wore loose.

Frankie was impressed with Ryman's kindness, his gentle tone. As cold as he was, he took off his coat and put it round Eva's shoulders. She didn't argue. Drawing on her cigarette, she spoke harshly as if he'd done something wrong. Just her way, Frankie supposed, though she couldn't swear to it. She heard the word *politsiya*. Maybe the girl had changed her mind about speaking out. Frankie hoped not. Potentially, she was the only witness who could ID the man who'd murdered her childhood friend.

Ryman glanced up at her. 'She's scared, really scared.'

'But willing to talk?'

He gave a nod.

'Can you ask her when she first saw the man?'

He did, then said: 'She was setting up camp on Friday night when she heard footsteps approaching. If this was your offender, he was in a hurry. She could hear police cars in the distance, more than one, and the guy was using the corner of the building as cover.'

'Where did he come from?'

'Croft Street, a stone's throw from your crime scene.'

'I'm aware of the geography, Sarge. Which way was he heading?'

'That way.' Ryman was pointing towards Carliol Square. 'She says she heard a bleep and saw a flash of light. Seconds later, a vehicle sped away. She doesn't know if he was in it or not. It was travelling at speed and the windows had privacy glass.'

Frankie pictured the scene in her mind's eye, wondering about the sequence of events, hoping Eva's recollection could be relied upon. It was important to establish not only what the young Russian had seen and heard, but the exact order in which it had taken place. Frankie glanced at Ryman. 'Ask her if she heard the bleep, before, after or during the running.'

Ryman's brow creased. 'Why is that important?'

'Ask her,' Frankie said.

A brief exchange between Eva and Ryman.

'During,' he said.

'Did she seem certain or in two minds?'

'There was no hesitation. When you live like we do, observation is important. Those of us who don't do drugs or drink are more finely tuned than most. You can live or die by what you see and hear, Oli. Eva's clean, in case you were wondering. We're not all pissheads.'

That was good to know. Frankie's mind was elsewhere. A man on the run from a murder scene would be opening his car as he ran towards it. He wouldn't wait until he got there to do it.

'What kind of car was it?'

'Give her a break, Oli.' Ryman raised a hand. 'OK, OK, I'll ask.'

Again, he spoke to the girl. She gave a brief reply.

Frankie could tell from her expression that she didn't have a clue.

Ryman confirmed it. 'It was a dark-coloured four-by-four. That's as close as you'll get. Eva's not a driver, so she doesn't know cars. She was too busy watching her six in case the man she saw wasn't in the car and doubled back. There was no one else around.'

Frankie peered into the undergrowth. 'Wouldn't she be better choosing an archway to sleep under? Somewhere dry? Strength in numbers.'

'You'd think so, wouldn't you?'

'That's not the case?'

Ryman shook his head. 'Young lasses like Eva often go it alone. Arches are renowned for trouble, sexual assault, that type of thing. Sadly, girls her age are easy pickings, targeted even within our own community.' He swept and hand towards her makeshift shelter. 'This is as good a place as any for her to bed down.' He flicked his eyes left, directing Frankie's attention to a flight of paved steps that led on to the street behind.

Frankie nodded her understanding. Now she thought of it, she could see why Eva would choose this quiet corner of the city between the hours of darkness, one with an escape route should she need one. It wouldn't do to be cornered in a place like this. She'd chosen well.

'Wait here,' she said.

Frankie took the rear steps from the old drum tower, arriving in Carliol Square a second later. In the sixties, there had been a jazz venue here, appropriately named The Downbeat, a club to rival London's finest, featuring traditional artists like the River City Jazzmen, according to her grandfather. Towards the end of its life, it switched focus to Rhythm & Blues bands and he'd become a member. He talked about it with affection, though the building had since been demolished.

There were several car parking spaces and more outside the Euro Hotel. No CCTV that Frankie could see. She scanned the area, looking left and then right, her eyes travelling beyond the old Worswick Street bus station to the T-junction at the top. From there, the offender would have turned left. In seconds, he'd be on the central bypass, free to travel north or south. She pulled out her phone.

24

David yawned, wishing he'd gone straight home before the weather worsened. He was stuck in a long tailback of traffic heading north. The southbound carriageway was even worse, down to a one-lane crawl. Those without a utility vehicle had no chance of making their destination anytime soon. Those with one couldn't get past the vehicles that were struggling.

His mobile rang.

Frankie's name came up on the display panel the manufacturer insisting on calling an infotainment system, a stupid name that bugged the hell out of him. Knowing Frankie, she'd be wanting to smooth things over. She'd have to wait. He wasn't ready to talk, let alone listen to yet another grovelling apology. He ignored the call, letting it go straight to voicemail. She left no message. When she rang again, he couldn't ignore it.

Frankie was relieved when he picked up at the second attempt. She'd anticipated a knockback first time round. She wouldn't have called him tonight had it not been urgent. For the first time since they began working together, she was wary of engaging with him.

She took a deep breath. 'David, I found something I think is important.'

'I thought I told you to go home,' he said.

'You did.'

'So why didn't you?'

'I didn't think I'd sleep. Besides, I'd put some feelers out with a rough sleeper I met last night and said I'd be back to talk to him ASAP. It seemed like the ideal opportunity—'

'Why is this the first I've heard of it? Another thing you

declined to mention. This is becoming a habit—'

'David, don't be a twat. I know I'm not your favourite person right now, but you told me to do my job and that's exactly what I'm doing. I didn't tell you because there was nothing *to* tell. We don't have time for bickering. Do you want to hear this or not?'

David smiled to himself. Whatever reservations he harboured about her conduct, he couldn't fault her effort. Like him, she'd rather be working than at home. Hard though it was to admit, the two of them were alike in so many ways. Lately though, dragging himself away from the job had required less effort. He had Ben to return to. It was very different walking into a house that wasn't always empty. Frankie didn't have that.

'David. Are you there?'

'Yeah, I'm stuck on the A1 going nowhere fast. I can't move forward or make a U-turn. According to the radio, there are accidents ahead and behind me. Our lot are stretched, unable to reach casualties, so when you're heading home, stick to the coast.'

'I will, thanks for the heads-up.'

The traffic update came as no surprise to Frankie. Emergency services were struggling to cope in the worst December weather in a decade. She walked back the way she'd come, pausing at the bottom of the steps that led to the old drum tower. Even with her extensive self-defence training, she couldn't imagine bedding down here for the night, with or without a handy escape route.

David's voice arrived in her ear. 'What did your rough sleeper have to say then?'

'One of his pals, a young lass of eighteen, saw a man running along Croft Street on Friday night, shortly after ten o'clock. He was clearly spooked, looking over his shoulder. The girl heard sirens in the background as panda cars flooded the area. The timing fits. I think we might be on to something.'

'You've spoken to her?'

'I'm with her now.'

'Is she a credible witness?'

'I think so. Her name's Eva Sokolov. She's also of no fixed abode. We need to keep hold of her until I can find her a place to stay. I know someone who might be able to help tomorrow. In the short-term, could we find her a cell or cheap hotel room, a place to lay her head while we work out what she knows?'

David inched forward in the line of cars, irritated with his lack of progress, unable to see a hand in front of his face even with his wipers going full pelt. The standing traffic meant that snow was piling up on what was normally a fast-moving dual carriageway. Frankie was still talking, excited at the prospect of a breakthrough in the case. As intrigued as he was, he could tell she had more to say and suspected he wasn't going to like it.

'What aren't you telling me?' he asked.

She hesitated, proof if it was needed that his assessment was correct.

'Put it this way: I don't feel inclined to enquire into her status.'

'What? Are you on something?'

'No. Our guy saw her, David. Right now, he thinks he's home and dry. I'm guessing that when he's had time to think about it, or if he gets an inkling that we're on to him, he'll realise the mistake he made, remember his encounter with Eva and look her up. He can't afford loose ends. He could kill her. She needs our protection until we collar him.'

'Can she describe him?'

'In a fashion, as well as she was able . . . via an interpreter.'

'Interpreter?' David exploded. 'You *are* on something. Frankie, there's no budget for that. You know as well as I do—'

'We don't need one, guv. My informant is ex-RAF. He speaks Russian and will work for nothing. The two are friends and he's keen to help her and us in any way he can. He's a rough sleeper. A decent bloke though, I promise you. Is it OK to stick Eva in a cell overnight?' Her request drew a moment of silence. 'David? Did you hear what I said? She's a sitting duck if I leave her where she is. Potentially, she's our best lead.'

'OK, do it . . . And if anyone argues, refer them to me.'

'You're the boss.'

When he rang off abruptly, Frankie stared at her mobile in disgust. 'Great job, Frankie,' she mumbled under her breath. 'You're back on the A team. We'll crack on with your witness first thing in the morning.' Slipping her mobile in her pocket, she regretted her parting shot. Had he picked her up wrong, thinking she was having another go at him?

She wasn't.

Frankie swung round, spooked by the sound of coughing that came from over her shoulder. Her rough sleepers were standing in the dark at the top of the steps beside the old drum tower. Ryman had overheard. And even if he hadn't, he was intuitive, clever enough to have worked out that whatever was bothering her involved the man she worked for. It didn't take him long to voice that opinion.

'Your good bloke giving you a hard time, Oli?'

'Nothing for you to worry about,' she said. 'C'mon, we need to get you inside.'

25

Ordinarily Stone would have called Frankie back as soon as his phone signal returned, but not tonight. He'd said all he wanted to say. By the time he finally limped home, his nephew had lit the fire and prepared a meal. A first for him. Appreciating the time and trouble he'd taken – also wondering what his motives were – David was instantly suspicious. He kept his thoughts to himself. It wasn't right to lay into Ben because Frankie had pulled a fast one and put him in a mood.

He took off his jacket and joined his nephew in the kitchen. There was a pan simmering gently on the stove. David lifted the lid off, dipped the tip of his forefinger into the deep red sauce and licked it. 'Mm . . . tastes a lot better than I thought it would.' He glanced at Ben. 'Have I got time to nip in the shower?'

His nephew checked his watch. 'Just about, wanna beer?'

A nod. 'Make it three.'

'That bad?'

'Worse.'

Freshly showered, bare-chested with a pair of grey tracksuit bottoms on, David pulled an old T-shirt over his head and peered into the kitchen, asking if he could do anything to help. Ben had everything under control. David left him to it and wandered into the living room where he stood by the window looking out. A pretty scene. Still and silent. If it had been dry, he'd have gone for a run before eating, for no other reason than to work off his frustration. Instead, he turned away, threw a log on the fire and sat down in his nan's old rocking chair.

The satisfying hiss of air escaping the beer can calmed

166

him. He tossed the ring-pull on the table and took a big gulp. It went down a treat. In the heat of the room, his eyes were getting heavy. He yawned, tipped his head back and shut his eyes, wondering what time Frankie would clock off. She'd done well to find her witness and, though what she'd told him was far from a smoking gun, he was hoping it would take them somewhere.

He thought of Eva Sokolov too and the man she'd seen acting suspiciously on Friday night. Homeless didn't equal criminal. NFA she may be, but she'd be treated with respect, same as any other witness. If she had information to give, the least he could do was help her deliver it. The practicalities of finding her accommodation, ensuring that she stuck around for a trial, could be worked out later.

'You want to set the table, while I dish up?' Ben said as he walked in.

David opened one eye. 'Nah, lets slum it.'

Ben downed a fork on the arm of David's chair along with a half jar of mango chutney and a bit of torn-off kitchen roll. Seconds later, he was in the room with two plates. David took one of them, still mulling over his row with Frankie, wishing he'd handled it differently, even though she was in the wrong. He was betting that she felt the same way. Though she was working hard to make amends, the fact remained that she hadn't come clean when she ought.

Ben raised his beer can. 'Bon appétit!'

'Cheers.' With his plate on his knee, David dug in.

What Ben lacked in skill, he'd made up for in enthusiasm. All things considered – given the ingredients he had to work with – he'd made a fist of a veggie curry that his uncle had to admit he'd have been proud of if he'd cooked it himself. They chatted over their meal, mainly about the decorators whose paint pots he'd been forced to climb over on the way in, negotiating ladders and tool bags to get to the shower.

'I'm sick of this mess,' he said, eyeing the boxes piled

everywhere. 'Good thing I insisted on a fixed price. How long can it take two blokes to paint three rooms? I thought they had a new job to start.'

Ben spoke through a mouthful of curried vegetables. 'Word is, they'll be gone when you get in tomorrow.'

'So will my weekend,' David grumbled.

'You've been out all weekend!'

'That's beside the point.'

'That isn't all that's pissing you off though, is it?'

Failing to admit or deny it, David handed Ben his empty plate and stood up. 'I need to make a quick call. Great nosh, by the way. You've missed your vocation, son.'

As Ben left the room to fill their newly acquired dishwasher, David stood by the window, his back to the room. No let-up in the weather. He hoped that Frankie had made it home, or better still gone to stay with her parents, who lived a damned sight closer to Middle Earth. He was betting she hadn't. Her father would have questions she wouldn't want to answer . . . not tonight . . . maybe never.

David dialled Abbott's number.

Never more than a few feet from his phone, Dick picked up immediately. 'You want me back in, guv?'

'Why? You need a reason to escape?'

'Always.' Abbott chuckled. 'I'm on dog-walking duty. Have you seen it outside? My whippet took one look out the door and sat down in the utility room refusing to budge. What's up?'

Taking a swig of beer was a delay tactic. What David had in mind to ask would put the detective sergeant in an invidious position, dividing his loyalty between a long-term friendship with Frankie and the chance to show his commitment to the Murder Investigation Team and ultimately to their victim. Despite Bright's lack of concern over Frankie's former relationship with the IP, the head of CID wasn't yet aware of Wells' discovery or the call Frankie had kept to herself. Now she'd explained herself, David understood her reasoning but, as her SIO, he felt compelled to investigate the matter further – for her good as well as his own.

'I need a job doing,' he told Abbott. 'You're excused from the briefing tomorrow morning. I want you down at the Crown Court first thing. Ask around. Spend some money if you have to. Talk to the ushers and journalists, anyone you think might have known our victim. Frankie has given us her input, but I suspect we don't have the full picture. What I need is some independent background on Adams. If he was investigating something important, above or below the radar, someone must know what he was up to.'

'You think Frankie's wrong about him?'

'Let's just say I'd like to know what he was really like. She's too close.'

Abbott jumped to her defence. 'Surely if she was that close, he'd have told her what his big scoop was all about, assuming there was one. Guv, I don't think—'

'Do as I ask. And Dick?'

'Guv?'

'Keep it to yourself.'

'Understood.'

David hung up, turning from the window.

Ben was standing at the entrance to the living room, a sour expression on his face. 'What the fuck? If you're replacing Frankie with Abbott, don't you think you should do it face to face? If the boot was on the other foot, that's what she'd do. It's a shit's trick, sneaking around behind her back. Not only is it unfair on her, it's unfair on Dick. They're mates, in case you didn't know . . .'

David did know.

Ben was still going, getting more and more fired up. 'That's no way to treat either of them, Dave.'

David gave him a black look. 'Didn't your father ever tell you it's rude to earwig private conversations? Relax, Ben. I

169

have no intention of replacing her, with Dick or anyone else. Her job is safe . . . until I say otherwise. And I'll use my staff in whatever way I see fit.'

'Speaks the man who prides himself on integrity. Have the balls to front up and stop undermining her. She'll never forgive you. You know that, right?'

'Son, that's enough. Button it or get yourself to bed.'

'I'm not tired.'

'Well I am.' David was shattered, in more ways than one. 'I've lost my rag today already. Believe me, you do not want to see me lose it twice. I'm running a murder enquiry, not organising a tea party, so without sounding too ungrateful, mind your own business or ship out.'

'What the fuck did I do?' Ben flushed, eyes locking on to his uncle's.

David didn't answer.

'Fine, I'll pack a bag.'

Turning to leave, Ben lobbed a third beer across the room. David caught it in mid-air. He'd gone too far. The last thing he wanted was to fall out with Ben, let alone make him find someplace else to stay. They were family; the only family either of them had – after a shaky start, they were finally making a go of it.

David spoke up before his nephew reached the door. 'Ben, don't. I'm sorry. My beef isn't with you, it's with her.'

The discussion – or was it a row? – went on for a good ten minutes, neither willing to back down. Ben wasn't perfect, but he talked a lot of sense and was keen to build bridges. His mother died of cancer in 2012. In the aftermath of his father's sudden death a year and a half ago, leaving him an orphan at the age of eighteen, he'd behaved badly. The more David rejected him, the more obnoxious he became. Frankie had made them see sense. She'd come to their rescue, acting as mediator between man and boy.

Ben would defend her come what may.

He stopped pacing the floor and sat down, assuming the role of peacemaker. 'Dave, if you carry on like this, you'll lose more than your rag and I know you don't want that. Either of you. What the hell did she do anyhow?'

'I said drop it. What she did or didn't do is no business of yours. Anyway, I can't tell you, it's case-related—'

'So what? You asked me and Belinda for help, remember?'

'And you didn't know Chris Adams, so leave it out.'

'Too late. We're already involved.'

'Wells is, you're not. Are we clear?'

Stung by the comment, Ben dropped his head.

Guilt was like a stab in the chest for David. Since his nephew had gone to work with Wells, he was a changed lad. He'd found his niche, developing a thirst for a beefy investigation that would utilise his intelligence and good instincts. Nevertheless, David's reservations about Ben's choice of career had grown rather than dissipated. That was a conversation for another day. He held his tongue. It was late. He was too wired for another debate he suspected would turn into a shitstorm.

'Son, can we park this? I really need to get some kip. We'll talk tomorrow, I promise. Whether or not you're involved – in any capacity – is up to Wells, so long as it doesn't jeopardise my position as SIO.'

'Is that what Frankie did?'

No answer.

Ben's eyes were pleading. 'Whatever it was, I bet she never meant to hurt you.'

'This isn't personal—'

'Yeah, right. I'm young, not blind.'

David gave him a long, hard stare. 'How I feel about Frankie is not open for discussion, Ben.'

'You do feel for her, though, don't you? She means more to you than being a good bagman.' Ben already knew the answer.

26

It was late when Frankie reached the fishing village of Amble. She'd taken David's advice and followed the coast road, where the snowfall hadn't been as heavy, but even so the ground was covered by a blanket of white and the going had been slow. A combination of guilt and sadness competed for space in her head as she parked the car, resting her key fob against the entry console to her apartment block. She heard it click open. Ignoring the lift, she made her weary way upstairs to the first floor and let herself in.

It was warm inside, though tonight it didn't feel cosy. Unlike Sutherland's place, there was no Christmas tree in her living room. Who the hell had time? She'd be lucky if hers went up by Christmas Eve. She didn't care. Beneath and above her apartment balcony were all the twinkly lights she required from the boats in the harbour and the stars in the sky.

That would do her.

Pouring herself a drink, she slid open the patio door and slipped outside. Had she not been numb already she might have noticed the blast of icy air as she stepped out on to the balcony. The North Sea was black, like her mood, the lights on the boardwalks drawing lines on the surface of the water below. She wondered if David had made it to his home inland. He'd kept her on the investigation, but there was none of the usual camaraderie or friendly banter between them. She couldn't believe he'd hung up on her. Still, she'd got what she wanted, a bed for the night for Eva Sokolov. If he didn't care to extend his usual 'Night, Frank. See you tomorrow' then fuck him.

At least there would be a tomorrow.

In many ways, he reminded her of her dad, a good man, a detective she looked up to and admired. He could be bloody annoying at times, but then so could she. She tried not to think about their row, what she'd said, what he'd said, but even as she'd settled Eva in a police cell the argument kept replaying in her mind. Neither of them had held back. Open and frank had always been their way. Hopefully, their relationship would withstand this blip. And, if it didn't, she only had herself to blame.

Gulls screeched as they flew inland for shelter . . .

Frankie felt like screeching too, letting it all out. She clutched at the edge of her balcony, tightening her grip. The rail was freezing. She wanted her father. If anyone would understand her reasons for withholding Chris's phone call, her compulsion to investigate his death, he would. She didn't want to be locked out of the investigation – that was a given – though it had nothing to do with the opportunity to prove herself as a murder detective.

Hadn't she done that already?

Despite the plummeting temperature, sweat soaked the shirt beneath her jacket. She looked out over the marina, a view that always made her feel safe, a stillness that she needed right now when her body was shaking with inner rage. Unable to leave things in the air till morning, she took out her mobile to call David again – he was on speed dial.

She hesitated, her finger hovering over the call button.

She couldn't do it.

Putting the phone away, she went back inside and kicked off her shoes. She thought about calling Andrea – she was always willing to listen. Frankie glanced at the clock. Her sister-in-law was probably in bed, cuddled up to Rae, or doing something even more physical. The thought of sex depressed Frankie. As far as relationships went, she was a car crash. Andrea had shown her that it *was* possible to be a cop, fall hopelessly in love and have it all. Frankie thought about this for a moment. What did *she* have outside of the Job?

A big fat zero.

Turning on her electric blanket, she ran herself a bath and lay in the suds, trying to relax. Instead all she could think about was Ryman and Eva, who'd be kipping on a hard bed at Middle Earth. After spending time with them, Frankie's apartment seemed lonelier than ever tonight. Drying herself off, she stared at her reflection in the mirror and didn't like what she saw. Far from ready for bed, she threw on a robe and wandered barefoot into the open-plan living room, making her way around the island that separated off the kitchen area. She opened the fridge and closed it again.

There was nothing edible in there.

The open bottle of Malbec on the counter caught her eye. She poured herself another drink, draining the glass in one almighty gulp, the turmoil inside her head refusing to go away. Having eaten next to nothing all day, the hit of red wine made her feel decidedly woozy, but it blotted out the image of David's disappointed face.

One more drink and she'd reach oblivion.

27

Despite lying snow, major routes were clear. Even so, Frankie was late arriving at the incident room. Stone had beaten her in. Maybe he hadn't slept either. Mitch told her he was busy interviewing Eva and Ryman, a process that Frankie had assumed would fall to her. Rarely did SIOs take the lead interviewing witnesses, but David was hands on. She liked that and had no inclination to interrupt him mid-flow. He seemed to be taking his time, checking out her rough sleepers for himself. Fair enough. She was confident that Ryman could hold his own, one decent bloke to another.

She glanced at Mitch. 'Dick not about?'

'Haven't seen him.' DC Mitchell was trying unsuccessfully to hide a bacon sandwich under the statement he was reading. 'I assumed he was with the guv'nor. Why are you not in there?'

'You ask too many questions.' Frankie put her coat on. 'I'm going out.'

'Where to?'

'What did I just say?' Frankie admonished him with a raised eyebrow. 'If they get finished before I return, tell them I won't be long.' Leaning over his desk, Frankie lifted the statement, scooped up his breakfast and walked away, flashing a big smile as she glanced over her shoulder to witness the affronted expression on his face.

He'd get over it.

With time to kill and a renewed sense of purpose, she left the incident room bound for Newcastle. There was no point dwelling on yesterday's mistakes. Olivers weren't quitters, they were fighters. Frankie had a mind to prove that before the day was out. It suited her that David was tied up. It left her free to do her own thing.

The bacon butty was finger-licking good, the first thing she'd eaten since lunch yesterday. As she drove, her father rang again. He was nothing if not persistent. She felt guilty for ignoring his calls. She'd have to face him at some point. Later. Now was not the time to open up old wounds, for either of them. Unable to handle another inquisition – face-to-face or over the phone – she let the call ring out and then dialled Chris's mum instead, tying up the line in case her father called back. Susan had many questions, none of which Frankie could answer with any degree of certainty, beyond the fact that her colleagues were making progress and would update her as and when with more detail. The bereaved mother accepted this.

'Susan, before I go, has DC Abbott been in touch?'

'No. Well, he might have. I've been ignoring the phone unless it's a number I recognise. Journalists have been hounding me, day and night. Melanie suggested that we let the answerphone take messages.'

'That's very wise.'

'Why do you ask?'

'We've been told that Chris had a motorcycle he kept in a neighbour's garage.'

'Yes.'

'You wouldn't happen to know which one, would you?'

'No, sorry.'

'I'm told you didn't approve.'

'I didn't. If you want the truth, I gave him a lot of grief over it. I begged him to get rid. When I went too far and said it would kill him one day, he lost his temper.' Susan began to weep. 'He wouldn't give it up, but he knew I'd worry every time he went out on two wheels, so we came to an arrangement.'

'Out of sight, out of mind?'

'Exactly.'

Frankie understood where she was coming from. Some years ago, together with her shift, she'd agreed to take part in a charity sky dive, a thought that horrified her own mother. Julie Oliver didn't want to know when it would take place. In fact, she'd point blank refused to allow Frankie to speak of it in her company. The words 'ignorance' and 'bliss' figured in the equation somewhere. That irrational approach to danger made sense of why Susan hadn't mentioned the bike when Frankie first spoke to her. In Susan's head it didn't exist . . . because she didn't want it to. Or maybe she was too traumatised, not thinking straight having been told of her son's murder.

'Stupid really,' Susan added. 'If he didn't take his car, I knew.'

Frankie's heart was breaking for the woman on the other end.

'The bike can't be far,' Susan said. 'Chris had a new mate on the estate, another petrol head. She only moved in last summer. Her parents don't mind her riding. Sorry, I'm rambling, pet. Is it important?'

'Probably not. Do you recall when he last didn't take the car?'

'Friday gone.'

'OK, thanks. Sit tight, I'll call in later.'

'That's not necessary. I know how busy you must be. I should, I've known your old man long enough.'

'It's no trouble.' Frankie hoped she hadn't given herself away, sounding too eager to drop by and check that Susan wasn't back on the booze.

'No really, Frankie, there's no need. Besides, the weather is set to get worse. Anyway, I'm exhausted. I'm going for a lie-down. Melanie is calling in and your mum said she'd pop by at some point. I don't know if I can handle any more visitors. I'm OK . . . Please don't worry about me.'

Frankie *was* worried . . .

How many excuses did she need?

She wondered if Susan was keeping her away for a reason not included in the long list she'd trotted out, or if *she* was jumping to conclusions again. She'd done a lot of that lately and it had to stop. There was no evidence that the woman on the other end had returned to her old ways. If there had been, FLO Mel Fitzgerald or her mum would've been on the blower . . . unless that's why her father had called.

Shit!

Frankie had a vision of him sitting in his den, surrounded by his private murder wall, the thing he stared at on a daily basis as soon as her mother's back was turned. He'd been trying to figure out what had been missed in the investigation into Joanna's murder, a case he'd been ruled out of because he was the victim's father. Vital evidence he believed might have solved the case had inexplicably gone missing. A cover-up. He wouldn't stop searching for it until they brought him out in a box.

The ringing tone stopped.

Frankie took a long, deep breath, trying and failing to sound upbeat. 'Hi, Dad. It's me.'

'Is that the same me I've been trying to reach for two days?'

She stopped at traffic lights, engine idling. 'I'm flat out. You know how it is.'

'I was never too busy to talk to your granddad.'

'So you're a saint and I'm a sinner. Is this going to take long?'

'Where are you?'

'City Road. Does it matter?'

They talked briefly, Frankie asking his advice to make him feel needed, but omitting to tell him how things really were, what a mess she'd made of the last twenty-four hours, and the current state of her relationship with her DCI. Her dad liked Stone and would side with him, given half a chance.

'By the way,' she said, 'did Dick call you about Chris's motorcycle?'

'He did call, but I was getting my hair cut.'

'I'm not the only one ignoring calls then?'

'What about his bike?'

'You wouldn't happen to know where he keeps it, would you?'

'Sorry, no.'

'Any houses you can think of near you that changed hands in the summer?'

'I'll check it out.'

'Dad, you're retired. We have detectives—'

'Consider it done, love.'

Frankie smiled. He couldn't let the job go if his life depended on it. He rang off, but not before he'd got her to promise to drop by and see her mum, who was as worried about her as Frankie was about Susan. The good news was that there had been no sign of her falling off the wagon.

Small mercies.

28

Stone took an immediate liking to Stuart Ryman. It came as no surprise; Frankie had vouched for the guy, and he trusted her instincts. Eva Sokolov, David wasn't so sure of. He hadn't understood a word she'd said but her body language betrayed her impatience. Throughout the interview her hands and gob were working overtime, which made it heavy going. David resisted the urge to look at his watch. He had a million things to do before the morning briefing. The team was still short on bodies – none of the sicknotes rushing back to work – Abbott out on his instruction, Frankie probably pissed off that she wasn't conducting the interview herself. She'd found these two – one of whom might turn out to be their star witness – and for that David would be forever grateful. In retrospect, perhaps Frankie would have done a better job.

Sensing his frustration, Ryman looked up.

'Bear with us,' he said. 'Eva doesn't understand why Oli – I mean DS Oliver – isn't here, why she's being asked the same questions she answered last night, or why it's important to go over familiar ground. She wants to help but, between you and me, she's had dealings with the police in Russia. It appears they were far less accommodating than here in the UK. She's also wary of the tape.'

'It's basic procedure,' David said.

'I told her that. I'm not getting through. She's shit scared.'

'Tell her she's here voluntarily. She can leave whenever she wants, but I need the recording. It'll have to be verified and transcribed by a professional.'

'Is that necessary? I did this for a living once.' Ryman rubbed at the growth of stubble on his chin. 'Trained by the RAF, if that helps.'

'You're also of no fixed abode.'

'Which means I couldn't possibly be of any use to a busy DCI, I suppose.' Ryman shook his head. 'Look, I'm not being a smart-arse. I know all there is to know about rules and regulations. I'm used to all that bureaucratic bullshit. I'm here, aren't I? Not to put too fine a point on it, I'm as good as it gets. Wouldn't it be easier all round if you added me to your list of accredited interpreters?'

'I can't do that, even if I wanted to,' Stone said. 'You have a personal connection with Eva. I need someone completely independent who can verify her statement when she makes one. Should we find the man she saw – assuming he's our killer – her testimony will be used in court proceedings. If I let you do it, any half-decent defence barrister would tear it to shreds. It would be inadmissible, you must see that.'

'Yeah, you're right.'

Ryman pushed his chair away from the table and got up. Eva went from semi-relaxed to meltdown in an instant. Grabbing for his hand, she held on to it, speaking in rapid bursts, presumably afraid that he was going to abandon her.

'Sit down, Sarge. You're panicking her.'

Ryman didn't move. 'I thought you said you wanted a professional.'

'In due course. Right now, all I need is an open channel of communication. You know her, which means you'll have deeper insight into her life. You have her trust and that's more important than calling in a stranger. She'll clam up if we do that and this interview will be a waste of her time and mine. What seems to be her problem anyhow?'

'She's wary of men—'

'She seems all right with you.'

'OK, she's wary of you then!' No offence was meant and none was taken. Ryman sat down, a quick glance Eva's way before he refocused on Stone. 'I explained that you're the SIO. From that point on she got it in her head that you're a badass who'll send her packing on the next flight to Moscow.'

'That's not going to happen. She has my word on it.'

'Words are meaningless to her, guv.' Ryman lifted a hand, fending off a response. 'OK, OK, I'll try.'

He spoke to Eva in a reassuring tone. Whatever he said seemed to have the desired effect. She visibly relaxed, a tear rolling down her face as she met David's gaze for the very first time since he'd entered the room, a small nod acknowledging that she'd received his message – moreover that she believed it to be genuine.

David smiled at her, then glanced at Ryman. 'Would she like a break? I have other things I can be getting on with.'

As Ryman spoke to Eva, David ran his eyes over the girl's skinny frame. Last night, Frankie had made sure that her two witnesses had been fed, given a medical check-up, allowed to shower and provided with fresh clothes. Of the two, Ryman looked in better shape, but they were both knackered. Only to be expected, having slept in the cells. They had been warm and safe, but the custody suite was noisy, never a place to be recommended for a good night's kip. Eva was emaciated, wearing an outfit David had seen his 2ic in many times. Perhaps that explained why, during the time he'd spent with the Russian, he'd been unable to get Frankie out of his head.

29

Frankie parked in Sandgate behind the law courts and walked down the bank on to the Quayside, grabbing a take-away coffee en route. The River Tyne was choppy, a floating body of gun-metal grey flowing east from the city centre. Mesmerising. Icy. Comforting nevertheless. She wondered how David was getting on with her witness and whether Eva Sokolov had remembered anything new about the man she'd seen hiding in the shadows on Friday night in an attempt to evade capture.

Binning her empty paper cup in the nearest trash can, Frankie turned away from the river and climbed the steps to the impressive Crown Court, her second home. Many serious crimes had been tried there since it was built in the late eighties. As the glass lift made its ascent to the top floor, she peered down to the spot where she'd been standing a moment ago. The lift doors opened. She got out, checking her mobile. There were several work-related emails, including one from Bright. As yet, nothing from David, Dick or Mitch.

The press office was a shit-pit with three groaning desks and someone's cast-off old-school metal filing cabinet. It hadn't changed since the first time Frankie had seen it, aged sixteen. Her father had dumped her there while he gave evidence in a court case, unable to leave her in the police office in case anyone more senior arrived. Frankie remembered the chaos, the fog of smoke, the banter among the three journalists based there full-time, while others came and went between court sessions. Only the pay phone in the corner was missing. Now, like then, it was a soulless conference room with smoked glass and crap lighting guaranteed to give those working there a migraine by three o'clock.

A young man – who looked ten but was probably in his twenties – got up and sauntered towards her. He was the new boy she'd heard about, pale and thin with short cropped hair, not much taller than her. He was wearing a smart blue suit, a pristine white shirt, top button undone, his navy tie loosened at the neck and pulled to one side. Who could blame him? Compared to the temperature outside, the room was unbearably hot.

'Can I help you?'

'Depends. Where can I find Andrew Fellows?'

'Who's asking?' The elongated A and what sounded like an R that didn't belong in the word 'asking' gave away the fact that he wasn't local. 'You do know this isn't a public area, right?'

Frankie glanced around. 'If it was, you'd need to employ a cleaner on grounds of health and safety, mate. Lucky for you, I've had all the relevant injections. I'm practically bombproof.' She threw him a wide smile. 'Don't panic. This is home from home for me, like any nick I ever worked in.' She held up her warrant card. 'DS Frankie Oliver, Murder Investigation Team.'

He returned her smile. 'I'm Lee . . . Ridley.'

'Nice to meet you, Lee.'

'If you're here for the murder trial, you'll be disappointed. Jury's still out. They failed to reach a verdict overnight. You did know one of the jurors has been discharged?' He didn't wait for an answer. 'He was rushed to the RVI this morning – suspected heart attack. The rest are split. The judge has agreed to accept a majority.' Finally, his brain caught up with his mouth. 'Anyway, Fellows isn't covering it, I am.'

'I'm not here for the trial, Lee. It's Fellows I'm after.'

His face registered a hint of disappointment.

A mobile began to vibrate behind him. He shot across the floor like his pants had caught fire, snatching it up as if he'd been waiting for the call. 'Ridley, yeah, it is.' He laughed. 'Who else would it be? No, nothing doing as yet . . . dinner sounds great. Eight o'clock?'

Frankie cleared her throat.

Remembering that he'd left her standing in the doorway, Ridley said: 'Hold on, I've got company . . .' Covering the speaker with his free hand, he glanced in Frankie's direction. 'Fellows is in Court 3 – His Honour Judge Pickford presiding.'

'Then I'm in luck,' Frankie said. 'Unless he quit, there'll be a short adjournment while he nips out for a fag, sooner rather than later.'

Ridley lifted a thumb. 'Guaranteed.' Putting his feet up on the desk, he resumed a conversation that was far more important than she was.

Frankie took a seat outside the courtroom with neither the will nor the inclination to go inside and haul Fellows out. She checked her inbox again. Answered a few emails that required a brief response, before checking iMessage. Still nothing from the incident room. The briefing wouldn't go ahead until she and David were available. He'd call her as soon as he was done.

If she was lucky.

She rang the incident room. 'Mitch, do me a favour. Ring round the local hospitals. Get them to check their admissions for the past two days. I know they're stretched. Tell them it's urgent. I'm trying to locate a homeless man known locally as the Doc. He's Ryman's friend. He's six four, bald, wears a Davy Crockett hat to keep out the cold. I know it's a long shot. It's all I have. Actually, that's not all. Tell them he's a former hospital porter. They might try harder to find him.'

'Is he a witness too?'

'We won't know until we find him, will we?'

'Gotcha.'

'Any joy from the boss?'

'No, he's still tied up.'

'OK, thanks. See you later.'

As Frankie hung up, the door to Court 3 opened, the proceedings halted for a witness to be called. A frustrated usher repeated the name 'Terence Munro' three times and got no response. She shook her head and disappeared back into the courtroom.

Munro was for the high jump.

Pickford wouldn't tolerate a delay, for any reason.

Frankie pictured him red-faced, barking orders to the police bench, issuing a warrant for the man's arrest. Seconds later, right on cue, the door swung open again, a uniformed officer checking the waiting area, a final call for Munro, before he rushed off to look for him. Frankie chuckled under her breath. If she had a quid for every time she'd left a courtroom to trace a witness she'd be a very rich woman.

Some movement in her peripheral vision.

Glancing along the corridor – expecting to see the missing witness rushing her way – she did a double take, recognising the distinctive gait of someone she knew striding along with a female court clerk by his side, her flowing black gown billowing in her wake as she tried to keep up. Neither of the pair noticed Frankie sitting there.

She was already off her chair.

Tailing them, she could see they were deep in conversation. Further along, they stopped walking, the man with his back to her. Frankie moved closer. There was nowhere she could hide and get close enough to listen in, though she sensed the verbal exchange was not going well. She decided to intervene and see what response she got.

'Dick?'

Abbott swung round, as surprised to see her as she'd been to see him, though trying his best to hide it. Taking leave of him, the clerk wandered off. He didn't try and stop her, a sign that they had said all there was to say.

Abbott took a step forward, a guilty look on his face.

'Frank, what are you doing here?'

'You took the words right out of my mouth,' she said. 'I thought you were with the guv'nor interviewing our new witness.'

'What witness?'

Frankie's jaw almost locked as he confirmed her suspicion. 'Well, if you don't know, you've not been to the incident room, which means you've been given a job by Stone that I don't know about.'

'Is that a problem?'

'It is if it involves me.'

'It doesn't.'

'Not even remotely?'

Abbott stalled.

In her head, Frankie answered her own question. There could only be one reason why he was there. As a young couple approached, Abbott stepped aside, waiting for them to move away before continuing the conversation.

'You OK?' he said to Frankie. 'You seem on edge.'

'That's because I am. Now give.'

'There's nothing to give—'

'That's bullshit. Don't insult me, Dick. I'm not in the mood.'

'I can see that . . .' Tilting his head towards his right shoulder, he surveyed her warily. 'You going to have the gloves off with me now?'

'If I have to.'

'Then shouldn't we take it somewhere less public?'

Frankie scanned the busy corridor. 'Maybe we should.'

The police room was empty when they arrived. Abbott clicked the door shut and turned to face Frankie. She didn't say anything, just waited impatiently for the low-down on his discussion with Stone, her face set like granite. Only once had he lied to her in order to protect himself. The memory disturbed him. She could count on his honesty now. Whether she'd like it or not was another matter. If she carried on like this, she'd alienate herself from their boss and the rest of the MIT.

'Frank, I don't want to fall out with you—'

'Then don't. The boss called you last night, didn't he?'

'Yes. He asked me to do some digging. Fill in the gaps in Adams' background—'

'What gaps? I gave his background at the briefing.'

'I know—'

'So?'

'So what?'

'So, I don't like people going behind my back.'

'He's not. He's worried about you. That's all there was to it.'

'Bullshit! I wasn't born yesterday. He's undermining me—'

'No, he's not! Look, I understand why you're angry . . .' Abbott shifted his weight from one foot to the other. 'This is not what you think. C'mon, how long have we known each other?'

'Too bloody long.'

The comment stung. 'Look, whatever is eating the two of you is nowt to do with me. At your own admission, it'd been a while since you'd seen the IP, much less spoken to him. If you hadn't—'

'*If?*' She glared at him. 'I told you I hadn't. Same as I told Stone.'

'Fine. Then it stands to reason that the people he worked most closely with might know something you don't. Isn't that why you're here?' Abbott could see how hurt she was to have been left out of the loop. He was merely following orders. He hoped she'd realise that and drop the attitude . . .

She didn't.

'And Stone thought you'd be the best person for the job?' When he didn't respond, Frankie fired off another question. 'And he said what? "Keep shtum, this is between you and me", or did he have the balls to come right out with a clear-cut, "Don't tell Frankie."'

'What would you have me do, Frank? I'm new in and he's the boss—'

'Yeah, and I'm his 2ic.' Frankie studied the guilty expression Abbott was trying to mask. She wasn't happy. 'You should've backed me up.'

'I did . . . don't I always?' Abbott took a moment, fighting hard to control his rising temper, pissed off that she was questioning his loyalty. 'Can I help it if he thinks you're too close to Adams? He was adamant, Frank. Let's face it, he wasn't the one withholding information. He has good cause to be cautious over the stuff Wells found in the notebooks.'

'Yeah, stuff *you* said would all blow over—'

'Oh, gimme a break. And, while you're at it, give him one too. It's his neck on the line, not yours. You're being paranoid, you need to calm down and think this through.' Abbott had to convince her that her place as 2ic was safe and that everyone valued her, including him. 'Look, you didn't hear this from me—'

'Hear what?'

'Stone has your back.'

'You could've fooled me.'

'He has. After you left the incident room last night, we were delayed in the car park. Some idiot had blocked him in and I was trying to locate her in the station. While I was waiting for her, Bright arrived unexpectedly. I overheard every word of their conversation. Stone said nowt about Adams calling you, neither did he mention the photographs crime scene investigators found at his home.'

'He'd hardly shaft me while you were there, would he?'

'Is that what you think he's doing? You're wrong, Frank. He's covering for you, if only you had the sense to realise it.'

Frankie swept a hand through her hair and looked away.

Abbott could see how anxious and highly strung she was.

Understandable, given the fact that her professional and personal lives had collided in the worst way possible. He'd witnessed the same emotional response from her father when Joanna was murdered.

This was déjà vu.

Frankie took a deep breath. He hadn't yet won her over. Her mood was shifting in the right direction. 'Maybe next time you could warn me, eh?'

'There won't be a next time,' Abbott said. 'And do yourself a favour. Don't go shouting your mouth off when we get back to base. By the way, I found nothing of interest here, not from court or admin staff, press or the probation team. Whatever Adams was working on, he kept it to himself. We're wasting our time hanging around any longer.' He winked at her. 'Last one to Middle Earth buys lunch?' It was a game they played often, a game he always won.

Finally, she climbed down.

'You're on,' she said.

30

There was a lull in proceedings as she walked into the incident room shortly after Abbott arrived at Middle Earth. Despite her head start, he'd outdone her again, bypassing the mid-morning traffic, taking the back streets to avoid the snarl-up on the coast road. Her downcast expression had little to do with the fact that she was footing the bill for lunch or the mini-spat they'd had at the Crown Court. Over the years they'd had worse and survived. No, he suspected it was because she hadn't slept, a consequence of her row with Stone the day before. Dick hadn't a clue what was going on with those two. The sooner it ended, the better for everyone. She'd fucked up – and everyone knew it, especially her. It was hardly a hanging offence.

Frankie stood in the doorway, eyes scanning the room. All around her, detectives were downing tools, ending phone calls, handing out briefing notes, anxious to get going, their hard work finally bearing fruit. Across the room, Indira Sharma was standing at the photocopier, printing out a two-page report from the technical support team. Given her eager expression – the fact that they had been examining the contents of Chris Adams' computer files – she suspected the document contained evidence that might take the hunt for his killer a step closer to a result. Ordinarily, she'd have marched right over and asked for sight of it. Not this time. Today, she felt unworthy of the position that allowed her first dibs, not to mention guilty at letting her team down. She was dreading the briefing. David's office door opened. She took a deep breath.

*

David made a beeline for Frankie, handing her a note. Reluctantly, she took it, acting like the half sheet of paper was contaminated with a toxin that might kill her or, worse still, that she'd just been handed her marching orders. She didn't open it as she took her seat beside him, preferring to do so without an audience. Understandable, he supposed. He didn't know how she'd take his message, given that she'd bumped into Abbott at the Crown Court. Dick had warned him that she knew what he'd been up to and why. He hadn't dropped her in it. That wasn't his style. David's gut feeling was that his two detective sergeants had shared a harsh word or two.

He'd lay money on it.

His 2ic looked broken, isolated from the rest of the Murder Investigation Team. David wanted the old Frankie, not this one. The dynamic between them had shifted seismically since their row yesterday. The frostiness was obvious to all. Unable to handle it, he called for order, work being the thing that most floated her boat. Once she got involved in casework, her focus was absolute, as she'd proven last night after they had all gone home. She wasn't one to bear a grudge and neither was he.

There's always a first time.

He kept his input brief and to the point: a rundown of his interview with Eva Sokolov, which had taken far longer than he'd anticipated. 'She could so easily have been missed,' David said. 'And would have, had it not been for Frankie's intervention. We have her to thank for finding Eva – and Ryman for acting as unofficial translator.'

'Is she reliable?' Dick asked.

'Seems to be. I'm told she's in better shape this morning than she was when Frankie brought her in last night. She's undernourished, as you might expect. She was borderline hypothermic according to the doctor. Left to her own devices, she might not have survived the night.'

*

Frankie had been listening intently. There'd been a bluish tinge to Eva's lips and hands when they arrived at Middle Earth, which was why Frankie had asked the police surgeon to check her out. Though she wasn't being held in detention as such, Frankie didn't want the custody sergeant ending up with a stiff in the cells by morning. She was covering her back, following procedure, ensuring that if medical intervention was required, Eva would receive it. Her chances of finding a permanent hostel placement were slim. And Ryman's weren't any better; as a healthy male, he was way down the pecking order for a place to stay, a warm bed, a roof over his head, basic human needs. Plans to end the plight of people like them had failed miserably. And yet, across the country, local authority homes stood empty, boarded up and secure, keeping people out.

David was still talking: 'Eva gave a description of the man we're looking for. He was wearing a grey fleece with the letters HH on the front and a wide light stripe down both sleeves. We also have height and build. A big bugger, she said. If we can pick him up on CCTV, we'll be able to track his movements through the city and hopefully lift him.'

A detective at the rear of the room spoke up. 'Sounds like Armstrong to me. What was he wearing at PTMY?'

'White dress shirt, smart pants,' Frankie said. 'He's Mr Cool, a dedicated follower of fashion. Still, it's worth checking with Chris's mates to see if he had a bag with him during the drink-spilling incident.'

'Good call,' David said.

Frankie felt prickly. Was he patronising her or was she being oversensitive? 'I wouldn't hold your breath,' she said. 'Armstrong wouldn't be seen dead in fleece.'

'Every thug needs a handy change of clothes,' he said.

A chuckle went around the room like a Mexican wave, Frankie the only one who didn't appreciate the comment. 'There's no doubt that he's capable of offing someone,' she said. 'And Collingwood is of the opinion that whoever carried out the attack would've been covered in blood. Armstrong's not stupid enough to hold on to evidence that, if found in his possession, would implicate him in a murder investigation, is he? He'll have got rid, for sure.'

'Assuming he was involved.' Abbott's tone was flat.

Frankie had been watching him. He seemed troubled by the direction in which the briefing was going. He was right to remind the team that – while witnesses had placed Armstrong within feet of the victim shortly before his death – there wasn't a shred of evidence linking him to the crime scene.

'Was there something you wanted to add?' she asked.

'Are we any further forward with the weapon?'

Frankie knew the question was loaded. 'Why ask when you know the answer?'

'Collingwood said the knife may not have been manufactured in this country. Eva is Russian, Ryman ex-RAF, so he's probably travelled extensively. Just throwing it out there.' The implication that Frankie and David had been taken for a ride hung in the air.

David considered this for a moment. In interview, the rough sleepers had come across as genuine, and Frankie seemed to think they were, though Abbott had made a valid point. As a detective, he was sharper than the blade recklessly plunged into the victim's chest on Friday night.

Across the room, officers were exchanging glances, quietly whispering opinions, preparing for the enquiry to turn on its head. Frankie was deep in thought, her expression hard to read. She met David's gaze, a brief non-verbal message passing between them: have we been hoodwinked?

She kept her voice low. 'All options are on the table, right, guv?'

'Absolutely. Call Collingwood as soon as we're done. We need the provenance of that knife ASAP.'

'Will do.'

David could tell that she was holding back, taking Dick's theory on the chin, rather than rubbishing it to the team. Having built up a rapport with the witnesses – Ryman in particular – she appeared to be giving it serious consideration. Or was she hesitating because she'd already made a mistake and didn't want to make another? People acted differently when exposed to criticism. He hoped her loss of confidence wouldn't last and felt the need to support her. He parked the thought, raising his voice above the growing din.

'Any other thoughts?'

The statement reader, Rob Mather, looked up. 'Wouldn't it be hilarious if it turns out to be them and we'd given them bed and board last night . . .' He took a verbal swipe at Abbott. 'Maybe we'd all be better off without a social conscience, Dick.' Without waiting for a response, he switched his attention to Stone, his expression more serious. 'Tell me you didn't let them go, guv.'

'They weren't in custody.'

Mather placed a hand on either side of his head and formed his mouth into an O, feigning *The Scream*. 'I won't tell Bright if you don't.'

No one laughed.

David studied Frankie. She had no clever retort or putdown handy, though her face was set in a scowl. She was itching to put Mather in his place. So why didn't she? Restraint had never been part of her DNA. David concluded that she'd had her fill of angst and wasn't about to invite more. Mather was still winding people up. David turned to face him. 'Why would Ryman concoct such a story and bring Eva to our attention if either one was involved?'

'Maybe they're playing games,' Mather said. 'Let's face it, it wouldn't be the first time an eyewitness – a star witness even – has been found to be the perpetrator, would it?'

'It's never happened on my watch.' David shut him down. 'Shall we move on?'

Indira raised a hand. 'Forensics say there are no prints on the IP's car, barring his own. And Technical Support have finished analysing the data on the computer they found in the boot. I have their report here.'

'Why haven't I had sight of it?' David said.

Indira was blushing, as she always did when she was in trouble, or thought she was. David glanced at Frankie, almost a roll of the eyes. She shook her head: she hadn't seen the report the aide was alluding to.

'It just came in,' Indira said quickly. 'Minutes before you arrived. I'd have brought it to your attention sooner, only Frankie was out and about, and your door was closed. That usually means you don't want to be disturbed, guv. I knew you'd want copies available for the briefing.'

'And you thought you'd read it while you were doing that.' It wasn't a question.

Indira didn't know where to put herself.

Frankie jumped to her defence. 'It's called multi-tasking, guv. The way I taught her.'

She may as well have told David to back off and give the young constable a break. Indira handed them each a copy of the report and turned away, distributing more among the team who were taking the piss relentlessly. With her back turned, Frankie caught David's eye – Do you have to be so hard on her? – flicking her head towards Indira. The nod he gave in return was so slight, it was almost imperceptible.

Frankie smiled. 'PC Sharma?'

Indira swung round, her colour rising even further. 'Sarge?'

'To save time, perhaps you'd like to précis the document for us.'

She pointed at her chest. 'Me?'

'Why not?' David said. 'You're the only one who's read it.'

Now the team were laughing . . . and so was Frankie.

Indira wasn't sure whether the SIO was joking or being serious. Still, Frankie could see how proud she was to have been asked. It was unprecedented for one so new and inexperienced to address the Murder Investigation Team on a matter this important, a task that would normally fall to a more senior officer. Nevertheless, she was confident that Indira was up to the job. She couldn't help noticing that Mitch was none too happy about it. He'd been waiting for the opportunity to demonstrate his growth as a detective, also under Frankie's direct supervision. Tough. Served him right for handing Indira the task of photocopying.

'Get on with it,' Frankie said. 'We haven't got all day.'

Indira took the floor as copies of the document were passed around the room. 'The tech team have established that most of the stuff on the IP's computer is work-related, as you might expect. There were a few short stories and a number of features that have never appeared in print or online. Titles unrelated to criminal cases were cross-checked with the *Corchester Herald*. No joy—'

'No surprise there,' Frankie said. 'Fox didn't rate him.'

'They also checked Google, with the same results,' Indira added.

'Titles often change on publication,' David reminded her.

'The text wouldn't.' Frankie focused on Indira. 'Did they check that out?'

'They did. A word search on the net recovered nil results. None of the stories referred to a conspiracy theory – or anything like it. One file piqued their interest when set against what we already know.' Indira tapped the report in her hand. She was on a roll. 'On page two, about halfway down, you'll find reference to a woman called Nancy. No surname, but she could be the N we're looking for . . .'

David asked her to pass on his thanks to Technical Support.

'Actually, there's more, guv. Along with Nancy's name,

they found an attachment, an image of a woman who's been roughed up. It's timed and dated: 1945 hours, September twenty-fourth, 2016. And there's a cryptic note: *She's ready*. No idea what it means. Again, the image was cross-referenced with the *Herald* in case it had been used by them. It hadn't. There's a copy of the photograph in the report.'

Everyone turned to the page to study the image, including Frankie. It had been taken in bad light, inside what looked like a potting shed. Behind the subject, there was shelving covered in cobwebs, terracotta pots of all shapes and sizes and what looked like a rusting milk churn lying on its side.

She looked up. 'Surely Chris's images would be synced to his computer. If he'd taken that photograph, it would automatically download as soon as he connected to Wi-Fi.'

'We don't know that he did,' Indira said. 'Technical Support said it arrived via email, a fake address set up on a guerrilla mail account by someone who was technically savvy.'

David turned to Frankie. 'Was Adams that clued up?'

She shrugged. 'No idea.'

Indira sat down. 'Technical Support are still on it. Don't count on a result, guv. They're not confident they can trace it.'

Swearing under his breath, David took a moment to digest the new information, keeping his focus on PC Sharma. 'When you said, "no joy" what exactly did you mean? The articles weren't published, or they weren't found on the *Herald*'s database? It seems odd that his ideas wouldn't be filed there for future reference, doesn't it? A mate of mine is a writer. She says she never throws anything away she might use further down the line.'

'That's a good point.' Frankie glanced at the report. 'It's not specified here, guv.'

'Then maybe we need to clarify that.'

She was nodding. 'Leave it with me.'

'Maybe Adams was in the habit of working on a computer we haven't yet found,' Indira suggested.

'Good thinking.' Frankie smiled at her. 'If I was working on something secret, I'd use a public one, in a library perhaps.' She turned to look at David. 'Guv, we need a sequence of events linked to the time and date that photo was taken.'

'OK, get on to Fox. Find out what Chris was doing that day. Dick, phone the FLO. Get her to ask Susan if he was in the habit of using a library and, if so, which one. Mitch, get yourself down to Westgate Superbikes. Liam Wiley was close to the IP. Ask him if Adams ever mentioned anyone called Nancy.' He turned back to Frankie. 'I wonder if this woman is a whistle-blower.'

31

When he walked into the small café in the city centre where he'd agreed to meet Wells for breakfast, Ben was wearing noise-cancelling headphones that made him look more like an airport technician than her most recent recruit. She assumed he was listening to music, but his mouth was moving, so probably not, unless he was singing along. He stood in the doorway for a second, in another world, head bowed, blond hair flopping over his eyes. From across the room, she couldn't hear all of his side of the conversation, but his tone of voice was enough for her to make an educated guess as to who he was talking to. He'd been agitated when they spoke earlier. Frankie Oliver and his uncle had fallen out. They had probably fallen in by now. If that was the case, it had passed Ben by.

Ending his call, he walked towards her. Shrugging off a worn overcoat that had once been expensive, he unwound his scarf and slid on to the seat opposite. Placing his headset on the table, he picked up the menu and began to read, an avoidance tactic Wells had seen many times.

So that's how it was going to be.

'You're late,' she said.

'Sorry . . .' He looked up. 'I had to get the bus.'

'Still not speaking to David then?' Wells shook her head. 'Didn't I tell you to back off?'

No reply.

'If you'd taken my advice, you might have saved your bus fare. Either step off his toes, or you can kiss goodbye to the wheels he's buying you—'

'I don't give a shit. He's a nob.' Ben's mouth was pinched tight. 'He had a real go at me last night.'

'Sounds to me like you deserved it.'

'I did not! It's not funny either . . .' Ben was scowling and didn't pause for breath. 'Whatever Frankie did or said, she deserves better from him. Honestly, I thought he was bigger than that. I mean, what is his problem?'

'He's been good to you—'

'Until last night when he practically threw me out on my arse.'

Wells looked up as a waitress approached. 'He'll have a fry-up, a strong black coffee and white toast. Don't skimp on the butter. He likes to lay it on thick . . . especially today.'

Ben blushed.

Confused by the double entendre, the waitress glanced at him.

He gave a nod and she moved away.

'If it weren't for David, you wouldn't be sitting here with me,' Wells said. 'Remember that.'

'Like he's ever going to let me forget it. He encouraged me to get a job – in fact, he insisted on it. And now I'm working with you he's laying the law down, preventing me from doing it. He wants it all ways, just like my old man. For someone who doesn't rate himself as a parent, he's playing a blinder.'

Belinda laughed. 'In a way, he is your old man now, Ben. No offence, but for someone as switched on as you are normally, you're acting like a twelve-year-old stamping his feet because Dad wants to spoil his fun. The world doesn't revolve around you. People fall out. Get over it.'

'I was trying to help.'

'Going the wrong way about it, I imagine. Put his back up and you'll get nowhere. Take it from someone who knows.' Wells understood where he was coming from. Her relationship with her own father had always been difficult. The more she kicked against his idiotic view of the world, the more authoritarian he became, until she finally took off and he severed all contact. They hadn't spoken for years. 'You need to make it up to him.'

Ben scowled at her. 'Believe me, I tried.'

'Try harder.' Pushing away the remains of a Continental breakfast, Wells leaned forward, hooking a slender forefinger through the handle of a ridiculously large mug that had enough liquid inside to satisfy every customer in the room – and then some. She could hardly lift it with one hand. 'So, are you ready to quit bitching and do some work?'

Shamefaced, Ben took a long, deep breath. 'Yeah, rant over. Sorry . . . What are we doing today?'

'I'm following up on Chris Adams. I thought I might set you free for a day or two. It'll do you good to shadow someone else for a change.'

'What?' He looked crestfallen. 'You don't want me along?'

'It's not a two-person job—'

'That's bullshit! It was yesterday . . .'

Wells tuned out his objections as David's voice arrived in her head: 'His fascination with the IP – whose life seems, in many ways, to mirror his own – worries me, Belinda. His involvement in a case I'm investigating can't continue. It's not only incestuous, it's unhealthy. Frankie was once close to Adams. Bright knows it. If it comes out that my nephew is meddling in a police investigation, I'll be for the high jump.'

'Oh, I get it,' Ben said. 'He called you, didn't he? He wants me off the case.'

'I've made my decision,' Wells said.

He pleaded with her to change her mind. She didn't. An all-day breakfast landed on the table. He never touched it.

32

Frankie left the incident room as soon as the briefing was over. It had gone well, all things considered. She made her way to the locker room and sat down, taking a moment before she slipped David's note from her pocket. Taking another moment before unfolding. It was short and to the point:

> You, me, a drink tonight? Seven o'clock if that suits. No worries if you've other plans. D

Frankie felt herself tear up. He was as keen as she was to patch things up and return to normal. She texted him: **I'd like that. Seven is fine.**

A reply: **Great. Your shout.** ☺

Done, she texted.

They were going to be OK.

Buoyed by the prospect of a meeting with him outside the office environment, Frankie headed to her desk and logged on. She was about to begin typing when her mobile rang, her father's name appearing on screen. Momentarily, she considered ignoring it, then decided that would be rude. Scooping the phone off her desk, she pressed to receive.

'Hello, Dad, how's it going?'

'Better than yesterday. You actually took my call.'

'Is there a point to this conversation or am I hanging up?' She was smiling when she said it.

He chuckled. 'I know where you'll find Chris's bike.' He reeled off the address. 'If you're coming yourself, I'll get the kettle on.'

Frankie stared blankly at her computer screen. 'It'll need a SOCO's eye over it.' She never used the CSI acronym when talking to her old man. He hated the Americanism. If Scenes of Crime Officers were good enough for him . . .

'Did I teach you nothing?' he said. 'I'm offering you an excuse to leave Middle Earth and have coffee with your old man before you forget what he looks like.'

'And I need one, Dad, but we're short-staffed and I'm up to my eyes.'

'With what?'

Frankie suppressed a giggle, her tiredness melting away. 'Confidential enquiries. That's all you're getting. Thanks for the information. I appreciate it.' Promising to call round as soon as she was able, she ended the call. On the other side of the incident room, Mitchell was loitering near the murder wall. 'Mitch? Have you got a minute?'

'Sarge.' He walked towards her.

She handed him the address. 'My dad found the IP's bike.'

'How did he manage that?'

'Didn't ask . . . Not sure I want to know. Give the CSIs a call, will you? I need someone over there ASAP.'

'Does the guv'nor know?'

'He will when you tell him. By the way, is there any news on the Doc?'

'He hasn't been admitted to any hospital, dead or alive. That's positive news, I suppose.'

'OK, I'll tell Ryman.' Mitchell didn't move away.

Frankie waited. 'Was there something else?'

There was no smile accompanying his nod. 'I spoke to Helly Hansen. The fleece jacket Eva described the suspect wearing was an old one, circa late eighties, which means we have zero chance of IDing the person who purchased it.' He may as well have added, unless they're really old.

'Not necessarily,' she said.

'You think? I wasn't even born then. Were you?'

'Ever heard the saying: "need to know basis"? Get out of here before I do you for insubordination.'

He spoke over his shoulder as he put some distance between them. 'I'll take that as a yes then.'

Frankie's eraser hit the back of his head.

Chuckling, she concentrated on her computer. She loved working with Mitch, watching him gain in confidence, week in week out. He was an asset to any team: enthusiastic, motivated, nice to be around. Typing the name Nancy into the Missing Persons database, she pressed return, waiting for the page to load. Only one hit popped up: Nancy Carver. Widow. Reported missing, 25 December 2016.

The attached image seemed to get bigger the more she looked at it.

Frankie held up the photograph Technical Support had lifted from Chris Adams' computer, comparing it with the one on her screen. Though they looked similar, due to the injuries to Nancy's face, the DS couldn't swear that it was her. The file had a PNC marker, which meant that every force nationally would be aware of it. Reading through the digital version, she made extensive notes, then left her desk to find the hard copy. It took two hours to locate it.

In the incident room, Frankie sat down, telling the team she needed space and didn't want to be disturbed unless it was urgent, then opened the misper folder and began to read. What she found made her heart race. Pushing the file away, she hit her keyboard again, searching for the cryptic notes Wells had transcribed from Chris Adams' notebooks. Scrutinising the two, side by side on a split screen, excited and appalled her in equal measure. She picked up the phone.

David answered immediately.

'I found something,' she said. 'Fancy a walk?'

They hit the beach at Tynemouth, their second office. Lying snow had melted and the sun had come out. It was still freezing, the way David liked it, a cold wind blowing hard off the North Sea, angry waves crashing to land. Apart from a few dog-walkers, there was no one about. There had been no awkwardness in the car, but Frankie had kept her powder dry, making him wait until she'd properly gathered her thoughts. Pointing to a large piece of driftwood, she invited him to sit down, then took a seat beside him.

Slipping her sunglasses from her bag, she put them on.

David had finally run out of patience. 'Is this about the mysterious Nancy by any chance?' He'd registered the way she'd perked up during the meeting at the mention of a fresh lead and assumed she would be eager to pursue it.

'There's no flies on you, guv.'

'We'll find her, Frank.'

'I may already have.'

David looked at her, intrigued.

'I don't have conclusive proof, so don't get too excited.' Frankie pulled a bobble from her wrist, gathered up her hair and tied it in a ponytail to keep it from blowing across her face. 'Given your suggestion that Nancy might be a whistle-blower, coupled with the fact that someone with the initial N seemed to trigger Chris's radar, I thought it might be worth searching missing persons and analysing the two. I found one woman who fits the bill.'

'Name?'

'Nancy Carver. The majority of Chris's notes were dated and so is the photograph the techies found on his computer. The woman in that photo is pretty bashed up, but I think it's her. The facial injuries look fresh, so I reckon the assault must have happened on or shortly before September twenty-fourth last year. By November, Chris was excited – or possibly horrified – by the gross breach of trust he was investigating. If you remember, he was still waiting for specifics in December. On Christmas Day, Nancy was reported missing. The timeline fits, David. Whether or not it's connected to our murder case is another matter.'

'Who reported her missing?

'Her son, James.'

'JC?'

'Very good! Except he's as Geordie as you and I.'

'Says who?'

Frankie narrowed her eyes. 'I've done my homework.'

David grinned. 'Just checking.'

'Anyway James raised the alarm when she didn't turn up for dinner. He called her several times and got no answer. When he went over to check on her, a stranger answered the door. Nancy had sold up and cleared off at the end of October. Bizarrely, he had no idea she'd moved, and neither did his sister. They'd had several phone conversations over the intervening weeks and months, and yet Nancy had failed to mention it.'

For the first time since he'd launched the enquiry, David felt adrenalin pumping through his veins. 'What checks were done?'

'They were low key initially. She wasn't a priority case—'

'Why?'

'She'd told her former neighbours that she was moving away and wanted a fresh start. They reported that she was happy about it, though they were surprised that she left no forwarding address. They had lived next door to her for fifteen years.'

'Presumably, this was fed back to her children.'

'Yes. Nancy's daughter was more willing to accept that her mother might have chosen to bugger off and do her own thing. Rachel told investigators that her mum hadn't been the same since her father passed away in 2010. The son, James, disagreed, insisting that something had happened to her, that she wasn't the sort to abandon her family and take off. She doted on her grandkids, his kids.'

'Corroborated by the neighbours?'

'Friends too. James didn't appreciate being told that people just upped sticks and left sometimes. Consequently, more checks were carried out. Officers traced Nancy to a furnished let in Blanchland via a trawl of the electoral register. They received no reply at the door. Subsequent visits drew a blank. She'd paid her rent upfront until the end of December. Our lot visited her workplace and were stymied there too. She'd handed in her notice – more proof, if it were needed, of her intent to make changes. There's a copy of her handwritten resignation letter in the report dated the second of December.'

'Verified by the family?'

'And her employer.' Frankie pulled her collar up against the biting wind, her attention drifting fleetingly to the open sea and beyond to the horizon. 'The case was downgraded further when it transpired that Nancy had applied for a new passport and a working visa for the States. Rachel said it had always been her dream to go there and that her late father would've approved. Obviously, James had to accept this, though he wasn't happy about it. I reckon she was planning to spend Christmas with her family and then move abroad when her rent was due on January first.'

'The case was written off?'

'As much as these things ever are. She's still logged as a missing person, but no one is actively looking for her. There was no suggestion of foul play.'

'Until now.'

'Precisely. Chris had no contact from N over the Christmas holidays. Understandable if she was with her family, only we know she wasn't. By January, he started to get worried. After that there's no mention of her in his notebooks until June when he writes "Unable to proceed"—'

'Because she's no longer in the country,' David said.

Frankie's voice broke as she uttered, 'Or worse.'

David went quiet. There was something bothering him, a lingering doubt. 'Chris's notes indicated a large target group, running into hundreds or thousands, of what we don't yet know. I thought it might be human trafficking or similar—'

'So did I, but if Nancy Carver is N, I think it more likely that we're talking about a different demographic. She worked in an upmarket private residential home and had done since her husband died. She was a senior care manager who, by all accounts, loved her job. An ageing population is a huge issue across the pond, as it is here. There are job opportunities over there for anyone interested. Maybe that's what drew her to America, though I'm beginning to think she might not have made it. I suspect she was running away – and not from her family—'

'Whoa, back up. You think the numbers referred to senior citizens?'

'Or the sheer volume of care homes nationally. Without access to Chris's investigative notes, we're screwed. If Nancy *was* his informant and someone was trying to silence her, what else would she be talking about? If we can ID her as the woman in that picture, then it's feasible that Chris was looking into the wholesale exploitation of the elderly.'

'For fuck's sake.'

'I know . . .' Frankie locked eyes with him. His nan had meant a lot to him. She felt the same way about her own grandparents. 'I can't bear to think about it either, and if his notes are anything to go by, neither could Chris. I told you before, he was kind and caring, a champion of the underdog. The last entry Wells pulled out of his notebooks suggested he was lost, unsure where to go next. I reckon his call to me was a last resort, a cry for help that I stupidly ignored. If that turns out to be the case, I'll never forgive myself.'

'You couldn't have predicted this,' David said. 'No one could.'

'That doesn't make it any easier to take.' She looked away, a moment of heartbreak and sorrow.

Resting a hand on her arm, David gave it a gentle squeeze. 'You did good today, Frank. You should be proud. If your theory is right, it represents a major breakthrough for us.' As she turned to face him, he took his hand away. 'Dinner's on me tonight. You earned it.'

33

Back at the office, David updated the troops while Frankie contacted the Passport Office to request a copy of Nancy Carver's passport application. The document had been paid for and processed, sent out to her Blanchland address on 15 December 2016. Scans of both the passport and application arrived in Frankie's inbox minutes later. She made copies for the team, asking every MIT detective to examine the photo ID independently.

All but one agreed that it was her.

David withdrew to his office, taking Frankie with him. 'We need to talk to the family,' he said. 'Question is: son or daughter?'

'Her son was described in the misper report as, quote, "over-emotional at the time she disappeared, bordering on unpleasant", unquote. The description irked me when I read it. What the fuck did they expect? His mum went missing at Christmas. Her presents were still lying under his goddamn tree. I can't imagine anything worse, can you?'

David shook his head. 'Given her ability to see the bigger picture, maybe Nancy's daughter should be our next port of call. It's cowardly, I know, but maybe she'd be better placed to break the news to her brother.'

'I agree. Her married name is Hooper.' Frankie held up a note. 'I have the address.'

Rachel Hooper lived in a suburban housing estate on the western edge of the city, an unremarkable semi-detached home with a small front lawn overlooking a kids' play area where the remnants of several snowmen of varying sizes were beginning to melt.

Halfway up the garden path, Frankie's mobile rang.

She stopped walking, a worried glance over her shoulder. 'It's Dick.'

'Ignore it.'

'You think? He knows where we are.'

'Well, make it quick and tell him his timing is crap.'

Frankie pressed to answer. 'Dick, this had better be good.'

'Are you there yet?'

'We're standing in the front garden, man. What is it?'

'An urgent call from the Passport Office. It completely threw me.'

Frankie listened carefully to what he had to say, putting a hand out to prevent David from approaching the house. He waited, tapping his watch impatiently. She nodded her understanding.

Abbott was still talking.

'Jesus!' she said. 'OK, I'll tell him. Thanks for the heads-up.' Frankie hung up.

'Tell me what?' David asked.

Too late.

The front door opened. A woman appeared on the threshold, stick thin, with an oval face and sharp green eyes. There was no doubt in David's mind that she was the woman they had come to see.

'You lost?' she said. 'Doesn't surprise me. It happens all the time. This estate is like a bloody maze.'

The SIO was on the back foot, with no opportunity to question Frankie about the call from Abbott. Without looking at his 2ic, he sensed her hesitation. Whatever Dick had said to her wasn't good news, the word 'Jesus' a dead giveaway. Now they had been discovered in the garden, David had no choice but to push on.

He took a step forward.

'We're looking for Rachel Hooper.' He knew he'd already found her. She was the double of her mother.

'Then you're in luck,' she said.

'Hello, Rachel. I'm Detective Chief Inspector David Stone and this is DS Frankie Oliver.' Names and ranks would suffice. David had no wish to add to the woman's distress before they got inside. He pointed into the hallway. 'May we come in for a moment? We'd like to talk to you.'

A flash of anxiety. 'Yes, of course.' Rachel showed them into the kitchen and turned to face them. 'Would you mind talking in here? My husband is asleep on the sofa. He's recovering from a long bout of pneumonia. It's taken him months to get out of bed. I'd rather not send him back there.'

'I'm sorry to hear that,' David said. 'In here is perfect.'

'Would you like some tea, coffee?'

'We're fine, thanks.'

Declining refreshments went with the job. For some reason the general public almost always offered it, even in the most bizarre circumstances: having been informed of a loved one's accidental death or the arrest of a family member; to give the guilty thinking time; and, for the majority, as a delaying tactic when faced with information they didn't want to hear. David had Rachel pegged in the latter category. He couldn't imagine what was going through her mind.

He was about to get started, when she said, 'I'll pop the kettle on in case you change your mind.' She went to the sink, turned on the tap and spoke with her back to them as she filled the kettle, then transferred it to the stove and lit the burner beneath it.

She walked towards them, inviting them to sit, pulling out a chair for herself at the head of the table. The *Journal* was lying open in front of her, a cryptic crossword half done. 'I get very few visitors,' she said. 'Most people assume I'm at work. Those that know I'm not, think I'm too busy looking after Stan to socialise. How can I help you?'

'DS Oliver and I are investigating the death of a young man in Newcastle City Centre on Friday night.'

Momentarily, Rachel's eyes settled on the newspaper. 'I read about it. Poor lad.' She paused. 'I'm sorry, but what has that to do with me? I don't know him. At least, I don't think I do.'

David chose his words carefully. 'Among his possessions was the photograph of a woman we believe to be your mother.' He took in Rachel's shocked expression. 'I'll be honest with you, Rachel. We don't yet know how one thing fits with the other, or even if the two incidents are connected. As a result of what we found, we're looking again at your mother's disappearance.'

'I'm sorry?' Confusion reigned. 'There must be some mistake. She's out of the country . . . in America. I haven't spoken to her. Your lot seemed to think she wanted out. I respected that and didn't try to find her, unlike my brother, James. He still thinks something awful happened to her—' She stopped talking abruptly, eyes homing in on Frankie, the most combative expression David had ever seen from a potential witness.

He glanced at his 2ic.

For a moment there was deadlock. Total silence. David had seen that look on Frankie's face before. She was getting ready to deliver a blow he knew would knock Rachel Hooper sideways.

Guaranteed.

'Rachel, your mother isn't in America. I'm sorry to have to tell you that urgent enquiries have been made. Immigration officials have confirmed that there is no record of her entering the United States since—'

'No! There must be some mistake, an admin error or something.'

Hoping she was right, David was about to offer to have them check again.

Frankie got in first. 'I wish I could give you better news, but I'm afraid that's impossible. The passport she applied for was returned to the Passport Office by her landlord. Her rent had been due on January first. He gave her a few weeks' grace, then went to the flat and let himself in. I gather he found the envelope containing the passport unopened on the mat. I'm so sorry.'

The whistle on the old-fashioned kettle was deafening. Monotone. Like a flatlining heart monitor. Rachel stood up and turned away, grabbing hold of the kitchen bench to steady herself as she muted the offending noise. Her head went down. Her shoulders shook.

She was weeping uncontrollably.

With her back turned, Frankie mouthed the word 'sorry' to David, compassion flooding her face. He rolled his eyes – not your fault – the photograph of Nancy burning a hole in his breast pocket. Rachel turned to face them, wiping her eyes, apologising for her loss of control.

'Does James know?' she asked.

'Not yet. We thought it best to approach you first.'

Nancy pulled a paper tissue from her sleeve, blew her nose and sat down at the kitchen table, looking up at the detectives.

'Would you like me to call him?' Frankie said.

'No.'

David took over. 'Rachel, I have to tell you that the woman in the photograph I referred to has been badly assaulted. The image is distressing to look at, but we need a positive ID. Would you be willing to look at it? Or would you rather we showed it to another family member, if not James then someone else—'

'No, if anyone is going to see it, it should be me. James will go to pieces. He's sensitive. I'll do it.'

David slipped the image from his pocket and passed it to her.

A sob was all the confirmation they needed.

34

The major incident room was fuller than it had been of late, but there were several strangers working alongside the regular team members. Given the MIT's depleted human resources, Bright had commandeered detectives from other teams less stretched. Not all met Frankie's approval. One was utter rubbish, someone recently transferred to the CID whose father happened to be a superintendent. Frankie resented that. No one had ever done her any favours when she followed her old man into the job. She wanted officers of high calibre, not those who felt entitled. She needed detectives who were able to make decisions when she wasn't around to do it for them. She'd briefed them all herself, delegating the most urgent enquiries to Dick and Mitch, the grunt work to the incomers. They had received the message loud and clear: heads down or close the door on your way out.

Seconds turned to minutes, minutes to hours, everyone pulling Nancy Carver's life apart. Her bank account was used to purchase goods on 1 December 2016: Christmas gifts for her grandsons, a toy truck from Fenwick's Northumberland Street store, a trampoline from John Lewis online, both delivered to her son's address in readiness for Christmas. Would she have bothered, if she'd known she'd never see them opened or enjoyed? Given the fact that she doted on her grandsons, Frankie found it hard to believe that she'd bunk off, cutting all contact and without saying a word.

Dick approached, interrupting her train of thought, a downcast expression on his face. 'Nancy's phone went dead on the second of December last year.'

'Then we're looking for a body.'

'Probably.'

'I cannot believe that bank and phone checks weren't a priority action when she went missing.'

'She was an adult, Frank. You said yourself, all the signs pointed to her upping sticks of her own free will, setting off on a new adventure. And don't forget, the daughter didn't see anything odd in her moving away without telling anyone where she'd gone. It's no wonder the missing persons report got filed; they came to the conclusion that she didn't want to be found.'

'I know the feeling,' Frankie carped.

'Me too, but you know what it's like—'

'Yeah, I also know how it should be.' Her tone was laced with contempt. 'If the nominated officer had done his fucking job properly, her family might not have been left in limbo wondering why she'd pissed off without saying goodbye. I bet you a pound to a penny she was dead by then.'

She glanced over Dick's shoulder. David waved at her as he left the incident room bound for HQ, a meeting with the head of CID. As the double doors swung shut behind him, she refocused on Abbott.

'Read this.'

'What is it?'

'It's a breakdown of Nancy's bank transactions. The account has been used regularly since she went missing, the maximum amount withdrawn from cash machines in various locations in and around London – almost thirty grand—'

'Maybe she'd decided that America was too far away.'

'Or maybe she was forced to hand over her PIN and someone is helping themselves to the proceeds of her house sale, taking it little by little so as not to alert bank security. Thieving bastards. If she was still alive and living in the south, why hasn't she been to see her family?'

'I can't answer that.'

Frankie could.

She pointed to the A4 sheet in his hand. 'There are no bank

transactions for services: gas, electricity, TV licence on that sheet. Not one. No rent, hotel or garage bills being paid, no new phone contract. And before you say she could be a Pay As You Go customer, consider this. Before she went missing, she paid everything by Direct Debit, everything—'

'Hold on a minute, Frank.' Dick walked over to his desk and plucked a report out of his in-tray, 'Nancy taxed her car online at the end of November 2016 – not something you'd do if you're planning to sell up and go abroad. The duty was due on December first—'

'The vehicle was road legal until the beginning of this month?'

He nodded. 'Like I say, she could have had a change of heart. I know for a fact that the car wasn't transferred to another keeper or it would have been registered with the DVLA. Her Fiat was an old banger, a rust-bucket worth nowt according to her daughter. For all we know, she could still be mobile, moving around, using cash to pay her bills.'

'I'd love to believe that, Dick. I really would. But I can't see it, can you?' He wasn't as hopeful as he was making out. 'Get on to Nancy's service provider. I want the exact location of where her phone was when it went dead. Quick as you can. And while we're on the subject of phones, what's the SP on Chris's device? It's high time his service provider updated us—'

'They did, that's the other thing I was going to tell you. Chris made umpteen calls to Nancy's number starting late September last year, continuing up to and including the eve of his death. None were answered. If he was so worried about her, why didn't he report it to us?'

'Yeah, well he tried, didn't he?' Frankie took a moment. 'I can't imagine why he'd wait months to do it, though.'

'Maybe he thought she'd got cold feet. She never reported the assault, I checked. In fact, she's not in the system in any capacity. Chris had access to records too, don't forget. At the very least, he'd have known she hadn't pursued her attacker through the courts.'

Frankie palmed her brow, her other hand on her hip. 'What a mess.'

'There could be any number of reasons why he didn't involve you earlier. Maybe she'd sworn him to secrecy and he didn't feel he could break a confidence.'

'Or maybe she didn't trust the police to investigate it properly.' There was a hard edge to Frankie's voice. 'If her disappearance is anything to go by, she'd be right. As depressing as it sounds, we're not the first choice any more. Public perception has shifted. Trial by media is the name of the game nowadays. It has more impact. Journalists have taken over.'

'They don't know they're born,' Dick said. 'They can ask their poxy questions off-camera, interview anyone they like and shout loudly about it in the press without fear of reprisals or complaint. They're not hog-tied by PACE the way we are.' He was referring to the Police and Criminal Evidence Act, a piece of legislation that regulated police powers and safe-guarded public rights.

'You may not like it, but PACE is a good thing, even if it doesn't always feel that way.'

'Keep telling yourself that, Frank. If Nancy Carver thought that Chris Adams would get results where we wouldn't, she was woefully mistaken. They both were.'

She didn't argue. 'Do we know who called Chris when he was standing in the queue at the ATM?'

'We have a number. I'm about to chase it up.'

'I won't hold my breath.'

'A wise move. We have zero chance of it taking us anywhere.' Abbott walked away in a strop.

Frankie watched him go. He was rarely this despondent. He was tired. They all were. She didn't blame him for a moment of despair, any more than she blamed Nancy Carver for not reporting the assault or Chris Adams for not coming forward.

They were a pair of amateurs, doing what they thought was right.

Whatever they had got themselves into, the DS was convinced it had claimed both their lives.

35

Stone left force headquarters feeling bruised following a lively exchange with Bright. Reporters had been bending the ear of the Press Office, screaming for a result or, failing that, a detailed update. His predecessor was in the habit of providing one. In no uncertain terms, David had been told to pull his finger out.

As he drove to Middle Earth, he grew more and more convinced that he'd find answers to Chris Adams' murder if he kept his focus on Nancy Carver. When he got back to base, he bypassed everyone in the incident room, including Frankie, and went straight to his office to lick his wounds.

Pouring himself a cup of strong black coffee, he sat down at his desk and logged on to the internet, typing in the name of the residential and nursing home where Nancy worked. According to the home page, Bastle View was privately owned, an eighteenth-century Grade II listed country estate belonging to local landowner Sir Giles Bradbury, a third-generation financier.

The advertising copy detailing what residents could expect was slick and seductive. Those who could afford it would enjoy far-reaching views over the tranquil Redesdale Valley, an idyllic setting for the elderly and infirm . . . unless there was something sinister going on inside.

David studied a photograph of the impressive grand entrance hall. Portraits – or copies of oil paintings, he couldn't tell which – lined the walls of a curved staircase, presumably of Bradbury's ancestral line. David wondered if the present generation retained quarters there, a wing, perhaps, separated from the main house.

Somehow, he didn't think so.

'Jesus!' he whispered under his breath.

The annual fee was astronomical. Only the well-to-do need apply. The accommodation was divided between retirement apartments and cottages, depending on the level of care required, with an on-site manager to provide support, and a range of activities on offer for those who cared to socialise with other residents: coffee mornings, arts, crafts and music groups and regular trips to the theatre and places of interest.

If it sounded too good to be true, it probably was.

He sank into his chair, considering the plight of those who were dependent on others for their care. Countrywide, offences against the elderly were on the rise – fleecing, swindling, scamming – so much of it going on that police and crime commissioners were calling for them to be recorded as hate crimes, along with the other five protected categories: disability, gender reassignment, race, religion and sexual orientation.

David needed to pay the home a visit.

Checking his watch, he decided to put it off till morning. It was almost six o'clock. The return journey would take at least two hours, more time than he currently had available. Besides, there was nothing to be gained from questioning the night staff. He wanted eyes on the managers, who, he assumed, would only be around during the day.

He picked up the phone and made a dinner reservation for seven thirty in one of Frankie's favourite eateries. She deserved some downtime and he didn't want to disappoint her when she'd worked so hard to progress the case. It was because of her diligence that they were looking at Nancy Carver and he wanted her along when he visited Bastle View. They would go together first thing in the morning.

36

Frankie and David enjoyed each other's company over a bottle of red. It was good to be away from the oppressive atmosphere of the incident room at Middle Earth, free of the awkwardness that had dogged them recently. There was no mention of the phone call she'd received from Chris. Grateful for that, Frankie found herself relaxing, her sense of humour returning. It was shaping up to be quite a night, two mates enjoying each other's company as if their falling out had never happened.

David ate as though he couldn't remember when he'd last been fed. In the hour before they had left the office, the incident room had been a hive of activity as, one by one, the actions he'd delegated at the briefing were completed and passed to the receiver, Pam Bond, AKA 007. The investigation had suddenly come alive.

Sensing his gaze halfway through their meal, Frankie looked up from her food, then down at her clean silk shirt, expecting to see a dribble of tarragon-infused hollandaise. Nothing there. She wiped her mouth on a white linen serviette. Nothing there either.

'What?' she said, picking up her wine.

'Are you sure about Eva and Ryman?' he asked.

She eyed him pointedly over the rim of her glass. 'I thought you said no shop talk.' On the journey to the restaurant, he'd told her that he wanted her to take the weight off, have some fun, and leave the investigation behind. Fat chance now she'd let her guard down.

'You're right, forget it.'

'Lighten up, man. I was joking! You know I never switch off. Besides, my old man says it's compulsory when you're in the middle of a murder investigation. Or, in his case, even when you're not.' She grinned, though it pained her to think that her father couldn't enjoy his retirement like his peers. He quizzed her relentlessly about her job, unable to leave the past behind.

David pushed his plate away. 'So, do I get an answer?'

She shrugged a shoulder. 'What do you think?'

'I reckon they're genuine but Dick has reservations.'

Frankie forked her last slice of beef fillet, happy that he'd come down on the side of the homeless. 'We've met them, David. Dick hasn't. He's bound to be wary. By his own admission, Ryman was very close to the crime scene. That doesn't make him guilty of murder. He's a top bloke, like you . . . on a good day.'

'You have no misgivings?'

'About you? Plenty. Ryman, no.'

He laughed.

She did too, except hers was forced. Disquieting snippets of a recent conversation replayed in her head – a flash of doubt she'd experienced when treating Ryman to free nosh in Dabbawal. *This is not you wasting police time trying to find her a crib for the night, is it, Sarge? You think I'm dicking you around?* Was he? Frankie didn't want to believe it – she liked him – but anything was possible. She'd been lied to before by people she'd grown to trust. When it came down to it, what did she know about him?

'You don't seem too sure,' David said.

'I had no idea I was so transparent.'

'I'm a mind reader.'

'OK, so there was a moment when I doubted him, but if Ryman intended to rob someone he'd have picked a better spot with direct line of sight to the NatWest cash machines. From where he was sitting, he couldn't have seen what was going on in the queue or pick out anyone dispensing enough cash to warrant a serious assault. I checked.'

'Unless he'd moved a few yards from his usual doorway. He's a big man too.'

'Admittedly, but so is the Tank.' Frankie knew that her guv'nor was playing Devil's advocate and felt the need to support her point of view. 'Armstrong constructed an alibi he knows we won't disprove. His dodgy mates who work the door at the Escape nightclub saw to that. Dick said they corroborated his account word for word. They're in his pocket. No question. And Armstrong had motive too, don't forget. No, what concerned me when I questioned Ryman, the second time around, was how far he might go to protect Eva Sokolov.' An image of that eerie space, tucked away at the rear of Plummer Tower, arrived in her head. The makeshift shelter the Russian had built to protect herself against harsh winter nights more akin to Siberia than the north-east of England. 'I was there when he woke her up, David. She was scared stiff. Genuinely scared, not some joker trying it on with the police.'

They danced around the subject for another half hour, finishing a delicious dinner and ordering coffee before the conversation inevitably wound its way back to work, firstly to Chris Adams and what he'd been up to that may or may not have led to his death and then to Nancy Carver and whether the two of them were in cahoots to expose fraudsters targeting the vulnerable on 'an industrial scale', if Chris's notebooks were to be believed.

A sickening thought.

Frankie hadn't spoken for a good few minutes. She was staring into her wine glass, a serious expression on her face, probably sifting the evidence, trying to piece together a credible scenario, a plan of action to take them forward. David couldn't read minds but he could see the wheels turning in her head. She looked up, a question on her lips. 'Can I say something?'

'Fire away. You don't usually ask for permission.'

She made a face. 'I was thinking—'

'Does it hurt?'

'Sometimes.' She grinned. 'Seriously though, when we began the investigation we were looking to Fox for answers and he wasn't forthcoming. We've been working on the assumption that he's telling the truth, that he knew nothing about a scoop, that he and Chris just didn't get on, a clash of personalities. What if there's more to it than that? What if Fox is part of the problem?'

'You're suggesting a cover-up?'

'I don't know. Maybe I've been watching too many conspiracy movies. Maybe I should take up origami.'

Despite the joke, David could see that she still had her investigator's hat on. 'Go on. Run it by me.'

She leaned closer. 'Fox said that Chris wanted his name above the fold, that he wasn't good enough to achieve it. What if he was getting too close to something his editor didn't want him meddling in? I've got a bad feeling about him.'

'Hold on a minute, Frank. It makes no sense that he'd turn down the opportunity to expose abuse of the elderly. Why would he pass up on the chance to lead with an article that might go viral and save his failing newspaper? He may be an exacting boss—'

'He's a prat.'

'In your opinion.'

'Wells doesn't like him. You trust her instincts . . . even if you don't trust mine.'

David studied her across the table and didn't respond right away. When she looked away, he knew he'd lost her. Shame. They spent so little time together outside of work, he didn't want to spoil the moment. Her intuition was sound, but a gut feeling wasn't worth squat without hard evidence.

She knew that.

'Sleep on it,' he said. 'If you think it worth pursuing, tackle him on it in the morning.'

'I intend to.' She still wasn't present.

Slipping her phone from her pocket, she checked the screen. It was unlike her to do that when she was off-duty in a social setting. It irked him to think that he didn't have her full attention.

'Am I keeping you from something?' he asked.

'Yeah . . .' At last, a smile. 'I always date two at a time. Doesn't everyone?'

'Only two? You're missing out,' he teased. 'Is that what this is, a date?'

Frankie grinned. 'You were the one sending secret notes.'

What she said next knocked him for six.

'We should go.'

David checked his watch. 'It's early . . . Frankie, I wasn't being serious—'

'Neither was I. You want an Andrea Corr doppelganger. I'm looking for someone a bit more edgy.'

'What?'

'Doesn't matter.' She held up her mobile. 'I'm worried about Mitch. He still hasn't checked in.'

'He has . . .' David felt himself relax, pleased that he'd come up with a reason to hang out with her longer. 'Sorry, I meant to tell you. It slipped my mind. I saw him in the gents before we left the office.'

'And?'

He gave Frankie side-eyes. 'He had quite a conversation with your man Wiley.'

'Did he know about Nancy Carver?'

'No.'

'Bugger.' Frankie took a sip of her drink. 'There's no logic to any of this. Don't you find it odd that Chris didn't mention her or his big story and yet he confided in Wiley on personal matters – i.e. me?'

'Not now I'm in possession of all the facts, no.'

'What facts?'

David topped up her glass before answering. He had information to share, some of it of a delicate nature that she could take one of two ways. He wasn't sure which way she'd jump. He was wondering how to handle it and whether he should disclose it in such a public place or wait until they were on their way home.

She was waiting for a response.

Placing the bottle on the table, he dropped his voice to avoid being overheard, intending to share the delicate stuff first. 'Would it surprise you to learn that Wiley would prefer me to you.'

'What?' Her eyes widened. 'He's on the other bus?'

David threw her a nod.

'No chance for me then.'

Now David understood.

'Ha!' He grinned. 'You might not float Wiley's boat, but he *really* liked Mitch. He made it obvious that he was both available and open to offers. Mitch was cool with it. Just as well we didn't send Mather, eh?'

Frankie stifled a grin. 'Now there's a complaint waiting to happen!'

'Can you see the logic now?' David could tell she wasn't yet following his chain of thought. 'I have a theory, if you're interested.'

'I'm not sure I am. Since when is a witness's sexual preference relevant to a murder investigation?'

'It's not – and I can't prove any of this – but Wiley broke down when he talked to Mitch. Apparently, he had a thing for our victim – unrequited. I think Chris fed him a story about you to make it clear their relationship was only ever going to be platonic.'

Frankie looked away, a picture of Wiley floating into her head. She remembered her first impression of him, sitting astride his motorcycle, the effect he had on her. He didn't fit the stereotype of a homosexual man and, stupidly, she'd made assumptions about him based on what she saw, pegging him as straight. Surprising, when her sister was in a relationship with Andrea, her best friend and police colleague. They hardly fit the profile either. Frankie had seen the odd looks they received when introducing themselves as partners. Things had moved on for those in same-sex relationships, but not fast enough. In many walks of life, there was still a stigma attached to it.

You were the one.

Frankie said: 'Now you mention it, Wiley's attitude towards me was laced with resentment. I assumed he'd formed the impression that I was a cruel bitch, ignoring Chris's overtures.'

'Even though there were none?'

'Except in his head. Like I told you, I was completely blindsided by Wiley's revelation, trying to work out what to do about it. I didn't know how you'd take it.'

David dropped his head on one side. 'Is that how you see me, as an ogre?'

'No! Of course not.'

'What then?'

She didn't answer.

'I think it was jealousy rather than resentment you encountered, Frank. Wiley could never have Chris because he'd been led to believe that you were standing in his way. Does it make you feel any better, knowing the truth?'

'A little.' She changed the subject. 'Did Mitch ask if he knew where Chris was a week past Saturday?'

A nod. 'They rode to Keswick for the day. Chris had no injury. They got back late, around half ten. Susan confirmed it. As we know, she doesn't like him riding, especially in the dark, so she waited up. She saw no injury when he arrived home. At eleven thirty next day, he took his kit and headed out to footy but didn't show at the ground. He turned up at home at around three forty-five bruised and with a swollen eye, lied to his mother and again to Fox when he turned up for work on Monday morning.'

'So, he was definitely injured on Sunday—'

'Yes. Taking his kit wasn't a ruse, Frank. He *was* intending to play football. I'm certain of that. He switched arrangements at the last minute.'

'How can you be so sure?'

'The ANPR picked up his motorcycle at eleven forty-three travelling north-west on the A696 towards Belsay where he plays football. He doesn't stop. He carries on towards Otterburn and Jedburgh, then they lose him. He must've turned off before the Scottish border on one of the minor roads where there are no cameras. ANPR clocked him again travelling south-east at around three fifteen.'

'Jesus. He could've been anywhere.'

'Not quite. I suspect someone lured him to a point in the central belt of the borders, otherwise he'd have taken a faster route home. If he'd gone towards the coast, he'd have travelled back via the A1. If he'd gone further west, he'd have used the A69.'

'If he remained in the central belt, there's little chance that we'll be able to identify exactly where he went.'

'Precisely. Dick has been through his bank accounts. Chris bought nothing that day on his bank card, not even petrol. He could have paid cash, of course, but it'll take months to canvass every village and hamlet in that area.'

'And he wasn't followed?'

David shook his head. 'That Sunday the A696 was practically empty.'

Frankie picked up her bag, pulling out the call list supplied by Chris's service provider. She scanned the page for the date in question and looked up. 'He received a call from an unregistered mobile at eleven forty-five. The last call he'd received was from that same unregistered number minutes before he accessed the ATM, the call Fireman Sam overheard. Minutes later the phone went dead.'

37

The Bastle View Residential Nursing Home was surrounded by extensive gardens, lakes and woodland. Although the SIO had shown Abbott the images in the brochure he'd found online, they couldn't compare with the actual view of the building as his car snaked its way around a bend, revealing a glimpse of the house through poplar trees lining the long driveway. The snow was still on the ground here, deep in Northumberland, small drifts visible against a stone wall that wrapped itself around the property.

'Wow!' Abbott glanced at DC Mitchell. 'How stunning is that?'

Mitch couldn't take his eyes off it. 'Am I too young to put my name down?'

Abbott chuckled. 'Keep playing the lottery, son.'

The smiles slid off their faces as they remembered why they were there. Until they found further evidence, at best the Murder Investigation Team were working on a strong suspicion that all was not well behind the magnificent facade. They had no hard evidence, which was why Frankie had suggested they go in undercover, acting as father and son, prospective clients looking to place a well-heeled family member there.

'What the fuck!' Mitch yelled. 'Back up!'

Responding to the DC's warning, Abbott braked hard, nearly standing his car on its end. Peering through a gap in the trees, he couldn't believe his eyes. Investigative journalist, Belinda Wells was exiting the front door, dressed to kill in a suit and high heels. Usually she was strictly jeans and sneakers. Dick could think of only one reason for the change . . .

She was here incognito.

He watched her descend the stone steps, shoulders straight,

head held high, like a woman with an inflated opinion of her own importance. Trotting along behind her was an equally astute-looking businesswoman, also suited. They came to a halt alongside the row of high-end vehicles in the parking area at the front of the property. All smiles, they shook hands. Business concluded.

'A done deal,' Abbott said under his breath.

Mitch glanced at him. 'That Audi A8 Wells is getting into doesn't belong to her. She drives an old Golf.'

'Not the impression she wants to give,' Dick said.

'Blimey! She's a shrewd operator—'

'That's not what the guv'nor will call her. He'll go apeshit when he finds out what she's been up to.' Finding reverse gear, Abbott backed up at speed. 'Give him a bell. He may want to rethink his strategy.'

As Frankie drove, she thought about her evening out with David, specifically how it ended. Despite the shop talk, she was pretty chilled by the end of the night, the warmth and motion of his car sending her off to sleep on the way home. David's hand on hers woke her with a start. Blinking away the glare of streetlights, she suddenly realised that they had arrived in Amble and were stationary.

She pictured him in the driver's seat, eyes fixed on her, a wry smile on his face. He'd said he'd had fun and that they should 'date' more often, making a joke about what good company she'd been on their journey to the coast. Ignoring his sarcasm, she'd climbed out of his vehicle. She didn't ask him up for a nightcap. It was late – it had been a long day and they were both on-call – one of them had to remain sober. She remembered looking back at him through the car door, thanking him for dinner and wishing him goodnight.

'Are we good?' he'd asked.

'We're good.' She smiled then. 'See you in the morning, guv.'

She arrived at the *Corchester Herald* offices around ten o'clock, parked in a bay reserved for staff and bypassed security as if she owned the place. When challenged by a member of staff in the newsroom, she held up her warrant card and walked on without a backward glance. Ignoring the fact that the editor-in-chief was busy on the phone, she knocked on his office door, turned the handle and let herself in. This time she wouldn't wait around. He wasn't the only professional with a job to do.

Fox looked up, an irritated expression on his face. 'I'm going to have to call you back.' He ended the call. 'DS Oliver, what can I do for you?'

'Apologies for interrupting. Could you spare a moment to talk to me?'

'Do I have a choice?'

'No, sir. I don't think you do.'

'Then you'd better be quick. I have a meeting scheduled in ten—'

'What I have to say won't take long.'

'I can't imagine why you need to see me. I've told you all I know.'

Frankie wasn't sure if he had. Was the editor Wells had described as 'a worm' being defensive or his usual, objectionable self? Closing the door behind her, Frankie approached his desk. Today there were no newspapers strewn across the surface, no notepads, just a cardboard coffee beaker and the remains of a half-eaten, over-ripe banana, the smell of which made her stomach churn.

Fox sat up straight, crossing his arms. He seemed to have aged ten years since she'd last seen him. He had the look of a man under immense pressure. Was he hiding something? Or was it more straightforward than that? In his industry, no news was definitely not good news.

'I gather you're making headway,' he said. 'Is that why

you're here?' He didn't wait for admission or denial. 'I thought you were done with your questions.'

Frankie dropped her bag on the floor, sat down and crossed her legs, a relaxed pose. She flipped open a notebook, revealing a handwritten list. He was too far away to read what was on it: hairspray, bath oil, toothpaste . . . She looked up, poised to write down his responses. 'I have one or two more to put to you, if that's OK?'

'About Adams?'

'Among other things.' Frankie pointed at the paper and pen in front of him. 'You might like to make a note of this, sir. I need a detailed account of his movements for the twenty-fourth of September last year, including his diary appointments so I can trace the people he might have been in contact with, his internet searches, all documents created or viewed that day. And I'd like it as soon as possible.'

Fox stopped scribbling and looked up. 'May I ask why?'

'I'm not able to share that information.'

He threw down his pen. This was not a man who was accustomed to being kept in the dark. Frankie was in control and he didn't like it. Maybe he had a problem with women. He glanced at his watch, a not so subtle reminder that Frankie was on the clock. 'You do know that I've had a number of enquiries from your technical support team already, DS Oliver?'

'I'm glad you brought that up.' Frankie chose her words carefully. 'I've now had sight of their report. I gather that, aside from his usual follow-ups on court proceedings and a series on gang culture and gratuitous violence, not one of the articles Adams had written over the last couple of years appeared in your newspaper.'

'That's correct.'

'None of his other stuff was published?'

'Not that I'm aware of.'

'If you don't mind me saying so, I find that astonishing.'

'You shouldn't.' Fox shifted uncomfortably in his seat.

'Until yesterday, we had a very experienced features editor who dealt with that side of things. She'd be best placed to advise you of the reasons that prevented his work getting through. Ours is a very competitive business. Every word counts and only the very best make it.'

'Until yesterday?'

'Trish Dolan is no longer working here.'

'Then I'd like her details.'

Fox took a moment to write them down and handed Frankie a note. Making a steeple of his fingers, he rested his chin on them. 'It's not true that *all* of Adams' submissions were rejected out of hand. One or two of his ideas that reached my desk were decent. As I recall, they were bumped when more important news items came in. That's the nature of our business, I'm afraid. Ask any journalist, TV or print. They'll tell you the same thing. It'll come as no surprise to you that we need to drop one ball and pick up another occasionally.'

'Quite, although in my line of work a murder victim always takes priority. The MIT will stop at nothing to bring an offender to justice. I'm sure you, as Adams' former employer, would accept nothing less.' Seeing that he'd got the message, Frankie moved on. 'I suspect that the articles we found on Adams' computer – those unrelated to his job here, I mean – are the tip of the iceberg. I expect that many more will have been created while he was at work in this very building. I take it they'll still be on your system?'

'I assume so, but your colleagues specifically asked if the items they found had ever been published in the *Herald*. They hadn't.'

Definitely defensive.

Time to turn the screw. 'I'm particularly interested in the articles that never made it into print.'

'Why?'

'Because I believe that one of them may have led to his death.'

Fox checked his watch again. He couldn't wait to offer up the excuse that she'd run out of time.

Frankie wasn't done yet. 'Did your IT staff search his draft folders?'

'Probably.'

'You didn't check?'

'Not personally, no. I've been rather busy trying to rescue my newspaper and keep hold of my staff.' Taking his specs off, he shook his head: Mr Sincerity. 'I've had to let one or two longstanding employees go this week with immediate effect. Trish Dolan was one of them. It's never a nice thing to put people you admire on the dole.'

Frankie refrained from saying 'You're breaking my heart'. She suspected he knew exactly what checks had been undertaken, that he was in possession of all the facts and was withholding information. 'If Adams was investigating a major news story, as we first thought, I'd like it found,' she said. 'Would you be willing to allow our IT bods to trawl your mainframe for anything with his name attached? I'd rather not have to apply for a warrant.'

Fox caught the threat. His glasses were back on. They couldn't hide his nervousness. 'I'm telling you now, there was no big story—'

'I beg to differ, sir.'

'Can I give you a piece of well-meaning advice, DS Oliver? It would be unwise to take what his mother said as gospel. As I told you—'

She cut off a further attack on Susan Adams. 'Relax, Mr Fox. My information is based on evidence retrieved from his personal computer. I'm following the evidence trail, and that has led me to you.'

'I already told you, I wasn't aware of any breaking news, neither did I sanction an investigation of the scale and scope you alluded to in our earlier discussion. How many more times do I have to tell you that Adams was a junior staff member with ideas above his pay grade? I'd be very surprised if he had column inches worth printing, though it might help if I knew the content of the so-called story you're referring to.'

'I'm not at liberty to discuss it.'

'Then I don't see how I can help—'

'Humour me a second.' Frankie uncrossed her legs and leaned in closer, never taking her eyes off him. 'Assuming for one moment that he did have a major news item to report, could the information perhaps have been deleted?' She paused a beat, before adding, 'In error or deliberately?' Her comment drew a flash of anger, as she'd known it would.

'It could,' he said warily, 'but why would it? We're struggling to survive here. I can assure you, I'd have bitten his hand off if there was anything remotely worth following up.'

Frankie still wasn't sure she trusted him. Was he trotting out a well-rehearsed line to save his skin? It was hard to imagine that he'd risk everything in some kind of cover-up. 'You stated that you had your finger on the pulse of the *Herald* and that you'd have known if an employee was working off-grid.'

'Absolutely!'

'Well, it seems that you are very much mistaken. You see, I'm fairly certain that Chris Adams *was* flying beneath your radar, Mr Fox. Either you knew about it or you didn't. Which is it?'

'Are you accusing me of impropriety, Detective?'

'I'm not accusing you of anything, sir.' She was hinting at it though.

'Good, because libel is much more than a five-letter word.'

Fox obviously thought his integrity had been questioned – and he was right. Frankie had calculated that it would be the surest way to rattle him, which had been her intention all along. Now he was dying to know what she knew, or thought she knew, and she wasn't about to share. Experience had taught her that there was a time to push a witness, co-conspirator or full-blown suspect – and a time to back off.

David had given her permission to conduct the interview as she saw fit. He'd also advised her not to go in too hard, too early.

That was good advice.

Her mind was a jumble of unanswered questions. Was Trish Dolan the intimidated female she'd seen lurking near Fox's office door during her first visit? Did she know something? Was that why he'd let her go? Frankie checked her watch and stood up to leave. 'It seems my ten minutes is up.' She threw the editor a smile, thanking him for his co-operation. His self-imposed time constraint suited her needs perfectly. She needed more information before she tackled him again and was hoping that Dick and Mitch might supply it when they returned from playing father and son at Bastle View. They should be back by now. Her questioning of Mark Fox was far from over.

38

David pulled up sharp as he entered Jesmond Dene House, Newcastle's only independently owned boutique hotel. Wells was standing at the check-in desk. He wouldn't have recognised her from the rear had Abbott not shared a description of how she was dressed when she left Bastle View in someone else's car. Ordinarily, her style was more casual, but she blended right in with the other guests milling around in what was, by anyone's standards, a great place to stay, nestled in a narrow, wooded valley on the River Ouseburn.

'Belinda . . .' He leaned over, whispering in her ear, so close that she could probably feel his breath on her neck. 'Fancy seeing you here.'

Her red lips parted as she swung round. 'David!' Clearly, she was expecting someone else. She left the 'What are you doing here?' unsaid, but David answered anyway.

'You first.'

'I'm having lunch with a friend . . .' She arched an eyebrow, a wicked smile on her face. 'A male friend, as it happens, someone I've had my eye on for a while. I know that'll come as a blow. I'm afraid he got in first. You're quick or dead in this game.' She thumbed over her shoulder, lowering her voice. 'I was about to ask if they had any rooms available . . . in case we need a lie-down afterwards.'

David was in no mood for games.

'Oh, c'mon. You're such a prude.' She winked at him. 'Actually, you look like you could do with a good meal and a lie-down yourself.'

'I haven't come to eat, sleep or get my leg over, Belinda. I've come to ask what the hell you think you're up to—'

'God, keep your voice down. I may not have much of a

238

reputation, but I'd like to keep what little I have. What's wrong with you?'

'I think you know.'

'I don't think I do.'

She did.

Stone moved her away from the desk and other customers. Wells was cool, a great journalist. She knew better than to try and bluff him. She'd already made the jump, he'd bet his pension on it. She was buying herself enough time to come up with a credible explanation for not consulting with him beforehand.

'Is this going to take long?' she said.

'Depends how long you intend to hold out on me.' He gave her a filthy look. 'Unless Abbott is losing it, you were visiting a certain nursing home this morning.'

'Ah.' She grimaced. 'I'm slipping, aren't I? I should've been watching my six.'

'He didn't follow you, Belinda. He saw you leave. You should've called me if you were planning to go there.'

'You want the gloves off with me now?' She locked eyes with him. 'First Frankie, then Ben, now it's my turn? Be very careful, David. You need your mates around you.' Shifting uncomfortably, she pointed along the hallway. 'Let's sit in the bar. These stupid heels are killing me.'

'Residents' lounge. I need you sober.'

She rolled her eyes. 'You're no fun.'

'So I've been told.'

'Yeah, probably more than once. Wait here a second . . .'

Ordering tea from a waitress who'd walked through from the restaurant, she retraced her steps to reception, telling the check-in clerk where she'd be if anyone came looking. Aware that David was eavesdropping, she omitted to give a name. Turning on her heels, she followed him out and along the corridor, joking as they reached a cosy lounge with oak panelling on the walls and ceiling and leaded windows overlooking a magnificent garden, an oasis in the suburbs, a stone's throw from the busy city centre.

She glanced at the door, then at him. 'Actually, it might play to my advantage if my new squeeze sees me with a young stud like you.'

'You're incorrigible.' Wells had always been direct. She saw something she wanted, she went for it. David smiled at her as she sat down on the couch beside him. 'I really hope it works out for you this time, Belinda.'

'Oh, please! I'm looking for fun, not a yoke to hang around my neck.'

He didn't believe her. She'd never taken anything seriously. Nor had she found a soulmate to share her life with. Love was universal. A basic need. She wanted that, as much as he did. Right now, she seemed oblivious to the silence that had opened up between them.

'You don't think this is too much?' She was referring to her clothes.

'No,' he reassured her. 'You look stunning.'

'Wish I could say the same for you.' She grinned. 'Late night with Frankie?'

'How did—'

'Ben.'

That made sense. His nephew and Frankie texted frequently.

A waitress arrived with their tea on a silver tray, a white teapot, tiny milk jug and sugar lumps in a bowl. Wells poured, making him wait until she was ready to talk, handing him a cup and saucer with a dainty shortbread biscuit on the side. Popping hers in her mouth, she looked up at him.

'Relax, David. You'll find another Jane.'

He was taken aback. Clearly, she was not as preoccupied as he'd first thought. Unwilling or unable to go there – probably a bit of both – he changed the subject. On the way to see her, something had been bothering him. He had to ask . . .

'Have I got a leak in my team?'

'Not that I'm aware of. Why d'you ask?'

'Well, if no one's feeding you information, how in God's name did you manage to get to Bastle View?'

'I drove—'

'I'm serious, so start talking. Have you been trailing us? Has Ben?'

'Do me a favour!' She threw down the gauntlet ready to go into battle. 'Who got there first, you or me? I'm good at what I do, you know that. And so is he. The only help I received came from you. Chris Adams' notes gave me a head start, so don't start bitching or falling out with my newest recruit.'

'Those notes were confidential.'

'And they still are.' She paused, a puzzled look. 'How did you find me, if I'm allowed to ask? No one knows I'm here.'

'Except Ben.'

They both laughed.

Wells checked her watch, her eyes drifting through the window momentarily. The dene was bathed in winter sunshine, a haven of nature and tranquillity. A car drew up outside. David wondered if it was her heavy date arriving.

It wasn't.

Finally, she paid attention and came clean. 'The information I retrieved from the notebooks was date-specific. My guts were telling me that Adams was on to something big. It didn't take me long to work out that the 'something' involved vulnerable people of one type or another. There were only so many scenarios available. Then, as you know, events took a turn for the worse. He lost contact with N over Christmas. I figured that if his informant had gone missing, I could trawl missing persons' articles at my paper, specifically forenames beginning with the letter N or the initials JC. There were none of the latter, but Nancy Carver's name came up, so I started digging. Don't look at me like that! It's what I'm paid for, same as you. Our feature mentioned her workplace and the timing corresponded with what I knew of your IP's investigation.'

This was a rerun of David's earlier conversation with Frankie.

Wells now had her professional head on, all thoughts of her lunch date forgotten. 'Though the clues pointed to Nancy leaving the area of her own free will, her son was and still is unconvinced. He claims the police did nothing to find her when she disappeared and made a personal appeal on the Missing People website, talking to anyone who'd listen. He said—'

'You interviewed him?'

'Why wouldn't I?'

'Because he's grief-stricken.'

'He was happy to see me take an interest.'

'Still, you shouldn't meddle in people's lives, Belinda. You may have given him false hope.'

'What I gave him was the truth. It's time someone did.' She made no apology for following her instinct. 'The more I found out about his mother's disappearance, the more convinced I became that it was somehow linked to your victim. I don't know the ins and outs of it yet, but I'm as sure as I can be that Adams was killed trying to write an exclusive highlighting an issue we should all be concerned about. And you're of the same opinion, or you wouldn't have sent Abbott to Bastle View. I assume you found Nancy on your misper database?'

'Frankie did.'

'There you go. That should tell you something. Look, we did an in-depth piece on Nancy's background shortly after she went missing. All the local papers did, with one exception . . .' She paused before delivering the sucker punch: 'The *Herald*. You didn't know that, did you?'

'No, thanks for the heads-up.'

She was one step ahead of him.

They both knew it.

'Frankie is with Fox now,' David said. 'She doesn't trust him.'

'You think he's part of a cover-up?'

'The thought had occurred to us.'

'He's a slippery customer. You're right not to bank on his honesty. He's a lowlife, a pariah in the newspaper business. No one believes a word he says . . . or in this case, doesn't say.' Wells paused. 'And just so you know, I'm not trying to score points here. I don't give a shit who discovers what, and nor should you. We're on the same page and neither of us believes in coincidence, do we? We need to work together on this, David. Nancy was a good woman, a strong woman.'

'That's not what her daughter told us.'

'I thought you weren't into meddling.' She stared at him. 'What did she tell you?'

'She said her mother was anxious.'

'A difference of opinion then.' Wells brushed aside his concerns. 'No offence, but women pick up cues that men often miss. James Carver might not have noticed her anxiety, but confirmed she was very low after his father died. They all were. He said that his mum had fully recovered and was trying hard to adjust to her new circumstances. He insists that at no point had she become so depressed that she'd have considered taking her own life. In his opinion, there was no suicide risk. I agree with him.'

'It doesn't work like that. People who top themselves don't always flag up their intentions, especially to relatives. Many leave no note. They do it because they can . . . Because they've had enough . . . Because they have reached the end of the road.'

'Fine, I stand corrected. Be honest, though: you don't be-lieve Nancy Carver killed herself or ran off to America, do you?'

He shook his head. If suicide had ever been a theory, the image Technical Support found on Adams' computer had put paid to it. David wasn't about to share that with Wells, but if she was talking to family members, she'd find out soon enough.

'We can debate this all day long,' Wells said, 'but Nancy's son is adamant that she would not have taken that route, neither would she have left the area by choice. If she ran away, it was because someone was after her. And before you ask, I didn't mention her when I paid Bastle View a visit.'

'Did you make an appointment or go in on spec?'

She rolled her eyes. 'What do you take me for? I told them I was looking to get my mother into a home – which happens to be the truth.' She cleared her throat, palmed her brow, the light leaving her eyes, a moment of heartache. 'She doesn't even recognise me nowadays.'

David had no idea. 'I'm sorry to hear that.'

'Save your sympathy for her.' Wells' sadness quickly turned to anger. 'David, I've been in and out of these institutions a lot lately, enough to tell the difference between good and bad. Despite the testimonials on their poncey website, there's something not right about Bastle View. They didn't seem to have any vacancies until I told the new manager that my mum was loaded and had dementia.'

39

Neither Wells nor Stone had noticed Ben slip into the seat behind them and open up a newspaper. They were locked in conversation, one that revealed much about the dead reporter whose life, even though they had never met, Ben identified with. He liked the sound of Chris Adams, a champion of the underdog. For the first time since his row with David, Ben felt he understood the pressure his uncle was under to solve this murder and why he'd attempted to keep *him* away from the investigation.

David was worried for his safety – as simple as that.

Some people thrived on risk. Ben was no exception, and yet he experienced a feeling of blind panic as it sauntered through the door in the form of the bloke Wells was having lunch with. Turning his head away gave Ben eyes in the back of his head; as the newcomer approached the journalist and detective, the scene was reflected in a well-placed mirrored cabinet. Fortunately, Wells only had eyes for the man now vigorously shaking hands with Stone.

Seconds later, introductions dispensed with, the three moved out into the corridor, David peeling off for the main entrance, Wells and her date turning the other way. Letting out a breath, Ben lowered the newspaper he'd been hiding behind. That was a close call, one that might have had dire consequences had he been discovered spying on them, though he'd prefer to call it a conscientious move on his part. Nevertheless, he was acutely aware it may have signalled the end of his days shadowing Wells and would most definitely have landed him in trouble with his uncle.

Counting himself lucky that he wasn't looking for a new job and a new landlord, an idea that he might help solve a murder rapidly began to form in his head. More research was required first. Ensuring that the coast was clear, he left the hotel bound for Jesmond, a short walk away.

In Café Nero, he ordered a latte and a warm almond croissant before opening up his laptop and logging on to Safari. There were so many jobs listed, he got the distinct impression that residential care struggled to keep its workforce. There were literally hundreds of vacancies. The more he studied them, the more convinced he became that he wouldn't want to apply for one of these positions in real life, despite the offer of a free uniform. Masquerading as a university dropout was what he had in mind, which was exactly what he'd been before he went to work with Wells.

Confident that he could pull it off, Ben felt a rush of adrenalin surge through his body. He was beginning to understand what it was that drove his uncle and Frankie Oliver to breaking point. Being part of something that would make a difference and bring justice to victims was giving him a high the like of which he'd never known.

Taking a long, deep breath, he continued to study the screen. Dealing with the physical and emotional needs of the elderly was taxing work and the shifts were long. The pay was even worse than he'd anticipated – almost 70 per cent of the posts on offer brought in less than fifteen grand. This was minimum-wage stuff with limited career opportunities; only those who lacked the incentive or wherewithal to enter nursing or management would apply. Given the cost of residential care, and the fact that it was devouring the life savings of those too ill or too old to care for themselves, it was shocking that care providers were paid so little.

Ben clicked on a job description.

Using his initiative? *Wasn't that what he was doing?*

Working under pressure? *Most definitely.*

Compassion? *He could do that.*

Could he go the extra mile? *Hell, yeah.*

Respect? *What the fuck? Was it even possible to teach someone respect for others? Surely that was a prerequisite, the very essence of any nursing job, and especially one that involved dementia or end-of-life care.*

According to the text, no training was required. Lucky for him, it was all done in-house. As he read on, he became increasingly concerned about the plight of those no longer able to live independently, wondering exactly what Chris Adams had intended to expose. If Wells was right and there was something sinister going on behind the respectable facade of Bastle View, Ben wanted in on the story.

Keeping his fingers firmly crossed, he scrolled down. Care homes right across the region had posted advertisements. He was only interested in one.

Bingo!

Care Assistants, Northumberland. (4 x posts) Immediate start at Bastle View Residential Care Home. We provide specialist care to elderly and frail adults in an unrivalled location. Salary upon application. Driving licence an advantage. Previous experience not essential as training will be given. An enhanced DBS check will be required.

Perfect!

Or maybe not . . .

When Wells took him on, she'd insisted on a basic CRB check to ensure that his record was clean. That wouldn't cut it with Bastle View. The Care Quality Commission had seen to that. The home was duty-bound to ask for a more thorough look into his background from the Disclosure and Barring Service – a necessary precursor to any job that involved teaching, working with a vulnerable group, kids or the elderly. It took him less than five minutes to apply. Once that was done, he made an appointment for immediate interview while he waited for approval to come through. Three days and he'd be in there. No question.

40

Frankie had missed two calls from David. It sounded like he was in transit when he left a message to call him immediately. She was hoping that Dick and Mitch had learned something of interest from their undercover operation at Bastle View, enough to form an impression, one way or the other, on its regime and legitimacy. She was disappointed to learn that they'd been forced to abort their mission because Wells had beaten them to it. Still, David sounded upbeat when she returned his call. There must be a tale to tell. Preferring not to talk on the phone, they arranged to rendezvous in town.

She parked the car on Richardson Road, entering the city's Exhibition Park through the north gate. David was sitting where he said he'd be, on a south-facing bench beside the boating lake. It reminded Frankie of August Bank Holiday when they'd attended the Newcastle Mela, an annual celebration of Asian culture, a festival of music, art and cuisine. The memory was a good one, a happy one, so powerful it conjured up the contrasting aromas of Pakistani, Bengali and Indian food floating on the breeze that day, the vibrant colours of traditional dress, the sound of musicians warming up on stage. In reality, the park was empty, the water like glass.

Despite the silence, David hadn't heard her approach along the tarmac path, or if he had he'd chosen to play dead. He was leaning back, arms crossed over his chest, feet crossed at the ankle, shades on, his face raised to the winter sun. A moment of silent contemplation. Looking nothing like the SIO she worked with on a daily basis, he could've been anyone: a tourist taking a break from a walk around the city walls; an ex-pat on a trip home paying homage to Newcastle

United – St James's Park was across the lake – a man waiting for the girl of his dreams to arrive.

'You awake?' she said.

'Just about . . .' He opened his eyes. 'Though a couple of more minutes and you'd have found me sending the zeds up big style. I didn't sleep well last night.'

'Detectives sleep? That news to me.'

He wasn't the only one to have experienced a restless night. She'd lain awake until the small hours, tossing and turning, angry with herself for having checked out in the car on the way home, not making the most of their downtime together. And when she'd finally given in to exhaustion, the intrusion of the alarm was unwelcome.

She still felt lousy.

Handing him a cardboard coffee beaker she'd picked up from a garage on the way into town, she sat down. 'It's black. I thought it might keep warmer for longer.'

Taking it from her, he opened the lid, steam escaping into the cold air as he did so. 'It's fine.'

'It was a question of take it or leave it, I'm afraid.' She took a sip. 'Urgh! Maybe leave it would be the better option. It's gross.'

'No grub?' He glanced at her hands. 'Call yourself a bagman?'

'I'm the best you'll get, mate.'

Frankie binned her coffee in the nearest trash, then sat down again, listening carefully as he confirmed that Wells' ill-judged visit to the care home wasn't what he'd wanted. For all that, it had borne fruit, the journalist expressing her doubts about the way the institution was run, adding that a brain disease – where memories, problem-solving and language skills were lost – could bypass a long waiting list and get you in . . .

'Even quicker if you happen to have a full bank account.'

'That's sick,' Frankie said.

'Don't worry, I'll make sure that we investigate the bastards, whether or not we can link Adams' death to whatever is going on there.'

'Don't you mean *if* there's something going on—'

He cut off her scepticism. 'Wells had a bad feeling about the place, Frank. Present company aside, there's no one whose gut instincts I trust more than hers. And another thing . . . The *Herald* was the only newspaper not carrying the story of Nancy's disappearance.'

She turned her body to face him. 'Are you sure?'

'Positive.'

'Did that come from Wells too?'

A nod. 'Relax, I just got off the phone to James Carver. He confirmed that he contacted every local rag when his mother went missing. Every one of them agreed to run it, including the *Corchester Herald*, except in their case it never happened. I'd like to know why and whether our victim was the reporter Carver spoke to.'

'Fox isn't going to tell you—'

'We'll see about that.' David fell silent, considering what to do. 'It'll be interesting to know if he has any connection with Sir Giles Bradbury or if the *Herald* is in any way linked to Bastle View. I can't imagine how. It needs investigating.'

Frankie bit her lip. 'Actually, I might have overstepped the mark with Fox earlier.' She put on her sorry face. 'I might have suggested that we were poised to turn over his office until we find what we're looking for. I might even have threatened him with a warrant if he didn't agree to let us analyse his database. OK, I did threaten him, in the nicest possible way.' There was a pause but the roasting she was expecting never materialised.

'Good work! Is he sweating?'

'What do you think?' She gave a wry smile, calmer now. 'OK if I give the Technical Support the go-ahead? I'm keen to gain access to the *Herald*'s computer system at the earliest opportunity. It's the only way we're going to pin him down.'

'Do it!'

'I did.' Frankie blushed. 'Half an hour ago.'

David laughed.

'It's going to take a while, days, possibly even weeks. In the meantime, I'd like to look into Bradbury's background to see if he's got any guilty secrets.'

'Good plan. And, while you're at it, find out about his knighthood—'

'I did that already. He got it for services to charity.'

'So did Jimmy Savile.'

Frankie shuddered involuntarily at a name that made her skin crawl. She hoped they were not about to open up a Savilesque can of worms when delving into Bradbury.

41

David's phone rang a couple of times before they left the park. Abbott had heard from the FLO. According to Susan Adams, her son wasn't in the habit of using a library, other than to borrow books and do his research. He didn't trust the security of public computers. They were too easily hacked by ten-year-olds. Stone chuckled, but Frankie's head went down as Dick ended the call. She was still carping about the one-step-forward-two-back reality they faced on every murder enquiry when Sharon Bailey, the Crime Scene Manager she'd sent to examine Chris Adams' motorcycle, came on the blower with more positive news, an exciting development she felt might prove crucial in the hunt for his killer . . .

'Hold on a sec.' Stone looked around, making sure no one was in earshot. Finding the coast clear, he put the phone on speaker so his 2ic could listen in. 'OK, shoot. Tell me you found his motorcycle.'

'Thanks to DS Oliver's dad, we did.'

Frankie rolled her eyes. 'Keep him the hell away from that garage, Sharon.'

'Oh, you're there!' the CSI chuckled. 'Is the pavement far enough? He was standing guard with the key and a clipboard when my lads arrived, taking names. He's even written out a continuity of evidence statement. He's very thorough, your old man – quite a character.'

'Tell me about it. Have you made a start on the bike yet?'

'No, but I found a digital flash drive hidden inside the motorcycle helmet that was perched on the seat. It belongs to your IP. I confirmed that with the tenant. I only have her word for it at the moment, but DNA will confirm whether she's telling the truth. The helmet and flash drive have been logged, photographed and are on their way to Forensics as we speak. The bike will follow as soon as I'm done.'

David and Frankie looked at one another.

'It's going to take a while to get them processed,' Frankie said. 'Lab technicians are flat out.'

'They are,' Sharon confirmed. 'But you're in luck. Following the intervention of a certain retired polis not a million miles from here, they've agreed to push it up the queue.' She was laughing as she said it. 'I'm told it's hard to argue with a juggernaut.'

'Damn right!' Frankie said proudly.

'Wish I had his pull,' David said. 'You think we could coax him out of retirement?'

'In a nanosecond.' Frankie was less concerned about her father's meddling than she'd been moments ago. Though she had many friends on the force, and in Forensics too, she hadn't yet mastered his art of persuasion.

'I'll crack on,' Sharon said. 'Let you know as soon as there's anything else to report.'

David turned to face Frankie. 'Put Technical Support on standby. As soon as Forensics are finished with that flash drive, I want the contents downloaded immediately. Tell them to ping us over a copy as soon as they're done.'

She was already making the call.

42

While Stone was catching up with Collingwood, and before going in search of features editor Trish Dolan, Frankie thought she'd look up Ryman, for no other reason than to put his mind at rest. She hadn't located the Doc but could reassure Ryman that he wasn't lying in a hospital ward, or worse, the morgue. Frankie didn't think Ryman had been pulling a fast one or that her assessment of him was way off the mark. Policing taught detectives to query everything and everyone – Dick was no exception and he was right to question her assessment – but she'd learned to trust her gut. In Ryman's case, she still did. He'd been desperate to spare Eva Sokolov an early death. That's all there was to it. Frankie would lay money on him being legit.

The detour took only a few minutes. Ryman was nowhere to be seen on Northumberland Street, which didn't surprise her. He'd make himself scarce during the day for fear of being moved on. If he got into an altercation with anyone, he'd be slapped with a Community Protection Notice or Fixed-Penalty on the grounds that his anti-social behaviour might have a detrimental effect on the quality of life of others, regardless of who actually started the argument. It was unfair, a fact of life for a lot of homeless people, though Ryman had avoided criminal convictions for begging, loitering or fighting thus far.

Remembering what he'd said about spending time at the Central Library, she made her way past the crime scene, up the ramp and into the building. She found him sitting on his own, in a quiet corner, a raft of newspapers spread out on the table in front of him, a library user like any other, causing no one alarm or distress, educating himself, keeping up with current affairs.

'Can I join you, Sarge?'

Lowering his newspaper, he threw her a wide smile. 'Blimey! You look knackered.'

'That's because I am.' She sat down with a weary sigh. 'I can't stay. I just wanted to let you know that there's no news on the Doc. We've checked all the city hospitals—'

'No sweat, I saw him last night.'

'He's fit and well?'

A nod.

Frankie was relieved to hear it.

'Sorry, I would've called. I ran out of cash. The Doc managed to find a hostel for a couple of nights to escape the worst of the weather. Now the sun is shining, he's back in the underpass with his mates. Daft though it may seem to you, that's where he feels most comfortable.'

'Mates are important to everyone, Sarge.'

'Do you still need to speak to him?'

'No, I only came to update you, payback for the enormous help you've been. Without you, we still wouldn't have a credible witness.' They were still trawling CCTV in the hope of picking up their suspect wearing that distinctive fleece, either before or after the fatal attack a hundred yards along the road.

'How is Eva?'

'Cosied up in bed, thanks to you. You're a diamond, Oli. I appreciate all you've done for her.'

'Likewise,' Frankie said. 'We're nowhere nearer to identifying the man she saw, but what she told us is very helpful and we're following it up. All we need is a good image and we're in business.' Frankie didn't tell him that there had been no CCTV sightings yet. He didn't need to know. And she was still hopeful that the MIT might catch a break from it. 'She hasn't remembered anything else since she spoke to DCI Stone?'

'Not that I know of.' Ryman was staring at her intensely. 'I liked him, your boss.'

'Yeah, he's cool . . . most of the time.'

Across the room, library staff were moving a mobile shelving unit to make room for a display someone had taken a lot of trouble to put together. There was an author photo pinned in the centre, cover images and information of where and when it would take place picked out in multi-coloured lettering. It looked interesting for those with the time to attend.

'Are you any further forward with your investigation?' Ryman asked.

'We're working on it.' Frankie stood up. 'I'd love to stay and chat—'

'No excuses necessary, Oli. A trip to the nick was evidence, if it were needed, of how busy you are.'

'Call me, anytime.' She slipped a tenner under his newspaper. Seeing his embarrassment, she said: 'It's not charity, Sarge. I need an open line to my star witness.'

43

When David arrived at the morgue, Beth Collingwood was hard at work, but not on a cadaver, for which he was eternally grateful. He'd had enough of blood and guts to last a lifetime. No strawberry-coloured scrubs today. Beth was in her office, casually dressed, her head in a medical science textbook. Peering over the top of purple-framed specs that matched her funky hair, she asked him to wait a moment while she finished up.

'Almost done.' She pointed across the room. 'There's a carton of fresh orange juice in the fridge. Help yourself while you wait.'

'Thanks.' David noticed two clean glasses on top. 'Want one?'

'Yes, please.' She looked up. 'Unless you prefer coffee?'

'No, juice is perfect.'

He poured their drinks and sat down, wondering how Frankie was getting on in her search for an employee recently made redundant from the *Herald*, a woman she thought might add to the growing pile of background information on their victim. Even if Frankie met a brick wall, he was hoping that the flash drive CSIs had found tucked into the lining of Adams' motorcycle helmet might contain specifics on what the journalist had been working to uncover before his death. David could think of no other reason he'd hide the item in such an obscure place if it wasn't part of his investigation.

Five minutes later, Collingwood's hefty volume closed with a thump, enveloping her in a cloud of dust. She coughed into her hand, reaching for her glass. David noticed a tiny dragon tattoo on the inside of her forearm. It surprised him that a woman who spent all day cutting up bodies would ever allow anyone to damage her own delicate skin.

'David? Are you in?'

'What? Yes, sorry, I was miles away.' He wiped a thin film of perspiration from his brow and paid attention. 'You have something for me?'

'Well, I assume you've come about Mr Adams,' Collingwood said, pulling a file towards her. 'I have the PM results here. I'll skip the full details of the examination and get to the important bits from your perspective. What we have is a knife wound at 125 centimetres from the heel, oriented in the ten to four direction in clock-face terms, and just to the left of the mid-line of the front of the body. The wound measures 2.4 centimetres edge-to-edge. The knife went in between the ribs, missed the cartilage and penetrated to a depth of 13 centimetres before coming to rest in the fifth thoracic vertebra.' Collingwood looked up to ensure that the SIO was still with her, then carried on. 'Unluckily for Mr Adams, the weapon penetrated his right ventricle and he bled out in his chest. As I told you after the post-mortem, he'd have been dead in minutes. Nothing paramedics could've done would have saved him, even if they had been on the scene when he was stabbed. The really interesting thing though is the unusual nature of the wound.'

'How so?'

She slid across a photograph taken during the post-mortem. 'Can you see the curved shape of the wound track?'

A nod.

'Normally, I'd expect to see a wound that is roughly tapered from the entry point to the tip, with either one rectangular edge and a V-shaped edge, or two V-shaped edges.' She used her pen as a pointer. 'Here we have one rectangular edge, here a V-shaped one on the skin surface. You're looking for a knife with one blunt edge and one sharp edge – as opposed to two sharp edges like a dagger. The injury to the body isn't straight, it's curved'

'Just to be clear, Beth. You're saying that the wound track into the body wasn't made with a straight-edged knife?'

'Precisely. This wound wasn't made with a kitchen knife, or any other conventional blade. It's highly unusual. I've run it past Sarah Hainsworth, she's a Professor of Materials and Forensic Engineering at Aston University.'

'I know the name,' David said.

'You should. She's worked with police forces nationwide.'

'I read about her somewhere . . . Wasn't she involved in identifying the skeletal remains of Richard III?'

'That's her.' Uncrossing her legs, Collingwood got up and moved towards her bookshelf. Pulling a thick file towards her, she retraced her steps. 'The research Sarah has carried out on tool markings is very specific, enabling her to deliver a detailed analysis of wounds inflicted on a body in order to identify potential weapons and their sharpness. Stabbing and dismemberment is her thing—'

'She sounds utterly charming.'

Collingwood laughed. 'You really crack me up.'

'No, seriously, she sounds like my kinda girl.'

'We both need women like her, David. Her contribution in her field of expertise cannot be overstated. She's been looking at a range of knives from European countries and the wounds they make, travelling the globe to talk about knife crime. She is a very busy woman. Fortunately for you, she also happens to be a good friend of mine.'

'Well, I won't take the piss if you don't bore me with the science. Can she help us?'

'She can, and she has.'

'More to the point, is she willing to attend court and defend her findings?'

'If called upon to do so, yes. As expert witnesses go, she's right up your street.' The pathologist sat down, leaving the file unopened on her knee. 'I think the two of you will get along.'

'If she can get across the complexities of her research in layman's terms, enough to convince a jury, that'll do me. Whoever caused the death of Chris Adams isn't going to cough, Beth. I want to put him away where he can't do it again. Whether Professor Haynes and I like each other is neither here nor there.'

'Hainsworth. For God's sake, get her name right!' Collingwood dropped her head on one side. 'You OK? You're very grumpy today.'

'I'm sorry . . .' Stone wiped his face with his hand, wishing he'd caught forty winks beside the lake in Exhibition Park. 'I don't mean to be rude, but I have a press conference later and God knows what else waiting for me at Middle Earth. I didn't sleep, I haven't eaten today – apart from a shortbread biscuit the size of a ten-pence piece – I'm being run ragged by my guv'nor.'

'Shall I tell you about this wound then or have you just come for a moan?'

'Go on, what does the good professor have to say?'

'Well, for a start, she agrees that a curved knife made this wound, something like a Karakulak or a Yagatan—'

'A what?

'They're knives, David. That's all you need to know. Rather than being straight from the tip to the handle, the blade of a Bulgarian Karakulak tends to be slightly curved. That would account for why the wound here doesn't run straight from the entry point to the vertebra. The Yagatan is Turkish, also a curved blade. Sarah tested both.'

'Are you telling me it's one of these?'

'Or something very similar. She ruled out other possibilities because they were too curved or too wide to have made this injury. The ones she's identified are really sharp and capable of creating the wound I found during my examination. She can't say for certain. If you find the knife we'll be able to check the dimensions and create some experimental wounds.

Hopefully, we'll come up with a positive match to those I found during the post-mortem.'

'Thanks, Beth.' He pointed at the report in front of her. 'Can I have a copy of that? I need to go share this with Frankie.'

She handed one to him. 'What you need is the knife.'

44

The sky was dark overhead by the time Frankie left the library. As she walked to her car, her thoughts lingered on Ryman, what had happened to him, and how she might help him get his life back on track. He wasn't only bilingual, he was multilingual. Skills that many an employer would rate highly, including her own, especially as he was ex-RAF. As soon as she was able, she intended to work on him.

He was a bloke worth saving.

Rain spotted the pavement as she exited the Eldon Square precinct, big blobs of it, the beginning of a downpour. She quickened her pace, as did others. Three women without umbrellas were running to shelter in the Haymarket bus station, handbags over their heads, squealing and laughing. A car tooted as Frankie dashed across the road, rain bouncing off the tarmac as she took the shortcut up St Thomas' Crescent, to where she'd parked her car. She was out of breath and drenched by the time she got there.

The residential suburb of Fenham on the city's western edge was only a short drive away. Trish Dolan's front door opened before Frankie took her finger off the bell.

'Oh, hello!' A flash of recognition. 'Can I help you?'

The features editor was the woman Frankie had seen heading into Mark Fox's office when she first visited the *Herald*. She was of indeterminate age, blond hair cut short; upturned, feline eyes, framed by brows she'd drawn in with a darker pencil than required. It was a good look, a modern look that probably took ten years or more off her. She was wearing a red woollen overcoat, a black bag slung over her shoulder, a rock memoir Frankie recognised poking out of the top: *Life* by Keith Richards. A good read.

'A fellow Stones fan, I see.' *If there's an ice-breaker, use it,* Frankie's old man had told her long ago, advice she'd often put into practice since she'd joined the detective division. Common ground was never to be underestimated. 'Ms Dolan, I'm DS Oliver, Murder Investigation Team.'

'I know who you are.'

'Then you're also aware that I'm dealing with the death of your colleague, Chris Adams.' She pointed into the house. 'Could we go inside, out of the rain for a moment? I'd like to talk to you.'

Dolan pushed up her coat sleeve to check her watch. 'I'm sorry, I'd be happy to chat later. As you can see, I'm heading out.'

Frankie stood her ground.

The woman didn't seem perturbed, much less spooked by an unscheduled visit from a polis. Most people would be. It was as if she'd predicted that Frankie would arrive on her doorstep with questions. Dolan seemed in no immediate hurry to assist the detective with a warrant card still in her hand.

'Really,' Dolan said. 'I'd be happy to answer your questions later, but now is not a good time.'

'For either of us,' Frankie said.

'I have an appointment in half an hour.' Dolan gave a resigned shrug. 'Breast screening. I've already put it off once. They've had a last-minute cancellation and I need to get going. My car's in for a service. It's in a worse condition than I am.' The smile didn't make it to her eyes. 'It'll take me all that time to get there.'

Frankie glanced at her car. 'Can I drop you? We can talk on the way.'

'Sure. I hate public transport.' Dolan rolled her eyes. 'I always get stuck in the seat with the chap who encroaches on my personal space. No bloody respect. I'm thinking of moving to Madrid.' She paused. 'You read that, right?'

Frankie gave a nod, a wry smile. The practice of manspreading had been banned in that city earlier in the year. A hashtag drawing it to the attention of the public had gone viral. And rightly so. The UK hadn't yet caught on. 'You're safe,' she said. 'There'll be no micro-aggression in my car. I can't reach the pedals with my legs wide open.'

A hearty laugh from Dolan.

She proffered a hand. 'I'm Trish, pleased to meet you.'

'Frankie.' The handshake was solid.

Turning on her heel, the detective led the way down the garden path, the redundant editor following close behind. Taking her key fob from her pocket, Frankie blipped the locks, opened the passenger door for Dolan, then ran around to her side of the car and got in, drying her hands on her strides before grabbing her seat belt.

Dolan was still smiling as they buckled up.

'Where to?' Frankie asked.

Dolan gave directions to a hospital in North Tyneside, not far from Middle Earth, a clue that she wasn't heading for a routine appointment but possibly a yearly screening, having had a scare – or worse. She didn't mention it – and neither did Frankie – but what she said next confirmed the detective's suspicion regarding the state of her health . . .

'I can't quite get my head around Chris's death,' she said. 'I've had to contemplate my own recently, but he was so young, so full of life, a great kid with a bright future.' There were no tears, just the heavy weight of grief reflected in Dolan's eyes. 'Despite the age difference, we were mates as well as colleagues: played the odd round of golf, enjoyed the occasional dinner date, that type of thing. We got some odd looks, I can tell you. If I'd been his age, he mine, no one would have given us a second glance, but an older woman in the company of a young male? Well, you'd have thought I was Jennifer fucking Lopez. I mean, I'm older than his mother!'

'No!'

'Yup.' Dolan pouted her lips. 'Fox didn't like it, of course. Chris told him to back off. I told him that what we did outside of work was none of his business. The more he complained, the more we played on it. I even rode pillion once or twice to the office to rub it in. I became a bit of a speed junkie.'

'You've got more guts than I do. They're dangerous—'

'So is walking across the road. Besides . . . I'd rather go out with a bang than a whisper.'

The comment made Frankie's throat constrict. Dolan reminded her of Wells. A good laugh. A sharp brain. A positive attitude. No pushover. Then Frankie remembered the first time she'd seen her, heading into the office of her editor-in-chief; she hadn't looked at all happy on that occasion.

The DS took a moment to consider this. Had she mistaken the cause of Dolan's concern? Perhaps it was a work issue, nothing to do with Chris. Perhaps she'd known she was on Fox's hit list for redundancy before the axe fell.

Head-checking the rear-view, then the wing mirror on her side of the car, Frankie pulled out into fast-moving traffic on Fenham Hall Drive, speed restrictions ignored by drivers making their way east towards the city. Dolan needed the space to chat and Frankie was happy to let her. She spoke of the fun she'd had with Chris – especially on the bike. Exhilarating to hear her tell it – trips over the Scottish border, skirting Kielder Water, stopping at the highest point to gawp across Wauchope Forest at the stunning view towards Carlin Tooth and Hartshorn Pike.

'Sounds wonderful,' Frankie said.

'It was. He was great company.'

Frankie's stomach rolled over.

She'd missed this part of his adult life, and a whole lot more, she imagined. She couldn't help wondering if the editor was aware of the history between victim and murder detective. Maybe she was and was too polite to say so . . . unlike Liam Wiley. Maybe Dolan was glad of it, taking comfort in the fact that it would drive Frankie on to find the bastard who murdered him.

'If you've never been,' she added. 'You should go. It's jaw-droppingly beautiful up there. Tranquil doesn't come close to describing it. It's about as far off-grid and as close to nature as it's possible to get. Chris really loved it. He joked that the place reminded him of Fox.'

'Sorry?' A quick glance at her passenger as Frankie slowed for a red light. 'You've lost me.'

'He said they both made him feel small.'

'You got that right, I—' Frankie was about to say she could imagine him saying it but managed to pull back before giving herself away. 'Fox is not a man you warm to, is he? To be perfectly frank, I found his lack of compassion for a murdered colleague astonishing. I can say that now he let you go, right? What exactly is his problem?'

'He's a snake,' Dolan said. 'He doesn't need a reason to take against you. It's his default position, unless you're a somebody . . . then he's as far up your arse as he can get. He measures people by what they do, not who they are. If you have Doctor, Professor, Lord or Lady in front of your name, you're quids in.'

'Detective Sergeant didn't count,' Frankie said bluntly.

'It wouldn't . . .'

Frankie fell silent.

Was Dolan talking about anyone in particular . . . Sir Giles Bradbury for example? Taking the Western bypass, heading for the coast road, she accelerated into the fast lane, passing a lumbering skip truck with an overloaded cargo that looked like it might topple on to the tarmac at any moment. An accident waiting to happen. She wondered how the MIT were doing, whether Technical Support had made their presence felt at the *Herald* and weighed the odds of them discovering any connection between the two men. If it was there, they would find it, but it was the information on that flash drive Frankie was most eager to get her hands on.

45

The Victorian house, built in 1870, was not as grand as Cragside, Lord Armstrong's pile in Rothbury, but from what Ben could see of Bastle View from the outside, it came a close second. Well off the beaten track, surrounded by a formal garden and acres of land, it had no convenient shop or local amenities nearby, no handy bus route. With no private wheels to take him there, Ben had got off the bus and been forced to walk half a mile from the main road. The isolation of the place was as sinister as it was wonderful.

A woman in a pristine suit greeted him warmly, offering tea, asking him to wait until called. Thanking her, Ben took a seat on a bench that must've been a century old, the smell of linseed oil triggering a memory of his great-grandmother's cottage. It was hard to remain relaxed under the stern gaze of Sir Giles Bradbury's ancestors staring down at him from the walls, one of the oils a full-length portrait of a man on horseback, an austere expression on his face. These were not so much works of art as statements of wealth designed to impress those walking through the finely carved front door.

Ben had researched the charitable status of the place during his long journey to the sticks on public transport, a bus that stopped at every small village on the way. The Care Quality Commission had rated the residential home as outstanding, performing well and meeting their standards. The CQC report was not available to view online, but he'd noticed the ratings on the way in, a legal requirement. Above the huge oak door was a CCTV camera; anyone sitting where he was, be they job applicant or potential resident, was possibly under surveillance.

Turning his head away, he smiled at two bored young

women to his left, presumably rival candidates. He tried a friendly approach. 'Just as well there's more than one post on offer. . .' He glanced around the hallway. 'Pretty fancy, eh?'

'Aye, if you're into that type of thing,' the one sitting closest said. Broad Geordie and proud of it. She stretched her knitted miniskirt down towards her knees, lowering her voice. 'It took me hours to get here.'

'It's possible to live in,' Ben said, the very thing he was after.

'Yeah, I saw that. Me mam said I should give it a try. She wants rid o' me.' She giggled. 'Don't think she should crack open the bubbly just yet, mind.'

'I'm Ben.'

'Courtney.'

The other girl sat staring straight ahead, ignoring them. She was cute with flaming red hair and the bluest eyes Ben had ever seen. She reminded him of model and actress Lily Cole.

'And you are . . . ?' Courtney said.

'Gemma . . . Radcliffe.' She took out her phone and stuck her earplugs in. It was tantamount to slamming the door on the conversation.

Looking like she wanted to punch her lights out, Courtney turned to Ben and said: 'That's plain rude! It's not like we're in competition, is it? Three jobs. Three applicants. We're sorted, right?'

'Four posts,' Ben reminded her.

'Same difference.'

'Unless they've already interviewed candidates we're not aware of,' he said.

He hoped not. If that was the case, the odds of him getting a foot in the door were longer than he first thought. He was half-hoping for a cat-fight, caught on camera, to nudge the pendulum his way. Given the nature of the home and the wealth of the majority of the people living in it, in theory he stood a better chance than either of the girls. His accent was verging on cosmopolitan, his father's job having taken him abroad as a kid. Years later, when they landed back in the north-east, he'd been teased about being a posh boy. Ordinarily, it was a label he detested, however, it might give him the edge today. On top of that, he was communicative. Gemma wasn't. He'd made every effort to smarten himself up for the interview. Courtney hadn't. She seemed nice though and he hoped she'd get a job too. She was a talker, which might help if she saw or heard something she didn't like.

Right now, she was leaning towards him, almost whispering.

'Don't say owt . . .' Her eyes darted left. She meant to Gemma. 'I lost my job at the Co-op on Friday. It was only packing shelves, so I wasn't arsed, but I hope I don't have to take old people to the bog or owt. I'd gag.'

Ben pressed his lips together, fighting hard to keep a straight face. 'You haven't worked in a care home before then?'

'No.' She panicked. 'Have you?'

'No, you're safe.'

Gemma ripped out her earphones. 'I have.'

'Well, good for you!' Courtney said. 'You might even crack a smile if you try hard.' Turning away, she continued whispering in Ben's ear. 'To be honest, the wifey in the job centre wasn't too confident of me getting this job. Nothing ventured, she said, whatever that means. They said no qualifications were necessary, so she rang up regardless. Another tick in a box, I suppose.' An eye-roll. 'They're supposed to encourage you to find employment, not take the piss.' She caught Gemma's eye. 'What's up? You look like you chewed a wasp.'

Ben felt sorry for Gemma. He was sure there was a personality under the surface, but she was uptight, incapable of relaxing. The door to the library opened, the woman in the suit appearing on the threshold.

'Courtney, you can come in now.'

Smirking at Gemma, Courtney stood up and followed the suit.

With her gone and Gemma not talking, Ben sat quietly. He had more to worry about than a successful interview. From what he could gather, Chris Adams had unearthed a can of worms and paid the ultimate price for doing so. Going under-cover had seemed the best way to find out exactly what was going on, and to uncover evidence he could feed to David. But if he got the job, he'd have to find a way to explain his absence to Wells, otherwise she'd rat on him to his uncle and then all hell would break loose. He could almost hear Belinda's voice in his ear. 'It's your call . . . David won't like it.'

Ben didn't give a shit.

46

They had been driving for almost fifteen minutes. For the sake of expediency as much as anything else, Frankie forced her personal feeling aside and tried to focus on the task in hand. She needed to know if Chris Adams had spilled the beans on his investigation – and she needed to know now. Enough with the memories, she thought but didn't say, keen to steer the conversation in a different direction. She was about to do so when Trish did it for her . . .

'Anyway, you didn't put yourself out to listen to me ramble on about Chris and what a fine fella he was. He's dead and there's bugger all we can do about it. I've written to his mother. I thought I should, because Fox sure as hell won't. What did you want to talk to me about?'

'I think you know.' Time was too short to go the scenic route.

Dolan didn't answer.

She knew something.

All Frankie had to do was extract if from her. She tried again. 'Trish, talk to me, please. I'm aware of how painful this is for you, but I'm struggling to make sense of his death.'

'Makes two of us.'

'Then work with me.' Frankie glanced to her left. 'Why didn't you come forward when he was found dead?'

'I thought it was a straightforward mugging outside a cash-point. That's what you fed us, isn't it?'

The DS had heard a lot of bullshit from seasoned journal-ists during her career, but this was way off the scale from Dolan. 'It didn't occur to you that it might have something to do with what he was working on?'

Trish turned her head away.

Frankie let it go. The woman had enough on her plate: a possible medical emergency, a lost job and God knows what else. 'OK, let's not dwell on that, but it's high time you unburdened yourself. There's more at stake here than solving his murder. You know that, deep down, don't you?'

A resigned nod from her passenger.

'Chris gave you the gist of what he was working on, didn't he?'

'Only very recently. I told him to tread carefully, especially with someone as high profile and well connected as Sir Giles I-have-my-fingers-in-more-pies-than-Desperate-Dan Bradbury. I met him once, at a charity function.'

Frankie glanced her way. 'What's he like?'

'Flash. You know the type. Money equals power equals an objectionable prick with no morals, a man who thinks he's God's gift to the likes of you and me.'

'You rate him, then.'

'He's barely human.' Trish's fingers were halfway down her throat, a gesture that underlined her distaste for the man. 'If I were you, I'd look into his financial affairs. That's what I told Chris to do.'

'And did he?'

'I don't know.'

'You have reason to believe Bradbury is in trouble?'

'He turned his inheritance into an old people's home. In my book, that means that he can't afford the upkeep.'

'That's quite a jump—'

'Believe me, the man is no philanthropist. He's heartless, in it for what he can get. It costs a fortune to take up residence at Bastle View, triple the average cost of residential care. He'll employ excellent nursing staff, but he won't pay them a bean over the going rate. He's keeping up appearances. It's working too . . . A knighthood? Do me a favour! It's an unearned honour, in my opinion. The only beneficiary I can see is him. That home is a goldmine with a stream of moneyed individuals on the waiting list, ready to pop their clogs and bequeath their hard-earned dosh to Saint Bradbury for the benefit of those coming after them.'

'I've seen the testimonials,' Frankie said. 'Doesn't sound like a home where the elderly are being ill-treated—'

'Depends on how compliant they are.'

'You have proof of that? Did Chris?'

'That was what he was driving at.'

'Has it occurred to you that Bradbury might be an astute businessman? It's his property. He can do what he wants with it. According to some, the place is a premium establishment with a fine reputation, second to none—'

'On the surface. Dig down. Sewers tend to be below ground.'

'Wow, you really don't like him, do you?' Frankie didn't let on that she'd heard negative rumours too. 'I take it you've done some research of your own.'

Trish nodded. 'Not that I got very far. Bradbury is a clever man. One with enough clout to cover his tracks, financially at any rate. I hope you have more luck.' She ran a hand through wet hair. 'You know what concerned Chris most?' She didn't wait for an answer. 'That place is home to a lot of elderly folk who might die if they're moved out of familiar surroundings, others who might suffer if left in there. He was caught between a rock and a hard place. I cautioned him against putting any-thing in writing that might be considered defamatory.' She glanced at Frankie. 'Advice I'm sure you would've given, had he confided in you.'

She knew.

'I did it to protect him,' Dolan added. 'He had no proof of wholesale abuse, only allegations from a woman he'd never met before. Nancy Carver could've been a fruitcake for all I know.'

'Except she's missing,' Frankie said.

'Presumed dead, more like!'

The DS admitted that she thought so too. 'You didn't have any doubts when Chris told you of her disappearance?'

'Stupidly, I thought she'd changed her mind, run away and no longer wanted the role as informant.' A dispirited glance in Frankie's direction. 'I was duped by the fact that she'd made arrangements to move abroad – the very reason your colleagues didn't try too hard to find her. Chris didn't believe she'd emigrated any more than you do.' Trish shook her head. 'Anyway, I suspect you're in possession of more detail than I was at the time.'

'We know she was bullied at work—'

'Welcome to my world.' Trish shook her head. 'Fuck knows how many times Fox has gone for me over the years. Are you telling me none of your colleagues have gone beyond the pale?' She paused. 'No, I didn't think so. My editor-in-chief once threw a paperweight across the room because I'd missed a deadline. Had I not ducked in time, it might have killed me.'

'That's appalling.'

And probably true . . .

Frankie had witnessed similar behaviour within her own organisation, senior colleagues who'd lost the plot, resorting to physical violence, many who'd got away with it because the person on the receiving end was too intimidated to make an official complaint. She didn't share that with her passenger.

Trish twisted in her seat, the better to communicate with her driver. 'As I said, Chris couldn't prove a damn thing. Well, that was the case the last time we spoke about his exposé.'

'He had a photograph. The abuse Nancy suffered went way beyond a momentary loss of temper, Trish. She was beaten up, quite badly—'

'So I understand, but there was no evidence of who'd hit her.'

'We don't know that—'

'She didn't report it, did she? Except to him. That's hearsay, right?' Dolan didn't stop for breath. 'And even if she had, what could you have done, realistically? It would amount to her word against the man or woman alleged to have caused her injuries. Without additional evidence, a reasonable expectation of a conviction, the CPS wouldn't have taken it anywhere. You have no proof either, or we wouldn't be having this conversation.'

Frankie had to concede she had a point.

Dolan added, 'Chris was obviously closer to the truth than I thought. Believe me, I never considered for one minute that he was in danger. Well, not until I saw his facial injuries when he walked into work on that Monday morning. I warned him to back off. He wouldn't listen. He didn't tell me who was responsible for the assault, but when Fox exposed the lie that it hadn't happened during his football match, I knew that someone had leaned on him, a warning shot. After that, he clammed up and wouldn't talk to me.'

'Why didn't you come to us?'

'Why didn't you call him?' Trish snapped.

Frankie received the comment like a stab to the heart. There was only one way that Dolan could know she'd ignored the call and that's if Chris had mentioned it. She wondered what he'd said – what they had both said – what Dolan was thinking now. Frankie didn't ask. She felt ashamed for letting him down . . . It was unforgivable, not the action of a true friend.

Trish took in her sad expression. 'Sorry, that was uncalled for.'

'No, I deserved it.' Frankie changed down, eyes front. 'Did Fox know any of this?'

'Not from me he didn't. I gave Chris my word that his suspicions would remain confidential.' Dolan checked her watch, pointing through the front windscreen. 'Pull over, please. I need some air.'

'Don't be silly, it's pouring. I'll drop you at the entrance.'

'We've made good time. I don't want to get into the clinic

early. I can't bear the look of pain on their faces. If it's all the same to you, I'd rather walk the rest of the way.' Gathering her bag from the footwell as Frankie coasted to a stop, Dolan withdrew a telescopic umbrella. 'I need to clear my head before I go in. Besides, there's nothing quite like the sound of raindrops. My grandma says they bring new life. She's ninety-seven. As fit as a flea. Still gardening.' She reached for the door handle.

'Trish . . .'

Dolan glanced over her shoulder, one foot outside the car.

'Whatever you're facing today, good luck.'

A brief loss of composure, a nervous smile. 'You too, Frankie. Remember, you're not to blame. Chris should've acted well before he did. He was in too deep. I told him so. It was my idea that he call you. He could have, should have, reported the matter sooner. And you're right, this case is way bigger than his murder.'

47

At Middle Earth, Stone glanced at the digital clock on the wall, wondering what was keeping Frankie. His press conference had gone well, in part due to Collingwood's intervention. Professor Sarah Hainsworth's input had been clear and concise, and while he didn't mention specifics, he was able to state with absolute certainty that he was making progress, enough to put the wind up the offender he was hunting. He or she would be watching the press for updates. The news also boosted a flagging team, giving everyone cause for celebration.

The MIT were on the right track . . . finally.

'Any news on the CCTV?' he asked Abbott.

Dick shook his head. The detective who'd been given the task of identifying the man wearing a distinctive fleece on the night of Adams' murder had drawn a blank. 'She still has a lot of footage to go through yet, guv. She's shut in an office at HQ and says she's not coming out until she finds him. She's the type to remain positive in the face of bad odds, even if I'm not.'

David knew what he meant. It was possible to circumvent the cameras to avoid being seen, approaching the crime scene from the rear, which would suggest someone with local knowledge, a savvy offender who'd identified blind spots. No city had total coverage.

'Was there anything else, guv?'

David shook his head. 'Let me know if you hear anything.'

As Abbott moved away, the door to the incident room opened.

Frankie walked through it, soaking wet, drying her hair on a paper towel she'd picked up from the locker room on the way in. Checking the murder wall was an automatic response, the first thing she did whenever she returned to base. It was a practice she drilled into other squad members, for there was no better way to ensure that they hadn't missed anything important. Seeing very little change, she threw the paper towel in the trash, combed her hair with her hands, tying it up in a ponytail.

In David's office, they pooled intelligence over a sandwich and a cup of coffee. As she debriefed him on her conversation with Dolan, Frankie was buoyed by the fact that all roads appeared to be leading in the same direction.

'There's more work to be done before we can begin questioning staff at Bastle View,' she cautioned. 'Either Bradbury is complicit in what's going on there – *if* there is something going on there – or he's totally in the dark. Either way, the responsibility for how that home is run lies with him.'

'The fact that Trish Dolan doesn't like him isn't enough.'

'As it happens, she doesn't like Fox either. If the miserable git is withholding information, he'll be shitting himself with Technical Support crawling all over his mainframe.'

They both responded to a knock at the door.

Abbott poked his head in. 'Sorry to interrupt, I thought you should know about this.' Approaching the desk, he unfolded an Ordnance Survey map and spread it out flat, using his forefinger to indicate a patch of green, a large wooded area in the county: Harwood Forest.

Frankie was way ahead of him. 'That's where Nancy's phone went dead?'

Dick nodded. 'And where I reckon Adams went the day he was supposed to be playing football. There are no cameras out that way. No wonder the ANPR lost him. If the poor sod was in trouble, he could yell till his lungs burst and no one would hear him. If Nancy is dead, and Adams was on the case, you'd think whoever he was upsetting would want to silence him for good.'

'They did,' Stone said.

'Eventually,' Abbott said. 'What I meant was, how come he managed to survive Sunday's attack?'

'Maybe he managed to get clear and ran for his life,' Frankie said. 'He was supremely fit.'

David was unconvinced. 'So why didn't his attacker wait for him to return to his bike and finish the job? Chris could hardly walk home, could he? The place is a bloody wilderness.'

'That assumes that he didn't have the foresight to park up and walk,' Frankie cut in. 'I know that area well. There are any number of places to stash a bike – it's a damned sight easier to hide and much harder to spot than a car. Chris might have been an amateur sleuth, but he was far from stupid. He'd have anticipated the danger, wouldn't he? Planned an escape in case things got ugly. He'd have waited until the coast was clear before heading home.' Frankie turned to face Abbott. 'Remind me what time the ANPR picked him up on the return journey?'

'Three fifteen.'

'He was there a while then. If he *was* forced to hide, it would explain why he was away for over four hours that day.' Frankie took a moment to think things through. 'Whoever laid into him wouldn't risk waiting on the main road either, would they? They'd fuck off and use the back roads to make good their getaway.' She glanced at the map, picked up a pen and drew a dotted line from Harwood Forest to Bastle View.

All three detectives looked at one another.

'Jesus!' Abbott said. 'It's no distance.'

'I want a search team out there immediately,' Stone said. 'Quietly . . . No bells and whistles. We don't want to tip anyone off that we're interested. Make sure you send them out in plain vans. If you need to create a diversion to keep people away, do it. Dodgy roadworks, whatever it takes. It shouldn't be too hard to organise.' He glanced through his office window. It was pitch-black outside. 'Do it now, Dick. We want them in under cover of darkness and ready to search at first light.'

48

Ben was bored, laptop on his knee, flicking through TV channels. His body was on the sofa. His head was in deepest, darkest Northumberland, inside a certain home for the elderly. Gemma Radcliffe had gone in first. She walked out of the Care Home Manager's office looking pleased with her performance, beaming at him on the way out, less up herself than when she'd been waiting to be interviewed, wishing him luck as she left Bastle View. Maybe it was nerves that made her appear aloof beforehand.

Everyone deserved a second chance.

He continued flicking through a never-ending list of programmes he had no intention of watching, none of them spiking his interest. He leaned down, reaching for a bottle of beer he'd left on the floor. Having become warm in front of the fire, it tasted vile. He couldn't be arsed to get up and fetch another, so he necked the rest, primarily to take the edge off his growing impatience. Things could change in a matter of hours – not always for the better.

He'd left Bastle View feeling upbeat, knowing he'd given a good account of himself. At the time, he felt he'd made an impression, except now he wasn't sure. With every minute that passed, doubt crept in. He reran the interview over and over in his head. He should've said this or expanded on that. Considering the responsibility heaped upon those who looked after the old and infirm, the interview had been brief, now he came to think of it.

Fiona Fitzgerald, Nancy Carver's replacement, seemed pleasant enough. Was she also playing a part, hiding behind a persona? 'I'm curious about your change of direction,' she'd said.

'I thought you might be.'

She relaxed into her chair. 'The thing is, Ben, I'm looking for people who intend to stick around, people with real commitment. I have the residents to think of. They get attached to staff in a very short space of time. I can't afford to employ anyone who'll be gone in two weeks.'

'I understand, Ms Fitzgerald, and I can assure you that won't happen . . .'

Putting on his sincerity face, Ben had delivered the story about university not floating his boat, how he'd helped look after his great-grandmother towards the end of her life, how satisfying the experience was. In truth, he'd never had that much contact with her, much to David's disappointment, something Ben had regretted since the day she passed away.

'That's exactly what we're after,' the manager said.

Ben looked down at his laptop. It sounded convincing at the time, so much so he almost believed it himself. He began to wonder whether he'd underestimated the woman on the other side of the desk. More to the point, had Fitzgerald seen through him? If she had, she hadn't shown it. With the articulation of a top-notch saleswoman, she'd given a spiel about the home, the clientele, the values all staff aspired to. They shook hands afterwards and Ben was told that he'd be contacted by the end of the day.

He checked his watch. It was getting on for eight.

What was keeping her?

Half an hour passed, by which time Ben was beginning to accept that he'd flunked the interview, that his chance to help David had slipped away. Shame. Never in his whole life had he felt driven to do something this momentous. Chris Adams deserved his name above the fold and Ben was as determined as his uncle that he'd get it. Problem was, he didn't yet have a Plan B.

Forty minutes later, and no further forward, his eyes became heavy and he began to nod off. The sound of an email pinging into his inbox almost lifted him off the sofa. Ben sat up straight and took a deep breath before clicking on it.

Yes! He was in, with immediate effect, including live-in accommodation that would reduce his 'salary' the email said. He almost snorted when he saw the numbers – he'd struggle to call that pay.

'Tomorrow?' It came out like an exclamation.

'What about it?' David said.

Ben panicked. He'd been thinking out loud and had forgotten that his uncle was in the house, never mind the room. When Ben first moved in, Stone was rarely at home in the evenings, always finding an excuse to stay late at Middle Earth, to hang out with Frankie, Dick Abbott and the rest of the Murder Investigation Team. His uncle was doing less of that now. In the past few months he'd chosen to come home and build bridges.

Ben appreciated that.

Since he was a boy, David had been his hero. He'd not seen him nearly enough, but when he did, the guy was ace. On a family holiday, he'd taught Ben to swim, and how to nutmeg his dad. He bought him burgers at St James's Park, two if he asked for them. And, coolest of all – when his dad wasn't in – how to do wheelies on his bike in the middle of the road. He was a laugh, everything his old man wasn't, everything an uncle should be. Ben had never shared that with him. He knew, though, didn't he?

They were family.

Ben didn't glance over his shoulder for fear that his uncle would spot the lie on the tip of his tongue. On the way home on the bus, Ben had racked his brains for a feasible excuse to take a few days' leave from the newspaper, so as not to raise suspicion with David or Wells. With a bit of luck, he'd come up with a scenario that would satisfy them both.

'I've been invited down to Liverpool.' Best to keep it casual. 'A mate of mine has asked me to help him move house. Belinda has given me time off. Thing is, he needs me there tomorrow.'

'Is that a good idea?' David walked round the sofa and stood in front of him, arms folded, his back to the fire, his sensible head on. 'You've been given an opportunity, son. Don't blow it.'

Even cool guys had their moments.

'I'm not, Dave.' Ben kept his focus on his computer screen, avoiding eye contact. 'Belinda has stuff on and, for some reason, I'm surplus to requirements.' Given David's interference, the pressure he'd put on Wells to keep him away from his murder case, Ben knew the falsehood would ring true. 'I'm shadowing a colleague who's not a patch on her, so now is as good a time as any.'

When he looked up, it was David who looked guilty.

Sorted.

49

Frankie had declined a quick drink after work with David. God knows she could do with one or two. She'd already accepted an invitation to dinner with her folks, an opportunity to reassure her mum that she was functioning normally after the shock of turning up at a crime scene where she knew the victim – history repeating itself in the Oliver household – and also to thank her father for pulling strings on behalf of the MIT.

'You haven't eaten much, love.' Her mother seemed distracted.

Frankie pushed her plate away, feeling ashamed for wasting good food. Her mum had taken a lot of trouble to prepare one of her favourite dishes. The truth was, Frankie was too wired to eat. Her mind was on a forest trail where vans with human cargo were parked up, their occupants on starter's orders to find Nancy Carver's body.

'It was delicious, Mum. I'm stuffed.'

Julie Oliver didn't do what she always did and push her daughter to eat 'just another mouthful' or mention how thin she was looking, how pasty, how tired, how she should take a long holiday. Neither did she jump up to fetch dessert. No, like Frankie she was someplace else, deep in thought, a worried expression on her face.

Frankie glanced at her dad: what's wrong with her?

A shoulder shrug, his mouth turned down at the edges. 'Julie, you OK?'

'Mm . . .' She focused on Frankie. 'Would you have time to check on Susan before heading home? She's not answering my texts.' The implication was clear.

*

Across the road, Frankie opened the garden gate and cut round the side of the house to the back door, as she had as a kid. It was and always had been a direct route to Chris, the door never locked in this peaceful, rural community. She tapped on the door, then pushed it open and stepped silently into the kitchen. Susan Adams was rigid, facing away from the door, leaning over the sink, hanging on to the taps. She was shaking uncontrollably, mumbling incoherently.

'Susan? What's wrong?' Stupid question. Frankie rephrased. 'Are you ill? Shall I call the doctor?'

She didn't move or offer any response.

Frankie could see how distraught she was and didn't want to frighten her.

Had she even heard?

A small wall-mounted TV was on, actors dressed as Stormtroopers lining the route as people arrived for the European premiere of *Star Wars: The Last Jedi* at the Royal Albert Hall, the event hosted by Princes William and Harry, a cause for celebration apparently. On screen, crowds cheered, stars signed autographs, the press jostled for the opportunity to capture the moment on the red carpet. The flash photography was blinding as actresses posed in expensive outfits: Calvin Klein, Monse, Vivienne Westwood, Halpern, Tom Ford.

Bunch of prima donnas.

Using the remote, Frankie pressed mute, shutting off the noise. Susan's mobile was lying on the kitchen bench, the screen smashed, the casing damaged beyond repair, a white powdery substance on one edge. Frankie looked around, noting the dent where it had hit the wall, a sprinkling of plaster dust on the floor beneath it. She picked up the device.

Completely dead.

No wonder her mother hadn't been able to get through.

In Frankie's peripheral vision, a full bottle of vodka drew her eye, a single shot glass beside it. It felt like the saddest thing she'd ever seen. Susan's sobriety journey had taken forever. She wouldn't make it a second time. The condition of the phone and the vodka explained a lot. Her mum hadn't dared visit for fear of what she might find.

Frankie reached for the bottle.

Susan got there first, snatching it away from her. She was trembling, her expression a mixture of helplessness, anger and downright guilt, a tear-stained face, eyes barely able to focus. Had she been drinking or was this the effects of heavy-duty medication? Frankie couldn't bear the thought that the bottle now in her hand might not be the first, that Susan might already have stepped over the abyss and was about to throw her life away again.

Frankie pulled out a chair at the kitchen table. 'Susan, come and sit down a moment. I'll make some tea and we can talk. Come on, I'll get the kettle on.' She didn't move, just fixed the DS with hard eyes. Frankie said, 'You don't need to do this. You don't. Please, think it through. You can't go there again.' Her eyes were pleading. 'I care about you, Susan—'

'Oh, spare me the sympathy, Frankie. Isn't that what your fucking FLO is for.'

It felt like a slap.

Frankie took a step away, sensing that they were alone in the house, suspecting that Melanie had been sent packing and hadn't yet built up the courage to admit defeat. It wasn't that she'd failed in her duty to assist the mother of a murder victim. Some people in Susan's position wouldn't, couldn't accept help. Frankie wasn't getting through. Empathy wasn't working and, before she knew it, the unvarnished truth spilled from her mouth. 'You may as well put a bullet in your head, you know that, right?'

Tears were rolling down Susan's face. She'd survived the initial shock of receiving the death message, the viewing room at the morgue and what came after. In a matter of days, the alteration in her appearance was stark. She had dark circles under her eyes, lines where none had been before. She hadn't combed her hair or bothered to dress.

This wasn't looking good.

'Did *she* tell you?' It was like an accusation.

'No, though it's part of Melanie's role to look out for you.'

'Spy on me, you mean?' She may as well have said: Take your kindness and shove it up your arse. A glare. 'Is that why you're here? Because if it is, you can sling your hook. Unlike murder, drinking isn't a crime. I'm a grown-up.'

'So act like one. If you open that bottle, you'll regret it.'

'I can make my own decisions.'

'So that's it? No negotiation? You're going to crawl under your duvet for another ten years? You didn't find solace in drink last time. Exactly how do you think it'll help you now?'

For all the times Chris had talked about physical and emotional dependency on alcohol, Frankie had no idea what to do, what to say to a woman on the brink of a relapse. How exactly do you stop someone you care for falling off the wagon when they had no desire to hold on during a bumpy ride? With no time to prepare for such a pivotal conversation, it was Frankie who now felt guilty. She'd been a copper for so long she was used to firing from the hip, even if it sounded harsh. Susan was vulnerable and needed careful handling. It was no good talking to her if she was half cut.

'Are you sober?' Frankie asked gently.

'Yes, I'm fucking sober!' Susan pulled the bottle to her breast with two hands, like a child might cling on to a comfort blanket, yelling like a woman possessed. 'No one invited you here, Frankie. Get out of my house!'

Frankie stood her ground.

It wasn't the first time she'd been ordered from this very room. As a teenager, she'd fled from the drunk who couldn't control her temper, wouldn't accept that she had a problem that was ruining her life, taking her son down with her, a woman who could flare up at a moment's notice.

Frankie wouldn't flee this time.

Trying to calm the situation, she flicked the switch on the kettle and made a pot of tea. As she did so, there was movement behind her. Susan hadn't said a word. When Frankie turned around, she was sitting at the kitchen table, both hands like a vice around the vodka bottle. Frankie sat down beside her, rubbing her forearm, soothing her.

Ignoring sense, Susan tightened her grip.

'Look, I know it's hard to cope with loss, especially in these circumstances. You saw what it did to my parents, to me and Rae. There's not a day goes by I don't think about our Joanna. It hurts like hell. I carry on and so do they. It's what she'd have wanted us to do. Chris . . .' Frankie stumbled over her words, that feeling of helplessness returning, as if it had never gone away. 'Susan, he was so proud of you. Please don't let him down.'

'You think I haven't thought of that?' Susan eyed the vodka, her voice breaking as she spoke. 'It's been sitting there, staring at me all day. I haven't touched it, I promise you. That's not to say I won't.' She met Frankie's gaze. 'I'm weak. Always have been. I wish I had your resolve. I don't.'

'Yes, you do. You've proved that. He wasn't here all the time, was he?'

'I always knew he was coming back, in an hour, a day, a week. I feel crushed without him, Frankie.' She swallowed hard, a tormented expression. 'Sometimes I can barely breathe. There's nothing left for me now. Nothing . . .'

Frankie had been to that place. She'd experienced the heartbreak, watched her parents go into meltdown as life went on for everyone else, worried that the crisis would blow them apart as a couple – it almost did – and only realised how strong her feelings were for her sister after she'd gone. It was a dark time. At school, Frankie had worked hard and kept smiling, though it killed her. She lost weight and wore layers to bulk up so her teachers wouldn't notice and bother her mum and dad. After school, she used to sneak in the back door and hide in her room so they wouldn't know she was there, close the curtains and sit in the dark. It took all her resolve not to crumble now. Susan spoke, interrupting her thoughts . . .

'I'm sorry for yelling, but I can't do this alone—'

'You don't have to. I'm here, aren't I?' Frankie paused, taking it gently, trying to avoid going over the top. 'There's no need for apologies. We've had the gloves off before and I'm not one to bear a grudge, you know that. Let me call your counsellor and set up an appointment. In the meantime, Mum says there's a bed for you across the road, for as long as you need it. You can use my room if you can bear to share it with a bunch of superheroes.' Frankie gave a wry smile. 'Mum thinks I'm still twelve.'

The tears came then. Frankie held her arms out.

Susan fell into her embrace.

50

'They found something, guv.'

Stone listened intently as Dick Abbott gave more detail. He'd gone out to the search area to check on progress and, more importantly, to get behind the PolSA team. Officers were growing increasingly jaded, having spent hour after mind-numbing hour in freezing conditions that had returned to that remote part of Northumberland, making their task more difficult.

'On my way.' Slipping his mobile into his pocket, David was out of his chair, scooping car keys off his desk, pulling on a warm jacket. Frankie's eyes seized on him as soon as he yanked opened his office door. 'We're on,' he told her. 'Whatever you're doing, offload it.'

'Guv?'

'Grab your kit. Meet me in the car park.'

She didn't argue and was gone in a blink.

Detectives downed tools and ended phone calls, all heads turned in the direction of the SIO, intrigued by the urgency in his voice. No doubt they had their suspicions, but he chose not to raise their hopes or tell them why he was going out, even when the office manager pushed his metal-framed specs up on to his forehead and wandered over, a mug of steamy liquid in his hand. There had been many false alarms in David's career. This could be another.

'Charlie, we might be a while. Keep it shut, eh? And tell this lot to do the same.'

'Gotcha, boss.' Charlie, an old soldier, said no more.

David approached DC Mitchell's desk. 'Mitch, keep pushing Fox. He's been dragging his feet for long enough. Tell him if the information we asked for isn't on my desk by close of play he'll be escorted here to explain himself, in cuffs if he argues.' Without further comment, Stone followed his 2ic out of the incident room and down the main stairwell to the rear door.

It had taken the PolSA team a week to search the woods where Nancy Carver's phone went dead. Stone and Oliver had been up to Harwood Forest a few times themselves to check on progress, only to receive a weary shake of the head from the search team coordinator. It was an immense area, accessible to the public, with miles of woodland paths. It was possible to get lost there. To lose yourself in nature, to walk for hours without meeting another soul.

They found something, guv.

David had dreamed of hearing those four words as he slept. When they came, they sent shivers right through him, bringing with them a feeling of delirium that he might be closing in on a perpetrator who, he suspected, had committed more than one murder. At the same time there was a sense of foreboding, knowing the discovery was guaranteed to break hearts and draw criticism at the way a misper case had been handled.

Bad press was the least of his worries. He wasn't responsible for the actions of others, though he felt the disgrace as if it were his own. Frankie climbed into the passenger seat, buckled up, placing her phone on a dusty dash, a sideways glance as she waited for him to pull away.

'Is it a body?'

'Not yet.' David turned over the ignition, meeting her gaze as he checked that there was no one behind him. 'I'm guessing it's only a matter of time. They found a wing mirror belonging to a Fiat. It's metallic blue, Frank. Same model as Nancy's car. I don't believe it belongs to anyone else, do you?'

'Fuck! I knew it.'

They both fell silent as the miles flashed by. David didn't need to tell her that if they could find Nancy's car and match

293

the wing mirror, they were in business. One more piece to the puzzle falling neatly into place. Sadly, despite flagging the car as a vehicle of interest on the PNC, it hadn't been found. He suspected that it had been dumped somewhere it might never be found: in a river, a deep ravine, a lock-up. David chose not to dwell on the negatives. It was still possible that it had been left on a street somewhere and, because it was parked lawfully, no one had drawn it to the attention of the police. Now the vehicle licence duty had expired, the DVLA alerted, if someone tried to tax it, he might yet catch a break.

In the past few days, the enquiry had moved up a notch. Technical Support had reported on the data they found on Chris Adams' flash drive. It had proved illuminating: extensive notes on his conversations with Nancy, detailing his thoughts over her disappearance and subsequent efforts to locate her, and a lot more besides, including grid references, longitude and latitude, a postcode pinpointing the area now being searched. It was all there in black and white. Adams had not named the man or woman who'd assaulted him, whose initials were JC. Frankie had already ruled out Jesus Christ.

51

Taking a deep breath, Ben slipped his phone into his pocket and walked into a drawing room littered with walking frames of all shapes and sizes. In the foreground, three female residents, two in wheelchairs, and one male were playing dominoes at a square table. Behind them, a massive smart TV was on in the background, incongruous in its Georgian surroundings, the volume up so loud that he was tempted to turn it down. No one was taking a blind bit of notice of what was on. Edna, ninety-eight, was knitting, while others dosed off in high-backed chairs, out of it due to the amount of medication they were taking. He wondered if they would see the other side of Christmas.

Standing in the doorway, he imagined what the room would once have looked like, full of elegant, antique furniture and oriental rugs on the very best parquet flooring that was now laid bare. Light flooded in through windows framed with heavy drapes. The main focus of the room was a magnificent white marble fireplace with logs in the grate which, he suspected, hadn't been lit since the house became a residential home. An arrangement of poinsettias created a splash of colour in the hearth.

His eyes shifted to an eight-foot Christmas tree in the corner, beautifully decorated with red ribbons and silver baubles, with makeshift presents he'd been asked to place underneath, the empty boxes acting as a chilling reminder, if one were needed, that all that glitters is not gold.

The cliché was fitting.

In the past few days, Ben had spent a lot of time watching and listening for gossip, volunteering for shifts he had no need to work and wasn't being paid for, none of which had been viewed as suspicious. He hoped. He was new in, keen to create a good impression. That was all there was to it. Wells had been right though. Underneath a perfect facade, there was something off about the place, an underlying tension he hadn't yet got a handle on, except for one snippet of information he'd passed to the police for the attention of his uncle. Anxiously, Ben wondered if David had received it yet.

'Ben?' A male voice.

Startled, Ben turned to face Michael Matthews, a man he'd been warned not to get on the wrong side of by more than one member of staff. Ben was tall, Matthews taller, with fair hair, piercing blue eyes and a sharp jawline. He smelled of cheap aftershave and had a hard edge to his voice.

'Who were you talking to just now?'

Ben considered a lie, then told the truth, a smart move should Matthews confiscate his device. 'My uncle,' he said. 'I promised to let him know how I was getting on. I couldn't get hold of him, so I left a message.'

'Mobiles are not allowed while you're working,' Matthews said.

'Yeah, I'm sorry. It won't happen again—'

'It had better not. Leave your phone in your room when you're on duty.' Matthews glanced around the room, then turned to face Ben. 'What the hell were you gawping at anyway?'

'Nothing, I was—'

'There's no time for daydreaming here. Go and check on George and Molly. Their call bells are going. They've probably pissed themselves by now.'

'Sorry, I—'

'Just do it!'

Ben practically ran along the corridor, feeling the heat of Matthews eyes between his shoulder blades. It saddened him to think that many of the elderly never made it past the threshold of their living quarters, not even to eat, too frail or ill to venture out unaided. The upside was that, whenever he got the chance to spend a few moments in their company, they responded to a brief respite in solitary confinement, an opportunity to reminisce about their younger lives. One old man was particularly coherent, Molly and George less so, their memories – short and long-term – inaccessible these days.

Ben stopped walking, eyes widening as a figure appeared in front of him. George had left his room and was heading Ben's way, shuffling along in a pair of oversized slippers, each tiny step representing a monumental effort. His arms shook as he struggled to grip his walking frame. Only the top of his balding head was visible. Ben had never seen him on his feet – let alone out of his room. George was a fall risk if ever he'd seen one.

'George?' Ben kept it light. 'Where you off to in such a hurry? Training for the Great North Run?'

Slowly, the old man raised his head. With steely determination, he straightened up, as much as he was able, spindly legs in baggy trousers half bent at the knee. His eyes were tiny, the colour washed out against thin, ashen skin. The only way Ben could describe him was lost.

'Goodbye,' George said, his voice as weak as the rest of him. 'I'm going home now.'

Ben threw him a wide smile. 'Your room is this way, George. Here, let me help you.'

The old man appeared affronted. 'I don't live here!' He did and had for five years. 'Fetch my coat. I need to go. Maisy will have the tea ready.'

The comment threw Ben. Maisy was dead. 'Did you get sick of waiting?'

'That's what I said, she's waiting. I don't want to be late.'

'OK, well I'm here now, George.' Ben placed a hand on his shoulder. 'That's it. Gently does it.'

Fiona Fitzgerald, Nancy Carver's replacement, smiled at

her new recruit as she walked along the corridor going the other way. In the past week, she'd given Ben a brief induction, informing him of families who visited regularly, those who didn't and those he needed to impress. He looked down at the resident walking beside him. George never got any visitors. Such a shame. He was a nice old man, if a little muddled. He took a breather, leaning on his walking frame, looking up at Ben as if he'd suddenly appeared out of thin air and they'd never met before.

His expression was hard to read.

'Siiimon?' It came out like a desperate cry for help. 'I've been looking for you. Where have you been?'

Ben didn't answer. He had no idea who Simon was, only that it wasn't him. A son? A grandson? He stood there, tongue-tied, unable to respond, wishing he'd known more of the man's background, wondering if it would be wrong to pretend to be Simon for a moment or two. What harm would it do if it made the old man happy?

Confusion reigned on both sides of the corridor.

'Did you think I was dead?' George waited, his brow furrowed, a flicker of something in his watery eyes. 'Well, I'm not,' he said crossly, 'so you've no need to send flowers.'

The hint of a sense of humour bubbling to the surface made Ben want to weep. George made no further attempt to communicate with Simon. Neither did he mention Maisy or put up any resistance as Ben steered him away from the front door. By the time they reached his room, he seemed to have forgotten their conversation in the corridor. Settling him in his room, Ben made him comfortable in a chair overlooking the garden. A pat on the hand. That's all it took to calm him down. A bit of kindness before Ben moved on to Molly.

Though Ben was on a covert mission to help David Stone, observing staff as well as residents, it was talking to the elderly that kept him going. He'd heard stories of heroism during the Second World War; of careers in medicine, education and politics; time spent 'in service' for wealthy landowners like Sir Giles Bradbury. Ben had been blown away by the collective wisdom of the residents of Bastle View. Working there had made him see beyond the wrinkled skin and loss of mental capacity to the souls who lived within. It had altered his perception of his own grandmother, who'd driven an ambulance during WW1.

He wished he'd listened now.

52

It was a bit of a trek through the woods over uneven ground, the narrow dirt track fringed by trees and ferns on either side, offering little shelter from a biting wind sweeping down from the north. It was icy cold. Enough to seep through Stone and Oliver's clothing, attacking their bones, making their eyes water as they followed the coordinates they had been given by Control. The path was long, muddy and winding, unsuitable for anything but a four-wheel drive. David had chosen to leave his parked on the main road inside the perimeter he'd set up as a normal road diversion with the help of a contact at Northumberland County Council. He wanted to get a proper feel for the place, a decision he was beginning to regret. Frankie was struggling, her Wellington boots slipping and sliding with every step. David grabbed at her arm as she tripped over a root sticking out of the ground, losing her footing, grumbling as she tried to stay upright, falling into his arms, her face inches from his.

An awkward moment.

Blushing, she stepped away – looked away – her eyes scanning the forest briefly, before turning to face him, a wry smile on her face. 'Hope no one saw that or we'll be engaged before we reach Middle Earth.'

He held up his hands as if she was pointing a gun. 'I'll tell them you were seducing me.'

'In your dreams, pal!' Pulling up her collar, Frankie blew on cupped hands, avoiding eye contact. She began walking on the spot. 'God, I'd have been warmer if I'd walked into a fridge,' she moaned. 'Ryman and Eva must be made of sterner stuff. I'm bloody freezing!' She gave him a dirty look. 'Why anyone would choose to own a four-by-four and walk beats me. Come to think of it, anyone who'd choose to come here in the dead of winter wants their head read.'

'Nancy wasn't taking a stroll, Frank. If my maths is correct, she was running for her life. Her resignation letter was dated second of December. The mail found at her Blanchland address post-dated her final shift at Bastle View. This is pure guesswork, but I suspect she was followed. Someone got wind of the fact that she was on to them and silenced her. I reckon she turned off the main road in a vain attempt to escape. Who knows what happened thereafter. She must've been terrified—'

'If it had been me, I'd have carried on driving—'

'If it had been you, you'd have called the law. I agree with you. At the very least, the open road offered the possibility of eyewitnesses. There'd be none here. Even on a summer's day, you'd be hard-pushed to meet anyone. That's the attraction. I could be wrong. If I'm right, in her panic to get away, I reckon Nancy played right into their hands.'

With a shake of his head, David peered through the trees and into the undergrowth. A native red squirrel caught his eye, skipping silently from branch to branch. It was hard to imagine that this peaceful, idyllic place was Nancy Carver's final destination. Under the circumstances, he couldn't bring himself to describe it as a resting place. Suddenly, the beauty of his surroundings morphed into something more sinister.

Within minutes, they had reached a clearing.

A number of identifiable vans were parked in a semicircle, like wagons in a western movie. The search was ongoing in every direction. The wing mirror had been left in situ. Stone and Oliver made their way towards it. Despite the fact that over two million Fiat Pandas of the same series as Nancy's car had been sold, as far as they were concerned, they were visiting a crime scene. Based on no more than gut feeling, both were of the opinion that the PolSA team had found something of evidential value. Time would tell if they were right in that assumption.

The search team coordinator looked over his shoulder as they approached. 'Guv. Frankie.'

'Andrew.' Stone shook his hand. 'I appreciate your efforts this week. It can't have been easy for you.'

A shrug. 'My team are bulletproof, guv. Rain or shine, it's what they do.'

The SIO crouched down to examine the find, a left-handed wing-mirror, lying on the left side of the track. He looked up. 'Travelling this way then, away from the main road?'

'Yes, guv. The car probably hit a tree—'

'Or another vehicle,' Frankie interrupted.

'No.' David stood up straight. 'It's too narrow for two cars to pass here.' A glance at Andrew. 'Is that it?'

'No, boss. After I called you, we continued searching . . .' He pointed to a spot in the distance. Around one tree trunk, stakes had been placed in the ground, joined by crime scene tape that flapped in the wind. 'That's where the wing-mirror became dislodged from the vehicle. Looks like it anyway. We knew the height of the mirror from the ground. There's a corresponding deep gouge in the bark of that tree over there. One of my team found it a few minutes ago.'

'So how did it get here?' Frankie was talking about the mirror.

'You'd be surprised how far foreign objects travel if the car was being driven at speed. It's possible that it flew a fair distance.' David was speaking from experience. He used to be part of the Metropolitan Police's armed response team. They didn't hang around. He'd been involved in a number of car chases that had ended badly, where parts of crashed vehicles had flown like missiles in all directions, littering the streets of London, on one occasion smashing through the window of a nearby house. As an aside, he added: 'Or maybe someone picked it up and dropped it here.' He refocused on their PolSA colleague. 'What's the plan?'

'My team will fan out now to see what else is here. They have their instructions, guv.'

'CSIs are on their way?'

A nod.

David's phone rang. Taking it from his breast pocket, he checked the screen: *DC Mitchell*. 'I'll have to take this. Great job, Andrew. Pass on our thanks to your crew. Beers are on me when they're done.'

'Guv.' He moved away.

Stone heard him relay the message, giving encouragement to his team to keep going. It would be dark soon. They were losing the light. Pressing to receive his call, David lifted his phone to his ear. 'Mitch, what is it?'

'I wasn't sure I'd get you, guv.'

'Well, you're in luck. The signal is piss poor here, so be quick before it disappears.'

'Fox has turned over the information you requested.' Mitch chuckled. 'I told him what you said. He didn't fancy an away game.'

'Did he come up with anything interesting?'

'Not sure yet. Dick and I are working on it. Actually, that's not why I rang. There's something else you need to know. Are you free to speak?'

'Yeah, hold on . . .' Locking eyes with Frankie, David then glanced over his shoulder. In theory, the only people around were police personnel, but you could never be too sure. Flicking his eyes left, he moved towards the trees, putting the phone on speaker so she could listen in. A second head check. 'Go ahead, Mitch.'

'We received a tip-off, guv.'

'From whom?'

'Anonymous male. It turns out that seven years ago, an old man's body was found in an outbuilding on Bradbury's estate.

The consensus of opinion was that he'd taken refuge there, having wandered away from the home late at night. He was still in his PJs and died of hyperthermia before he was found. His name was Alfred – Alfie – Jenkins.'

'Verdict?'

'Accidental death.' There was a long pause. 'Guv, he was a retired surgeon with no next of kin. I've had sight of his will. Guess who inherited the lot?'

53

The detectives returned to Middle Earth for the briefing, David peeling off to his office to prepare, Frankie checking the murder wall before sitting down at her desk and logging on to her computer. She stared at the force logo, the anonymous tip-off worming its way into her head as it had throughout the journey back to base. It wasn't the notion that Alfie Jenkins had wandered away from Bastle View or even the possibility of a second whistle-blower that worried her. It was the fact that the anonymous caller hadn't contacted the front desk. He'd asked for the incident room, leaving a message for David specifically. Other than the Murder Investigation Team, only one person knew of the link between Chris Adams and Nancy Carver . . .

Oh, God!

Frankie's heart began to kick against her ribs, a wave of nausea sweeping through her. She got up and made her way across the room to the receiver's desk. Taking a moment to compose herself, she kept it casual, so as not to raise any eyebrows. 'Pam, the message that came in for the boss earlier. Did you take it?'

'No, one of the temps did . . .' Pam pointed her out. 'Her name's Claire. She's the civvi in the Christmas jumper. As you can see, she's popular. She has more red cards than Joey Barton. Me? I have this . . .' Pam held up a handmade Christmas card. Someone had drawn a smiley Santa on the front and stuck a bit of tinsel on with Blu Tack. 'Pathetic,' she grumbled. 'One of the lads put it there so I wouldn't feel left out. It's not even signed.'

'Quit bitching. It's one more than I have.' Smiling, Frankie glanced at Claire, whose desk was littered with seasonal greetings. A miniature tree was stuck to her computer monitor, complete with lights.

Frankie refocused on Pam. 'What's she like?'

'Efficient. And off to Lapland tomorrow. If you want to speak to her, do it now.'

'Can I see the message first?'

Locating the A4 sheet, Pam passed it over. Frankie read it in its entirety, her eyes seizing on six words at the top: Keen to speak to the SIO. The rest of the message was exactly as Mitch had repeated to David over the phone, word for word.

Claire was a pro.

Tapping the message, Frankie said, 'I'll let you have this back in a mo.' She crossed the room, trying not to show the stress she was under as she approached the civilian clerk. 'Claire, I'm Frankie Oliver. Sorry to interrupt. Have you got a second?'

'Sarge.' She took off her headset. 'I've heard a lot about you.'

'Likewise. I'm in a hell of a rush, so forgive my bluntness. You received this message today.' Frankie handed it to her. 'I want you to think hard and tell me exactly what the caller said to you on the phone?'

Claire glanced at the paper, then handed it back. 'Only what's written there. Is there a problem?'

'Not at all. I wish all messages were this detailed. One question. Did the guy you spoke to actually use the acronym, SIO? It could be important.'

'Yeah, he did.'

'He didn't mention the guv'nor by name?'

'No.'

'And when you asked him who he was . . . ?'

'He said he'd rather not say.'

'It says here . . .' Frankie read from the message. 'Youngish male, local accent, not broad. Can you give me any more detail, or take a stab at his age for me?'

'Twenties. Articulate. Polite.' She waggled her hand from

306

side to side. 'Nervous maybe. He wasn't on the line more than a minute.'

'Thanks, that's super helpful. Enjoy your leave.'

'Thanks.' Claire picked up her headset. 'I can't wait.'

Returning the message to Pam, Frankie glanced at David's office door as she returned to her desk, dialling Ben's number as she kept a lookout.

The call went straight to voicemail.

'Fuck!' She threw her mobile on the desk, then picked it up again, sending a brief text: Call me when you're free.

Staring at the phone, willing it to spring into life, she waited.

Nothing.

'Sarge, you OK?'

She looked up to find DC Mitchell standing over her. She gave a half-smile, hooking a rogue hair behind her right ear. 'Yeah, tired. You did good today, I'm proud of you.' If she hadn't been so fucking worried, she'd have been proud of Ben too. What was the stupid sod up to? Another glance at David's office door. Should she share her suspicion with him?

What if she was wrong?

She wasn't wrong.

Mitch was still loitering.

'Do me a favour,' Frankie said. 'Put a trace on that anonymous call, quick as you can.'

'First thing I did,' he said proudly. 'It's unregistered, the SIM card activated three days ago. Whoever it was wants to keep his identity a secret. He must've heard about what happened to Chris Adams.'

He'd inadvertently hit the nail on the head. That knowledge struck fear into Frankie. She stood up suddenly, her chair scraping across the wooden floor. Lifting her coat off her desk where she'd dumped it, she eyeballed the young DC, a knowing look. 'If the guv'nor asks where I am, tell him I won't be long.'

He checked his watch. 'The briefing—'

'I don't give a shit about the briefing. Now piss off and do as you're told!'

'Sarge.' Mitch walked away.

Grabbing her keys, Frankie charged out of the incident room and ran down the stairs, feeling guilty for having bitten his head off. She was tempted to drive to Bastle View, search every inch of it until she found Ben and haul him out of there, but she couldn't jeopardise the enquiry, so she did the next best thing and called Wells. The journalist answered on the third ring.

'Hi, Frank.'

Frankie's tone was scathing. 'Did you put him up to it?'

'Excuse me? What's up? Has Stone been rattling your cage again?'

Frankie could hear noise in the background. Wherever Wells was, she wasn't alone. 'C'mon, Belinda. Level with me. He's a kid. He's David's kid.'

'Frankie, what's happened? Is Ben OK? Where are you?'

'Meet me in the usual place. Fifteen minutes. Be there!'

Frankie hung up as a text message arrived: **Will do**.

She stared at the screen. No kiss? Unusual. Then again, in her panic to send Ben a text she hadn't included one either. Was she overthinking this? He was probably busy. Doing what, she didn't care to imagine. He might even be in Liverpool helping a pal, like he'd told his uncle. She bloody hoped so.

54

Pocketing his mobile, Ben hid the device beneath his mattress and left his room, heading for the staff canteen. He'd been careful not to show his hand all week. He'd found out about Alfie Jenkins purely by accident, on a wander through the grounds with another member of staff during a rare tea-break. They had come across an outbuilding and sat down next to it when the carer he was with happened to mention that one of her charges had wandered off in the night and taken refuge there.

As Ben walked along the corridor, he replayed the conversation in his head.

'A lovely man,' the carer had said.

Ben asked: 'Is he still here?'

A shake of the head, a downcast expression. 'No, he didn't make it. By the time we found him, the poor man was stone cold.' She'd stopped talking then, looking out across the grounds and woodland, a long, regretful sigh. 'Alfie really loved it here.' And that's where the conversation ended.

Ben turned left, heading away from the staff quarters and into the main building, wondering if Stone and Oliver were now looking into Alfie Jenkins' death. They needed more information and they needed it now. Playing dumb, Ben had raised a number of issues in the past few days, like questioning the bruises he'd seen on the arms of some residents, all of which had been passed off by his co-workers as perfectly normal.

'Their skin is thinner,' someone had told him. 'Don't worry about it, elderly people are prone to bruising.'

It was a reasonable response, supported by medical science, but nevertheless worrying. How you could differentiate between an accidental bruise and one inflicted by rough treatment was beyond his comprehension. The vulnerability of anyone dependent on others for their care, physical and financial, was astonishing. If he'd learned anything since his arrival at Bastle View, it was that he never wanted to grow old.

Over supper, gossip was rife. Unable to contribute, Ben dived in only when someone mentioned Fiona Fitzgerald, comparing her with her predecessor, a woman who everyone seemed to rate. Staff were guarded when he pretended that his mum knew Nancy Carver, the reason he'd applied to work there, acting surprised and disappointed on hearing that she'd moved on.

'I like Fiona,' Gemma chipped in.

'I don't,' a male nurse said bluntly. Steve Gibbon took a bite of his sandwich and spoke with his mouth full. 'She's a good-looking nowt, a penny-pinching bureaucrat who doesn't give a shit about the residents . . . or staff for that matter.' He glared at Gemma, picking bread from his teeth with his thumbnail. 'Have you ever seen her spend any time with the elderly? Because I sure as hell haven't.'

Gemma clammed up, a glance at Ben, a plea for help.

Having secured their jobs, the two had quickly formed a bond. Ben had been right about her. Underneath, she was a laugh, but he suspected that she wouldn't stick around for long. Despite her qualifications, caring nature and obliging disposition, she didn't fit in here. Everyone knew she was struggling. Privately, she'd told him that she wasn't cut out for the long shifts and was already considering her options. He'd told her to give it time. Secretly, he hoped that she'd leave at the first opportunity.

'Steve's right,' a carer said. 'Fiona isn't a patch on Nancy. She knew everyone by name, everyone, and they knew her. The residents were distraught when she disappeared. One of the old guys had a wobbler when he realised that she wasn't coming back. It took us weeks to calm him down. I don't think he's yet over it.'

Ben frowned. 'Disappeared?'

The atmosphere changed instantly, furtive looks passing around the room. It appeared that no one in the closed community believed that Nancy had moved on of her own volition. 'Her departure was sudden,' a nurse explained, lowering her voice. 'She was here one minute, gone the next. She didn't tell anyone she was leaving. We were all shocked to learn that she'd handed in her notice.'

'Can you blame her?' Steve carped. 'Petersen was giving her a hard time.'

'Who?' Ben kept it casual.

Steve ignored the question. 'I'd be out of here in a shot if he turned on me. He's a right twat.' He glanced at Ben. 'We think she was sacked. Staff turnover here is rapid, so keep your nose clean.'

'I don't think I've met him,' Ben said.

'Keep it that way.'

'Steve, you're scaring me.' Gemma was almost squirming in her seat. She glanced at Ben, like she didn't want to be there. 'I've not come across him either. Is he a nurse or carer?'

'Neither,' Steve said. He's Bradbury's estate manager, the only Norwegian I've ever met that I don't like. Do yourselves a favour and steer clear.'

55

Wells had beaten Frankie to Revolution. She looked up from her newspaper as the detective flung herself down on the chair opposite, lifting the shot of whisky that the journalist pushed towards her. Frankie downed the lot in one gulp and clashed the glass down on the table. Wells had seen her upset before, but never like this.

'Shall we start again?' Wells sat forward, leaning on her forearms. 'Frank? Has something happened to Ben? I gave him time off. You know he's in the north-west, right?'

Frankie's eyes gave her away.

'You know different?'

The detective rubbed at her temples, calmer now, but no less upset than when she'd arrived. Wells had already poked her nose into Bastle View without consulting with the MIT. It had infuriated David and Frankie too, though it had given them an in should they require Wells to carry on the pretence of finding a home for her mother, a cover story that was provably true should the home's administrators decide to look into it. Her mother *was* ill, requiring care . . . and extremely wealthy.

Wells was staring at her. 'Frank? What's going on?'

'We had a tip-off. Anonymous male. Details relating to a sudden death on Bradbury's estate. Historical. It came from an unregistered mobile, recently activated. Only you, me and the MIT know that we're investigating Bastle View, yet the call was marked for the attention of the SIO.'

'And you think it was Ben?' Wells relaxed. 'Don't talk wet.'

'This is not funny, Belinda!'

With a flick of the wrist, the journalist batted away Frankie's concerns. 'Go home, Frank. You've been working

312

too hard. I know this case is getting to you. And rightly so. Any abuse of trust is despicable. Preying on the elderly under the guise of looking after them, even worse. What you're suggesting, however, is impossible. Ben knew about Chris Adams, not his connection with Nancy Carver or her place of work. You and I followed the trail based on the information I found in Adams' notebooks. I didn't share that with Ben. David asked me not to. He wanted to keep the lad out of it.'

'Are you absolutely sure?'

'One hundred per cent. I went to the home alone. Ben knows nothing.'

Wells gestured to the barman, holding up one finger, ordering another whisky to be put on her tab. Frankie refused a second shot. She valued her licence and her job. She wasn't drinking another. She wasn't listening either. Her out-and-out refusal to accept that she might have misread the situation frustrated Wells.

'I can see I'm going to have to spell it out for you,' she said. 'Nothing I did for the MIT was written down at work. It was all done at home, so Ben couldn't have seen it if that's what you're thinking. I may have a penchant for younger men, but I'm not in the habit of screwing children. Day or night, Ben has never crossed the threshold of my place. Not once. So, if you haven't told him and David hasn't either, and he's been careful not to take work home, which I assume he has, then you're way wide of the mark.'

Frankie was far from satisfied . . .

She had to be sure.

'Will you do me a favour?'

'Will it put you out of your misery?'

'It might.'

'Fire away then.'

'You're well in at Bastle View. Take the tour. Talk to the staff and have a good look around. You're smart, Belinda. If

313

Ben is there, I know you'll find him. I'd go myself if I could, but I can't afford to show my hand.'

'Is that necessary?'

'I wouldn't have asked if it wasn't.'

'Frankie, you've got this all wrong. Ben is resourceful, but he's no genius. He'd have to be bloody well organised to land a job in that home, or any other, at such short notice. These places have security measures, a vetting procedure, guidelines to mitigate the risk of employing the wrong type of people.'

'Well it's not working at Bastle View, is it? Please, Belinda, I'm begging you. If you won't do it for me, do it for Ben.'

'No need. I told you, you're mistaken.' Wells picked up the drink that had been placed in front of her, a pouty smile at the barman as he collected her empty and moved away. Taking in Frankie's scowl over the top of her glass, Wells finally acquiesced. 'OK, have it your own way. It's a fool's errand – and you just spoiled a bloody good Scotch – but if it'll stop you fretting, I'll do it. Just remember you owe me and I intend to collect.'

Frankie planted a kiss on her cheek. 'I knew I liked you.'

Wells didn't ask if Stone knew what Frankie was up to. Why would she? The journalist was adamant: Frankie's assertion that Ben had gone undercover was illogical and would prove to be unfounded. Despite Wells' reassurances, Frankie's guts were telling her that she was right to be concerned. In trying to help his uncle, she was sure that David's nephew had placed himself at risk. Only one thought terrified her more. Keeping yet another secret from her SIO was a dangerous game to be playing.

56

The voicemail was brief: 'Frank, it's me. I'm about to start the briefing. Don't make me wait.' David sounded royally pissed off that she'd gone off-piste at such a critical point in the investigation. Lowering the phone, Frankie checked her watch: 19:35. The briefing would be over by now. He'd have wrapped up for the night and left by the time she got back to the office. No bad thing. By morning, she'd have thought up a plausible excuse.

Avoiding him didn't sit well with her.

Time and again, Frankie had promised not to disappear without warning. And what had she just done? She'd also told Mitch that she wouldn't be long and yet she'd been gone a while. She wouldn't put it past David to organise a search party if she didn't call him soon. For a moment, she wrestled with her conscience. Should she call and put his mind at rest, wait till morning and tell him the truth, or none of the above? Until she had proof, one way or the other, she didn't want to worry him. He had enough on his mind. Besides, Wells had been unshakeable: without access to confidential police intelligence, Ben couldn't have made a connection between Chris Adams and Nancy Carver.

He couldn't.

Her mobile rang and she checked the screen: David again. Her forefinger hovered between the Decline button on the left, the Accept button on the right. Ignoring both, the call went straight to voicemail. Frankie didn't bother listening to the message. She couldn't face another ear-bashing and needed time to think.

*

A shrill whistle took her attention as she wandered through the city. Frankie followed the sound. Ryman was standing on the pavement, on the opposite side of the street, his right arm raised in salute. She'd crossed over to speak to him. That chance meeting provided the perfect antidote to her foul mood, a kind word from her rough sleeper, a joke, a telling off for looking so forlorn. She deserved it. No matter how grim his life might seem to an outsider, he never let it get him down.

A text pinged into her inbox.

Bidding Ryman goodnight, she turned away, her eyes widening as she stared at the screen, the name BEN picked out in bold font above a short text that took her breath away – and not in a good way:

Look into Petersen. Bradbury's estate manager. Norwegian national. Nasty piece of work. x

'Jesus wept!' she mumbled.

What had Ben got himself into?

Unsure of what to do and in what order, she decided to call off Wells. One dead journalist was one too many.

Frankie sent her a quick text: **Ben has been in touch. False alarm. Stand down.**

A reply: **Is he OK?**

Yes. It wasn't a lie. **Gotta run. Speak later.**

Frankie glanced at her watch. It was almost 9.30 p.m. Before bumping into Ryman, she'd spent a couple of hours wandering aimlessly. The content of Ben's text forced her to refocus. It was now or never. Stone must be told. If he was at home, and she thought he might be, he was a fair distance away. Her car was parked beside Revolution where she'd met Wells. To reach it and save time, she hailed a passing cab.

'Collingwood Street,' she said as she climbed in.

The driver glanced in his rear-view mirror. 'You got money

to burn? It's only down the road, pet. No more than a ten-minute walk.'

'I haven't got ten minutes. And how I spend my money is my business, so drive!'

'Suit yourself.'

The car sped off, taking a left, then a sharp right, throwing Frankie around in the back. She pulled out her phone. David was on speed dial. She chose his landline for no other reason than to pinpoint his location.

He picked up immediately, no pleasantries, just: 'What are you playing at?'

'Guv, I'm in a taxi . . .' It was her way of saying she wouldn't answer questions. 'Sorry I missed the briefing. I've got a potential lead on our anonymous caller. You're not going to like it. We need to meet. Now. Stay where you are. I'll come to you.' She hung up before he could argue.

57

Frankie was as anxious to extricate Ben from the residential home as she was to reunite Nancy Carver with her family, dead or alive. As she drove north on the A1, an image of Nancy's facial injuries popped into her head, along with the words **She's ready** in Chris Adams' handwriting. Creating a fake email address to hide his identity was not only smart, it proved that he was taking Nancy's complaint seriously, covering his tracks so that he wouldn't be discovered. It was the kind of thing he'd do to help a woman in peril. Frankie hadn't yet worked out where and how the two of them had met. The Murder Investigation Team had established a link between Chris and Nancy through the phone calls he'd made, but no other connection that they were yet aware of. If Chris had taken the photograph of her injuries, they'd had personal contact, so why had he later showed his hand to the very people he was investigating? Only one conclusion made sense . . .

He'd got sloppy or over-confident.

Flooring the accelerator, going over the evidence as she continued her journey, Frankie wondered if the man Ben had described as a 'nasty piece of work' had caused Nancy's injuries. The photograph showing them was timed and dated 1945 hours, 24 September 2016. A Saturday. The image had since been blown up by Technical Support in the hope of identifying where it might have been taken. Detectives had searched her former home for an old potting shed and drawn a blank. There wasn't one at Chris's home either, but even if there had been Frankie knew it couldn't have been the one in the photo. Susan was a gardener, no shed of hers would have such a look of abandonment, its only purpose a hotel for spiders.

Frankie had been driving for twenty-five minutes. The case was as depressing as it was confusing. Most of the evidence was circumstantial. The information lifted from the USB flash drive found hidden inside Chris's motorcycle helmet had yet to be corroborated. With Nancy missing, presumed dead, they had no witness. What Frankie needed was hard evidence. With some idea where she might find it, she called Abbott from the car.

'Sorry to bother you at home, Dick. Can you talk?'

'Yeah, go ahead. My missus is out on the town. Christmas is coming. Who knew?'

Frankie laughed.

With less than a week to go, she hadn't so much as purchased a Christmas card and had no plans to do so now. Presents for her family would be bought on Christmas Eve if they were lucky. If not, it wouldn't be the first time that she'd delayed until January, not for the sales but through lack of opportunity. David had been shopping. A car for Ben.

Who else was there to buy for?

Frankie swung the wheel left, turning on to Rothbury Road, keen to get the lowdown on the briefing from her fellow detective sergeant. She didn't mention why she'd absented herself and Abbott didn't pry. He knew she'd have a good excuse, that she'd been working the case, following her intuition. He'd been in the incident room when she was quizzing Pam and Claire about the anonymous message, so he'd probably have guessed her absence was connected to that. Frankie was confident he'd have kept it to himself.

'Did Fox have anything of interest for us?' she asked.

'Not a lot,' Abbott said bluntly. 'The IP wasn't at the *Herald* on September twenty-fourth, though he must've attended the Saturday morning Magistrates Court session because he filed some remands in custody reports via email. Nothing major, overnight arrests mainly, including one on the Tank—'

'For what?'

'Decking someone outside a nightclub. Y'know, his usual Friday-night entertainment. Fox suggested that's why Adams attended court that morning. I gather he was on the overnight arrests mailing list. He took a particular interest in one or two regulars.'

'What happened to Armstrong?'

'He claimed self-defence and was released on bail when he appeared in court the following Monday. The slimy bastard got off on a technicality.'

'That's it? Chris had no diary appointments or internet searches we can follow up?'

'No. And there's no evidence that he created or viewed any documents that day. Sorry I haven't anything more compelling to share.'

'Is Fox being deliberately obstructive?'

'To be fair, I don't think he is. The boss's threat wound him up. He was cooperative when we spoke. Besides, a lot of what he told us is borne out by the data Technical Support retrieved from the *Herald*. I called Wiley to see if Chris was out with him on the Friday night. He was. One of their mates turned thirty that day and they had been for a nosh in town. Chris was his usual self, no outward signs of concern.'

Frankie wondered if Nancy had collared him at the Magistrate's Court. For eighty years the city's main police station had occupied the building next door. Was it possible she didn't know it had closed, its officers relocated to a new headquarters on Forth Banks? Had she wandered into the court on the off-chance of speaking to a copper and come across Chris instead? No, Frankie decided. Given the visual clues in the photograph, that theory didn't hold up. There were no potting sheds she was aware of on Pilgrim Street.

'Frank, you still there?'

'Yeah, sorry. Traffic is slow.' Not slow enough. The closer she got to David's home address, the more nervous she became.

He'd go ballistic when he found out what Ben had been up to. Changing down, she turned right towards Pauperhaugh, a peaceful hamlet on the River Coquet that was about to get noisy.

'You heading home?'

'Into a shitstorm more like. I'm on my way to see the boss.'

'You pulling the night shift now?'

'Something like that.'

'Anything I can do to help?'

'Can you turn back time?'

Abbott chuckled. 'You missed a briefing, Frank. It's not a hanging offence. How angry could he be?'

He didn't know the half of it. 'It would help if I was up to speed before I do battle. Any news on the weapon?'

'Not yet, but Technical Support found a deleted file on the *Herald*'s database on Nancy's disappearance. Begs the question why.'

'Did they find anything linking Fox and Bradbury?'

'Negative.'

'Any intel on who's been accessing Nancy's account? I asked the bank for a rush job.'

'And you got it,' Abbott said. 'On every occasion, a woman made the withdrawals, one clever enough to change her appearance or hide her face. She's not local either.'

'A block on the account might draw her out.'

'I suggested that but the boss wasn't having any.'

'Why not? There was an article in the paper only yesterday—'

'Yeah, I saw it.'

Someone fleecing a pensioner's account had made several calls to a bank in order to get a block cancelled and came a cropper when she couldn't answer the security questions. It prompted her to falsify evidence in the care home's database where she worked. She was now doing time.

'Well if it works,' Frankie said. 'What's the problem?'

'All withdrawals from Nancy's account were made within a twenty-mile radius of the North London borough of Haringey. Geographically, she never strays far from the N8 postcode, never uses the same cashpoint twice. Rarely uses ATMs at banks. We analysed the data. She might not be aware of it, but she favours three specific areas: Crouch End, Muswell Hill, Wood Green. Pound to a penny that's where she lives. The bank has flagged the account. They'll contact us when the next withdrawal is made. The boss is hoping that the same woman might be driving Nancy's car. If he's right, the ANPR will pick it up. He felt that a block on the account would scare her off.'

'Sounds like a good call.'

'The team thought so.'

Frankie glanced at the bottom left-hand corner of her windscreen where her vehicle excise disc used to be. 'Nancy's Fiat is out of tax now. That's the reason I called. A simple search on gov.uk would verify whether or not anyone tried to check its status.'

'We thought of that too.'

'And?'

'We struck lucky. A search was detected on Monday, sixteenth of January – three weeks after Nancy disappeared. Whoever took her car – assuming someone did – made sure it was a) shipped out of the area and b) road legal. Either they've forgotten to renew the tax, or they don't give a shit. And here's the even better news . . . We traced the IP address to Bastle View. That's grounds for a search warrant, right?'

'Yes!' Frankie punched the air in celebration. 'This is gold, man.'

'Too right,' Abbott said. 'The boss is ecstatic.'

'He should be.' It was a eureka moment for the MIT. They both knew it. Since the abolition of tax discs in 2014, more people were riding around illegally than ever before. Frankie suspected that the woman Dick had mentioned was one of them. 'Did you put a marker on the PNC?'

'Yup. If it's picked up, they'll stop and search.'

Frankie pulled up outside David's cottage, thanked Dick and ended the call, unable to keep the smile off her face. She took a deep breath and got out of the car. Despite the breakthrough, her next conversation was not going to be an easy one.

58

David had his phone to his ear when he came to the door dressed in button-fly jeans and a black close-fitting T-shirt that showed his physique in a way that a shirt never did. If what Frankie had come to say hadn't been so serious, she'd have joked that he was a shoo-in for the next Levi 501 advert. He beckoned her in and stood aside to let her pass, a brief smile as he closed the door behind her. He never mentioned the briefing. Whoever he was talking to was making his day.

She was about to unmake it.

Moving into the living room, Frankie took off her coat and dumped it unceremoniously on the floor. Ignoring her favourite rocking chair, she stood awkwardly with her back to the fire. Too busy with his call to notice her anxiety, David lifted his free hand, holding up an imaginary glass, then pointed toward the kitchen, miming: help yourself.

Frankie wandered away, for no other reason than to put some distance between them and practise her delivery. A bottle of red breathing on the kitchen bench reminded her of Susan Adams. Hoping that vodka bottle was still unopened, Frankie made a mental note to call her mum and ask how Susan was doing, then put the kettle on and made two coffees, strong and black. She could hear David's voice carrying across the hallway. He sounded upbeat.

It wouldn't last.

'Not at all,' he was saying as she arrived in the living room. 'No, no, I appreciate the call. Yeah, cheers, any time.' He hung up, looking pleased with himself. 'CSIs lifted minute paint scrapings from the tree where Nancy's wing mirror came off, assuming it's hers. There's a positive match between the two. They shared images with Fiat, who say it's most likely Blue

Lido Metallic, a popular colour in 2003 when the car was bought. They're sending samples for comparison. Talking of paint, what do you think?' He swept a hand around the room.

Frankie made every effort to show an interest, even though she hadn't noticed his new colour scheme on the way in. Home improvement was the last thing on her mind. 'It's lovely, David.'

'You don't like it?' He looked crestfallen.

'No, really, it's great.'

'So why is your expression telling me otherwise?'

Frankie couldn't raise a smile. It seemed bizarre to engage in small talk, given the revelation she was about to share with him.

David frowned at the coffee mug she handed him. 'You don't fancy a glass of wine either?'

'No, we have work to do.'

'On your potential lead?' He glanced at his watch. 'It couldn't wait till morning?'

'You'd better sit down.' The good mood drained from his face. His body tensed. He didn't move an inch. Sucking in a breath, under no illusion as to how he'd take the news of his nephew's interference, Frankie wasted no time getting to the point. 'David, Ben isn't in Liverpool.'

59

Alarm and confusion seized Ben, choking him, making every hair on his head stand to attention, producing goosebumps on his skin. He felt sick. The first thing he'd done when he left the canteen was to return to his room and send Frankie a text, before restarting his shift. When he'd returned a second time, lifting his mattress to see if she'd answered, his only means of communication with the outside world was gone.

Fuck!

In his rush to get out of the room before he was missed, was it possible that he'd pushed the device further under the mattress than he remembered? Ben rechecked, heaving it up by one corner with both hands, diving underneath in an attempt to locate it.

The mobile wasn't there.

A cloud of dust filled the air as the mattress landed heavily on the old-fashioned bedstead. With a growing sense of unease, Ben got down on his hands and knees to look under the bed, groping in the dark space beneath, hoping that the phone had fallen between the slats and on to the floor.

It hadn't.

He panicked.

If anyone had seen that final message, he was in deep trouble.

The feeling that he was under surveillance was like a stab in the back. Still on all fours, he glanced over his shoulder to check that he was alone in the dimly lit room. If his uncle was correct in his assumption that someone associated with the home had killed Chris Adams and Nancy Carver, they had nothing to lose and everything to gain by killing again.

Adrenalin pumped through his body as he heard footsteps approaching along the corridor.

Racing to the door, he killed the lights, then stood, his back pressed against the wall.

It all went quiet.

Ben blew out a breath, telling himself to get a grip. For a moment, he couldn't trust his senses. He pressed his ear to the door, unsure whether he'd imagined the sound of footsteps a moment ago. Fear did strange things to people. He strained to listen for a creak of ancient floorboards, someone breathing outside his bedroom door.

Nothing.

The only breathing he could hear was his own.

He couldn't see, but he could feel a presence. Leaving the light off, his eyes glanced at the narrow gap beneath the door, two distinct shadows making his heart pump faster. With every bone in his body he felt the need to arm himself. With what? The windowless room was like a black hole. He couldn't see a hand in front of his face. The sensation that someone was there was overwhelming.

What were they waiting for?

Inching his way across the room, Ben found his bed, lay down and shut his eyes, feigning sleep, mentally crossing his fingers, imagination in overdrive. In his head, he pictured a giant Norseman charging into the room with a weapon, stabbing him in the chest, ending his existence in this cell-like room that passed for staff accommodation in Bastle View.

Fear gripped him.

He'd never been so terrified in his life.

His plan to go undercover, dig up information that would help his uncle crack a murder case and shed light on the wholesale abuse of the elderly, financial as well as physical, had been insane. He knew now that David was right to keep him out of it. If only he'd listened. There and then, he promised that if he got out of there alive, he'd never again interfere.

The police were dealing with a vicious killer who'd stop at nothing to cover up his crimes. There was no knock before the door creaked open.

Ben froze as an arc of light flooded his room.

With eyes half-shut, he peered at the indistinct figure backlit by the stark tube lighting in the corridor. A woman? For a moment, he thought it was Fitzgerald standing in the half-light. Tension radiated from her. He held his breath, half-expecting her to stand aside to allow Petersen in.

A whisper. 'Can I come in?'

'Jesus, Gemma! You scared the shit out of me.'

'I'm sorry. I need to talk to you.'

She crossed the threshold, flicking the light on, closing the door quietly. This was not a good time. Ben wanted her gone. He sat up, trying to compose himself. Gemma was staring at him, and no wonder: he could feel the sweat running down his face. He wiped it away.

'Are you ill?' She placed a hand on his forehead. 'You're running a fever.'

'No, I'm just hot.' It sounded like a lie, even as he said it.

'Nonsense,' Gemma said. 'It's freezing in here. In my room too. I hate this place.'

She wrapped her arms around herself to demonstrate the point. A shiver, in case he hadn't got the message. For a moment, Ben thought he might come clean and tell her what he'd been up to, but it was too risky. The last thing he wanted was to place her in danger. He wanted her to leave. If anyone had seen her entering his room, they might jump to the wrong conclusion and decide that they were working together, a pair of amateur sleuths who needed shutting up. Guilt by association. But first there was something he needed from her.

'I don't suppose you have your mobile on you – I've mislaid mine, can't find it anywhere . . .'

60

Stone had made the leap immediately. Since then, he'd been fighting to keep his temper under control. So far it was working. He was looking out of the window, most probably willing Ben to turn the corner, praying that he would. Frankie couldn't tell if he was listening or if he was adrift inside his own head, imagining the worst-case scenario, as she had on the way over. There was no doubt that his nephew had placed his life in jeopardy, but she realised as soon as she voiced her fear that she'd made a mistake.

David lost it then.

He swung round, harsh words spilling from a mouth that was taut and ugly. 'At least one person has died on Bradbury's estate, a former member of staff is missing, presumed dead, and a would-be investigative journalist has been murdered. And *you* didn't think it a good idea to share Ben's where-abouts with me?'

Frankie glared at him. 'That's right, David. Blame me.'

'Who else would I blame? What the *hell* were you thinking?'

'I didn't have proof—'

'You had a strong suspicion, enough to go AWOL.'

'Are you going to listen or shout me down?' she said. 'Because that's not going to get us anywhere, is it? Look, as soon as Claire described our anonymous caller as "twenties, articulate and polite" I did think it might be Ben. I wasn't sure, so I did what I'm paid for and followed it up. I sent him a text—'

David's hands spread in a gesture of disbelief. 'You did what? Jesus, Frankie—'

'Oh, for God's sake, give me *some* credit. It was an inno-cent text. It gave nothing away. If it's seen by anyone else, it won't raise an eyebrow.'

'Did he reply?'

'Yes, in the same vein.' Frankie stalled. Ben had been stupid. She wanted David calm before she disclosed that fact. 'Like it or lump it, Ben has given us more than we had. He tried to speak to you, at the earliest opportunity. You weren't available, were you? So don't go off on one when you see him—'

Anger flashed in David's eyes. 'Don't you mean, *if* I see him?'

That painful reality stung. Frankie took a step backwards, turning away from him. In the past few months she'd witnessed a strong bond developing between David and his nephew. Like all relatives, they had had their moments, but were trying to make a go of it. They had formed a close relationship, where once they had been estranged.

David's next question was laced with venom:

'Did you tell him about the home?'

'No!' How dare he accuse her of that. 'Did you?'

'Not a word.' He stopped pacing. 'This has got Wells' name written all over it.'

Frankie shook her head. 'You're wrong. I spoke to her. She's as worried as we are.'

'She can also lie for England.'

'That's not fair! When has she ever lied to us, to you? She swears she knew nothing of Ben's plans and he knew nothing about the home—'

'So how did he find out?'

'I don't know. Wells said you wanted to keep him out of it and she respected your wishes. For what it's worth, I believe her. Mind you, I don't understand how he managed to get in there so quick.'

'I'll kill the little bastard when I get hold of him.'

'Yeah, that'll help.'

'I don't give a shit.' David wiped his face with his hand. 'I've had it with him, Frankie. As far as I'm concerned, he's overstayed his welcome. The sooner he moves out, the better I'll like it—'

'You don't mean that,' Frankie said.

'Believe me, I do.'

'He's trying to help.'

'Well he's not.'

'He's young, enthusiastic. You're blind if you can't see what you mean to him. He isn't doing it to help you, he's doing it for me, because of my relationship with Chris.' Frankie paused. She wasn't getting through. Time to up the ante. 'Look, I asked Wells to go to the home tomorrow morning to see if she could locate him and haul him out of there. I've since called her off. At the time,' she explained, 'I wasn't aware that you were in the process of securing a warrant—'

'Because you weren't at the fucking briefing!'

'OK, OK! I messed up . . . again.' Frankie sat down, elbows on her knees, head in her hands. When there was no response from David, she glanced up at him. If he had one strength, it was his ability to read a situation. He'd sensed that she hadn't told him the worst of it. She was about to prove him right. She stood, putting herself on his level before delivering the bad news. 'He sent me a second text, more specific than the first. He said that we should look into a man called Petersen, a Norwegian he described as "a nasty piece of work".'

'Oh great! He has NO fucking idea who he's dealing with.'

She flinched at the aggression in his voice. 'Stop yelling and let me think.'

He apologised immediately. He wasn't angry with her, he was angry with Ben for sticking his nose in where it didn't belong. Frankie rubbed at her temples, locking eyes with him. He was beside himself. Seeing him so helpless was hard to take, making it even harder to concentrate, but it was vital that she did.

One of them had to.

'Will you please sit and listen?'

He fell heavily on to the couch.

Frankie glanced at their untouched coffee. 'Actually, I'll take that drink now.'

She walked into the kitchen.

Grabbing the bottle and two wine glasses off the bench, she retraced her steps, returning to the living room. Pouring them both a glass, she handed him one. 'Ben will be fine, David. Try not to worry. We now have grounds to question the staff at Bastle View. Dick will have the warrant first thing. Then we go in, right?'

Nodding, David swallowed his wine.

'Something occurred to me on the way over here . . .' Frankie put down her glass. 'Alfie Jenkins' body was discovered in an outbuilding on Bradbury's estate. Do you know a better way to kill an old man than leaving him out in the cold, in his night clothes, then passing it off as a tragic case of dementia-related wandering? And it happened right after he changed his will. I accept that Alfie had no relations to leave his money to, but the home benefitted by just short of three million quid – his entire estate. That's quite a pay-off.'

The implication hung in the air between them.

David looked away, a deep breath, a chance to think. 'He left his estate to the home that looked after him. Is that so odd?'

'I don't know, is it?' Frankie glanced around the home he'd inherited from his grandmother. 'When your nan died, as well as including you and Luke in her will, didn't she bequeath small sums to her favourite charities? Most people do. How come Alfie, a retired surgeon with no family and a substantial fortune, left the whole lot to Bastle View? Surely he'd have wanted some of it to go towards research, to further the cause of medical science?'

'Perhaps . . .' David sighed. 'Though unless we can prove conclusively that his will was forged, we're on a hiding to nothing.'

Frankie had already moved on. 'We need to find that outbuilding and get a forensic team down there. Alfie was cremated soon after he was found and, given the time lapse, I'm not confident that we'll find any evidence he was killed there. But it's not too late for Nancy, is it?'

Stone frowned. 'What do you mean?'

'I suspect she was taken there too – a scare tactic to shut her up. It didn't work. Whoever roughed her up may have underestimated her. Thought they'd done enough. That picture we found on Chris's flash drive was taken in what we assumed was a potting shed, one that we haven't been able to find.'

'You think it could be the same outbuilding?'

'It's worth following up. If we're lucky, we might find someone at the home who's as unhappy with what's going on there as Nancy but who, given her disappearance, is now too scared to come forward.' David shook his head, unconvinced, so she delivered the clincher: 'I don't think that photograph was taken by Chris. I reckon Nancy went there after the assault and took a selfie.'

61

David felt numb after Frankie left. He'd fallen into bed almost immediately but was unable to settle, her suggestion that Nancy had deliberately left a clue keeping him awake. When exhaustion finally took him, he slept badly, tormented by dreams of a body lying on a mortuary slab; a coffin; Frankie's sadness as she looked on; a stand-up row with her, a combination of many, like several crossed lines, providing the soundtrack to his nightmare. As David peered at the body of his late brother, it morphed into Ben. He woke suddenly – in a state of confusion – soaked in sweat, heart pounding.

Rolling over, he glanced at the digital clock on his bedside table: 03:17. Incapable of rest, he lay in the darkened room, eyes fixed to the ceiling. All he could think of was the time Ben had come back into his life. It hadn't been pretty. He was a good-for-nothing, dope-smoking dropout, a waste of space looking for a handout, the kid indirectly responsible for his father's death in an RTA. Frankie had begged David to take him in, to offer him a home and security, warning him that without his support the lad was likely to end up in jail.

Think of Luke.

David's response to Frankie's comment echoed loudly in his head: 'My brother is a pile of ashes because of him!' Luke would have been safe at home if he hadn't got the call that Ben had collapsed following an all-night bender. He was racing to the hospital to be with his son when a lorry ploughed into him. The crash had put him in the same A&E department as Ben. Only one of them survived.

'The wrong one,' David had told her.

He bitterly regretted that now. At the time, he hadn't thought he'd ever forgive Ben. He had. Frankie had made him see sense, pointing out that it was unfair to blame him. Ben wasn't the drunk who'd driven the HGV that killed Luke. His subsequent rudeness and hostility, his drug-taking and provocation was nothing more than a cry for help. He was lost, an orphan in need of guidance. Finally, David had climbed down and taken him in, providing unconditional support, a home . . . and forgiveness, eventually. They were family.

They still were.

The idea that Ben might now be in danger was gut-wrenching. Like any other parent waiting up for a child who'd stayed out late without permission, David had mixed emotions now: anger that Ben had gone against his wishes; resignation that he was capable of making his own decisions; acceptance that he wasn't a kid any more. Time and again, David had encouraged him to grow up.

He couldn't have it both ways.

Robbed of the ability to sleep, he'd wandered into the living room. The two empty wine glasses were on the coffee table where he'd left them; the sight conjured an image of Frankie, visibly distressed, in his rocking chair. Feeling guilty for having yelled at her, David riddled the fire, threw a log on and sat down. The place felt empty without her, even lonelier without Ben.

62

There had been no further contact from Ben. David approached the residential home before dawn, taking Frankie with him. As they walked up the driveway, the lights were on in most windows, illuminating the surrounding area. To the left of the main entrance, David could see movement. Early risers were breakfasting in a huge conservatory, as good as any you'd find attached to a high-end country house hotel. The residents could have been mistaken for hotel guests, getting stuck in to a full English.

'It's hard to imagine a more peaceful scene,' Frankie said.

'I agree. C'mon. Let's hit them when they're least expecting it.'

More than anything, David wanted to find Ben, but he had a duty to expose whatever corruption was hiding beneath the facade of respectability, to protect a vulnerable group of elderly people as well as the staff who cared for them. The thought that anyone who'd taken up residence was being groomed to part with their cash by unscrupulous individuals made his blood boil. If, as he now suspected, that included physical abuse or death, his investigation was set to increase in complexity and scope. The ramifications, for him and for the MIT, were enormous.

A woman in a dark business suit and crisp white shirt was standing in the hallway when they entered the building. Her attitude was corporate. More like a banker or fundraiser, skills that might come in handy if money was more important to Sir Giles Bradbury than a kind word or gentle hand on the collective shoulder of the elderly. The Suit appeared to be expecting them, which put David momentarily on the back foot. He exchanged a glance with Frankie, then focused on the introductions.

'Ms Fitzgerald?'

'That's me.' She seemed surprised that he knew her name. 'You have me at a disadvantage. Have we met before?'

'I don't think so.' David had known who she was from the description Wells had given him. Still, it worried him that she'd come to greet them. With no time to indulge that thought, he said: 'I'm Detective Chief Inspector Stone and this is DS Oliver. We're investigating the disappearance of Nancy Carver, your predecessor. We'd like to ask you some questions.'

'You'd better come into my office then.'

A resident interrupted, a complaint that her Wi-Fi was only working intermittently. David's attention strayed as Fitzgerald asked her to report the problem to the admin office when it opened. He'd picked up the hum of conversation, the clink of cutlery, the voices of the staff toing and froing in the breakfast room. Some residents were making their own way along the corridor to join them, others with the assistance of staff. Ben was not among them.

'Inspector Stone?' Fitzgerald pointed. 'It's this way.'

As she began to lead the way, David caught Frankie's eye, flicking his head in the direction of the breakfast room. Nodding, she continued to follow him. She'd pick her time. Make an excuse or simply disappear. They stopped walking as a motorised wheelchair turned the corner at speed, blocking their way.

'Morning, Grace.' Fitzgerald's eyes were on the speedster, a non-verbal warning for her to slow down. 'How are you this morning?'

'Better, thank you.'

'Excellent! Enjoy your breakfast.'

They all stood aside to let her pass. When her wheelchair drew level, the old lady's smile melted away. Her voice was weak, her message less so. 'I hope no one has stolen my place, Mrs Fitzgerald.'

'There's room for everyone, Grace. The staff will sort you out.'

'I'll eat in my room if my usual spot is taken.' She took off, abruptly ending the conversation.

'If that sounded like a threat, it was . . .' Fitzgerald said. 'Some of our residents are territorial. They like to sit at the same table for all their meals, in small cliques, with like-minded individuals. Woe betide anyone who tries to push them out. They get anxious if they have to change places. Grace has been quite ill. At one point, we thought we might lose her.'

David wondered why she felt the need to share what he considered was confidential information. As Fitzgerald opened the door to her office, standing aside to allow him in, she poked her head out into the corridor, waiting for Frankie. She was nowhere to be seen. Fitzgerald's greeting at the main entrance made sense to David now. Her impressive office was at the front of the house with dark wood panelling and a huge window overlooking the driveway. She'd seen them arrive and had come to investigate, curiosity getting the better of her.

She was still hanging on to the door handle. 'Is your colleague not joining us?'

'DS Oliver will wait outside.'

'As you wish . . .' She shut the door, walked round her desk and sat down, a puzzled expression on her face. 'Please, make yourself comfortable. I can organise a bacon butty if you'd like.' She glanced at the grandfather clock. 'It's rather early.'

'That's very kind, I've already eaten.' A barefaced lie.

'I'm not sure I can be of much help to you. Nancy left over a year ago. She was gone long before I arrived.'

It sounded like an alibi to the SIO. 'There was no handover between you?'

'No, which was far from ideal from the residents' point of view. Nancy was very well thought of, so I had a lot to live up to. It took a while for me to settle in, but we got there in the end.' She paused. 'What makes you think she disappeared? I was led to believe she'd emigrated.'

'So was her family.'

Fitzgerald repeated her question.

'UK Border Control found no record of her having left the country.' David's expression gave nothing away. He'd been careful not to identify himself as the SIO on what was potentially a double murder case. He would in time. First, he had a request to make, and he was keen to gauge her reaction. Rather than risk disturbing the residents, he decided to focus on the office premises and outbuildings and keep the PolSA team out of the home for the time being. 'I'd like to carry out a systematic search of the grounds and examine your database.'

'Then you've had a wasted journey . . .' Fitzgerald was shaking her head. 'I have no authority to give you access.'

'Then I'll wait while you get permission.' David's smile had no substance. There was a short pause as they sat there, staring each other down. Abbott was in a meeting with a magistrate. He'd deliver the warrant as soon as he was able. In ten minutes or so, it would be light. David had already made up his mind that he wouldn't be leaving until he got his way. He pushed harder. 'This home is the last place Mrs Carver was seen alive. I'll need to talk to the staff, of course.'

'And the residents?'

'Not unless it's absolutely necessary. Let's get the search underway and then I'll let you know what I want.'

'Inspector, given the circumstances, I'm confident that our trustees will cooperate, but you'll appreciate that what you're asking is of great concern to us. If word gets out that you're searching here, it could damage the home's reputation—'

'You mean Sir Giles won't like it.'

'No, he won't. Bastle View is one of the best, if not *the* best residential home in these parts. We have a duty to protect our residents. What on earth will I tell them?'

'Nothing. We'll keep it low key.'

'Can you give me any more detail?'

'Not at the moment, no.' David pointed at the phone on Fitzgerald's desk. 'If you wouldn't mind . . . '

63

There was a sign on the door: The Austen Room. Turning the brass handle, Frankie pushed open the door, slipped inside and found the lights. As the name suggested, it was a library, the like of which she'd never seen, a lavish room, stuffed with antiques, shelf upon shelf of old books on science, medicine and history – some of them as big as half a paving slab. A beautiful partners' writing desk stood in the centre, a piano in one corner. The room had a faint smell of vanilla. She imagined children spending time in here over the generations, educated privately, ladies writing at the desk, quill pens and ink.

If Stone needed an interview room, this would do nicely.

For the umpteenth time, Frankie took her mobile from her pocket, buoyed to see a tiny red dot on the messages' icon at the bottom of the screen. It was good news – confirmation from Abbott that he had the warrant – nothing more. Switching off the lights, she went in search of Ben. No one challenged her as she wandered the corridors, though she noted CCTV. If anyone was watching, she'd be stopped. Let them try – the warrant was signed, dated and on its way. No judge worth his salt would argue with that.

Finally, she arrived back where she started, frustration getting the better of her. In the conservatory, meals were still being served. She scanned the room as she walked in. No sign of Ben there either. Worrying. Frankie was aware that her presence had been noted by staff going about their business. One in particular stood out, a young woman, a willowy redhead of about Ben's age who appeared hell-bent on avoiding eye contact. Her new uniform was too big for her, room to manoeuvre when shifting the elderly, Frankie assumed.

She studied the girl.

Yes, she'd do nicely.

Frankie's dad had given her the nous to sniff out the weak link in any organisation. She couldn't wait to put the bite on her, but it was important to establish rapport first. The red-head was heading her way. Frankie made a comment about how busy she was, clearing a space on the sideboard for her to put down the tray of precariously balanced dirty dishes she was carrying.

'Thanks,' the girl said. 'It's manic this morning.'

Frankie threw her a warm smile. 'Looks like you could do with another pair of hands.'

'Yes, we're short-staffed.'

They chatted for a few minutes. Then, like any other wait-ress, the girl turned to face the room, her eyes searching for a raised hand, anyone requiring assistance or finishing their meal. She shot off again, returning with another full tray. It was then Frankie noticed how drawn she was. If staff hadn't turned in, it occurred to her that the girl might be at the end of a shift, rather than the beginning. Frankie felt her pain. Being held over from night shift was a frequent occurrence when she was a cop in uniform.

'I'm Frankie,' she said.

The girl reciprocated. 'Gemma.'

'That's a lovely name.' Frankie kept it casual. 'Don't sup-pose you could slip out for a second?'

'Um . . .' Gemma bit her lip, a glance at her colleagues, none of whom were paying them any attention, wide eyes settling on Frankie. 'I'm not sure I can right now. I'll be in trouble if I'm missed.'

'I won't keep you long, I promise.'

'I daren't, I've only been here a week.'

It was an opportunity too good to miss. 'Then you must know Ben Stone. He's new too . . .' Casually, Frankie glanced around the room. 'I've not seen him this morning. Do you happen to know if he's around?'

Instantly agitated, the girl opened her mouth to speak, then changed her mind, stonewalling Frankie. This timid kid was rattled, on the edge of tears. The detective sergeant wanted to know why. For a split second, she doubted her intuition. The feeling didn't last. Forcing a smile she didn't feel, she pressed on with the conversation, hoping to win her over.

'He can be a pain in the arse. I can't tell you how many times he's fallen out with me—'

'We haven't . . . fallen out—'

A chill ran down Frankie's spine. 'Then why are you so upset?'

Suddenly, the floor became interesting.

Before Frankie had a chance to quiz her further, Gemma scuttled off to collect more dishes with Frankie's eyes on her back. Whatever was bothering her had something to do with Ben. Unsettling. To discover what it was, Frankie was prepared to slap the cuffs on her if necessary, except she couldn't afford to show her hand.

Forcing the issue would be counterproductive.

When Gemma returned, she kept her head down, scraping uneaten food into the bin, stacking empty plates on the sideboard. One slipped from her hand, crashing to the floor, sending shards of crockery in all directions, drawing the eyes of everyone in the room. There was definitely something on her mind. Her concentration was woeful.

'Here, let me help.' Frankie crouched down to pick up the pieces and tried again. 'It's just a plate, Gemma. Don't look so worried.'

She looked up. 'It's not the plate.'

'What then?' They both stood up. 'Look, if there's something bugging you, I'm a good listener.'

'Are you a copper?'

'Third generation. Why d'you ask?'

'Ben told me that the only family he has is in the police. He

343

wasn't specific, so I thought it might be you.' She waited for Frankie to confirm or deny it.

She did neither.

'I thought . . . what I mean is, if you're looking for him I—' She stopped talking as someone raised their voice from across the room, telling her to get her act in gear. He meant a dustpan and brush.

Gemma turned away to fetch it.

'Gemma, wait!' Frankie took a step forward. 'What were you going to say before?'

'I'm sorry, I have to go.'

Frankie loosely caught her wrist. 'Two minutes, please. Can't you step outside for a moment to—'

'I can't!' She pulled away. 'It's more than my job's worth to leave before my official break.'

'Then meet me in the library as soon as you're done.'

64

Fitzgerald put down the phone, her expression suitably apologetic. 'As I suspected, Sir Giles is in Honfleur. He has a home there. The board of trustees will convene this morning and get back to me. When they do, I'll be in touch.' Pushing her chair away from her desk, she rose to her feet, David's cue to leave.

He didn't.

'DCI Stone, I appreciate the urgency of your task, but our residents are frail and infirm. Their well-being is paramount. I'm sure you understand that our first duty is to protect them from unnecessary stress.'

David would love to believe it. 'They won't know we're here.'

'Even so, I need permission.'

Frustrated at the delay, he glanced out of the window. 'Actually, that might not be necessary.'

Fitzgerald followed his gaze.

Abbott's car had appeared on the driveway. Seeing David watching from the window, he tapped his breast pocket as he climbed out of the vehicle: he had the warrant. Seconds later, he walked through the door, handing the document to the SIO, who served it on Fitzgerald. Without fuss, or reference to the home's legal counsel, which is what David had anticipated might happen, she made his job easier, accepting the legality of the document in her hand.

Retaking her seat, she said: 'How can I help you, Inspector?'

'At 11.30 a.m. on Monday the sixteenth of January, a computer from these premises was used to access a particular website. As a result, I need to examine your database. I'd like details of anyone on duty or on the premises at the time,

345

computers in use, a list of employees, and anyone who has left your employ in the past two years. I also require the names and former addresses of all residents, including when they arrived, any who have since died, moved to other residential properties or returned home to live with family.'

'There are very few of those,' Fitzgerald said. 'We have very many requests to come in, but residents tend not to leave. None that are breathing anyway.' Fitzgerald stalled, unable to hide her embarrassment. She'd regretted the insensitivity of her last sentence as soon as it had left her lips. 'Surely all you really need are details of staff on duty at the time and date you mentioned.'

'With respect, Ms Fitzgerald, that's for me to decide. What I need is your full cooperation, along with everything I asked for, as quickly as possible.' He glanced at the computer on her desk. 'I take it this isn't the only computer on the premises? I noticed the general office on my way in, though the blinds were drawn. I assume they have one?'

'Yes, and there's another in the nurses' station.'

'Which I assume is manned twenty-four seven?'

A nod. 'It's a medical archive, a day-to-day commentary on the condition of those in our care. Given that the average age of our small community is eighty-seven, their circumstances are subject to change at a moment's notice. Nursing staff are required to receive and share medical data from or with other agencies so it's important that it's bang up to date.'

'I assume the computer is password protected?'

'Of course. We're very security conscious here.'

'Only medical personnel have access to it?'

'Correct.'

'Then it should be easy to identify who used it on the day of interest to us.' David held her gaze. 'Unless someone here isn't following protocol. Any idea who we might be looking at?'

'You need to ask the nursing staff.'

'I'm asking you, Ms Fitzgerald.'

'I'm sorry, I can't help you.'

'What about the computer in the general office?'

'It's purely admin.'

'Who has access to that one?'

'Everyone. Staff rotas are posted there. Residents pop in for a chat, the able-bodied among them picking up mail. Family queries are dealt with there. If we bring in outside contractors, that's where they report.'

'Office hours?'

'Nine till five, closed on a weekend, though they finish tomorrow for the holidays and will reopen on the second of January.'

'They might receive a bonus this year.' Reacting to a raised eyebrow, David explained: 'A technical support team will be arriving shortly to examine all three computers.' He pointed to the one on her desk. 'Who else uses this terminal?'

'No one.'

'And when you're not here?'

'The door is locked. I'm the only keyholder.'

David thought that strange. Nancy's resignation letter was found on her desk. Had the door been left open when she walked out? Or had someone seen her leave and accessed the office with a key Fitzgerald either failed mention or didn't know about? David wondered if Ben's version of what went on here would differ from the one he'd been given. He couldn't wait to talk to him.

'Are there any occasions when you've left the office unattended and not locked up?'

'I can't recall, though I'm careful.'

'Have you taken on any new staff recently?' David had to ask.

Fitzgerland frowned. 'Is that relevant to your enquiries?'

'Please answer the question.'

'We have two new members of staff.' She mentioned Ben

and a female whose name Stone hardly registered. Confirmation that his nephew was employed there sent a shiver right through him. Fitzgerald hadn't clocked his anxiety. 'I'll get you those lists.'

Pulling her keyboard towards her, she typed in a command.

Leaving his seat, David walked round behind her, to check on what she was doing.

'Is there any CCTV on the premises?' he asked.

'Yes, in all general areas.'

'Did Nancy Carver live in?'

'No, I don't believe so.'

'Was she particularly friendly with anyone? Was there anyone she didn't get on with?'

'You'd have to ask around, DCI Stone. As I said, we didn't work together.'

Fitzgerland didn't look up. With eyes firmly on her computer screen, fingers planted on her keyboard, her attention elsewhere, David was pleased for the opportunity to recover from news that had sent him reeling a moment ago. Still, he was here now, able to ensure that Ben would come to no harm.

65

Gemma appeared fifteen minutes later. Fearing recriminations – and in return for the promise of confidentiality – she
sat down and promptly broke down. It was hard to watch.
Even harder to listen to her sobbing and, for a moment,
Frankie thought she might lose it too. These were the actions
of a young woman who was scared stiff. What of, the detective had yet to establish. It was a bleak moment, a pivotal
moment.

It was going to hurt.

Sitting down beside the girl, with a feeling of dread creep-
ing like the pox across her skin, she took hold of Gemma's
hand, willing herself to focus before her own emotions got
the better of her. 'Take your time and start at the beginning,'
she said. 'You'll feel better once you get it out. Whatever it is,
I can sort it . . . but only if you tell me everything.'

Could she sort it?

Frankie wasn't sure that she could. 'Is this about Ben?'

Nodding, Gemma, took a tissue from her pocket and dried
her eyes. 'I saw him last night. I went to his room to warn
him that Petersen had been asking for details of his shift pat-
tern. He's not a nice man. We'd been told to stay away from
him. He'd stopped me in the corridor. It frightened me.' Tears
erupted and ran down her cheeks, two black lines of mascara
staining porcelain skin. 'Ben was in a state, lying in the dark
when I got there, looking like he'd seen a ghost. He was hot
and trembling, even more petrified than I was – and that's
saying something. He tried to cover it up. I could tell he was
lying. He said he'd mislaid his mobile and asked to borrow
mine. I didn't have it with me.'

Frankie felt sick.

If Petersen had set eyes on that mobile, he wouldn't necessarily have seen that Ben was on to him – the device was secure – but, somehow, in the pit of her stomach, Frankie knew that he had.

Her mind flew backwards.

This wasn't the first time she'd received bad news about a member of David's immediate family. June eighteenth, 2016 was imprinted on her memory. On that day, she'd taken the call from Traffic with the news that his brother, Luke, had been in an RTA and hadn't survived. David had been in another room, unaware of the unfolding drama, just as he was now.

How the hell would she tell him that Ben was here and in trouble?

The expression on Gemma's face was one she'd witnessed many times before. The girl had more to give and, right this minute, Frankie wasn't sure she wanted to hear it – but hear it she must, the sooner the better.

'Did Ben tell you why he was in a flap?'

Gemma shook her head. 'I said I'd fetch my mobile and bring it to him. He refused, said it wouldn't be smart. He practically frogmarched me from the room. He said we'd be in deep shit if anyone found us together, that it was against house rules.'

'Is it?'

'Yes, only that's not why he wanted rid of me.'

He was protecting her.

'And you've not seen him today?'

'I didn't expect to . . .' Gemma broke down again, choking on her words. 'After I left him, I went to my room. I couldn't sleep. I got up to get a drink. That's when I saw him leave with his bag on his back.' Her eyes were empty. 'He was running.'

66

Frankie knocked on Fitzgerald's office door. David looked up as she entered. He was standing behind the care home manager, while her fingers flew over her computer keyboard. Behind them, a printer spewed out A4 sheets that Frankie assumed were details of her staff and historical duty rosters. The link between the IP address of Bastle View and the search for Nancy Carver's vehicle on the public database, after she'd handed in her notice, was the reason they had applied for and secured a warrant. David was following the evidence. He couldn't leave Fitzgerald alone in the office for fear that she might tamper with it.

'Guv? Have you got a minute?'

He shook his head. 'Not now.'

'There's been a development,' Frankie said, code for something serious.

He apologised to Fitzgerald. 'Would you mind waiting outside for a moment?'

She got up and left them to it.

Now that they were alone, Frankie almost bottled out, in two minds whether to break the news or wait until they reached Middle Earth. That could be hours yet. She'd passed Abbott in the corridor. The search of the grounds was already underway, Technical support summoned to examine the computers. She had to do it now.

'What is it?' There was a hint of irritation in David's voice.

There was no other way to say it. 'Ben left here at midnight—'

'Thank Christ for that!' Relief flooded his face. 'He's been in touch?'

'No.' Frankie's heart skipped a beat. 'He'd lost his phone

and was asking to borrow one. He was seen leaving by a member of staff . . .' She stalled. 'He was in a hurry and was followed out by Bradbury's estate manager. Ben's not been seen or heard of since and neither has Petersen. Jesus, David! What are we going to do?'

He didn't react, a bad sign, though she could tell that the news had shaken him. It had shaken her too. She wanted to tell him not to worry. She didn't. Not only would it sound like bullshit, it *was* bullshit – he had every reason to be concerned for Ben's safety. Calmly, he walked over to the printer, sifting through the sheets of paper in the output tray until he found what he was after.

He looked up. 'Petersen isn't listed on the staff register. That's odd. I want eyes on him. You know what to do.'

'David—'

He cut her off. 'Do it, Frank! There's no time for weeping and wailing. Don't you dare crumble on me now. Ben wanted in. He's in. End of—'

'He's nineteen! He's your kid.'

'Stop it.' He turned away, palming his forehead. 'I can't deal with this now.'

'Are you serious?' Frankie spat out the words. 'You're fucking unbelievable, you know that? What the hell is wrong with you? We have all we need to wrap things up here. You know we do. It's only a matter of time. What's more important than finding Ben?'

He rounded on her. 'Keep your voice down! You should've thought of that—'

'What?' The implication that she was somehow responsible knocked her sideways.

'You had to push it, didn't you?' His eyes were like heat-seeking missiles finding their target, exploding with devastating results he chose not to notice. He was looking for a scapegoat and he'd found one. 'When you asked Wells when she was going to give him a proper job, didn't you see

352

the look on his face? He thinks he's fucking Superman.'

'How fucking dare you!' Frankie glared at him. 'You're right, I did encourage him. I wasn't the only one. As I recall, Wells gave him the job as a favour to you. I didn't come here for a slanging match, but hey, I'll take the blame if it makes you feel better. I really don't give a shit. Whatever way this falls, remember Ben was trying to impress you. Have you forgotten what it was like when you first joined the force? The danger, the intrigue, because I sure as hell haven't—'

'That's different. We were wearing a uniform. We had back-up.'

'Yeah, and we thought we were indestructible. It's called youth. As for me, I've given up trying to impress you. It doesn't work. And, for the record, you're woefully short of impressing me right now. Ben is more important than one or even two victims we can't bring back to life. You need to drop everything and find him before it's too late. If you don't do this right, you'll never forgive yourself.'

'Are you done?'

She threw her head back. 'Not even close.'

David didn't budge. 'Look, we can't drop everything. We're in the middle of a murder enquiry. Give Wells a call and see if she's heard from Ben.'

'She hasn't. She would've been straight on the blower.'

David wiped his face with his hand. A big sigh. 'I still want you to call her.'

'Why?'

'She was given a tour of the building. Ask her if she remembers Fitzgerald locking the door to her office.'

Frankie didn't even try to hide her frustration. 'What for?'

'She told me her office is locked when she's not in it. Theoretically, mine is too. . . except when I forget because I'm juggling more balls than I can cope with, like now. Just ask her, eh?'

'Why is that a priority? We've got more important—'

'It isn't. It might keep us both from going crazy, Frank.' During a moment of heartbreak and regret, neither detective spoke. What else was there to say? Unable to stand the weighty silence, David was first to break the deadlock. 'Who was it that saw Ben leave?'

'Gemma Radcliffe. She and Ben arrived on the same day.'

'When I'm done with Fitzgerald, I'd like to talk to her.'

'She's in the library waiting.'

'Good. Keep her there.' Stone paused, considering. 'Circulate a photograph of Ben and call Andrew. Tell him to split the PolSA team in half and get the dog section in.'

It was the right call.

Frankie felt like bawling. David hadn't apologised for what he'd said. She could see that he was sorry and so was she. She left the room then, leaving the door wide open, telling Fitzgerald she could go back in. Frankie didn't expect the remainder of their meeting to go well. David wanted answers. If Fitzgerald couldn't supply them, in his present mood, he wouldn't hold back.

67

Frankie made the calls. Wells hadn't seen Ben. Half of Andrew's search team were on their way. As she hung up, three technical support civilians arrived in the hallway, one of whom was an old copper she knew. Geraldine (Geri) Hayes had returned to that role, following her retirement from the force, a move many officers had wangled on their way out the door. Extra pocket money. Frankie didn't know the other two that well, so she addressed Geri first.

'There are only three computers in the building. The SIO is happy that you examine them in situ. It was that or shut this place down. None are to be used until we have what we want, with the exception of the nurse's station, and then only with one of you on hand watching every keystroke. Understood?'

Geri gave a nod.

'The general office is due to open at nine,' Frankie added. 'Dick will send them packing so you can work in peace.' Frankie thumbed over her shoulder. 'Can one of you hang around the care manager's office? That's the first door on the right? Whatever you do, don't disturb the SIO. He's interviewing and will let you know when you can go in.'

'And the nurse's station?' Geri queried.

Frankie pointed in the opposite direction. 'That way.'

The tech team split up, setting off in opposite directions, loaded down with equipment. Abbott hung around, desperate for an update on Ben and Petersen. Frankie shook her head. He knew as much as she did. She held his gaze, replaying the row with David in her head. If fatherhood hadn't been forced upon him – and by extension, motherhood on her, since Ben had neither – she'd march into Fitzgerald's office and tell him that he was way out of line.

'He took it well, then?' Dick never missed a trick.

'The guv'nor?' She tried for a smile. 'It was nothing, just a few issues over child discipline. Did you ever see *Meet the Fockers*? That's us. A complete mismatch. How do you do it, Dick? Parenting has to be the worst job in the world. I mean, who in their right mind would put themselves through it?'

'There is a flipside.'

'Oh, yeah?' She pulled a face. 'I must've missed that in the dos and don'ts manual.'

Resting a hand on her shoulder, Dick gave it a squeeze. 'Keep the faith, Frank. If he thinks he's in danger, Ben will be lying low, keeping his head down. If Ryman can survive the cold, he can.'

'I hope you're right.'

'I am. And when we find him, you can kick his arse for putting you through it.'

'I look forward to it.'

'I didn't only come with the warrant, Frank.' She raised an eyebrow, prompting him to carry on. 'Indira's been digging. She retrieved the coroner's report on Alfie Jenkins, the old surgeon who died here seven years ago. The outbuilding we're looking for is the one where he was found.'

'You're kidding!'

'Nope. We have photographic evidence to prove it. Nancy must have twigged. That's why she went there to take that photograph. She was one gutsy woman.'

'Yeah, she was. Grab the CCTV footage from last night before it disappears, internal and external. When you have it, join me in the library. I've had it with kids today. I may need a babysitter.'

Abbott took off in the direction of the general office.

Heading for the library, Frankie slipped her mobile from her pocket and punched in a number.

'DC Mitchell.'

'Mitch, its me.' She took a few minutes to updated him on

developments. The investigation had moved up a notch, in pace and complexity. The pressure was on the MIT to keep up. 'Drop whatever you're doing,' she said. 'The boss wants eyes on Bradbury's estate manager, Jan Petersen. We need anything and everything you can find on him. I don't have a date of birth. If I find it, I'll let you know.'

'Have you seen Sir Giles?'

'No, he's incommunicado.'

'He'll make his presence felt as soon as he hears that we're searching the grounds.'

'Probably. In the meantime, make Petersen your priority. If necessary, get Indira to give you a hand.'

'Roger that.'

Abbott closed the general office door, CCTV footage secured in an evidence bag. As he approached the library, the door was yanked open from the other side. Frankie came racing out, so fast she nearly knocked him flying.

'Gemma's gone! C'mon, we need to find her.'

They searched the communal areas for a good half-hour. The girl was nowhere to be found. A middle-aged nurse pushing a drugs trolley along the corridor beamed at Abbott. Dick returned the greeting. Always popular with the ladies, he seized on the opportunity to quiz her. The answer she gave didn't surprise Frankie . . .

'Gemma excused herself from duty – she's not feeling well.'

That was one way of putting it. She was terrified. When Abbott showed ID, the nurse liked him even more, tripping over herself to help, grabbing a member of staff to take them to the accommodation block.

The nurse only had eyes for Abbott. 'I'd do it myself if I wasn't dispensing medication.'

As she turned away, Frankie dug her fellow DS in the ribs with her elbow. 'I saw that.'

'What?'

'You winked at her.'

'You got your escort, didn't you?'

On the way to the staff quarters – a converted stable block away from the main building that had little to recommend it – the skinny guy they were following grumbled continually that young kids these days didn't have the work ethic. Given Ben's current predicament and Gemma's useful information, the comment irritated Frankie.

She whispered to Abbott. 'Get this dickhead out of my sight before I do or say something I might regret.'

'Join the queue,' he said.

Gemma's door was locked.

'Can you get us in there?' Abbott asked.

'Believe me,' the skinny guy said. 'You're better out here.'

Frankie gave him side-eyes. 'Excuse me?'

He glanced at her feet. 'You'll be OK, Miss. You have boots on. I'll get the key.'

'While you're at it, get one for Ben Stone's room too.' He left them, retracing his steps, returning a few moments later with the keys she'd asked for. Frankie held out her hand. 'Which one is Ben's room?'

'Three doors down.'

'We'll take it from here.' Frankie waited for him to move off before turning the key.

Gemma's room was smaller than a police cell, an unmade single bed, a small built-in wardrobe and little else. No washing facilities or toilet. No window. No personal items on show. Frankie checked the wardrobe. Empty. She turned to face Abbott, opening the door wider so he could see that Gemma had cleared off.

His eyes travelled around the room. 'Can't say I blame her.'

'Me either, but the boss asked me to keep hold of her. Dammit!'

'On foot, she can't have got far.' Dick held up his car keys. 'Try the bus stop.'

He lobbed them at her. Frankie caught them in mid-air. In exchange, she handed over the key still in her hand. 'The search team are up and running. They need a hand. As soon as the dog section arrive, take them to Ben's room. When they're done, I want them out there looking for him without delay.'

'Leave it with me, now go!'

She ran out of the accommodation block, blipping the doors open as she approached his vehicle. The wheels sent a cloud of dust high into the air as she took off at speed across the gravel driveway. Given that Stone was with Fitzgerald, with a good view of the car park, it occurred to Frankie that he might think the worst. In her rush to get out of there, she hadn't realised. He might think something had happened to Ben. Braking hard, she stopped short of the main road, punching in Abbott's number.

He picked up immediately. 'You found her?'

'No, but be sure to tell the boss why I left.'

'Gotcha.' He didn't require further explanation.

'Thanks, I'll not be long.'

She might: she had previous for it.

Dropping her mobile on to the passenger seat, she turned left on to the main road. Gemma was like a speck in the distance. Before Frankie could catch up with her, a text alert drew her attention. Swearing under her breath, she pulled up sharply and scooped up her mobile, the search team coordinator's s name appearing on the screen: Andrew. The content of his message flipped her out:

We've found a body. Call me.

68

Stone's mind was in turmoil. As yet, he had no image of Jan Petersen, the man he was keen to question on three counts: the disappearance of Nancy Carver, the brutal stabbing of Chris Adams and, more recently, the absence of his nephew from Bastle View. Hopefully, the MIT were on the case but, now that Frankie had described Ben on the run at midnight, at risk from the shadowy figure following close behind, he couldn't get the image out of his head.

David felt like he'd failed his nephew; failed his late brother. It seemed like only yesterday when Ben was born. David remembered the pride in his brother's eye, the joy at having fathered a son, and something else he couldn't get a handle on. With tears in his eyes, Luke had held the child like it might break. It was then that David realised that the small precious bundle in his arms was completely dependent on his parents, that what he hadn't been able to nail in his brother's expression was raw fear. As grown up as Ben was now, for the first time in David's life, he could identify.

Pushing the thought away, he refocused on the care home manager, a woman he considered had more to give. 'Ms Fitzgerald, I appreciate that you've been here less than a year. I'm trying to work out why your predecessor left without serving notice and then promptly disappeared. During your tenure, have you heard any gossip that might help me establish the truth of it?'

'No, though the staff were all shocked by it.'

'Is there anyone employed here you have reservations about?'

She was shaking her head.

'No one?'

'No.' She sat motionless. David waited, the intensity of his stare getting to her prompting her to add. 'If that were the case, I can assure you they wouldn't be on my staff.'

David took a moment. He knew little of Fitzgerald. She might be an innocent witness caught up in his investigation. Equally, she could be complicit in what was going on within the home. Though the interview wasn't being recorded, he couldn't afford to put a foot wrong or ask any leading questions. A wig at court would tear him to shreds if he did. Neither could he hint that he was interested in Petersen in particular. It would be unwise, if not downright dangerous. If Fitzgerald was in cahoots, he wasn't about to hand her the means to tip off the Norwegian.

David had to find another way.

Through the window, he spied a gardener clipping a hedge, an idea occurring. He consulted the staff list Fitzgerald had given him, making her wait. In every case, the name had a job description next to it, a date of birth, references and security checks, Ben's among them. Choosing to come at her from a different angle, he accepted the coffee she was offering, got up and stood by the window, looking out.

'The home is well-named,' he said casually. 'That's quite a view.' He turned to face her, a smile developing, a ploy to put her at ease. 'I have to say my office is rather less salubrious. All I can see from my window is a brick wall.'

She cracked a smile, the first since she'd re-entered the room, 'I have to admit, it's a wonderful outlook, not that I have much time to enjoy it.' Pushing her chair back from her desk, she crossed her legs, linking her hands in her lap. A relaxed pose, exactly where Stone wanted her.

Once again, he glanced out of the window, inching his way to the point he was about to make. 'There's not a leaf out of place,' he said. 'The gardens are pristine. That must take some doing.'

'Sir Giles is keen to maintain them as his family have for

generations. We have an army of volunteers who help out in summer. We hold an open day every July to raise funds. It's a popular event and not only for the local community. People come from miles around. On a good day, there's no place like it.'

'I can imagine.'

It was time to make his play.

Returning to his seat, David downed his coffee, placing the cup on its saucer. He shuffled the lists she'd given him. Leaning forward, he slid an A4 sheet across her desk. 'And yet, I notice that there are no gardeners listed here.'

She studied the document. 'My apologies. When you asked for the staff register, I thought you were interested in those who work within the home – the nursing, ancillary and admin staff. Manual workers come under Sir Giles' land management company, which is an entirely separate entity. I can certainly pull them off for you.'

'If you would, that would be enormously helpful.' He watched her closely as she printed them off, retrieving the list that emerged in the output tray, the original from her desk. 'Actually, there is one other thing I should've asked for and that's a list of vehicles, owned or used by the charity and the land management company you referred to and, of course, your own.'

She resumed typing.

David collected the list but didn't look at it, though he was itching to. He was hoping for the dark-coloured four-by-four, as described by Eva Sokolov driving away at speed from Carliol Square on the night his investigation began. If the windows had privacy glass he'd throw a party.

'I'm afraid I'm going to have to ask you to vacate your office for a while. I have a technician standing by to examine your computer.' He walked her to the door.

She spoke before he had the chance to open it. 'DCI Stone, can we speak off the record?'

He turned to face her. 'I can't make any promises.'

'I understand.' That's all she said.

He gave her a nudge. 'I don't think you do, Ms Fitzgerald. I could have lied to you just now. Instead, I handed you the opportunity to be straight with me. The choice is yours. If there is anything about this organisation or anyone employed here that you're unhappy about, now's the time to share it.'

An impasse.

'I'll take that as a no then.' He opened the door.

She pushed it to, as if she'd changed her mind, but still she wavered.

He gave her a verbal shove: 'Ms Fitzgerald, in my experience, loyalty can often backfire.'

Conflicted, she took in a breath, finally finding the courage to share what was on her mind. 'I'm sorry, I wasn't entirely honest with you before. I love working here, but I'm not a fan of the land management staff. I'd prefer to do the hiring and firing. That's not the case with them. Sir Giles takes personal responsibility for that side of things.'

'You two get on?'

'I have little to do with him.'

That wasn't an answer. Stone suspected it was the only one he'd get. He tipped his head on one side. 'Why are you telling me this now?'

'Because I'm not stupid.'

'Meaning?'

'Your presence here is making me nervous. I get the impression that you are investigating something more serious than Nancy Carver's disappearance. Am I right?'

He looked at her.

She seemed sincere, but fifteen years in policing had taught Stone never to accept things at face value, when to speak and when to remain silent. Faced with the possibility of prosecution, Fitzgerald could be playing him.

69

Meltdown. Frankie glanced through the front windscreen, blinking into the distance. Gemma Radcliffe was nowhere to be seen. Swearing under her breath, Frankie checked her watch. She'd been sitting in the car for a full fifteen minutes since that text came in, frozen, literally and metaphorically. Anyone else might have said that a time jump was impossible, except she knew different.

We've found a body. Call me.

With both hands, she gripped the steering wheel, her knuckles turning white, the taste of bile in her mouth. The time jump worried her. It hadn't happened since she was a kid. A psychological response to trauma was the medical diagnosis, a cognitive reaction to her sister's death, accompanied by disorientation and intrusive thoughts of the event, even though she wasn't actually there to witness it.

And now, as she sat in Abbott's car, she imagined another crime scene, equally appalling: a woodland grave, a whistle ringing out deep in the forest, a hand raised alerting Andrew to a gruesome find. The image was incomplete, lacking a locus. He was in charge of both PolSA teams. That's what had thrown her into chaos, causing her to shut down temporarily. She knew that now, but which location was he talking about: Harwood Forest or Bastle View? The question induced a harrowing image that knocked the stuffing clean out of her.

A sob left her throat.

It couldn't be Ben . . .

It couldn't.

Unable to breathe, her mind wrestled the unimaginable. If it wasn't Ben, then why had Andrew sent the text to her, instead of the SIO? She knew he hadn't done both. David would have called her, arranged a rendezvous. As she forced herself to focus, realism kicked in, a hard truth she didn't want to acknowledge: a fresh body would be easier to locate than one that had been buried a year ago.

We've found a body. Call me.

Frankie didn't want to make that call. On the other hand, she wanted to shield David from the traumatic experience her father had gone through when he was called out to a crime scene, only to recognise his daughter's body. A body wasn't a casualty. A body meant death. The final curtain. Let it be Nancy . . .

Please God, let it be Nancy.

It was a moronic thought, cold and calculating, a disgusting thing to pray for. Frankie cried, not for Joanna, Ben or Nancy, but for what she had become. Climbing out of the car, she placed her hands on the roof, gulping down cold air. She had no right to choose between the two. Nancy had family: a loving daughter, Rachel Hooper; a traumatised son, James Carver, who'd never believed that his mother had left him of her own free will. Frankie had been waiting less than a day for news of Ben. Nancy's children had been waiting for what must seem like a lifetime.

Frankie's mobile rang in the car, startling her.

The screen came to light. She opened the door and leaned it, scooping it off the passenger seat: *David*.

Maybe she'd jumped the gun and was panicking unnecessarily, maybe he was already at the crime scene and was about to bend her ear for going AWOL; maybe he knew already.

Taking the call, she shut her eyes, lifting the device to her ear.

She cleared her throat. 'Guv?'

'Hi, Frank.' He sounded upbeat.

He didn't know.

70

Abbott waited nervously in the library with no idea of what was going on. When Stone dropped everything and legged it out of there, he didn't stop to explain, just gave instructions to find Petersen, keep in touch with the incident room and keep the pressure on Technical Support. Stone wanted information on whoever had accessed Nancy's car on the gov.uk database and he wanted it yesterday. The grave expression on his face as he left was a dead giveaway. The fact that neither he nor Frankie had returned or been in touch confirmed that something significant was going down.

It wouldn't take a super brain to work out what it was.

With a heavy heart, Abbott opened his laptop and logged on to the force database, inputting Jan Petersen's details from the list Fitzgerald had reluctantly handed over to the SIO. With little information, Mitch had a drawn a blank. Hardly surprising. Now they had a date of birth and a mini-backstory, they were good to go. Abbott was hoping he might get somewhere.

He didn't.

Petersen had no form, at least not in the UK. Like everyone else, Abbott was now convinced he was the man they were after. The pieces of the puzzle were all fitting together, information coming in thick and fast.

After a quick search for a telephone number, Abbott called the Norwegian Police Service in Oslo, where Petersen had once lived, allegedly. He was put through to a detective who worked in the National Criminal Investigation Service, better known as Kripos, a specialist organised and serious crime unit – both of which applied in the case he was investigating. He gave his name, rank and the telephone number for the switchboard at his force HQ, so she could verify his identity and call him back, which she did immediately. With links to Europol and Interpol, she spoke perfect English. Just as well. His knowledge of languages, other than his native tongue, was non-existent. Her name was Toril Sand and she was based in Bryn.

'How are you spelling your name?' he asked.

'T-O-R-I-L – and then sand like you get between your toes on the beach.'

'If you're lucky.' Dick wrote her name down.

'Sounds like you need some downtime, Richard.'

'Be sure to mention that to my guv'nor,' he said. 'Only my mother calls me Richard. My friends call me Dick.'

'That I can spell.' She had a filthy laugh. 'How can I help you?'

Abbott had liaised with the Norwegian police before and had formed the impression that they shot straight from the hip. He did likewise. 'I'm trying to trace one of yours we want to interview in connection to a murder enquiry.' He gave Jan Petersen's details, including the references he'd produced to get his current job.

'I'll take a look.'

'Thanks. If you can't get hold of me, you need to speak to DS Frankie Oliver.' He gave Sand the number of the incident room and Frankie's email address in case she wanted to send anything.

'I'll do what I can.'

As she hung up, Abbott's mobile rang in his hand: it was Mitchell. Ignoring a knock at the door, Dick leaned back in his chair and put his feet on the mahogany writing desk. It was already dark outside. He could see his reflection in the library window and liked what he saw. He was in the wrong job.

He pressed to receive the call, faking a posh accent. 'You're through to the Austen Room. How may I help?'

Mitch ignored the attempt at humour. 'I can't raise the SIO or Frankie. Any ideas?'

'They're busy. Hit me with some news that won't depress me. I'll pass it on.'

'The Met picked up Nancy's car, minus a wing mirror, and arrested the woman driving it. No ID as yet. Beyond Nancy Carver's cash card, she had nothing on her. She's not said a word, but the detective I spoke to has shared her photograph internally. We might get something from it. The car is on a transporter on its way up the M1 as we speak.'

'Good stuff. Send a male/female escort to pick the woman up.'

'Already taken care of.'

'Impressive. I'll let Frank know you were listening. When the car arrives let me know.'

'You won't be back?'

'Unlikely. There's too much going on here.'

The door opened. Geri Hayes poked her head into the room. Seeing that he was on the phone, she raised a hand, an apology for the interruption. He beckoned her in, gesturing for her to take a seat and returned to his call.

'Any news on the knife?'

'Not yet,' Mitch said. 'I can't see us finding it now, can you?'

'Miracles happen . . . apparently. Anything else?'

'Yeah, Gemma Radcliffe is safe and well. We sent a uniform to her parents' address. She'll sit tight and make herself available for a formal interview.'

'I'll tell Frank. Keep me posted, mate.'

The line went dead.

Geri eyed him from across the room. 'Good news?'

Abbott waggled his hand from side to side. 'We don't have the case wrapped up yet, but the pieces are falling into place. You?'

'We're done. We pulled the internet searches for January sixteenth. The general office and the nursing station were both in use at the time the gov.uk website was accessed. Whoever was responsible used Fitzgerald's office.'

'You're certain about that?'

'One hundred per cent.'

'I'd get up and kiss you if I wasn't so comfy.'

Geri grinned. 'Loving the tycoon impression. You want a coffee?'

'There's no champagne?'

'Later. We're not home and dry yet.' She added, 'CCTV in the communal areas is overwritten once a month, so we can't ID who made the search, assuming it wasn't her.'

71

The crime scene had been cordoned off by the time Stone and Oliver arrived in separate cars, tape flapping in the wind, drawing a line from the dirt track to the deposition site. It was imperative to create a sterile forensic corridor, where potential paths of exit and entry of suspects may have taken place, though the possibility of evidence collection after such a time lapse would be negligible. Much of the evidential material would have been lost or compromised.

Harwood Forest had never seemed so menacing.

A huddle of freezing officers stood on the periphery awaiting instruction. The finder who'd viewed the body assumed that it was the person he'd been looking for, though all agreed that it was hard to know for sure. The woman, or what was left of her, was lying face up in a shallow grave, covered in soil and leaves. There was evidence that one leg had been gnawed at by animals.

Frankie crouched down beside the body, careful not to touch anything. One glance and she knew. She looked up. A nod to Stone: the PolSA team had found Nancy Carver. With a hand covering her mouth to stop herself from wailing, Frankie stood up straight, overwhelmed by self-loathing for having wished another woman's life away. There were not enough negative adjectives in the dictionary to describe her conduct.

Reprehensible didn't come close.

No matter which way she read it, there simply was no justification. The weight of David's attention forced her to concentrate. If he expressed one word of sympathy for Nancy, Frankie would fold.

Turning away, she scanned the scene, noting that they

were close to the location where the Fiat's wing-mirror had become detached. The MIT had yet to confirm that it belonged to Nancy's car, though in Frankie's reckoning there was little doubt. David's theory that she'd been followed from her place of work and silenced had always been the most likely scenario.

Shutting her eyes, listening to sounds of the forest, Frankie played the scene in her head, wondering what nightmarish thoughts had gone through Nancy's mind that night. In her imagination, she pictured Nancy fleeing for her life, stumbling and falling in the dark, trying to get away. It was a petrifying image, a hideous way to die. She had no realistic possibility of escape against a man like Petersen. By profession, he was nothing more than a glorified hunter, arranging shoots for the landed gentry's entertainment.

'Frank? You about ready?'

She swung round. 'Yeah. Uniform personnel are on hand to guard the scene. There's nothing more we can do here.'

David was nodding. 'Andrew, once the remains have been removed, stand down for the night and resume a fingertip search at daybreak.'

Reluctantly, he agreed.

There was a reason why Andrew was so down in the mouth. Once his crew had found their target, contamination had become an issue. There was no possibility that they could team up with their colleagues at Bastle View, even though the second search area needed more boots on the ground. Bradbury's estate was huge.

David was already walking away, head down as he made his way to his vehicle.

Andrew glanced at Frankie, a knowing look, an apology on the tip of his tongue. Aware that Ben Stone was missing, there wasn't one of his team who wouldn't have preferred to stay on and assist.

'The situation must be killing him,' he said.

Frankie locked eyes with him. 'It's killing us all.'

'I'll get another team out to Bastle View at first light.'

'Thanks, Andrew. Appreciate it.'

As he moved away, Frankie caught sight of David behind him. He was alone, noting down his observations while they were fresh in his head. He looked like she felt: lost and miserable, another death chipping away at his spirit. She knew the feeling. The Job took no prisoners. Sooner or later it would grind them down and they'd leave. Not today, tomorrow or even next month, but it would happen – as it had to her father.

She called out to Andrew.

He swung round, retracing his steps.

'Need a favour,' she said. 'Can you ask one of your guys to drive Dick's car back to base for me? I can sort a lift out for him later. Looks like my guv'nor could do with some company.'

72

All that seemed like hours ago. Frankie felt like she was moving in slow-motion. When she and David had left the crime scene, there was only one place it was appropriate to go and that was to the western edge of the city, to the home of Rachel Hooper, Nancy's daughter.

Frankie called ahead to warn her that they were on their way. Beyond that, she hardly spoke on the journey. When she did, there was no mention of Ben for fear it would upset David. He didn't choose to speak of his nephew either, for exactly the same reason. The atmosphere in the car was grim.

Rachel had the foresight to call her brother and ask him to join them. They were both waiting when the detectives arrived. They entered the house with one task in mind, to warn Nancy's family that a body had been found before the press got hold of the news. It was the best they could do – the only thing they could do.

'Is it her?' James Carver's eyes were like dark pools of water.

'The jewellery she was wearing would suggest so,' Frankie said. 'I'm so sorry. I realise how distressing this is for both of you. While we cannot say for certain, you must prepare yourselves for the worst.' She expected an angry outburst, recriminations, finger-pointing. It didn't come. Rachel slipped her arm around her brother's shoulder. James Carver was stoical, as was she. It seemed that they were already resigned to their mother's fate.

With the post-mortem already underway, Stone and Oliver headed to Bastle View, relieved that a difficult conversation was over for now. It was one they would return to in due course, when a full medical examination had been carried out and the process of formal identification could take place. A couple of miles from the residential home, David's eyes strayed to his rear-view mirror, the sight of blue lights fast approaching from behind.

He slowed the car.

A Traffic vehicle shot by.

'Must be nasty,' Frankie said. 'That was Andrea.'

'Was it?' Her sister-in-law was the last person David expected to see tonight. As she took a sharp bend in the road and disappeared, he checked his wing mirror. More blue lights. 'She's acting as escort.' His voice broke as he said it. 'Take a look for yourself.'

Frankie swung round to look over her shoulder.

David sat motionless, a chill passing through him, hands welded to the steering wheel. A Rapid Response Vehicle passed them at speed, then another Traffic car, and another, sirens blaring to warn other road users that they were coming through. Ramming his vehicle in gear, David waited for two other vehicles to pass, then took off after them, throwing Frankie back in her seat. He didn't need to verbalise his thoughts. She'd done the maths.

A couple of minutes later, Stone drove through the main gates of Bastle View, then braked hard, coming to a stop halfway along the driveway. The scene that greeted him was not what he'd expected. There was no medical crisis or fire, no police vehicles or RRV outside the main entrance, no paramedics. For a split-second, he thought that his eyes had deceived him, that the convoy of vehicles had sailed right by, that stress had caused him to hallucinate their entry on to the estate, that his terror and confusion was part of a bad dream and that he'd wake at any moment. Had it not been for the faces at the windows of the residential home, staff and residents peering out from within, he'd have been convinced of it.

'So much for keeping a low-profile,' Frankie said.

She was staring intently across his body and out of his side window, flashing blue lights reflected in her eyes, an expression of horror on her face. When David turned his head that way, he was met with his worst nightmare imaginable. Whatever had summoned the emergency services in such numbers was happening within the extensive grounds of Bradbury's estate.

It seemed to take forever to make sense of the scene.

The convoy had turned right and driven across the immaculate lawn towards a drystone wall that separated the gardens from grazing land and the woods beyond. He watched the lead vehicle move out of the way in a north-easterly direction, allowing the RRV through; the second car taking up a position directly behind it; the third, mimicking the first, though in reverse, this one sweeping in a wide south-easterly arc, parking up facing Andrea's vehicle, their headlights illuminating the landscape.

'David?' An icy hand found his.

He didn't look at her. He was too busy watching paramedics jumping out of the response vehicle, climbing the wall and legging it across open ground towards the woods. 'It's not looking good, Frank.'

'They're still running, guv.'

He knew what she meant.

David pulled over to let an ambulance pass. It followed the others, did a U-turn and parked up, ready to make a quick getaway. As they watched, Andrea jumped out of her vehicle, pulling on her coat. She vaulted the wall and ran towards the treeline, shouting orders at her team.

Depressing his accelerator, David drove on. Foot to the floor, he bumped over the kerb, tearing up the grass, getting as close as he could to the other vehicles. Across a four-acre field, flashlights in the woods were like pinpricks in the darkness. It was impossible to work out what was going on.

His imagination did it for him.

'Jesus Christ!' It came out like a whisper.

Frankie snapped her head around. 'Stay put!'

Before his four-by-four had properly come to a stop, she was out of the car, arms pumping, fists curled into hard balls of pent-up aggression as she raced across the lawn. Unable to move, David watched her cover the ground in double-quick time.

She pulled up sharply.

Out of breath, she bent double, hands on knees, head lifted, eyes focused straight ahead. She felt for her coat pocket, then glanced over her shoulder. She was staring right at him, a curious look on her face, as if she was about to return to the car. It was then he noticed her radio on the passenger seat. She'd left it in her rush to get out of the car.

Picking it up, he turned it on and changed channel.

Andrea's voice was unmistakable: 'Mike 7003 to Control: We have one casualty, semi-conscious. I repeat, one casualty. Ambulance now on scene. Stand by for an update.'

'Control: That's received.'

Clutching the radio, David grabbed his coat from the rear seat and got out of the car. The north wind bit into his face and made his eyes water. Left out in the cold for the best part of eighteen hours, hypothermia and dehydration – two silent killers – would be an issue for Ben, in addition to whatever other injuries he might have suffered, David knew that it was a race against time to get him medical help. With his focus on the pinpricks in the distance, David pressed to transmit . . .

'Mike 7125 to 7003. How bad is it?'

There was a moment's hesitation while he waited for Andrea to respond. 'Mike 7003: casualty has lost consciousness, query head injury, broken femur.' She didn't elaborate.

He wanted more detail. Will he live? was the burning question, though he didn't press her on it. He wasn't giving up on his nephew yet. Ben was super fit. He was tough. In his short life, he'd made mistakes, but he'd overcome them. He'd survived the death of his parents and a whole lot more besides. He'd survive this.

Wouldn't he?

With his mind seesawing between hope and desperation, David took off towards the drystone wall. As he reached it, Indira slipped her arm around his 2ic. Frankie was shivering uncontrollably, her lips blue with the cold. He could see the distress on their faces and wondered if they knew something he didn't. To his left, police dogs barked excitedly. Like the PolSA team, the canines had found their target. Their handlers were patting them, returning them to their transportation unit, rewarding them for a job well done. They were the unsung heroes of the police service. Many lives had been saved because of them. Mentally, he crossed his fingers, praying that this would be the case tonight.

'Guv.' Indira pointed.

Frankie took a step forward.

Indira held on to her.

'Get off me!' Frankie yelled.

'Frankie, stop it!' David said. 'Indi's right. We can't touch him.'

'I don't want to touch him. I just want to see him.' Her wild eyes stared at him. 'Guv, we have to. It might be the last chance we get.'

The harsh reality of her words sent blood rushing through David's ears blotting out all but white noise. Putting a hand on the drystone wall to keep himself upright, his attention switched to the woods. The flashlights were getting closer. Seconds later, they cleared the treeline, voices calling out in the darkness. Four of Andrew's search team emerged carrying a body on a stretcher. They were moving quickly.

73

David woke with a start, reliving the moment when that stretcher emerged from the woods. Instinctively, he'd had the foresight to realise that Ben still had a pulse. If he'd been dead, there would have been no need for Andrew's men to rush him to the ambulance. In fact, they wouldn't have moved him. They'd have waited for someone like him to arrive on the scene; an SIO high on adrenalin, who'd be buzzing at the prospect of a new murder enquiry, as David and Frankie had on countless occasions in the past.

He knew the narrative well and yet, from the get-go, his investigation had given pause for thought. Life was cheap. Too cheap. It could vanish in an instant, causing untold damage to those left behind. No one could look David in the eye as the procession passed him by, because Ben might have suffered internal injuries that could, potentially, kill him before he reached the hospital.

Yawning, David pulling himself up out of his chair. He checked his watch – two a.m. – then refocused on the patient in the bed. Out in the cold, Ben's body temperature had fallen below a critical thirty-five degrees, the reason he'd passed out. Once they warmed him up, he'd regained consciousness, his confusion quickly disappearing. His SATs were low and he required oxygen. He had a broken leg, cuts and bruises, but he'd live. He had not been assaulted. The stupid sod had fallen thirty feet down a ravine in his rush to get away from Petersen, whose name was the first word that came out of his mouth, before admitting that he'd overheard David talking to Wells in the Jesmond Dene Hotel, mumbling an apology before he fell asleep.

*

David's eyes found Frankie's as he walked into an incident room where detectives were flat out, making and fielding calls, updating HOLMES, the computer system on which all major enquiries were run. Last night, she'd refused to go home and was asleep in the corridor when he left the hospital ward. He'd taken her home and spent the night at her place, arriving at Middle Earth in time to hold an early briefing with the MIT.

There was much to do.

The SIO had given the PolSA team instructions to locate all outbuildings on Bradbury's estate, to enter and photograph, nothing more. He'd sent Abbott out to Bastle View to keep an eye on things while Frankie liaised with detectives in the Met. David and Indira had been interviewing the woman who'd been caught driving Nancy's car, having accessed a cashpoint machine in Crouch End. By the look of her, Frankie couldn't wait to get off the phone for an update.

He was about to disappoint her.

Hanging up, she walked towards him, a spring in her step. Impressive, given that she'd been up half the night. 'How did it go?'

He shook his head. 'She hasn't said a word.'

'You didn't expect her to cough, did you?'

'I'm glad you find it so amusing.'

'Lighten up, David. Her name is Amanda Williams. Date of birth: seventeenth of April 1985. Our Met colleagues matched her prints. The duty inspector gave them authorisation to search her flat. They found a huge amount of cash, a bundle of credit cards and a whole lot more they or we can throw at her.'

'Anything belonging to Chris Adams?'

Frankie shook her head. 'Beyond Nancy's credit card, they found no proof that she had any links with Petersen. She may have been sending him money, but I doubt it. Indications are that she was a fence, receiving the card in exchange for cash. Upfront money would suit him, wouldn't it? Less risk. One thing's for sure, she won't have lost out on the deal.'

'She has previous for it?'

'Yup. She's on SOCA's watch list.'

'Well, they haven't been watching her very closely, have they?'

'Only recently has she come to their attention.' Frankie explained that the Serious Organised Crime Agency suspected that Williams was part of a network of offenders involved in the manipulation of the elderly, many of whom were dying of shame having been scammed and placed on a sucker's list, their names bandied around by corrupt cockroaches looking to gain access to their bank accounts. 'That's why, when we asked the Met for help, they took it upon themselves to keep watch on Williams' three favourite cashpoint machines. With or without her cooperation, she will be charged.'

'That's something, I suppose.'

'We're after bigger fish than her, David.'

'I know.' He let out a big sigh. 'There's nowt doing on the CCTV either. Petersen wasn't daft enough to walk into shot on the exterior footage and, according to Gemma Radcliffe, he collared her inside the staff accommodation block where there is none.'

'Bummer.'

Indira interrupted. 'Frankie, there's a call on line one. Detective Sand?'

'Good, I've been expecting her.' Frankie stuck her tongue in her cheek. 'How did you like shadowing the SIO this morning?'

Indira burst out laughing. 'It was a no-reply interview.'

'I'm pulling your leg. You can sit with me next time. You might learn something.'

David chuckled.

Indira wiped the smile clean off his face. 'Guv, Detective Chief Superintendent Bright is on his way up. Bradbury is back from France, making waves. It seems he's none too happy about the state of his lawn.' They were all laughing now.

74

Frankie walked to her desk and sat down, hoping that the Norwegian police officer could give her some background on the man the MIT were keen to interview – no matter how small. Humans liked to talk. They were also creatures of habit. The more you knew about them, the more chance there was of apprehending them. She'd once arrested a guy in a betting shop following an off-the-cuff remark by someone who'd told her that he'd bet on two flies walking up a wall. He'd been on the run for months and his gambling habit had not come to light, despite extensive enquiries.

She picked up the phone. 'Detective Sand, this is DS Frankie Oliver.'

'Good morning. My name is Toril. How are you today?'

Frankie's eyes were on David. He was smiling at Indira. 'Better than yesterday.'

'That's about as good as it gets in our line of work, is it not?'

'It is.' Across the room, David was walking away. 'Did you find our man Petersen?'

'Yes, I did.'

Scooping a pen off her desk in readiness to take notes, Frankie pulled a notepad towards her. The door crashed open and Bright marched in. For Frankie's benefit he made winders with his hands. Then like the ex-military man he was, he pointed at his eyes with two fingers, then at the SIO's office, a gesture that her presence was required. She threw him a nod, then focused on the Norwegian.

'You have something for me, Toril? I hope this doesn't sound rude, but I'm feeling the heat this end. I've been summoned by the head of CID. He's not a man you want to mess with, if you get my drift.'

'You may have a bigger problem than that,' Sand said. 'Unfortunately, along with Jan Petersen's birth certificate, I found his marriage and death certificates. Jan Petersen is a common name in our country, like John Smith is in the UK, so it's possible that there is more than one with the same birthday. But not, I suspect, the same references from the same company. The documents DS Abbott sent me check out, but only for a dead man. Clearly, you're dealing with a case of stolen identity.'

'Damn.' Frankie's eyes were on Stone's office door. 'Actually, now I come to think of it, that makes sense.'

'In what way?'

'We've been looking for an illegal immigrant with the initials JC, not JP. It's been driving me mad for days. Look, I've got to go. Can you email copies of what you found?'

'On its way to you.'

'Thanks, I'm sorry to have troubled you.'

'No apologies required,' Sand said. 'It's good to reach out to colleagues across the North Sea. We are practically neighbours, right? Best of luck with your investigation, Frankie. If you're ever in Oslo, look me up. If you get your man, or even if you don't, we'll raise a glass of Akvavit.'

With that, Toril Sand was gone.

The continuous dialling tone in Frankie's ear was like a flatlining heart monitor. She threw her pen down, wincing at the empty notepad in front of her. 'Bollocks!' she said.

The two senior officers were deep in conversation when Frankie slipped into the room to join them. Sir Giles Bradbury had been on the blower to Bright, having acquired his name and designated number from Northumbria's Deputy Chief Constable, a man he knew through his charity work. It was nothing more than a buck-passing sidestep by an officer with his eye on promotion to the top job. It was rumoured that the man in overall charge of the force would retire in the spring and the deputy didn't want to rock the boat.

'Beyond the fact that we have a search warrant,' Bright said, 'Bradbury knows nothing. He refused to talk without his solicitor present. I want to make this clear, he's not someone either of you will warm to. He's a man of considerable wealth and a formidable reputation, but he gets no preferential treatment. None whatsoever. Assuming it works for you, he will present himself here at two o'clock. I expect you to treat him with respect or you'll have me to answer to. As far as I can see, you have no proof that he's involved in a criminal act of any kind.'

'That's the current state of play,' David said.

'Watch yourselves,' Bright said. 'He's angry.'

Frankie grinned. 'You know me, sir. I love a good scrap. As it happens, I'm free at two . . .' She glanced at David, a mischievous grin. 'How about you, guv? We wouldn't want to tear up his reputation when we've already ruined his lawn, unless we absolutely have to.'

'Always the joker, Frank. Your father would be so proud. However, this is no laughing matter. Bradbury is well connected, about as high-profile as you'll find in this community.' Bright glanced at Stone. 'David, keep *her* under control. If she shouts her mouth off, can her.'

Frankie couldn't keep the smile off her face. 'I'll behave, sir. I promise.'

'You'd better. By your own admission, Bradbury is not yet in the frame. Having had an unpalatable conversation with him less than an hour ago, in which he tried to throw his weight around, I'm willing to accept that he may be guilty of mistreating employees. Powerful men often do, but would he stoop to murder? I don't think so somehow.'

'He would if he was trying to protect his empire,' Frankie said. 'He might not do it himself. Why would he? He has enough money to pay someone to do his dirty work. That makes him no less culpable. If he's inciting violence, never mind ripping off the elderly, he's equally guilty under the law.'

'Really . . . I had no idea.'

Frankie ignored his sarcasm. 'Sir, DS Abbott and DC Mitchell have been at the home all day questioning staff. They've been met with a wall of silence. They're convinced that the estate and care home employees know more than they are prepared to share.'

'Then keep digging. Find the proof and I'll back you all the way.'

'Thank you,' David said. 'That means a lot, sir.'

The door opened without warning. Indira landed in the room as if she'd been shot from a cannon. 'Omigod! I'm so sorry, sir. I, I didn't realise you were still here.' She didn't know where to put herself.

'I don't think we've been introduced,' Bright said.

'PC Indira Sharma, sir.'

'Ah, the new aide.'

'Yes, sir.'

'I've heard a lot about you.' Bright was doing his best to put her at ease. 'DCI Stone tells me that you'll make an excellent detective, so if you have something important to tell us, you'd better spit it out.'

'Petersen has been arrested, sir.'

'That's a great opening line.'

'Thank you, sir. DS Abbott is bringing him in. I was told to tell DCI Stone that he lives in a former gate lodge on the north side of Sir Giles Bradbury's estate, so there's no need for a warrant to search his home.'

'Is that where they found him?' Stone asked.

'No, guv. His Land Rover was spotted on the A696 near the airport. Whether he was heading there, we don't know. He had no passport on him. Traffic were alerted. Inspector McGovern heard the call go out. She organised a rolling road, but in the end it wasn't necessary. Petersen didn't try to outrun them. I'm not sure what he meant by it, but DS Abbott said it was a good move on his part.'

'It was . . .' Frankie grinned. 'He wouldn't have got very far with Andrea in the driving seat.'

'I have more good news.' Indira kept her focus on the most senior officer. 'Sir, in every respect, Petersen's four-by-four matches the one seen by the witness Sokolov on the night Chris Adams was murdered.'

'Yes!' Frankie almost whooped.

'Welcome to the MIT,' Bright said. 'You enjoyed that, didn't you?'

'Just a bit, sir.'

Bright checked his watch. 'I'm needed at HQ. PC Sharma, nice to meet you. Keep up the good work.'

'Yes, sir. Thank you, sir.'

David and Frankie stood up as the detective chief superintendent made a move. Indira Sharma followed him out, a quick glance over her shoulder at the others as she left the room, wide-eyed and with a cheesy full-on grin, stoked that she'd finally been introduced to the head of CID.

75

'So, what's the plan?' Frankie asked excitedly as soon as she and David were alone. She smelled blood and couldn't wait to get started. Glancing at her watch, she didn't wait for a reply. Instead, she proceeded to tell him what she had in mind. 'It'll take a while for Dick to bring Petersen in. Even longer to process him. The detention clock is ticking once he's in the nick and on the custody record. Ordinarily, we'd want a forensics team turning his place over—'

'Ordinarily?' He gave her a pointed look.

'Why wait?' she said. 'David, CSIs will take forever to get their act into gear this close to Christmas. They're flat out. You know that. That doesn't stop us grabbing a couple of forensic suits and searching Petersen's house before we interview Bradbury at two. It wouldn't be a bad idea to sling the Norwegian in a cell and let him sweat a while. He's dead, by the way.'

'Come again?'

'Detective Sand called me as Bright arrived. Whoever Dick has arrested, it's not Jan Petersen. He may not even be Norwegian. Maybe that's why he didn't run, because he knows that we have no fucking idea who he is. There might be something in his house that'll help us ID him.'

David was already off his seat.

Had it not been for Frankie's sharp eye, the SIO would have missed the gate lodge. Having overshot the place, he stopped the car, put his four-by-four in reverse gear and pulled into a passing place on the single-track road. Grabbing Petersen's key off the dash, he climbed out and walked back towards the lodge, Frankie overtaking him, keen to get inside. With a gloved hand, she rattled the elaborate forged iron entry gate.

'Damn! It's locked. Is there only one key?'

David checked his pocket. A nod.

She blew out a breath, frustration getting the better of her. 'We'll have to drive all the way round and come at it from the other side.'

'Sod that,' he said, undeterred.

'Hey! Where are you going? You can't abandon me—'

'Hold on a minute.'

He walked to his vehicle, reversing it half on and half off the road, so that the tailgate was abutting the entrance gate. Getting out, he climbed on to the bonnet, on to the roof and over the gate as nimbly as an experienced burglar.

'Nice one,' Frankie said.

'Thanks, now shift the car.' He tossed his car keys over the gate.

Frankie caught them in her left hand. 'And how do you propose I get over?'

'I'll see if I can find something to pop the padlock from this side.'

By the time she returned, the gate was open slightly. She slipped through the narrow gap, a wry smile on her face. The gate lodge would have made the perfect romantic hideaway. It was a single-storey cottage, much like David's, tucked to one side of a separate entry on to the estate that had not been used in decades, trees and shrubs concealing it from view, overgrown ivy surrounding the tiny windows.

They took off their outdoor gear, stashing their coats and shoes outside the property, then put on forensic clothing and nitrile gloves and went inside. The hallway was a shit-pit, muddy boots discarded on the flagstone floor, a coat and gloves. A Barbour jacket and tweed stalker's hat hung on a huge rusty nail sticking out of the wall. The living room wasn't much better, the small kitchen either: dirty pots in the sink, a half-eaten sandwich lying on the bench, a dirty tin cup and several empty beer bottles.

'He must smoke like a trooper,' Frankie said. The place stank of fags and sweat.

'It's also like a fridge. See what you can do in here and in the living room. I'll check out the bedroom and bathroom, assuming this place has one.'

'No chance. There'll be an outside netty in the rear yard . . . if you're lucky.'

'You can do that then.' David took in her grimace. 'Joking! I'll take the bog and the bedroom.' The search was finally underway.

76

What Frankie found at Petersen's gate lodge gave her much to smile about. As she and David left the house, a crime scene investigators' van pulled up outside. The occupants jumped out, surprised to see a couple dressed in forensic gear already there. Stripping off her white suit, Frankie joked that they were too late, that the hard work had already been done. She listed the important stuff the SIO wanted examined urgently and where exactly it could be found in the house.

'We've not removed anything.' She held up her phone. 'We have all we need right here. Oh, and there's a locked gun cabinet in the rear hall. Make sure it's empty when you leave.'

David called the hospital on the way to Middle Earth, asking to be put through to Ben on the ward. While he waited for the connection, he tapped the speaker icon so that Frankie could join the conversation. She was itching to talk to his nephew. Hearing his voice was the only way she'd stop fretting.

'Hello.'

'It's me,' David said. 'How you doing?'

'I'm OK, Dave. A bit groggy, sore ribs, an aching head. They ruled out concussion. I'm expecting to be discharged later.'

'You gave us quite a scare,' Frankie said.

'Don't you worry about me, Frank. I bounce, apparently. Any chance one of you can pick me up if I text you when they discharge me? It'll save me having to wait for an ambulance. Besides, even if they take me home, I can't get in. I lost my key.'

'No can do,' Frankie said. 'Thanks to you, we're tied up.' It was her way of praising him. What he'd done was foolish, but she reckoned he deserved to get out of bed before the recriminations began. 'I'll call Wells, see if she can collect David's key and bring it to you. She might even take you home if she's still speaking to you.'

'Did you get Petersen?' Ben asked.

Momentarily, David lifted both hands off the steering wheel, raising them to the heavens, a sideways glance at Frankie. 'Does this kid ever learn?'

Ben laughed. 'I heard that.'

'Well hear this. It's rude and sometimes dangerous to earwig other people's conversations.' David was smiling when he said it.

It didn't stop Frankie from thumping his upper arm and giving him a dirty look. 'Yeah, we got him,' she said. 'Now all we have to do is nail him. You've been a great help, Ben.'

'I've been well rewarded.'

'By whom?'

'Your mam and dad, grandma and granddad popped in. I have enough homemade cake to feed the crowd at St James's Park.'

Frankie smiled. 'Has Wells been in?' She'd texted her from the car on the way home from the hospital to put her mind at rest.

'She was here when I woke up,' Ben said. 'Scared the living shit out of me.'

David snorted. 'You deserve a telling off, mate.'

'No, it wasn't that. You should see her without her slap on. No kidding, I almost lifted off the bed!'

David and Frankie laughed.

Ben was going to be fine.

77

Stone and Oliver split up, having spent an hour agreeing their strategy. The men they were about to interview were very different. How the detectives went about the task would be central to the successful conclusion of their investigation. David would tackle Bradbury with Mitch as second chair; Frankie and Dick would interview Petersen; Indira acting as go-between, relaying messages if any news came in during the process.

Timing was key.

At the exact moment that Bradbury walked into Middle Earth with his brief, Frankie and Abbott took off for the cells, Indira to the observation room with Pam Bond, the receiver, who had read everything on the case. The next few hours were going to be critical.

Stone and Mitch stood up as Sir Giles Bradbury and his solicitor were shown into Interview Room 1 by a female PC. The visitors both pulled out a chair and sat down, stony-faced, David and Mitch retaking their seats, the latter turning on the recorder on the console adjacent to the table they were sitting at. The SIO had no notes. All he had to say to Bradbury was filed away in his head. Bright would get his way. Sir Giles would be treated with the utmost respect.

'Sir, thank you for coming in. I'm DCI David Stone, and this is—'

Mitch gave his rank and name. 'DC Raymond Mitchell.'

David focused on Bradbury. He was immaculately dressed in a dark blue suit and striped regimental tie, a handsome man with an impenetrable gaze who reminded him of actor Jason Isaacs. The SIO never took his eyes off him. 'I'm recording this interview for easy recall. You have a solicitor present.

For the tape, would you please identify yourselves.'

'Sir Giles Bradbury.'

'Trevor Mansfield . . . Mansfield, Elliott and Associates.'

'Thank you,' David said. 'Mr Bradbury, you are here as a voluntary attender, which means you may leave at any time. I'm sure Mr Mansfield will have explained this to you.'

'He has.'

'Before I begin, do you have any questions?'

'Not at this stage, no.'

Frankie Oliver had administered the caution and gone through the formalities. The tape was running. Unlike David, she had a file in front of her. For now, she didn't open it. Her suspect had declined legal representation and given his name as Jan Petersen, along with a date of birth belonging to a dead man, stating that he was Bradbury's estate manager.

So far, so good.

Though she had enough evidence to keep him in custody beyond the initial period of detention, she couldn't prove that he – whoever he was – was responsible for selling Nancy Carver's credit card to Amanda Williams, the woman recently picked up by Met Police who was refusing to answer questions. Now Stone and Oliver knew she was driving a dead woman's car, they had more ammunition to throw at her.

She'd come across . . . eventually.

Frankie couldn't prove conclusively that her suspect had searched the gov.uk website in order to flog the car to the same woman to make an extra buck. Whatever he was doing for Bradbury, it would appear that Petersen had a sideline going.

'Could we perhaps start at the beginning?' she said. 'Jan Petersen is not your name. What is your name?'

He didn't answer.

She didn't expect him to. 'Well, let's move on then, shall we?' She tapped the folder in front of her. 'In this file, I have irrefutable evidence that you stole Jan Petersen's identity and

392

references and used them to obtain employment at Bastle View. That constitutes a criminal offence called pecuniary advantage.'

'I don't understand.'

'I think you do. Let me make it clear for you. In the UK, it's against the law to make false representation in order to gain financially.'

'I didn't.'

'The Norwegian authorities say you did.'

'Sir, you're probably wondering why I wanted to talk to you, so let me explain. I'm investigating the violent death of a young man found in Newcastle city centre on Friday the eighth of December. As a result of my enquiries, I have reason to believe that his death is connected to the disappearance a year ago of a woman whose body was discovered buried in Harwood Forest yesterday. The remains have since been identified as Nancy Carver, an ex-employee of yours.'

'And what has that to do with me?' Bradbury asked.

Stone ignored the question, firing off one of his own. 'Do you have any knowledge of how she ended up there?'

'No, of course not. What are you suggesting?'

'Bear with me a moment. I'm hoping that you might help me establish the facts of the case. You knew of Mrs Carver's disappearance?'

'I'm aware that she left my employ suddenly, causing untold inconvenience. Beyond that, I had no interest.' Responding to the perturbed look on David's face, Bradbury quickly back-pedalled: 'Though I am, of course, sorry to hear of her death. Buried, you say?'

'Yes, so we're not talking suicide.'

'Poor woman.' Bradbury waited.

'Were you consulted over the appointment of her replacement, Ms Fitzgerald?'

'No. That is a matter for the trustees. I own Bastle View. I don't run the place.'

'I understand. And how well do you know your staff, generally speaking?'

'I don't. As I just stated.'

David waited until Mitch stopped taking notes. 'Leaving aside the care home staff for a moment, is it the case that you take personal responsibility for the hiring and firing of manual workers employed by your land management company?'

'You didn't ask about them.'

He was right. David hadn't. 'Please answer the question, sir.'

'Yes, that is correct.'

Mansfield interrupted. 'DCI Stone, if there is any point to this line of questioning, please get to it. Sir Giles is a busy man.'

Bradbury was angry, as Bright had warned. David could see it in his eyes. Off the record, Fitzgerald had confirmed her dislike of land management staff, but sidestepped his questions about the man on the other side of the table who was cold and intimidating to look at. Trish Dolan, the features editor who'd lost her job at the *Herald*, had described him as immoral, a man she considered to be – how had Frankie put it? – barely human. David was beginning to think that she was right.

'I do have a question,' Bradbury said. 'I'd like to know why the police are crawling all over my land, questioning staff and upsetting elderly residents. I've taken years to provide a safe and peaceful environment where they can live out the rest of their days. I'm the last person to stand in the way of a police investigation, Detective Chief Inspector, especially one as serious as you outline. I'm entitled to an explanation as to what it is that has led you to this point, surely.'

'I'm afraid I can't give specifics. I can only apologise unreservedly for any inconvenience to you or distress to your residents. Believe me when I tell you that it was never my intention to make our presence felt. Last night's medical emergency could not have been foreseen. A sniffer dog found one of your employees badly injured on the estate. With a life at risk, a rescue operation was our only option. Rest assured that my officers will keep disruption to a minimum from now on.'

'That's the very least I expect.'

David bristled. He didn't even ask after Ben.

'Can you vouch for your man Petersen?'

'That's a loaded question, if ever I heard one. Jan is a bit rough around the edges, but he's a loyal employee, exceptionally good at his job. He wouldn't be working for me if he wasn't.'

'I was thinking more in terms of his status here in the UK.'

Mansfield stopped twisting his pen through his fingers. 'DCI Stone, you seem to be hinting at some impropriety. If you have something to say, out with it.'

'As you wish. Sir Giles, I have reason to believe that Jan Petersen is using a stolen identity, and may even be in the country illegally—'

'Nonsense!'

'I'm afraid so. It appears that the references he provided to obtain his current job were not his. Furthermore, and perhaps more worryingly, some of your care workers are wary of him. Would you have any idea why they are warning the new intake not to mix it with him?'

'Are they?' He glanced at Mansfield. 'I must say, this is all very worrying. Maybe I don't know Petersen as well as I thought.'

Frankie took a moment. 'Do you have, or have you ever owned, a grey Helly Hansen fleece jacket with a light stripe on the sleeve?'

The suspect shook his head. 'No.'

'Have you ever worn or borrowed one?'

He crossed his arms over his chest, a bored expression. 'No.'

It was a provable lie that would come back to bite him.

'You seem very certain.'

'I've answered the question.'

'You have – and I will now demonstrate that you are not being truthful. Following your arrest, I searched your home. In it, I found a box of old photographs. The images are of poor quality, but I'd like you to take a look at one of them for me.' Frankie opened the file, pulling out a blown-up image which she passed across the table. 'I'm showing the suspect a photographic exhibit. 'Can you explain, for the tape please, what I've just shown you?'

The suspect stared at the photograph. He didn't pick it up, neither did he speak.

'That is you, is it not, wearing the jacket I described? I don't expect that you still have it, but I have reason to believe that you were wearing it on the night of a murder I'm currently investigating. I have a witness who saw you and the car you drove away in, a dark-coloured four-by-four with privacy glass, exactly like the one you were driving when arrested this morning.'

Bradbury hadn't made much effort to stand up for Petersen; in fact, he'd distanced himself from his estate manager at the earliest opportunity, though being careful not to abandon him entirely or point the finger at him too quickly. Bright was right, David had nothing to tie Bradbury to any misdeeds, though he remained convinced that the landowner was the driving force behind the murders of Nancy Carver and Chris Adams and so very nearly Ben. David now had a call to make. He decided to give Bradbury enough rope to hang himself.

'I won't keep you much longer. It would help greatly if we could speak confidentially, nothing I tell you must leave this room.'

'You have my word.'

'I'm sorry to have to inform you that Jan Petersen has been

arrested and is currently being held on suspicion of murder of the young man I mentioned earlier. I am looking into other serious matters, other victims.'

'Good God! Who?'

Stone feigned indecision. 'Some years ago, your charity received a substantial amount of cash following the accidental death of a Bastle View resident on your estate. A retired surgeon named Alfie Jenkins.'

'That's possible. We receive many donations from residents. Why does that concern you?'

'You're looking into my client's financial affairs?' Mansfield said. 'That's outrageous!'

'Mr Mansfield. Let me reiterate. Sir Giles is here voluntarily. He has been kind enough to assist me with these very serious matters. He is not implicated in these offences, so please let me continue.' David turned his attention to Bradbury, who seemed to be relaxing the longer the interview continued. 'I'll be straight with you, sir. The evidence against Petersen – I don't yet know his real name – is mostly circumstantial. Put it this way, I don't yet have a smoking gun. Unfortunately, no weapon has been recovered for the murder of the young man I referred to at the start of this interview. I'm looking for a knife, a very specific knife, and I wonder if you've ever seen him with such a weapon.'

Bradbury took a moment to consider his response.

'Sir, I need all the help I can get.'

'DCI Stone, I . . .' The pause was for effect. 'As you can imagine, I'm finding it hard to take this all in. I have seen Petersen with knives on several occasions. In his role as estate manager, he takes groups out on the estate hunting and fishing and I often join them. I'm horrified by what you've divulged here today. I'll give it some serious thought . . .' He glanced at the expensive Hublot watch on his wrist. 'But I'm afraid that's all I have time for.'

David tripped over himself to thank him for cooperating.

Bradbury wasn't the only one who liked to fish.

78

David peered over the edge of the ravine, the place where Ben could so easily have lain undiscovered for days had the police dogs not found him. It was a long, steep drop with a stream running through it, little vegetation and no easy access out, a landscape characteristic not uncommon in the county. No wonder it had taken the search team a while to get to him. The man passing himself off as Jan Petersen may not have assaulted him, but it was clear he'd been tracking him. Petersen hadn't touched Gemma Radcliffe either, only intimidated her, asking about Ben's shift patterns. Both would testify against him when the case came to court.

David turned to look at Frankie. 'There's more to put to both suspects, but we're building a strong case.'

Before she could answer, her phone rang: Mitchell.

'Well hello,' she said. 'Does this mean you've stopped sulking?'

Frankie grinned at David. Indira Sharma had made a good impression in the office and Mitch's nose was out of joint. She'd noticed that he was feeling threatened, trying hard to impress. Nothing wrong with a bit of healthy competition to get the best out of her protégés.

'There's stuff happening,' he said.

'Stuff? Could you be more specific?'

'The PolSA team have found several outbuildings that may be of interest, one in particular we might want to take a look at. Whoever uses it has been smoking dope in there. They're sending images through. Oh, and the nurse Gemma Radcliffe mentioned wants to talk to you.'

'Is he with you now?'

'No, he's on duty at the house.'

'Name?'

'Steve Gibbon.'

'Call him. Tell him I'll be right there.'

David and Frankie arrived at the residential home fifteen minutes later. Gibbon was pacing the hallway, a worried look on his face. Having seen the commotion the night before, and heard the morning news, he'd decided he had to act. They took him into the library. Before the door was even closed, he proceeded to tell them that he'd seen Nancy with an eye injury he suspected had been inflicted by Petersen. While Gibbon hadn't witnessed the assault, he'd seen the estate manager arguing with her the day before, grabbing her roughly by the arm.

'And you didn't challenge him?' The question had come from Frankie.

'No, I should have—'

'Yes, you should.' She looked at him as if to say: what are you, man or mouse?

Gibbon hung his head in shame. David shook his head at Frankie: Give the guy a break. She stared him down: He doesn't deserve one. And all he'd given them was another piece of circumstantial evidence. Still, it was enough to keep them chipping away at the case.

'When was this exactly?' she asked.

Gibbon thought for a moment. 'End of September? A little earlier, I can't recall the exact date, but the next day she had a nasty injury to her face. It was a couple of months before she left without telling anyone why she was leaving or where she was off to. Given the injury she sustained, I wasn't surprised to see her go.'

David said: 'You're sure it was the next day?'

'Positive. I asked her who'd done it. She wouldn't say.'

'Are you prepared to make a statement to that effect?'

'Absolutely, if Petersen is responsible, for the assault or her death. I'm sorry, I should have acted earlier. I didn't have the balls. It's her, isn't it? The body you found in Harwood Forest?'

'What makes you think that?'

'I may be spineless but I'm no dimwit. This is a small community, DCI Stone. Things like that don't happen around here.'

'Well, clearly they do.'

79

They took Gibbon's statement before heading to Middle Earth, talking shop as usual. When did they ever do anything else? Their dinner date seemed like moons ago to Frankie. She was first to arrive in the incident room, Stone having stopped in the corridor to chat to another DCI. The room was more buoyant than she'd left it. Desks were standing empty, telephones being ignored. Detectives had downed tools. They appeared to be celebrating, chatting, definitely not working. Some were huddled around one desk, an atmosphere of euphoria permeating the room, as intoxicating as it was infectious.

As Stone followed Frankie in, he pulled up sharp, his mouth dropping open. Detectives dispersed, big smiles all round as they returned to their desks to resume work. As the gap opened up, Mitch and Indira were high-fiving, no longer competitors trying to outdo one another.

'What's going on?' David asked.

'We're throwing a party, guv.' Indira was sitting on Mitch's desk, legs dangling, crossed at the ankle. She jumped down. 'We scored a hat-trick.' She held up three fingers to demonstrate her point. 'Mitch has been studying the photographs Andrew's team sent through from Bradbury's estate.' She glanced at her new bestie. 'Go on, Mitch. Tell them.'

'One image caught my eye,' he said. 'A dilapidated outbuilding on Bradbury's estate which is, without doubt, the location where the photograph of Nancy Carver was taken, the one we originally assumed was a potting shed, but which Frankie thought might not be. Take a look for yourselves.'

Swivelling his chair around to face the other way, Mitch tapped his keyboard, bringing the screen to life. David and

Frankie leaned in, peering over his shoulder. It was all there, the cobweb-covered shelving, the terracotta pots, the milk churn lying on its side, exactly as it appeared in the photograph retrieved from Chris Adams' digital flash drive.

'Good work!' Frankie said.

Mitchell turned to face them. 'Indi has even better news.'

Indira couldn't wait to share it. 'I've been concentrating on the images CSIs found at Petersen's home. I recognised a location.' Scooping a file off Mitch's desk, she removed a copy and held it up for them to see. It was an industrial scene, a foreign coastline, a large port, a lot of cranes, smoke belching from chimneys. The image had been taken across a large expanse of water. 'I have one just like it, taken from the stern of an Ijmuiden ferry.' She picked up her phone, accessing the image.

They were almost identical.

David and Frankie exchanged a glance. Intrigued, the SIO congratulated Indira.

'This might give us a head start in identifying Petersen—'

'Hold on,' Mitch interrupted. 'Indi held up three fingers, not two.'

Indira continued: 'Given that we think Petersen may have arrived here illegally, it occurred to me that he might not have bought a ticket, so I did an internet search for trouble on that route. There wasn't much: a Dutch stag group going wild in the ship's nightclub; á Brit placed in the holding cell going the other way who was off his face; weather events, that type of thing. And then I came across this.' She handed over a local newspaper report, dated 12 January 2009:

A Bulgarian stowaway was held by the ship's crew on a passenger ferry en route from the Dutch port of Ijmuiden, twenty miles from North Shields. The coastguard were alerted as the man had fallen ill. It is believed that he is now being held by UK Border Force.

'One of the knives Professor Sarah Hainsworth identified was Bulgarian.' David was looking at Indira. 'Did you find out anything else?'

She nodded. 'He was never held by UK Border Force.'

'What?' David's head went down.

'He escaped before they got there,' Indira explained. 'They managed to lift prints from where he was found hiding. He has an extensive criminal record: a string of violence and intimidation offences dating back years. He's wanted for the murder of a woman in Burgas, a town close to the Black Sea. His name is Julian Chinova.'

'JC,' Frankie whispered under her breath.

'Yeah,' Indira said. 'Your mate's notes were spot on, Sarge.'

David locked eyes with his 2ic. 'We need to up our game, Frank. These two young 'uns are knocking spots off us.' He dismissed the Murder Investigation Team. They were done in and had homes to go to. It had been a long day. Tomorrow would be longer.

80

Stone and Oliver made their way to the cell block bright and early, David peeling off to an interview room while Frankie went to fetch the man who'd been calling himself Petersen, asking the custody sergeant to wake him up. The custody suite was noisy, people yelling, doors banging, keys turning in locks. This close to Christmas, it was mayhem in there. She signed the custody record as the prisoner was handed over, excited at the prospect of a second interview, a chance to keep up the pressure on the man they were convinced had murdered two, if not three, innocent people on someone else's behalf. Now they knew his identity, they had leverage.

David was on his feet, facing the door when they reached the interview room. As the prisoner stepped over the threshold, taking in the change of personnel, his step faltered slightly, a worried glance over his shoulder at Frankie, the first sign that he could see the writing on the wall.

She led him to a chair. 'Take a seat, Mr Chinova – or shall I call you Julian?'

He threw himself down, spreading his legs, dark eyes fixed on Frankie as she sat opposite. He never took his eyes off her, even as she introduced the SIO. Cautioning the suspect, she asked again if he wanted legal representation. This time he accepted the services of the duty solicitor. A sensible move on his part.

The detectives adjourned.

An hour later, they were good to go.

'Mr Chinova, are you ready?'

A resigned nod.

Frankie began by listing the evidence chronologically. She

wasn't able to include surgeon Alfie Jenkins, in that. He'd been cremated. There was little chance she would ever prove that his death was anything other a tragic accident. In due course she would try. For now, she intended to concentrate on what she might prove.

'Mr Chinova, are you familiar with the name Nancy Carver?'

'Yes, I know her. She used to work at Bastle View.'

Frankie cautioned him. 'I am arresting you on suspicion of the murder of Nancy Carver.'

'I'm sorry, I'm not following . . .' The duty solicitor eyed the senior officer. 'DCI Stone, I was told that Mr Chinova had been arrested on suspicion of the murder of Christopher Adams.'

'I'm coming to that.' Frankie passed a photograph across the table describing her actions for the tape. 'I'm showing Mr Chinova a photographic exhibit. As you can see, this image is timed and dated on the twenty-fourth of September of last year and clearly shows facial injuries to the subject, Nancy Carver.' She kept her focus on her prisoner. 'Mr Chinova, are you responsible for those injuries?'

'I don't assault women.'

'Perhaps you forgot. No? OK, it was a long time ago. Would it help you to remember if I told you that I have a witness who saw you arguing with Nancy Carver the day before this assault took place? A woman whose body was discovered in Harwood Forest yesterday, where *you* buried her on the day she disappeared.'

'Nothing to do with me.'

'OK, let's move on then. The Murder Investigation Team has been very busy since your first interview and we have a lot to get through.' Frankie consulted the file in front of her. 'You initially gave your name as Jan Petersen. Can we at least agree on that?'

'That is my name.'

'I beg to differ. It is, however, the name you've been using since you entered this country illegally on January twelfth, 2009 on a DFDS ferry sailing from Ijmuiden to North Shields.'

Chinova's eye began to twitch.

'On that day, you escaped the custody of the ship's crew. Your fingerprints were lifted from the part of the vessel where you'd been hiding. Prints that match those taken at the time of your arrest.' Frankie took an A4 sheet from the file, pausing as if she was reading it, making the suspect wait. She looked up. 'It would appear that you have quite a criminal record in Bulgaria and one outstanding warrant. I thought you said you didn't assault women. It says here that you do.'

The suspect didn't answer.

He was doing his level best to look bored. Frankie could see that he was rattled. No doubt about it. Despite her opinion of this man, she was the exact opposite; unruffled, in no particular hurry to nail him for the death of Nancy Carver and her estranged childhood friend.

'Mr Chinova, your escape from the ferry is well documented.' Frankie passed the information to his brief, hardly stopping for breath. 'What's more, your true initials were contained in the notebooks of a journalist investigating the residential home where you have been employed since July 2009, a young man you viciously attacked in Newcastle on December eighth, a man who died from his injuries.'

No response.

There was a knock at the door.

'PC Sharma has entered the room,' Frankie said.

Indira passed a hand-written note. She passed it to the SIO and then retreated.

David opened it, read it, then passed it to Frankie. The note was brief:

Message from Bradbury. He once caught Chinova smoking dope in a disused barn on his estate. He

*sometimes stashes his gear there. Bradbury wonders
if this is where you might find the knife.*

'DS Oliver, given the interruption, I'd like a word with my client,' the duty solicitor said.

'As you wish.' Frankie gathered up her papers.

Stone followed her from the interview room.

81

It took them the rest of the day and a good part of the evening to finally break the suspect down, stopping every now and then so that he could be fed and use the bathroom. It had been heavy going for all concerned, but Chinova was weakening with every second that passed. It angered Frankie that she didn't yet have a shred of evidence against the man she was convinced had been pulling the strings, the man with the cash to engage the services of one of the best legal minds in the north-east. Not only was Bradbury not around to support his employee, he was actively trying to put him away.

'You were seen hiding on Croft Street moments after a young man was stabbed to death. You were wearing a distinctive jacket that you denied owning and yet we have a picture of you with it on.' For the benefit of the brief who had not been present at the first interview, she again showed Chinova a photographic exhibit of him wearing the fleece. 'This evidence is pointing in one direction only. I don't think your boss is impressed. His reputation is at stake here.'

Chinova's jaw bunched as he clenched his teeth. His head went down. He was showing signs of distress, a thin film of sweat on his upper lip, a slight tremble in hands he couldn't keep still.

Frankie had found her trigger.

Under further interrogation, Chinova admitted to disposing of Nancy's body, not killing her. It was rubbish. He was lying. 'Why, Julian?' It was the first time she'd used his first name, an attempt to bridge the gap between them. 'Why, after all this time, would you do anything that would jeopardise your freedom? For years you've had a roof over your head, an idyllic spot in which to live. You drive around in a high-end vehicle. You have money. You had everything to gain and nothing to lose by staying out of trouble.'

He sighed, wiping his face with his hand. 'He told me to do it.'

'Who did?'

Frankie could feel her heart kicking against the inside of her ribs. She could feel the heat of David's gaze on the side of her face. Could sense the discomfort from the brief sitting across from the SIO. She didn't look at either of them. She knew the answer but needed Chinova to say it. And finally, it came.

He shut his eyes, exhausted by the questioning.

'Bradbury,' he said.

'You could have refused.'

'He threatened to expose my past.'

'He knew you were a fugitive? How?'

'I had no papers when I asked him for work. He said it didn't matter, that he had other people on his books that were in the same position and were unfortunate like me. It was his idea that I should change my name. He said he had connections. That he could give me a new identity, one that no one would question. He said that whatever I'd done, it didn't matter, that if I was honest with him, he'd look after me, that I'd have a job for life.'

The word 'life' would soon mean something else entirely to her prisoner. Frankie had no sympathy for him. Because of him, James Carver and Rachel Hooper had lost a loving parent; Susan had lost an only son and with it her reason for living; Frankie had lost an old friend. And who knows? Maybe one day they would be able to prove that Chinova had deliberately locked Alfie Jenkins in an outbuilding and left him there long enough to freeze to death.

Frankie was angry when she should have been ecstatic. Two murders or three, what Chinova had done was deplorable and indefensible. Whatever allegations he made against

409

Bradbury, Frankie knew that a clever lawyer would argue his cause, possibly even convince a jury that Sir Giles had been duped by a good-for-nothing loser after giving him a job out of the goodness of his heart.

'Shame you can't prove that, Julian.'

His eyes darkened.

82

An admission of guilt from a suspect was progress, but it took Stone and Oliver only as far as first base. The MIT still had to prove that Chinova had actually murdered his victims in cold blood, taking him through his actions moment by moment. His continued detention was authorised by the superintendent – a rubber-stamp job, bearing in mind the seriousness of the allegations. Stone and Oliver still had work to do.

Before the MIT left for the evening, the SIO called the squad together for a short briefing. When it ended, Abbott volunteered to liaise with Andrew, whose search team had mapped every single outbuilding on Bradbury's estate. Dick's task was to find and retrieve the murder weapon.

As the hours ticked by with no news, Frankie continued to question the suspect. He admitted to having assaulted Nancy Carver. He said that she'd been asking questions about things that didn't concern her, that she'd pleaded with him to help expose Bradbury.

'She asked the wrong guy.' Chinova grinned when he said it.

Frankie held her breath . . . one, two, three seconds, struggling to keep her emotions in check, dismissing the urge to leap across the desk and punch his lights out. Despite the seriousness of his position, the arsehole seemed to be enjoying this. Now he'd started talking, she couldn't shut him up.

'I gave her a slap, a warning to stop digging. She wouldn't listen. The woman was desperate.'

'And you told Bradbury.'

'He's my boss.'

'And he said what?'

'He told me to keep an eye on her. I found her resignation

letter and knew she was planning to run, so I followed. She was a gutsy woman. She said she'd never stop talking, that she'd spoken to a journalist who knew what was going on. I think she thought it might save her. It didn't. What was I to do?'

Frankie didn't give him the time to get off on it. 'What did you do?'

'I struck her with the butt end of my rifle.'

Inwardly, Frankie shivered.

Another smile from the Bulgarian. 'I went back to my Land Rover for a spade. I think you know the rest.'

Frankie did. She'd viewed the post-mortem report before resuming her questioning. As expected, Beth Collingwood had ruled out accidental death. Nancy had received a blunt force trauma to the side of her head, a serious but not fatal injury. The bastard had buried her alive.

'Did she tell you which journalist she'd been speaking to?'

'She didn't have to. I had her phone, didn't I?'

'You called Chris Adams?'

Chinova shrugged. 'I convinced him that I'd fallen out with Bradbury and was going to help expose him. The idiot actually believed me. We met, but he soon realised that I hadn't come to chat. He can run like a bastard. He wasn't hard to find. His name is listed in the *Herald*.' As he continued to fill in the blanks, Stone and Oliver were content to listen. In the end, he said: 'I bided my time and stuck him as soon as he left the cashpoint.'

Frankie stood up. She couldn't listen to another word.

83

Last night, after they'd finished the debrief, David had asked her to go for a drink before they called time. Frankie had declined. She was done in. Despite the late hour, she'd reminded him that Ben had been discharged and was waiting at home with his tail between his legs, begging David to go easy on him. The lad was sleeping when David entered the house, but awake before he left for work. They breakfasted together.

This morning, congratulations seemed inappropriate. Frankie had worked hard to get Chinova to cough, but his testimony alone wasn't enough to arrest Sir Giles, let alone convict him, though the suspect insisted that he was telling the truth, that if he was going down, he was taking Bradbury with him.

David glanced across the room.

Frankie was at her desk, preoccupied, with one eye on the door. She perked up as Dick sauntered into the incident room with a bit of a swagger and a broad smile, a dozen pairs of eyes trained on him. The weapon wasn't all he'd found. A cheer went up when he told them what it was.

Armed with a photograph of the knife, David took Frankie to his office, arranging a conference call with Sarah Hainsworth, the engineering professor who'd so helpfully identified the kind of knife they were looking for. It took her no time to confirm that their find was a Bulgarian Karakulak, a traditional shepherds' knife. Beth Collingwood would now be able to take precise measurements and match it to the wounds inflicted on Chris Adams. That was all the detectives needed to hear.

*

Sir Giles Bradbury's housekeeper opened the door to a property he'd purchased before turning Bastle View into a residential home for the elderly. They were shown into his study and told to wait. It was a wonderful room with a view over rolling countryside. The owner arrived moments later, extending his hand to the DCI, a warm smile on his face. David shook hands with him, though Frankie could see that it pained him to do so. The detectives looked on as Bradbury walked around his desk, hitched up his trousers and sat down, offering tea, inviting Stone and Oliver to make themselves comfortable.

Both remained standing.

David glanced around the room. Like the library at Bastle View it was grandiose; a facade designed to impress its visitors, decorated and furnished to a very high standard.

'I take it you have news, Detective Chief Inspector.'

'Yes, sir. Thanks to you, the Murder Investigation Team have made excellent progress. We have a lot to thank you for. We've now recovered the weapon and charged your employee with not one, but two murders: that of your former care manager and the young man I referred to when we first spoke in the company of your solicitor, Trevor Mansfield.'

'Former employee,' Bradbury corrected him. He stood up. 'Well, thank you for letting me know, DCI Stone. I'm pleased to have been of service. Perhaps now we can all get back to normal.'

David eyed him with contempt. Bradbury was a snake. There was no expression of sympathy for the family of a woman who'd worked for him for years. 'Sit down, please, sir. I'm not quite finished.' He threw Frankie a nod, her cue to proceed.

The landowner was shocked as she began to administer the caution. 'Mr Bradbury, I am arresting you on suspicion of the murders of Nancy Carver and Christopher Adams . . .'

In the interview room at Middle Earth, Bradbury and Trevor Mansfield were waiting when Stone and Oliver arrived to conduct the interview, this time in the chaos of the cell block. The detectives felt like they had lived in that grim room for days, but both were ready for the final push, David taking the lead this time – or at least, that was the plan, if only he could get a word in edgeways.

'Stone, you are making a big mistake,' Bradbury said. 'Whatever that toerag has told you, I can assure you it's slanderous. These deaths have nothing to do with me. The idea is preposterous. You must see that.' He glanced at his solicitor. 'Trevor, do your job.'

'Calm down, Giles. Let's see what the SIO has to say.'

'Mr Bradbury, I'm going to show you a number of photographs.' David spread them out on the table. 'You may recognise this building as one that is situated on your land.'

'Yes, of course I do. I own it.'

David pointed to one of the photographs. 'Do you see the knife here, sir?'

'Yes, of course I do. I'm not blind. Get on with it.'

Frankie eyeballed the suspect. 'Mr Bradbury, these images were all taken from the same angle, with the same camera, at the same location. As you can see, they are time-and-date-stamped.'

'What is your point?'

'Will you now look at this image?' She handed him a photograph that hadn't been on the table. 'The knife wasn't there two days ago when crime scene investigators first entered the property. It is now. Which tells us that in the intervening period you went to those premises with that knife and placed it in that location for us to find, a deliberate attempt to incriminate your former estate manager.'

'I did no such thing!'

David took over. 'Mr Bradbury, outside of this police

station, only two people knew that we were looking for a knife in connection with this offence. The information was never made public. As you can see, it's a very specific knife that I was careful not to describe when we spoke the day before yesterday. The two people who knew about it were you and the man masquerading as Jan Petersen, who we now know to be Julian Chinova, a Bulgarian national. You knew that already, didn't you?'

'I did not.' Bradbury's head dropped.

He knew he was done for and so did Mansfield.

84

On Christmas morning, Frankie stood in David's tiny cottage, staring out of the window, the fire crackling in the grate behind her. The radio was on and she could hear Ben singing along in the kitchen, cobbling together something decent to eat. There would be no turkey and trimmings, no crackers to pull or presents to open, but there would be joy. Ben was alive and that was all that mattered. Falling into that ravine had saved him from certain death.

The thought of it made Frankie shiver.

The previous evening, she'd waited with David on the corner of Northumberland Street for someone else who'd survived a close encounter with Chinova. He should've silenced Eva Sokolov when he had the chance. He'd underestimated her, written her off as a down-and-out who wouldn't want to go near the police, let alone help them. The fleece jacket may never be found but her eyewitness testimony had provided a vital piece of evidence that identified him as the person responsible for the stabbing of Chris Adams, allowing detectives to chip away at his lies.

Frankie's mobile rang out as they stood there.

'Leave it,' David told her. 'You'll regret it if you don't.'

She hesitated, a disappointed expression on her face. 'Maybe they're not coming.'

He smiled. 'They're coming.'

As the snow began to fall on the streets of Newcastle, Frankie had fallen silent, reflecting on the coming weeks and months, gratified by the fact that Chinova and Bradbury would get what was coming to them, the latter especially. A son of the landed gentry, he should have known better. She wondered how a man who had so much would risk everything to get more. His actions had ruined more lives than his own.

Nancy Carver's family and Susan Adams would never again see their loved ones and it would be some time before they could bury their dead, but thanks to the hard work and commitment of a depleted Murder Investigation Team they would get 'justice' in the eyes of the law – a word that was meaningless to Frankie. There was nothing fair or reasonable about murder. Her sister's killer was out there somewhere. If they found him tomorrow, Joanna wouldn't suddenly re-appear. She was gone. No key turning in a lock, no cell door slamming, would ever make up for that.

Amanda Williams had been charged with receiving stolen goods. Frankie had been right about her. Once she realised that she'd been driving the car of a murder victim, she was quick to distance herself from Chinova; a man she'd picked out in an ID parade as the one she'd met in a Manchester hotel car park where the dodgy transactions had taken place. She'd since been escorted to London to face further questioning from the Serious Organised Crime Agency who now believed they had enough evidence to convict a syndicate of offenders who were ripping off the elderly.

The investigation into the suspicious death of retired surgeon Alfie Jenkins would continue into the New Year, as would forensic examination of Bradbury's financial accounts. No doubt they would make interesting reading. David had vowed that vulnerable elderly residents who'd been fleeced would be reimbursed. A team of experienced detectives were being lined up to question them. It would be a slow process. Litigation might take several years. Some residents didn't have that long. They might die before the truth was revealed, but it gave Frankie peace of mind to know that while the man driven by greed began a lengthy sentence, in time the families of his victims would receive recompense through the courts.

There was no evidence to support the view that Fiona Fitzgerald had anything to do with Bradbury's master plan. Chinova had admitted to the Internet search from her office, lasting less than forty-five seconds – another mistake by the Bulgarian who'd evaded the police for years and who'd probably spend the rest of his life in jail.

So far, detectives had found nothing to implicate editor Mark Fox in any of this. If he'd concealed any wrongdoing by Sir Giles, he'd been careful to cover his tracks. The technical support team would continue digging, but Frankie didn't expect it would lead anywhere. David had taken the view that the editor's dislike of Chris Adams was born of jealousy, a downward slide, a fading career. In Chris, Fox had recognised his younger self, an enthusiast with the skills and potential to rise to the top of his profession. Such a waste.

Before Frankie left Middle Earth, Trish Dolan, the former *Herald* features editor, had been in touch to congratulate her on the successful resolution of an investigation that began with that same young journalist. Trish looked forward to the day that Bradbury, a man she considered unworthy of the honour bestowed on him, would be stripped of his knighthood. Before she hung up, she shared some good news of her own. She was now officially in remission and in the market for a new job. Wishing her luck, Frankie had passed on Wells' details, promising to put in a good word for her over the holidays.

Frankie was the first to spot Eva and Ryman as they turned the corner. They were dressed up, a sight to see, thanks to a last-minute whip-round by the MIT, a small thank you for assisting the police. As the two men shook hands, David caught Frankie's eye over Ryman's shoulder. His smile made her heart sing. The investigation had taken its toll on their relationship, but they too had survived. A pre-Christmas drink in a warm pub was what they all needed.

There would be no celebrating for Susan Adams. She'd wept when she heard the news that Chinova and Bradbury had been charged with her son's murder. Now able to begin the grieving process, she'd spend a sober Christmas with Frankie's parents. As far as Frankie was concerned, there was no better place to be. If anyone could make her believe that life was worth living, they could.

Ousted from her bed in the Oliver household, Frankie had accepted an invitation to spend Christmas Day with Ben and David Stone. Her eyes scanned the quiet street, wondering what was keeping her boss. She turned from the window as Ben hobbled into the room with a glass of mulled wine in one hand and a crutch in the other.

'For you,' he said. 'Merry Christmas.'

'Merry Christmas.' She pulled the glass to her nose. 'Mm . . . smells delicious.'

'It's homemade, not that shite you get readymade in the supermarket.'

'Is it a bribe?'

'Do I need one?'

'Hmm . . .' Frankie raised her right forefinger to her lips, eyes on the ceiling as if considering a response. 'You're undoubtedly the hero of our investigation, mister, but you've yet to serve a penance. Deception cannot go unpunished. Tell you what, keep my glass topped up . . . all day, and it might, just *might*, let you off the hook . . . maybe.' She smiled at him over the top of her glass. 'Consider yourself my slave for the day.'

'Gimme a break, it's Christmas! *And* I'm a casualty. What

420

are you doing here, anyhow? I thought you'd want to be with family.'

'I'm in the way?'

'No! Why do you always twist my words?'

'That's harsh—'

'But true ... Dave does it all the time and it's bloody annoying.'

'Does he?' She lifted her glass. 'Are you not joining me?'

'I only had one hand. Wait there.' He retreated into the kitchen.

A car pulled up outside. Seconds later, the door flew opened. David walked in dressed in a Santa suit. Frankie burst out laughing. He looked ridiculous. She called out to his nephew. 'Ben, you have a special visitor.'

The lad poked his head out of the kitchen.

'I've never been a dad before,' David said. 'Will I do?'

Ben caught the double meaning. He grinned. 'You'll do.'

David smiled back at him. 'Drum roll, if you please.'

Ben pointed at him. 'For that?'

Gemma Radcliffe peeped out from behind his uncle.

Ben's eyes lit up. Christmas was shaping up nicely.

Frankie had so much to say to David. It would wait.

'Come with me,' David led them all to the door.

Parked at the kerb was a brand-new motor.

'For me?' Ben's eyes were like saucers. The smile slid off his face as he looked down at his leg in plaster. 'Oh bollocks!' He rounded on Frankie. 'My penance, right?'

Everyone laughed.

It had been three long months since Bradbury and Chinova had been charged and remanded in custody. In the meantime, David had moved on to another investigation and was discussing strategy with Frankie over a beer. Sitting together on the sofa, they were paying Ben no attention, though both were aware of what he had to do, just as he was aware that they'd talked Wells into allowing him to write an article that would put an end to a tragic case. Her editor-in-chief agreed – not that he had much choice in the matter. Ben smiled to himself. Who'd argue with Belinda?

He sat down at his computer and began to type . . .

Justice for murdered whistle-blower and the journalist silenced trying to help her

Two men found guilty of murder last week appeared at Newcastle Crown Court for sentencing this morning, both receiving a term of life imprisonment. Throughtout a lengthy trial, Sir Giles Bradbury and Julian Chinova blamed each other for the deaths of Nancy Carver and Christopher Adams, offences occurring a year apart. The jury deliberated for less than three hours, returning unanimous guilty verdicts on both defendants, convinced that Bradbury was the driving force behind both murders. In a statement afterwards, the Senior Investigating Officer, Detective Chief Inspector David Stone of Northumbria Police, said that his team were still investigating Bastle View and expected further charges to be brought against these men.

Ben spent two hours writing and another editing, tightening up the text, feeling under pressure to produce his very best work; not because it was a big deal to cover a case as important at this, but because of those affected by these tragic deaths: the victims' family and friends, the detectives who'd worked tirelessly to protect the vulnerable and speak up for the dead. Ben had witnessed firsthand the effect this had on David and Frankie but, most of all, he was determined to honour Chris Adams' efforts to bring the case to light. Pausing to reflect on what he'd written, he looked up. Frankie eyed him from across the room, an encouraging you-can-do-it nod that sent his fingers flying once more across the keys . . .

Her Ladyship Ms Justice Underwood described Nancy Carver as a brave woman whose selfless actions had triggered an independent enquiry into the way that care homes were run. Paying tribute to Chris Adams, who'd lost his life trying to help her, Her Ladyship told the court that if Julian Chinova was ever again a free man, he would face immediate deportation. Of Sir Giles Bradbury she said, 'You have abandoned all decency. There are no mitigating factors in this case. This was a despicable abuse of power against the most vulnerable in our society. A long period of incarceration is not only justified, it's mandatory.'

Aware that Bradbury's defence team had lodged an immediate appeal. Ben read through his article one final time. Sensing movement behind him, he was suddenly aware that he had company. With Stone and Oliver looking proudly over his shoulder, he paid tribute to a young man he'd never met, the journalist without whose evidence the MIT might never have been able to secure a conviction or put away his killer and without whose contribution this story would never have been told. Typing the byline, Ben ensured that Chris Adams would finally get his name above the fold:

Benjamin Stone and Christopher Adams

Acknowledgements

High five Team Orion: my wonderful editor, Francesca Pathak; publicist, Alainna Hadjigeorgiou; marketing guru, Lynsey Sutherland; designer Tomas Almeida and freelance copy-editor Anne O'Brien to whom this book is dedicated. I wouldn't be the writer I am without any of you.

To every single reader, writer, blogger, bookseller and librarian who has taken the time to organise or attend events, read, review and recommended my work to others – especially Forum Books who've launched every one of my titles in the village where I live – I appreciate all you do for me.

Thanks to Professor Sarah Hainsworth, personal friend, Pro-Vice-Chancellor and Executive Dean of the School of Engineering and Applied Science at Aston University whose knowledge of knives was invaluable in writing this book. And Garry Willey who I first met when he was a court reporter and I was a Crown Court Liaison Officer. His memory of Newcastle Crown Court is better than mine.

No dedication would be complete without tipping my hat to all at A.M. Heath Literary Agency, especially Oli Munson, agent and friend for almost a decade, who once read an unsolicited debut, saw potential and offered to represent me. There must've been a fairy sitting on my shoulder that day – it seems she's still there.

A big wave to my wonderful family: Paul, Kate, Max and Frankie; Chris, Jodie, Daisy and Finn; Mo – partner, collaborator and unsung hero – who I suspect would love to swap places with my keyboard but has never voiced that out loud. She is simply the best.